THE CRITICS LOVE DEBRA DIER!

PRAISE FOR MacLAREN'S BRIDE:

"Debra Dier will delight readers with her delicious love story. Meg and Alec are a passionate pair and the Scottish setting is truly romantic! Ms. Dier has written a thoroughly enjoyable novel that readers will love!"

—*The Literary Times*

"Debra Dier's delightful drama is definitely a historical romance reader's dream."

—*Affaire de Coeur*

"The talented Ms. Dier captures the English/Scottish animosity to perfection and weaves an exhilarating tale that will touch your heart and fire the emotions. Great Reading!"

—*Rendezvous*

PRAISE FOR LORD SAVAGE:

"Lord Savage is exhilarating and fascinating!"

—*Affaire de Coeur*

"Kudos to Ms. Dier for an unforgettable reading adventure. Superb!"

—*Rendezvous*

"Sensual, involving and well written, this is another winner from the talented pen of Ms. Dier."

—*The Paperback Forum*

UNFORGETTABLE LOVE

"What do you wonder?" Meg asked, appalled at the breathy sound of her voice.

Alec closed the distance, each movement filled with the sleek grace of a man certain of his prowess. "If you really have abandoned all your youthful notions."

Meg stepped back, her heel colliding with the closed door. She lifted her head, assuming a haughty pose in spite of the trembling in her limbs. "I can assure you, I have."

Alec smoothed his fingers over her cheek, spreading warmth across her skin. "You told me once you would never love another man the way you loved me."

Meg swallowed past the tight knot in her throat. "Children say the most outrageous things."

"Children do."

Alec nuzzled the sensitive skin beneath her ear. Meg tried to form a protest, but her brain wasn't functioning. Her muscles shifted without thought, her body melting against him.

"I need to know something," he whispered, sliding his hand into the curls at her nape, cradling her head in his big palm.

Meg stared up into his eyes, mesmerized by the flames simmering in the celestial depths. "What?" she asked, her voice sounding strange to her own ears.

"This." Alec lowered his lips to hers.

MacLaren's Bride

Debra Dier

LEISURE BOOKS   NEW YORK CITY

A LEISURE BOOK®

September 1997

Published by

Dorchester Publishing Co., Inc.
276 Fifth Avenue
New York, NY 10001

For my husband's clan, my extended family:
Korky, Faye, Gary, Carolyn, Cathy, Amy, Gene, Janice,
Mikel, Christopher, Mary Kay, Mike, Tara, Tecia,
Aunt Pearl, Johnny, Junie, John, Leah, Denise, Lynn,
Bob, Jeremy, Frank, Lisa, Emma, Lorraine, Charlie,
Aunt Helen, Uncle John, Georgia, Mike, Christopher,
Mike, Carl, "aunts" Lorraine, Sally, June, and Geno.
And all their families. You've made it a pleasure to be
part of the clan.

MacLaren's Bride

Chapter One

Scotland, 1815

"You can't be serious." Alec MacLaren rose from his chair near the fireplace in Sir Robert Drummond's library. He stared at his father's old friend, not quite believing what Robert had just asked of him. Yet the desperation in Robert's dark eyes left no room for doubts. And the obligation Alec had to this man left him little choice.

"I wouldn't be asking this of you if I thought there were any other way." Robert tapped the tip of his cane against the carpet beside his wing-back chair, burgundy and ivory wool dulling the soft thuds. "The girl has left me no alternative."

Alec glanced at the painting above the stone fireplace, where a pretty golden-haired fourteen-year-old girl smiled at him from the confines of a carved rosewood frame, her green eyes sparkling with innocent dreams. He remembered the summer it had been painted ten years ago. The summer he had marched off to war. The summer a young girl had confessed her love for him.

That warm July morning had been the last time he had seen Meg. Sweet, innocent Meg, so certain her childish infatuation would last until the day he came back from the war. He wondered if she had grown into the promise of beauty he had glimpsed in her youthful face. He wondered if she even remembered him.

Sometimes it seemed his life before that last summer was nothing more than an idyllic dream, a memory of heaven before he had been cast into hell by his own foolish search for glory. "If Meg's content with marrying the man, I'm not sure we have a right to stop her. Even if he is English."

"She's doing it to spite me. And she'll regret it. Lord knows she'll regret it."

Alec glanced at Robert. In spite of the recent wound that had nearly cost him his leg, Robert still looked as vigorous as he had since Alec was a boy. A few years past fifty, tall and lean, Robert had inherited the blond hair and fiery temper of his Viking ancestors. "You can't be certain. She might—"

Robert held up his hand. "The Englishman she's going to marry is your cousin Wildon."

"Wildon? Wildon Fethersham!"

Robert grimaced as though he had bitten into a rotten apple. "The same. Wildon Fethersham, Viscount Blandford. When her grandmother flaunted the fact Meg was going to marry an English viscount, I thought she was only trying to provoke me. The English witch likes nothing better. But Meg didn't deny it. My only daughter smiled and said it would serve me well to have an English son-in-law. Then she had the audacity to tell me she had always entertained the idea of an

12

elopement. Just to let me know she intended to marry the blackguard at her own choosing."

Meg and Wildon. The thought grated along his spine like sharpened fingernails. Alec suspected he knew the reasons Wildon had suddenly taken the notion to marry Robert Drummond's daughter. None of them were honorable.

"When I went to see her last week, I had hoped Meg might have sweetened some toward me. I had hoped she might come back home, where she belongs. I had hoped . . ." Robert's words dissolved in a husky whisper. He drew in his breath. "Lord, how the girl hates me."

Alec saw the raw pain etched on Robert's face. Nine years ago Robert had lost more than a wife he adored through the scheming of an ambitious woman. He had lost his only daughter. Last June he had lost the last shred of his family. His son Colin, Alec's closest friend, had died on the same bloody battlefield where Alec had nearly met his own fate. "Meg was fifteen when it happened. She doesn't know the truth about that night."

"I've told her the truth. She didn't believe me."

"Have you tried to talk to her about it recently? With some distance from that day, she might be able to see more clearly."

"It wouldn't make a difference. She doesn't trust me any more than her mother does. And now she wants to punish me for a crime I didn't commit." Robert squeezed the smooth oak cane until his knuckles blanched white. "The thought of that fortune-hunting bastard and my daughter . . . makes me want to kill something with my bare hands."

Alec knew his cousin too well to dispel any of Robert's fears. Wildon needed money. And Margaret Drummond had just become an extremely wealthy heiress.

13

Robert lifted one golden brow, pinning Alec in a challenging stare. "You know what that English dandy will do if Blandford gets his hands on Drummond land."

Alec knew all too well what his cousin would do if he got his hands on Meg's inheritance. He would rape the land, evict tenants—whose families had lived there for generations—to make room for sheep. Wildon had done it once. He would do it again. "Perhaps I could spend some time getting reacquainted with Meg. I might be able to change her mind, coax her without forcing the issue."

Robert shook his head. "I know you're accustomed to ladies tripping over each other to win your favor, but you won't charm Meg. The only reason she is going to marry that man is to spite me. She won't let affection get in her way. Trust me, Alec, there isn't time for fancy maneuvers. We must move quickly. I can't let that bastard get his hands on my daughter. He'll destroy her."

Even if Alec were not obliged to Robert for dragging him back from the brink of eternity, he would be obliged to save Drummond land from falling into Wildon's greedy hands. And he had to admit, he wanted to save more than the land. He wanted to save the girl he remembered from a time in his life when he still believed in innocence. Still, he couldn't reconcile his doubts or his conscience concerning Robert's plan. "I'll leave for London tonight. I'll bring her home. And then we'll see if Meg can be convinced to change her mind."

Robert frowned into the polished gold handle of his cane. "All right. We'll do this your way. But I'm afraid you'll see, Meg is too stubborn to change her mind. There is only one alternative."

An alternative Alec hoped to avoid.

* * *

Meg Drummond sat in the yellow drawing room of her grandmother's London town house, wondering if it were possible for a person to die from an excess of sugarcoated conversation. It wasn't enough for her grandmother to spend the spring in London. Lady Hermione Chadburne had to scamper back the first week of September, even though it was scarcely three months after Colin's death. Although they did not attend any of the more elaborate social functions, her grandmother insisted they did not "wallow" in deep mourning. Instead, Hermione made certain they fluttered from one party to another, like demented butterflies.

Meg suppressed a sigh of relief when her grandmother's dinner guest announced it was time he left. It was amazing how a few hours could drag into a few decades. She found that especially true when enduring the company of Lord Wildon Fethersham. She molded her lips into a polite smile as the man took her hand.

"I hope you might come for a ride through the park with me tomorrow morning." Wildon pressed his lips to the back of her hand, lingering a moment longer than propriety allowed. It was all she could manage not to jerk her hand free of his grasp. "I shall be desolate if you deny me the pleasure of your company."

Meg had to admit, Wildon Fethersham was certainly not unattractive, if one preferred his type. His light brown hair was carefully cropped and coaxed into the latest fashion—spilling over his brow in cultivated waves. He was average in height, slender, and his clothes were tailored by the best Bond Street had to offer. Meg, however, had never developed a taste for men who had the smooth, pretty looks of a pampered feline.

"I'm terribly sorry, Lord Blandford, but I have a prior engagement," Meg said, neglecting to mention that the engagement was with a novel she was reading.

Wildon drew his pretty features into a look of complete despair. "I fear I shall wither, like a vine denied the sustenance of the sun, if I must wait to see you until tomorrow at dinner."

Meg managed to maintain her smile. "Do be careful, Lord Blandford. You shall crush me with the weight of your flattery."

He smiled, looking pleased with himself. "I shall count the minutes until I see you again." He kissed her hand once more, bid a final farewell to Meg's grandmother and mother, then left the drawing room.

Lady Hermione Chadburne sat beside her daughter, Lady Joanna Chadburne Drummond, on a sofa in the shape of a sphinx. Hermione had decided last year to transport the yellow drawing room from London to the Nile.

Hieroglyphics covered the walls. Replicas of Egyptian thrones served as chairs. Each table was shaped like a small sarcophagus, complete with paintings of mummies. A pair of stuffed crocodiles guarded the entrance, beneath twin palm trees. Hermione Chadburne had a passion for interior decoration. No room in the house escaped her touch. Unfortunately, almost no room in the house existed in the same space and time.

The red saloon was a piece of China, filled with porcelain jars, mandarins, and pagodas. They dined in a medieval banquet hall. The music room was ancient Rome. And in her bedchamber, Hermione slept beneath a Turkish tent. Only by the grace of the Almighty had Meg managed to keep her grandmother from transforming her own bedchamber into a Greek temple.

Small and plump, dressed in a gown of black bombazine, her white hair crimped into ringlets beneath her white lace cap, Hermione stared at her granddaughter, like a queen displeased with the princess in the house. "I do wish you would encourage Blandford more, Margaret. You are perfectly cold when he is near. I wonder that he hasn't given up on you."

Meg refrained from telling her grandmother that the dear lady encouraged the man enough for both of them. "You needn't wonder overly much, Grandmama. Lord Blandford is enthralled by the beauty of my dowry."

Hermione lifted one white brow, her gray eyes chilly with reproach. "When I think of all the eligible young men who have asked for your hand, I positively shudder."

All the eligible young men Meg knew were either seeking a rich wife to fatten purses depleted through lives of excess, pompous aristocrats who wanted a suitable bride to extend the family bloodline, or boring puppies who yapped at her heels.

"Now you are busily working at sending a viscount packing." Hermione wagged her finger at Meg. "Mark my words. If you aren't careful you shall find yourself on the shelf. With no hope. You'll be a spinster."

Meg molded her features into a serious expression. "Do you think so?"

Hermione clasped her hands in her lap, her expression one of a celestial judge dooming a sinner to eternal damnation. "If you don't change your ways, Blandford will join the ranks of all the young men you have carelessly discarded. I'm certain of it."

Meg grinned in the shadow of her grandmother's gloom. "I do wish you could be more precise on exactly what I must do to convince him to peddle his title elsewhere. Nothing I've tried so far has done the trick."

Hermione's eyes widened. "You want to discourage him." She turned toward Joanna, who had been silent during their exchange. "She's your daughter. Aren't

17

you the least bit concerned she shall end up a lonely spinster?"

Joanna considered her words a moment before she spoke. "I'm more concerned she shall marry a man who will make her life excessively unpleasant."

Hermione pursed her lips. "You, of all women, should know the folly of following a foolish heart. It is better to follow one's head, and keep one's heart well guarded."

Joanna's smile pulled into a tight line. Although close to fifty, she looked years younger. Tall and slender, graceful in her movements, she had a few streaks of silver threaded through her light chestnut brown hair. A few lines marred a face still beautiful enough to draw the attention of more than a few admiring gentlemen. Yet, in the nine years she had been separated from her philandering husband, Joanna had never once broken her vows to the man who had broken her heart. "We mustn't judge all men by the treachery of one. Even though one must wonder if the male of the species is capable of monogamy."

An old bitterness stirred inside of Meg, like shards of broken glass. She curled her hand into a fist against the arm of the sofa. When she thought of all the pain her father had caused, she wanted to scream.

"In any case, we certainly mustn't try to force Margaret into a marriage that could well prove a disaster," Joanna said.

Hermione folded her hands in her lap, her voice gathering the strident tone of a misunderstood martyr. "I only want to make certain Margaret doesn't make the same mistake you did."

"I won't." Meg met her grandmother's curious look with a smile that felt as brittle as the dreams she had once held so dear. "I have no intention of marrying anyone."

Joanna glanced at her daughter, her green eyes filled with regret. "Margaret, I applaud your decision in being careful with this important decision. But I would hope you don't allow what happened to me to spoil your future."

"The past has nothing to do with this." Yet Meg suspected she could not completely escape the scars of the past.

"You mustn't close yourself off from the possibility of marriage to a fine young man," Joanna said. "You are still too young to consider becoming a spinster."

Although she wasn't ready to don a cap, Meg was hardly a chit straight out of the schoolroom. She had enjoyed six London Seasons, without once meeting a man who tempted her to leave the safety of her solitary existence. The simple truth was, she had only once thought of marriage. When she was too young to understand the true nature of men.

"If I met a man I wanted to live with for the rest of my life, I might change my mind. But I doubt that will happen." Meg looked from her mother to her grandmother. "And I can assure you, I would never marry a man who thought more of my inheritance than he did of me. I can think of nothing more dreadful than to marry for the sake of convenience."

"I can tell you something more dreadful, my girl." Hermione wiggled her forefinger at her granddaughter. "Being a spinster. Ridiculed by society. Looked down upon as some unnatural creature unable to make a suitable match. That is far worse than marrying a respectable gentleman. Such as Lord Blandford."

"Grandmama, I appreciate your concern; I truly do. I simply cannot imagine spending more than an hour in Lord Blandford's company. How could I possibly spend the rest of my life with him?"

Hermione waved aside her words with an elegant

19

sweep of her pudgy hand. "Once you are married, you shall have the freedom to do what you like. You needn't see your husband more than you wish."

Meg crinkled her nose. "I doubt even Blandford would excuse me from some of the more intimate duties of marriage."

"No need to be vulgar, my girl." Hermione flicked open her fan. "I need not remind you that I told your father you would be married to Blandford by the end of the year. As I recall, you did not deny it."

Meg shrugged, hiding the old pain beneath the mask of indifference she had cultivated over the years. For the past nine years she had tried hard to convince herself she no longer cared what happened to the father she had once thought the most wonderful man in the world. The father who had torn her world into shreds. "Let him believe it," she said, keeping her voice level. "Let him worry himself gray. Let him think his precious lands will fall into the hands of an Englishman."

Joanna shook her head. "No matter what has happened, Margaret, he is still your father."

Meg shrugged, as though the matter was of no concern, as though she didn't ache with the old wound. "Since he is seldom inclined to remember I'm his daughter, I see no reason to dwell on the fact."

"I can think of no better punishment for that Scots barbarian than to see his daughter married to an English nobleman." Hermione smiled at Meg. "If you were thinking clearly, my dear, you would see I'm right."

"I'm afraid I'm not interested in slipping my neck into a noose to punish Father."

Hermione stiffened, her smile vanishing in a florid expression of fury. She flicked her fan back and forth beneath her chin, fluttering the white curls framing her face. "Have you given any thought as to how foolish I shall appear to that man if you do not marry Blandford? I've already suffered enough humiliation at the hands of Sir Robert Drummond. I simply shall not suffer any more."

"Grandmama, perhaps you should have consulted me before telling Father I intended to marry Blandford."

Hermione waved her hand. "There is absolutely no reason why you shouldn't marry the man."

"Mother, I believe we have exhausted this subject," Joanna said. "Margaret is old enough to make her own decisions."

Hermione threw up her hands. "Very well. I shall not mention it again. Not a word. Far be it from me to try to dissuade the girl from making a tremendous disaster of her life. It's obvious she doesn't care if I appear the fool."

Silence descended over the drawing room, settling like frozen rain over the three ladies. Meg stared at a page in the novel she was trying to read, trying to ignore the nagging nibble of guilt she couldn't quite dismiss. Although her methods were a bit high-handed, she knew her grandmother wanted the best for her. Yet she couldn't bring herself to marry Wildon Fethersham. Not even to spite her father.

The ladies retired for the evening a short time later, without another word spoken about Meg's future husband. Although Hermione had kept her word, Meg was certain the discussion would rise from the ashes on the morrow.

An hour after going to bed, Meg was still awake, staring at the dark folds of the canopy overhead. The discussion this evening had dredged too many memories to allow for peaceful slumber. Too much bitterness to allow any comfort.

Less than a fortnight ago, her father had come to see

her, his second visit since his return from the war in August. Although a part of her wanted desperately to believe his sudden attention was due to the fact that he missed her, she knew better than to believe in miracles.

With the death of her brother Colin at Waterloo, she was now her father's heir. He wanted her to return to Scotland, to the home she had once loved. Not because he missed her. No, his motive had nothing to do with affection. He wanted to preserve his precious land. His daughter was merely a means to an end.

She threw the covers aside and climbed from bed. The soft flickering glow of the fire on the hearth guided her across the room, the thick wool of the blue and white carpet cushioning her bare feet. She pulled open the blue silk brocade drapes shrouding one of the windows overlooking the gardens at the back of the house. Moonlight rushed through the square panes, embracing her in silvery light.

She opened the window, welcoming the chilly air against her warm cheeks. It was a clear night, but the air carried a smoky scent. The air in London was never as sweet and clean as in Somerset. And Somerset could not compare to the Highlands. For all the years she had lived in England, and all the attempts at burying memories, she had never forgotten the scent of heather in the rain.

High above, the stars burned silvery holes in the black velvet of the sky. She found the cluster forming the constellation Orion, picked the brightest star, as her father had taught her when she was a child.

You see that star, Meg? That's our special star. When you've grown and you're away from me, you can look up at that star, and know I'm looking at it too, thinking of my little girl.

Did he ever look at that star and think of her? Her

throat tightened with the threat of tears. Lord, the reason she still allowed that man to hurt her was beyond her comprehension. She rubbed her arms, her hands sliding against the soft white lawn of her nightgown, fighting the chill of the evening. But she couldn't quell the chill of memories and broken dreams. One of these days her father would regret—

What was that?

Although she heard nothing, she sensed movement behind her, a shifting of air in the shadows. Shivers skittered across her skin, raising the fine hair on her arms. Someone was in the room. She started to turn. A strong arm whipped around her waist, dragging her back against a chest as hard as oak. She opened her mouth to scream. The intruder clamped his hand over her mouth, capturing the sound against his warm palm.

Fear shot through her, flashing along her nerves like electricity arcing across a wire. She struggled against her attacker, twisting in his powerful arms, a rabbit caught in the jaws of a hound.

"Easy," he whispered.

Desperate with fear she clawed at the hand clamped to her mouth. When that accomplished nothing, she swung her elbows back, ramming her attacker beneath his diaphragm. His breath whooshed past her ear. His grip slackened for an instant. With all of her weight, she plunged against his arm, breaking free, lunging straight for the open window. She gasped. She windmilled her arms, a fledgling falling from the nest.

"Damnation!" He grabbed her arm, dragging her back from the fall. He wrapped one strong arm around her, imprisoning her arms to her sides, while he clamped his other hand over her mouth. "Take it easy, Meg, before you kill yourself."

Memory stirred with the sound of his dark voice,

colored with the soft burr of the Scottish upper class. Meg froze in his powerful embrace. An intriguing scent of sandalwood and leather coiled around her. Her heart pounded; her skin tingled. She was certain she knew this man. Yet she couldn't gather all the pieces of the puzzle. Who was he?

"I'm not going to hurt you, sweetheart. It's me, Alec. Alec MacLaren."

Chapter Two

Alec! The room whirled around her. The heat of his body radiated through the fine white lawn of her nightgown, seeping into her blood, warming her, dissolving her fear.

"You remember me, don't you?"

Meg nearly laughed. How could she ever have forgotten Alec? She nodded, too stunned to do anything else.

"Now if you promise not to scream, I'll take my hand away from your sweet lips."

Meg nodded once more. He eased his hand away from her mouth.

"Alec?" She twisted her head, looking back at the man who still held her close against his chest. Moonlight spilled over him, spilling silver onto the thick black waves of hair that curled against the back of his white collar. The silvery light sculpted the sharply defined features of a face that could steal a maiden's fancy with one glimpse. Thick black lashes framed eyes as blue as a Highland sky. Eyes filled with a glint of mischief. Eyes that had haunted her dreams.

Excitement bubbled inside of her, like water in a steaming kettle. Until a few months ago she had believed the reports declaring Alec dead, killed on the battlefield at Waterloo, beside Colin. She had mourned this man, as bitterly as she had mourned the loss of her brother.

Only, Meg had never felt any sisterly affection for Alec. Not Alec. She had loved him with all her heart and soul. Loved him with the innocent intensity of a fourteen-year-old girl experiencing her first infatuation. But this infatuation had refused to die an orderly death. Since she believed in honesty, she had to admit that she still held a special place in her heart for Alec MacLaren. "What are you doing in my bedchamber?"

His lips tipped upward into a devilish grin. "As I recall, you said you'd be waiting for me when I came back home. Well now, I got home and you weren't there. So I came to fetch you."

Ten years ago she had made a complete cake of herself with this man, confessing her love, pledging her undying devotion. In the past ten years she had pictured exactly how she would behave when next she met Alec MacLaren. She would be cool, aloof, untouchable. Alec would see she had grown elegant in his absence. Refined. He would see she was no longer the naive child who adored him, but a woman. A desirable woman. He, of course, would fall desperately in love with her.

Although Meg had often imagined the day Alec would walk back into her life, she had never seen it quite this way. "You came to fetch me?"

"That's right." Alec released her, grinning at her as she pivoted to face him. "I have a coach in the lane behind your house, waiting to take you back home."

His words swirled in her befuddled brain. "You can't be serious."

Alec lifted one black brow, his expression drawing into mock severity. "Now, Meg, I took you for a girl who kept her word."

"I was fourteen!"

"Ten years is a long time to wait." Alec winked at her. "But wait for me you did."

Heat crept into her cheeks. There was more truth in his words than she was willing to admit. Too often she had caught herself comparing a suitor to her image of Alec—an ideal no man had been able to match. "I did no such thing."

He feigned shock. "Do you mean to say you're going back on your word?"

"Do you really imagine you can simply barge into my life and expect me to . . ." A disturbing thought struck her, as sharply as an open hand across her cheek. "You've been back from the war since August. Why did you suddenly decide you needed to *fetch* me?"

Alec shrugged, broad shoulders lifting beneath the smooth black wool of his coat. "It took a while to get my strength back."

The thought of his wounds sent a shiver through her, distracting her. Alec had been declared dead on the battlefield. His name had been printed in the *Times*, along with all the other officers killed in those last few days of battle. Meg knew Alec had been wounded terribly. He must have nearly died. Yet she couldn't see a trace remaining from his injuries. In fact, he looked . . . wonderful.

She was staring at the man. She knew it. Yet knowing and amending were two entirely different things. She tried to reconcile the image of the eighteen-year-old boy she had known, with the man he had become.

He was tall, even taller than she remembered. The black wool of his coat hugged the width of his broad shoulders. The snug fit of his buff-colored trousers molded narrow hips and long, muscular legs.

It wasn't at all proper to notice a man's physique, especially when that man had just invaded her bedchamber. But this man commanded her attention with an intriguing blend of elegance and power. The slender boy she had known had developed into a splendidly proportioned, powerfully built, terribly handsome man.

The glitter of amusement in his eyes told her Alec knew exactly how attractive she found him. He lowered his eyes, favoring her with a similar inspection. Meg felt his gaze as keenly as a soft brush of strong, masculine hands across her skin. His gaze slid in a warm caress from the lace just below her chin to her bare toes peeking out from the hem of her nightgown. Excitement surged in the wake of that gaze, setting her limbs trembling like leaves in a summer storm.

"You did a fine job of growing up, Meg," Alec said softly.

His darker-than-midnight voice flowed over her, making her warm and achy inside. Countless times Meg had imagined this man noticing her across a crowded ballroom. Alec wouldn't recognize her, of course; she had changed too much from the child he had known. But he would be drawn to her, intrigued by the elegant lady she had become. Of course, she had never once imagined Alec would storm into her bedchamber. The realization snapped her out of her besotted stupor.

The man thought he could snap his fingers and she would swoon, like a fourteen-year-old girl smitten with her first love. Well, he would see she was no longer the naive little girl he had left behind.

28

Meg marched across the room and snatched her green velvet dressing gown from the chair beside the bed. She threw on her robe and fumbled with the sash, painfully aware of the man who watched her every move. Still not feeling covered enough, she shoved her feet into her slippers. When she had regained some measure of composure she turned to face the rogue. He was smiling as though he were enjoying himself immensely.

She lifted her chin, assuming the haughty attitude she had learned her first London Season. She only hoped he wouldn't notice the way she was trembling. "You're here because of my father, aren't you?" she asked, voicing her worst suspicion.

Alec hesitated a moment, as if weighing his words before he spoke. "Your father needs to see you, Meg."

Alec's sudden appearance had nothing at all to do with any sudden need to be with her. Meg ignored the sharp twist of pain in her chest, telling herself it certainly didn't matter what Alec MacLaren thought of her. Still, it took every ounce of her willpower to keep her voice steady. "Since you were friends with my brother, I shall give you the opportunity to leave, without summoning a watchman."

"I'm not leaving without you."

"I'm not going anywhere with you."

Alec moved toward her with the slow, powerful grace of a man in command of his realm. "If I had known you would grow up to be so bonnie fair, I would have come to see you a long time ago."

The warmth in his eyes kindled an answering flame deep inside of her. In the past Meg had been told she was beautiful. Such flattery was common among men intent on claiming a wealthy bride. A woman would be a muttonheaded dolt to believe every silly scrap of flattery cast in her direction. Especially by this man. "Save

29

your false flattery. It shall have no influence, I assure you."

"It isn't flattery. It's the truth."

Although she realized she was not unattractive, she was not at all the ideal of true English beauty. She was too tall. Her hair was not a pale yellow. Instead of sculpted perfection, her nose had the unfortunate inclination to tip upward at the end. Although oval in shape, her cheekbones were too prominent to give her face that delicate, rounded appearance so adored. She certainly wasn't the ideal of feminine beauty. Yet this man made her feel beautiful with a glance. *Deceiving scoundrel!*

"I'm warning you, if you put one hand on me, I'll scream." She stepped back, too late.

Alec grabbed her upper arms. Before she could utter more than a gasp, he hauled her against his chest. In the next heartbeat he clamped his mouth over hers.

Meg pounded her fists against his shoulders, with all the impact of a butterfly ramming a lion. Alec didn't notice her protest. He didn't seem to care that she stood rigid, her lips sealed together. She curled her hands into fists against his shoulders. She would not be seduced by the rogue.

Alec slid his lips across hers in a lazy glide, as though he had all the time in the world. Heat kindled in the sweet friction, a delicious burn that simmered along her every nerve, melting her resistance. This was Alec holding her. Alec kissing her. Meg snatched at her scattering will. She certainly would not . . .

Alec touched the seam of her lips with the tip of his tongue, tempting her to open for him. His scent teased her senses, tugging at her in a curious fashion. She couldn't . . .

Her thoughts disintegrated in the warmth Alec kindled inside of her. He was so warm, a breath of summer in the depth of winter. Alec's kiss was nothing like those she had ever experienced before. Her prior experience involved a few swipes at her lips by over-zealous suitors. Men she couldn't even remember. Not the full charge of a man she had never forgotten. Nothing had prepared her for Alec MacLaren's kiss. Not even her dreams.

In dreams Meg had felt Alec's arms close around her. In dreams she had tasted his kisses. In dreams she had imagined desire. Yet dreams could not compare to reality. She had imagined desire a pleasant emotion, a little naughty, deliciously wicked. Desire was an attraction between man and woman, tugging one toward the other. Now she realized she had misunderstood. She had completely underestimated the emotion.

Desire was as powerful as a storm racing across the sea. Desire rushed over her, a savage wave, enveloping her, dragging her away from shore. Without realizing it, Meg had been waiting for this moment all of her life. Without thought she threw her arms around his neck, held him, afraid he would disappear like a phantom in the moonlight.

A low growl issued from deep in his throat. Alec pulled her closer, his powerful arms lifting her upward, until her toes barely touched the floor. She clung to him, sipping the potent elixir of his kiss, welcoming the startling slide of his tongue into her mouth.

Meg snuggled against his hardened frame, trying to get closer to the warmth radiating through wool and linen. She slipped her hand into the thick ebony waves at his nape, plunging her fingers into cool strands of silk. *Alec*. Her own precious hero.

Alec stiffened against her, his arms tightening around her. In the next instant he pulled away from her. She clung to him like a drowning woman. He gripped her upper arms and eased her away from him.

He held her at arm's length, as though he couldn't decide whether to push her away or draw her back into his arms. She stared up at him, dazed, as wobbly as a newborn fawn. For a moment he looked as confused as she felt.

Soon the confusion in his eyes dissolved into a glint of pure masculine pride. A smile slowly tipped one corner of his lips. Reality awakened with that smile, and poured over her, like a bucket of ice water. He touched her and she turned into a blithering idiot.

The man had come here at her father's bidding. Alec had plied his charm to manipulate her. Well, if he thought he could beguile her with a kiss, if he imagined he could coax her into following him like a besotted puppy, he was mistaken. "Leave this room at once."

Alec stared into her upturned countenance, seeing her fury, resisting the urge to pull her back into his arms. He wanted to kiss her prim little mouth until she opened for him again, until all the icy fury melted into sweet, heated desire. Yet kissing her again wouldn't be wise. No matter how much he craved the taste of her. He wasn't certain he could stop with one more kiss.

Alec had meant to soften her with that kiss, shatter her defenses. He hadn't expected to want her this way, with a need that clawed at his belly. He couldn't remember a time when a kiss had left him as shaken as a green recruit facing his first battle. He flexed his hands against her arms, wondering if Meg realized how close he was to tossing her back against that big bed and seducing her right out of her innocence. "Bonnie fair and shimmering with Scottish fire."

"Take your hands off of me," Meg said, her voice once more frozen into crisp English ice.

Even in the dim light, Alec could see the color riding high in her cheeks, the fury flashing in her eyes. His heated temptress had frozen into an icy English princess. One moment she was kissing him as though her world would shatter if the kiss should end. The next she was glaring daggers at him. Glaring at him with eyes as green as a Highland glen in springtime. Even in her fury, those eyes were beautiful.

He suspected Meg was almost as furious with herself as she was with him. Furious for allowing herself to surrender ground to the enemy. That kiss had spoken more eloquently than words. That kiss had managed to sear away most of his doubts about the plans he had made for this woman. No matter what she might think, Meg didn't belong with Wildon. She had too much fire in her. It was a mercy rescuing her from that fancy fop. Trouble was, she didn't share his opinion. "Come back home, Meg."

"If you don't leave this instant, I'm going to scream," Meg said. "You'll find yourself behind bars."

"I was hoping we wouldn't have to do this the hard way," Alec said, pulling a white silk scarf from his coat pocket.

Meg tugged against the grip of his hand wrapped around her upper arm. "What are you doing?"

"I apologize for this." Alec spun her around and released her.

"Alec MacLaren, I demand—" Before she realized his intention, he whipped the scarf around her mouth. She struggled, clawing at his hands as he tied the scarf behind her head.

Alec grabbed her wrists and drew them behind her. "Trust me, Meg. This is for your own good."

Meg screamed, her voice muffled by the silk gag. He pulled a second scarf from his pocket and tied her wrists together. She twisted and turned, trying to jerk her wrists from his grasp.

"Easy. You'll hurt yourself." He gripped her shoulders and turned her around to face him. Meg glared at him in silent fury. "I promise you, everything is going to be all right."

Meg mumbled against the silk.

"I'm sorry to be doing this. But you leave me no choice." Alec kissed her brow.

Meg lashed out, kicking his shin with her slippered foot. Alec scarcely felt the blow through the leather of his boot. She winced, a groan escaping her lips.

"Ah, Meg, in time you'll understand." Alec bent and tossed her over his shoulder. "This is all for your own good."

Meg squirmed and kicked, hitting nothing but air. Alec held her securely, his arm around her thighs, the warm curve of her hip against his cheek. The scent of vanilla mingled with a spice that was hers alone, teased him, tempted him. Desire stirred in his belly, swirling heat through his loins. He clenched his jaw, fighting the need curling deep inside him.

She wiggled and shouted, the sounds muffled by the gag. Yet Alec was certain he heard something about boiling oil in the muttered curses. This was for her own good, he assured himself. He carried her down the back stairs, across the kitchen, and out the back door, following the route detailed by one of the Chadburne maids, a woman only too willing to help him for a few pieces of gold.

Meg twisted and bucked. Right now she wanted to kill him, Alec thought. At the moment she was contemplating the ways she would do the deed. In time he would make her understand this was all for the best, he assured himself. He knew women. By the time they reached Dunleith, he would have her purring like a kitten. She rammed her knee into his chest. He grimaced with a sudden flare of pain. In the meantime, he made a mental note to keep sharp objects away from her.

Alec hurried along a brick-lined path leading to the lane behind the house. His elegant black traveling coach stood hitched to a team of four matched grays, waiting to whisk them away from town.

One of his servants opened the door to the coach, casting his master a smile. " 'Tis a bonnie night, milord."

Alec grinned. "Aye, Gordon. A bonnie, fair night."

Meg screamed against the gag. She twisted, her body stiff with rage. Alec carried his fair burden inside the coach. Gordon closed the door behind him. Meg wailed, bucking wildly on his shoulder.

As the coach lurched forward, Alec eased her to one of the seats. Meg tumbled back against the black velvet squabs, her unbound hair spilling over her face in a thick curtain of honey-colored silk. She sat up, stiff and indignant beneath a veil of hair.

Alec tried not to notice the way her robe and nightgown had twisted around her thighs, revealing the smooth curves of shapely legs, the delicate turn of her slender ankles. He stood for a moment, swaying with the rocking of the coach, trying to catch his breath. Until now he had thought he had regained all of his strength. Yet the dull ache throbbing in his chest reminded him of how close he had come to surrendering his place in this world. The trip from Dunleith had taken more out of him than he had expected.

Meg shifted on the cushion, trying to toss the hair back from her face. Alec knelt on one knee in front of her. "I'm not going to hurt you, Meg," he said, smoothing her hair back from her face.

When he saw the expression on her beautiful face, he nearly allowed the hair to slide back into place. Meg glared at him, her eyes narrowed to green slits, her lips taut over the gag, her cheeks high with color. The back of his neck prickled. Women were unpredictable at best. When angry, there was nothing in the world more dangerous.

Alec had ridden straight into the fire of French artillery, met sword with sword, faced death countless times on the battlefield. Yet the anger blazing inside this one slender woman sent a shiver along his spine. For a moment he considered keeping her tied and gagged until they reached Scotland. That thought quickly vanished when he realized how uncomfortable she was.

Alec told himself this was ridiculous. Meg was a woman. A slender slip of a girl. He could manage her. He tugged on the gag. Even if she was angry, he could certainly handle her, he assured himself. When he pulled the silk away from her mouth, she didn't say a word. She simply sat there, glaring at him as though she wanted to tear him to shreds with her bare hands.

He stared down into her furious green eyes and wondered what defense a man could use against an angry woman. He couldn't strike her. Any man who raised a hand against a woman was less than a coward. So what defense did that leave him? He had an uneasy feeling he was going to have to figure it out. Soon. "If you turn a wee bit, I'll untie you."

Meg turned on the seat, presenting him her stiff back. Alec lifted her hair, the silky strands sliding through his fingers, the scent of vanilla curling around him. Light from the interior coach lamps rippled through the long veil of silk, finding chestnut highlights nestled in the honey-colored strands. For a moment he became distracted, staring at her hair, resisting the urge to bury his face in the fragrant mane. He imagined the silky slide of her hair across his bare chest, images sparking desire, lust sinking claws into his belly.

She glanced over her shoulder, catching him staring

like an idiot at her hair. Alec dropped the tresses over her shoulder.

"I know you're angry now." He drew the white silk away from her hands, frowning at the red marks the binding had left on her wrists.

Meg pivoted on the cushion, fixing him in an icy stare.

Alec came to his feet. "But I'm certain, in time, you'll see—"

She lashed out, hitting his shin with the bottom of her slipper. He jumped back, before she could connect with something more vital. "Now, Meg, you—"

"Blackguard!" She scrambled from her seat and lunged for him, ramming his chest with her shoulder. Pain from wounds suffered in battle vibrated through him, snatching the breath from his lungs. Alec fell back against the cushions, taking Meg with him. She sprawled across his chest, her hip jabbing his ribs. Pain flickered with each bounce of her slender body against his chest, as she twisted and squirmed and pounded her fists against his shoulders.

"Damnation!" He grabbed her wrists and shifted, dragging her down to the cushions.

"Let go of me!" Meg bucked wildly, ramming his belly with her knee.

Alec swallowed a groan. Silently he cursed the night he had agreed to bring the hellcat home. He pinned her against the cushions, crushing her struggles beneath his body. "Enough!"

Instantly she stopped flailing at him. She lay pinned against the cushions, her glorious hair spilled around her face, her eyes wide with the sudden shock of having a man flush against her.

Alec admitted he was experiencing a shock of his own. The soft mounds of her breasts pressed against his chest, searing him through the layers of their clothing. He was aware of every place her body touched his, as though she were a flame burning him, searing temptation into his skin.

This wouldn't do. Not at all. He was a man who prided himself on his control. And he didn't intend to lose it. Not now. Not with so much at stake.

"If you can't behave yourself, I'm going to bind your hands and ankles and keep you tied up until we reach Scotland," Alec said, wondering what he would do if she called his bluff. "Do you understand me?"

Meg narrowed her eyes. "You wouldn't dare."

Alec lifted one brow. "Think again."

The gentle rocking of the coach rubbed her breasts against his chest, brushed her belly against his hardening frame, coaxing heat to shimmer through his blood. He had never seen anything as intriguing as Meg in a fit of fury, her eyes flashing fire, her breasts rising and falling with every angry breath. It made a man wonder what it might be like to divert all that fire in a much more pleasurable direction. And that was a direction his thoughts had no business taking, he reminded himself.

"We have a long journey ahead of us, Meg. We can pass the time pleasantly, or you can be tied up like an unruly animal. The choice is up to you. Are you willing to try acting like a lady instead of a shrew?"

"You have the audacity to criticize my behavior?"

"Well now, you have to admit you've hardly been behaving like a lady."

"Why you . . . you . . . get off of me, you big brute!"

Alec smiled. "Promise to behave?"

"I promise to make you regret the day you were born!"

Alec shrugged. "Then I guess I'll just have to . . . kiss you."

Her eyes grew wide. "No!"

He brushed his lips across her brow. "Change your mind?"

Meg turned her head, trying to escape his touch. "Let me go!"

Alec nuzzled the smooth skin beneath her right ear. "Ah, you smell good," he whispered.

She twisted beneath him. "Stop it!"

He flicked the tip of his tongue against her skin. "Hmmm, you taste good too."

"Let me go!"

Alec nipped her earlobe. "Do you promise to behave yourself?"

"Brute!"

He brushed kisses down the length of her neck. "Of course, I don't mind if you want to argue with me all night."

"Stop it!"

Alec pushed aside the lacy edge of her nightgown with his nose, nuzzling the soft skin at the joining of her neck and shoulder. Blood pounded low in his belly. "Are you this soft everywhere, Meg?"

"All right! I'll behave."

He lifted far enough to look down into her eyes. "Do you give your word? Upon your honor?"

Meg released her breath in an angry huff that brushed his face with heat. "Yes. I give you my word. Now get off of me."

Alec lingered a moment longer than he should, enjoying the heat of her, the scent of her, looking down into her eyes, seeing a glitter of something more interesting than anger in the green depths. There was a spark between them, a flicker of flame that could easily ignite and consume every chance for common sense. He couldn't allow that to happen.

Alec pulled away from her, feeling as though he were tearing away a good portion of his own skin. He watched her scramble to the seat across from him, her hair swirling around her hips. She sank to the black cushions and fixed him in a glare cold enough to freeze the depths of Loch Ness. He had a feeling this was going to be the longest journey he had ever made.

Chapter Three

Meg sat in Alec's coach, rubbing her wrists, glaring at the man lounging against the black velvet cushions across from her, his long legs stretched out to the side to accommodate their length. Alec was smiling at her, watching her like a wary lion not quite certain of his prey. The clatter of wheels and horseshoes filled up the silence stretching between them.

Strange, she was being kidnapped, but she wasn't frightened. Furious, but not frightened. Deep inside, she knew Alec would never hurt her. She, on the other hand, intended to make him regret the day he was born. "I thought you were a man of honor, Alec MacLaren. Yet you allowed Robert Drummond to convince you to kidnap me."

"He asked me to see you safely home." Flickering light from the coach lamp above him touched his face with gold, gilding the tips of his long black lashes.

41

"Your father is concerned about you. He wants to spend some time with you."

Meg glanced down at her hands, fighting the urge to scream. Not only had Alec betrayed her, so had her father. Once again. "My father is concerned about his precious land."

"You're his daughter, Meg, all he has left in this world," Alec said, his dark voice brushing over her like warm velvet. "He's concerned about your future."

"He is concerned I will allow his lands to fall into the hands of an Englishman. That's the only reason he wants me to come home."

"I won't lie to you. He is worried you'll allow Drummond land to fall into the hands of a man like Wildon Fethersham. He has seen what the clearances have done to the crofters. He doesn't want that to happen on Drummond land."

She squeezed her hands in her lap, wondering what her grandmother would say about the outcome of her little attempt to punish Robert Drummond.

Alec leaned forward, resting his forearms on his thighs, clasping his hands between his knees. "But that's not the only reason he wants you home."

Meg stared at his hands. They were such strong-looking hands, the fingers long and tapered, his skin kissed by the sun. The hands of a warrior. Yet his touch, even when he was quelling her struggles, had been gentle. A tremor rippled through her at the memory of those powerful hands touching her. She glanced away, staring down at her own tightly clenched hands. "I'm certain I don't care what reasons he might have. Unless he plans to keep me locked in my room, I won't be staying at Penross House."

"He needs you, Meg."

"Strange, he never needed me before."

"He has always needed you, and your mother. But neither one of you trusted him enough to believe in his innocence. You turned your backs on him."

Meg fixed him in a stare that had quelled many a presumptuous male. "You are hardly in a position to judge my actions."

Alec held her withering stare without flinching. "Your father told me everything."

"Then you know only his twisted version of the story."

"I fought beside Sir Robert Drummond for nine years. You learn a lot about a man in nine years. Your father is honorable. If it weren't for him, I wouldn't be alive."

After Waterloo the *Times* had been filled with tales of bravery. Daring tales of men who had risked their lives to vanquish Napoleon. During the war Robert Drummond had been decorated for valor. As had the man who sat across from her. So much for a hero's honor. "Robert Drummond's honor does not extend to his wife."

Alec frowned, a single line creasing the skin between his black brows. "The man is your father. I would think you could find enough trust in him to believe his side of the story."

Meg stiffened with the condemnation in his voice. Alec had no idea the pain Robert Drummond's selfish act had caused. Alec had never seen her mother sobbing in the middle of the night for the man who had destroyed her world. She had. Alec had never wept so hard he had made himself ill, wishing for a miracle. She had. Alec couldn't understand how betrayed she felt. She had trusted her father more than anyone in the world. Until the night he had shattered her trust and destroyed her family.

"You have no right to judge my actions," she said,

keeping her voice level. "I was there that night. I know what I saw."

"Things aren't always what they seem, Meg."

"That's true." Meg forced her lips into a chilly smile. "You appear a gentleman. You have been honored for your bravery in battle. Yet here you are, kidnapping a woman."

His lips tipped upward into a devilish grin. "I'm simply escorting you home."

"Against my will."

"Aye. Unfortunately, you don't have the good sense to return to your home on your own. I'm afraid the years you've spent in England have muddled your brain. Made you more English than Scottish."

"Why you . . . you . . ."

"But I have hope for you." Alec sat back, grinning at her, mischief glinting in his stunning eyes. "When we get you back to the Highlands, you just might be able to shed all that English skin of yours."

Meg clasped her hands on her lap. "Unfortunately, I have no hope for you, Alec MacLaren. You shall no doubt remain a barbarian. After all, it's in your Highland blood."

Alec wiggled his eyebrows. "Don't be forgetting, lass, some of that wild Highland blood flows through your own veins, mingling with all that English ice water."

"The ice manages to keep me civilized, MacLaren. At the moment, you should be thankful for it."

Alec chuckled softly. "There was a time when you liked me."

"There was a time when I wore my hair in braids."

Alec studied her a moment, a warm smile playing on his lips. "From what I gathered in your bedchamber, I thought you might still like me a wee bit."

How dare the man throw her own foolishness back in her face! "You thought wrong."

Alec leaned forward, so close she could catch the scent of sandalwood rising with the heat of his skin. "Meg, I know this isn't exactly a fine beginning, but I hope one day we can be friends again."

Friends. Such an insignificant word for all the affection she had once felt for this man. "It is not my custom to make friends with vile, deceiving . . ."

Alec held up his hands in a gesture of surrender. "Perhaps we can discuss this again when you're in a better mood."

A scar sliced a diagonal path across his left palm. The slender white ribbon of flesh trailed along the side of his wrist, disappearing into the cuff of his white shirt. In spite of her best intentions, she caught herself wanting to touch him, to trace the old paths of his wounds with her fingertips, to assure herself he was well and truly healed. *Foolish woman*. "I assure you, I shall never change my mind."

He studied her a moment, his expression growing serious. "I'm not your enemy."

"You will pardon me if I hold a different view."

Alec smiled, all the warmth of summer filling his blue eyes. "All things in their time. I'll keep my hope of changing your mind."

A sensible woman would despise this man. Unfortunately, there was something about Alec MacLaren that melted her sensibilities to mush. With a silent oath Meg crushed the tender feelings Alec evoked in her. He was a man. Worse, he was a Highlander. A woman would be a fool to trust one of his breed. Any woman who gave one of the barbarians her heart could expect it to be broken into a thousand pieces. She really must remember that.

"Since you arranged to kidnap me from my bedchamber, I suppose it's too much to hope you had

45

enough sense to bring some clothes along for me," Meg said, employing her haughtiest tone.

Alec had the audacity to grin at her. "I was willing to let you pack, but since you insisted on doing this your way, I didn't."

"I would hardly call being tossed over a man's shoulder and kidnapped from my house *my* way of doing things."

Alec shrugged. "I suppose we'll have to make do. If you'd like, you can borrow some of my clothes."

Meg stared at the man. "How in the world do you expect me to enter a posting inn dressed in your clothes?"

"Ah well, if that's all you're worried about, you needn't."

Meg frowned, an uneasy sensation gripping her stomach. "What do you mean?"

"Seeing we won't be stopping at any inns, there is no worry of anyone seeing you. No matter how you're dressed." His grin turned devilish. "Except me, of course."

Even though the seats were well padded and the big coach rocked gently on well-oiled springs, Meg knew how uncomfortable traveling would become in a matter of hours. "You can't mean to drive straight through to Dunleith?"

"We'll stop to change horses, of course, and for other necessities. But I'm afraid we can't stay overnight." Alec rubbed his thumb over his knee, glancing down at the buff-colored wool as he spoke. "Under the circumstances, I think it's the best course of action."

"You mean you're afraid your prisoner will escape."

He glanced at her. "I was thinking more about your reputation."

Meg frowned. "My reputation?"

"It wouldn't do for someone to see you at a posting

inn with a man who isn't your husband."

Meg sat back, all the blood draining from her limbs when she thought of the scandal that would explode should anyone glimpse her at an inn, escorted by an unmarried man. It wouldn't matter that the man was kidnapping her. It wouldn't matter that her honor was intact. She would be labeled damaged goods, no matter what the circumstances. She would never again be accepted in polite society. Her mother and grandmother would not be spared. They too would be shunned by the haute ton. Humiliated again by the man who had already caused her mother too much pain.

Alec leaned forward and took her hand in his warm grasp. "Don't worry, Meg. I'll make certain no one sees you."

There was such comfort in his touch, that gentle embrace of his hand, such concern in his dark voice. It was so tempting to keep her hand warm and secure in his hold. So tempting to rest her head against his chest. Pity all he could offer was a lie. She snatched her hand from his grasp. "Please forgive me if I find your reassurances less than comforting."

Alec studied her. For a moment Meg imagined seeing regret in the stunning blue depths of his eyes, a flicker of sadness that evoked a response within her. She quickly dismissed the infuriating instinct coaxing her to comfort him. She was the one who deserved comfort. Not that infernal brute. "My mother will be frantic with worry when she discovers I'm missing."

"I arranged to have a note delivered to her tomorrow morning."

In spite of the dread gripping her stomach, Meg managed a smile. "I'm certain a note from a kidnapper will put her mind at ease."

"I told her you were safe with me, and that I was escorting you home."

"My mother will not allow this to pass, MacLaren. She will send someone after me. You will find yourself behind bars."

Alec grinned, looking pleased with himself. "I'm hoping she decides to come after you herself. It's about time she became reacquainted with her husband again."

Meg stared at him a moment. "Are you playing matchmaker?"

"Would it be so terrible, Meg?" he asked, his voice low and soft. "If your mother found her way back to your father's arms, would it be so terrible?"

Meg turned away from his penetrating gaze, hoping Alec couldn't see the pain his careless words had twisted from her heart. The coach had made its way out of the confines of London. Beyond the window glass, moonlight rippled across the trees lining the road, splashing silver deep into the heart of darkness. The steady rumble of horseshoes and carriage wheels filtered into the quiet compartment. She was aware of Alec watching her, quietly prying into her thoughts. "I'm certain my mother has no intention of allowing that man to humiliate her again."

"Ah, lass, if you could only see how much your father misses his wife, you wouldn't be doubting his love for her."

"I doubt the sincerity of anything Robert Drummond does or says."

Alec released his breath in a long sigh. "I hope you learn to look beyond your own pain, Meg. It's the only way you'll see the truth."

Meg cast him a dark glance before deciding to ignore the beast. She turned down the coach lamp on her side, taking what little privacy the shadows afforded. Her father wanted to see her. *Fine.* When she saw Sir Robert Drummond, she would tell him exactly what she thought of his high-handed tactics. The man had gone too far. As for the blackguard he had sent to do his dirty work, she would make Alec MacLaren regret his part in this crime. She wasn't certain how she would punish the man, but punish him she would. If it took her until the day she died.

Alec leaned against the black velvet cushions, watching Meg fidget on the squabs across from him in her attempts to get comfortable. The air was chilly, but not nearly as frosty as the lady. He pulled a wool carriage rug in the MacLaren tartan from the narrow compartment behind his seat and tossed it over her knees. "You might be needing this."

Meg tossed him a chilly look.

He smiled, hoping to melt a wee bit of ice.

She turned her head on the padded back, dismissing him without a word.

Alec reached up and turned down the coach lamp, moonlight filling up the space as the flame died. This was all for her own good, he reminded himself. Still, he couldn't quite shake the guilt nipping at his heels. He wished he had come to see her months ago. Perhaps then they could have avoided this battle.

While Alec lay near death in a Brussels hospital, he had made plans to visit Meg. He wanted to give his condolences about Colin. He knew Colin and Meg had remained close through the destruction of their family. Yet Alec hadn't expected his own family to be destroyed while he fought for his life. When he came home, circumstances had prevented him from doing more than trying to put his own house in order.

Alec returned from the grave to find his family gone, lost in a fire that had destroyed the east wing of Dunleith Castle. Since the Ministry had declared him legally dead, his own identity was in question for weeks. His father's title and estates had fallen into the hands of the next in line: Wildon Fethersham, his all-too-English cousin. Unfortunately, his father's eldest sister had made the error of marrying an English aristocrat. From what he had seen, Alec had long ago decided Scottish blood did not mix well with the ice that flowed through English veins. Robert Drummond was a testament to what happened when a man lost his heart to a pretty English lady.

Not that Alec hadn't dallied with his share of Englishwomen. Yet he had never entertained the idea of taking one for a bride. English marriages were arranged for the sake of bloodline and wealth. Husbands sought refuge from their icy wives with mistresses. Wives took lovers. And the polite world looked the other way. Alec would have none of it. No, when it came to marriage he would find a fiery Scottish lass.

Still, during the past few months, while his body healed and Alec tried to shoulder all the responsibilities left to him by the deaths of his father and older brother, the pursuit of a wife had been the last thing on his mind.

Alec watched the moonlight stroke Meg's smooth cheek, and wondered how he might mend his bridges with the lovely lady. Meg was no longer the fiery little girl he had known. True, she had Drummond blood in her veins. But from what he could see, the lady was English from the top of her golden head to the tips of her dainty toes. Still, he wondered if the Scottish lass he had known still lived deep inside of this icy Englishwoman. For Robert's sake as well as his own, Alec had to try to find her.

Unfortunately, his experience with gently bred maidens was limited. His years in the army had given him a great deal of experience with ladies of a more worldly nature: lovely widows looking for excitement; pretty whores looking for gold. Although Alec had never sought it, he had gained a reputation for charming the ladies. Still, he hadn't exactly impressed Meg with his devilish charm. Perhaps he should have spent more time in London when he was a youth, gaining experience with her species.

Although Alec had visited London several times in the past ten years, he had never appreciated the allure of the Season. Members of the haute ton scurrying from one glittering ball to the next, like butterflies trying to sample every flower in a crowded garden. Aggressive mamas shoving shivering chits into the paths of eligible bachelors. Dandies preening like cocks in a barnyard. The entire English whirl did not appeal to him.

Instead of London, Alec had preferred to spend his few precious days of leave each year at home, in the Highlands. Now he acknowledged some regret that he had never gone to visit Meg. His reasons had seemed sound each time he had decided against going to see her.

The first year he hadn't wanted to intrude after all the trouble had happened with her parents. The next year he had listened to Colin's brotherly pride about the sister who had grown into a beauty and realized his friend was anxious for a match between them. At the time, Alec regarded marriage in the same light as he did pestilence and plague: something to be avoided at all costs. Avoiding Meg seemed the best way to avoid a complication he didn't want.

Alec hadn't been interested in marriage, not while he still had a commission. He was fighting a war, which meant his life expectancy was not the greatest. Although many men dragged their wives with them to the battlefields, he had never possessed a desire to

51

count himself among their number. The thought of his wife mopping up his wounds left him cold. And leaving his wife for months at a time didn't hold any appeal at all. He had always thought marriage could wait until his thirst for glory had been quenched. He had never realized glory could be such a bitter draft.

Meg shifted, propping her head against the side of the coach, muttering a curse under her breath as she tried to find some comfort.

"If you'd like, you can use my shoulder as a pillow."

Meg looked at him with eyes narrowed to emerald slits. "I assure you, I would sleep stretched on a rack before I would lean upon your shoulder."

Alec smiled beneath her icy glare. "If you manage to look past your pride and anger, the shoulder will still be here for you."

She tilted her chin at a militant angle. "I don't want anything you have to offer."

"How do you know, until you've sampled what I'm offering?" He gave her a devilish grin, one that had melted more than a few hearts.

Meg returned an icy glare. "I assure you, the less we have to do with one another for the next few days, the better I shall like it."

"And here I thought we could spend the next few days getting to know each other all over again."

"Since you saw no reason to renew our acquaintance over the past ten years, I see no reason why I should want to renew it now."

Had the lady guarded a small amount of affection for him all these years? Was that part of the reason for her anger? Alec decided to tease her, to see if he could break through all the English ice. "So it seems you really were waiting for me all these years."

Meg stiffened, her back pulling away from the seat. "I certainly haven't spent the past ten years breathlessly waiting for you to charge back into my life."

Alec grinned at her. Perhaps the lady protested a wee bit too much. "And here I was, thinking you had forgotten all about me. If I had known you were still in love with me, I would have—"

"Don't be ridiculous! I have certainly not been coddling some misguided infatuation for you."

He pressed his hand to his heart. "To know one of the fairest ladies in all of England was waiting for me while I—"

The carriage rug smacked his face. When the soft wool tumbled to his lap, he grinned at her. "It's good to see some fine Scottish fire still survives beneath all that English ice."

Meg pursed her lips. He could almost see her gathering the scattered fragments of her control, piecing together her icy mantle. "It is typical of a Scottish barbarian to enjoy the base emotions."

Alec winked at her. "You'll find, lass, there are one or two of the base emotions that can prove quite enjoyable."

Meg snatched the rug from his lap. "I don't plan to remain in Scotland long enough to discover any of them."

He leaned back against the cushions, watching her flick the dark plaid over her legs, spreading squares of sapphire blue and emerald linked by ruby and gold bars. "Wait until you take your first breath of Highland air, sweet with a morning rain. Until you see the sun touch the summit of Ben Lyon. Until you taste a sweet mountain spring. Then maybe you'll change your mind."

"I didn't lose anything in Scotland." Meg turned her head on the back of the seat, dismissing him once more.

Alec watched her, finding some jealousy for the

moonlight that brushed her smooth cheek. Slowly the tension eased from her face as sleep wrapped comforting arms around her. Thick dark lashes lay against her pale cheeks. Soft pink lips parted in a teasing way. He watched her sleep for a long time, wishing she would allow him to shield her from the bumps and the chill of the night.

They had a long road in front of them. Even though he intended to do his best to help, he wondered if there was any chance Meg would soften toward her father. If she refused to change her mind about marriage to Wildon, Alec would soon be faced with his own decision. One he wasn't anxious to make.

Chapter Four

"Oh, my goodness, I think I shall faint." Lady Hermione Chadburne sank back against a sphinx sofa in her yellow drawing room, placing a hand dramatically over her heart.

Joanna stood near the windows, staring down at a letter, reading once more the words she had read a dozen times since the missive had arrived a short time ago. "You had better not," she said, glancing at her mother. "I'm too distracted to tend to you at the moment."

Hermione cast her daughter an irritated look before once more assuming her tragic pose. "Kidnapped! Our little girl has been kidnapped. By a Scots barbarian. By gad, there is no telling what he shall do to her."

Joanna stared at the signature at the bottom of the white parchment, the name etched in an elegantly bold scrawl. "Margaret is with Alec MacLaren. I'm certain he won't harm her."

"How can you be certain?"

"You remember his parents? Douglas and Isobel, the Earl and Countess of Dunleith. Lady Isobel was a dear friend of mine." Joanna watched the rain stream down the windowpanes. "Alec is the last of the family."

Hermione waved her hand impatiently. "I'm not so old I've lost my memory. Of course I remember the earl and countess. Dreadful tragedy last summer. As I recall it happened soon after the youngest son was declared dead at Waterloo. Only, young MacLaren returned from the grave and stole poor Blandford's title from him. Now he has kidnapped my granddaughter. Dreadful man."

"Alec was close friends with Colin. I watched him grow from the time he was a babe. I know he won't hurt Margaret."

"If anyone learns of this, she'll be ruined. Utterly ruined. There won't be a decent family in town who will have her under their roof." Hermione flicked open her fan and started fanning herself in quick agitated movements. "And she won't be the only one ruined. Think of it. The scandal would be tremendous if anyone should know Margaret was alone with that barbarian."

Joanna's chest tightened with the gravity of the situation. She knew what it was like to be humiliated, to have people whisper behind her back. Adultery was common among the haute ton. Deserting a philandering husband was not. One was expected to glance the other way, to forgive, to carry on as though your heart had not been torn from your chest. The scandal in store for Margaret should anyone discover what had happened would be far worse than any Joanna had suffered. "We shall make certain no one finds out about this."

"It's Drummond who is behind this."

"Yes." Joanna curled her hand around the parchment, crushing the letter against her palm. "I'm certain he didn't care for the idea of Margaret marrying Lord Blandford."

Hermione shifted on the sofa. "You needn't give me that dark look. It certainly isn't my fault that barbarian you married has had Margaret kidnapped."

Joanna stared out at the rain-splattered street, watching a carriage plunge through a puddle. "No. I know exactly who to blame."

"Oh, how I would love to see Robert Drummond dangling from the highest bough of a good sturdy oak."

At the moment, hanging seemed much too generous for the scoundrel, Joanna thought. Over the past nine years she had tried to convince herself she no longer cared about that man. Yet Robert Drummond still haunted her. At night he crept into her dreams, holding her, kissing her, loving her. At odd times during the day, she would catch herself thinking of him, wondering if he ever spared her a thought. Did he miss her at all? Did he have any regrets? While he was away at war, she had lived every day in dread, praying both Robert and Colin would return safely. Robert Drummond had been her first love, her only love. And he had destroyed her. "Robert won't get away with this. I won't allow him to destroy my daughter."

Hermione stared at her with wide eyes. "What shall we do?"

"Pack."

Hermione blinked. "Pack?"

Joanna marched toward the door. "I intend to leave for Scotland in an hour."

The glow of morning slipped past the black leather shades Meg had drawn over the coach windows, spilling pale light across her lap. She had finished dressing

57

ten minutes ago. Yet she couldn't bring herself to leave the coach.

Earlier this morning, they had stopped at an inn to obtain provisions, change horses, and use the privy. Wearing one of Alec's greatcoats over her robe, and one of his hats drawn low over her face, she had sneaked about like a thief, terrified someone might see her. Fortunately, no one had.

A few miles north of the inn, they had stopped in a small clearing in a copse of trees near a stream. After informing her he planned to stay only long enough to freshen up and eat breakfast, he departed, leaving her the privacy of the coach. Soon after, a servant had delivered a tin of warm water, soap, a towel, and a portmanteau filled with Alec's clothes. Everything for the comfort of Alec's prisoner.

Meg fiddled with the top button of the shirt she wore. The shoulders of the soft white cambric fell halfway to her elbows. Since the cuffs had swallowed the tips of her fingers, she had rolled them and rolled them, until she had a pile of material at her wrists.

Meg smoothed a crease from the buff-colored pantaloons over her knee, the soft merino wool sliding against her palm. She supposed the pantaloons would reach midcalf on Alec. They bunched around her ankles. Made to fit him like a second skin, the soft wool managed to cling to her hips and hug her legs in a way she felt certain was far from flattering. Her curves had never been generous, and there was no way to conceal that fact in the pantaloons. She had used one of his starched white cravats to cinch the pantaloons around her waist, another to tie back her tangled hair. Her satin slippers completed the outfit.

All in all, she looked . . . ridiculous.

The scent of simmering sausage slipped into the coach, whispering to her hungry stomach. It growled in response. Meg slipped into a dark green riding coat, the sleeves swallowing her hands. As she rolled the soft superfine wool she decided there were two choices she could make. She could hide in the coach like a frightened schoolgirl, or she could face the rogue with her head held high. Even though she looked atrocious.

Meg drew a deep breath and flung open the door of the coach, assuring herself it didn't matter how horrible she looked. She certainly was not interested in what Alec MacLaren might think of her.

A few yards away from the coach, a short, stocky man was tending to the sausages over an open fire, as though he performed the task every day. Near him another servant was lifting a basket of scones from a wicker hamper. Both men nodded when they saw her, wishing her a polite good morning in a broad Scottish burr. Alec was nowhere in sight.

Meg drifted toward the stream, assuring herself it was only exercise she sought. A short distance from the coach, a small table had been placed beneath a tall oak tree. The white linen tablecloth rippled in the breeze. Sunlight spilled through the branches overhead, glittering on crystal glasses, ivory china, and polished silver. It all looked so romantic. Something dangerous stirred in her chest, an insidious monster fashioned from hope and need. If only . . .

No, she thought, crushing the warm feelings stirring inside of her. She wouldn't allow herself to wallow in regrets. Alec was a deceiving scoundrel. Like most men. She wouldn't permit herself to yearn for what might have been.

Meg continued walking toward the stream, wondering where Alec might be. Not that she cared, of course. If she never saw Alec MacLaren again, it would suit her just fine. If she weren't so brutally honest with herself, she might have actually believed that piece of fiction. Instead, she threaded her way through the trees, searching for the infuriating rogue.

The leaves of birch and ash rustled in the chilly breeze, lending harmony to the rush of water crashing over stone. She stepped from the woods into a clearing by the stream. That was where she found her quarry.

Alec stood by the side of the stream, his back to her. His broad, bare back. Sunlight glistened against golden skin, smooth, thick muscles rippling as Alec rubbed a towel through his wet hair. A pair of tight-fitting pearl gray trousers hugged his narrow hips, the long length of his legs, revealing every muscular curve.

Meg stared, dazzled by the sight of him. Alec was lean, his skin stretched tautly over muscle and bone. An artist crafting marble into the depiction of some mythical Greek deity could not have found a more worthy model. Except the perfection of this creation was marred by a single scar, a thin white line slicing across his left shoulder blade. Still, the scar didn't steal his raw male beauty. Only heightened it in some primitive way. Marked him as a warrior tested in battle, powerful enough to survive.

Alec turned, catching her staring like a demented spinster with her first glimpse of a half-naked man. The fact that it was true didn't help her composure. Yet she didn't turn away, as propriety, no matter how belated, demanded. She stared at his broad smooth shoulders, the thick muscles of his arms, the hard, chiseled planes and angles of his chest, golden skin shaded by black curls.

Although the sight of this half-naked man was riveting, it wasn't the sheer beauty of his form that gripped and held her attention. It was the sight of horrible scars carved into the golden skin of his arms, his chest, his shoulders. Violence had slashed with wild abandon across this man, leaving sharp-edged reminders behind.

Her throat tightened as Meg stared, unable to look away from him. A few of the scars were old, bleached white by age, but most were barely healed. So many wounds. Such horrible pain. How could anyone survive wounds that would leave such wicked reminders of war?

His lips parted, but not a word escaped. A pained expression crossed his features. For an instant Alec seemed utterly vulnerable, as though she had glimpsed some terrible dark secret, instead of the marks of valor. He turned away from her, shielding her from the ruined flesh. He snatched his shirt from a limb of an oak tree standing near the stream, then tossed the towel on a lower branch.

Meg stood staring at him, searching for something to say, while her instincts treaded a dangerous course. She had intruded on more than his morning toilette. She had glimpsed his pain. She fought the unforgivably foolish urge to slide her arms around his waist, to press her cheek against his proud back, to hold him close.

Alec pulled the soft white cambric shirt over his damp skin, keeping his back to her. "I wasn't expecting you."

Meg stared at his broad back, trying hard to retrieve a shred of her anger from the tangle of emotions inside of her. "I'm sorry, I didn't mean to intrude. I was . . . I needed to stretch my legs a bit."

"We've been a long time on the road." Alec fastened the buttons of his shirt, the tails flapping in the cool breeze.

"Yes. We have." She pulled his coat closer around her, breathing in the intriguing scent of him lingering on the soft wool, fighting the chill deep inside of her, in that place where she had hidden her dreams of marriage and affection and family. In the past nine years she had convinced herself a contented woman was one who need never be concerned with the quixotic devotion of the man she had married. A safe woman kept her heart well guarded. A smart woman never trusted a man. Any man. "Is it wise to bathe in the open when it is so chilly?"

"I'm accustomed to it. A soldier soon learns there are few niceties on campaign." Alec turned to face her, his shirt covering his scars, his devilish grin back in place. Yet Meg wondered if the smile hid other scars, those not so easily viewed. "I see you've found something to wear."

She was his prisoner, she reminded herself. Alec was here because of her father's treachery. Not for any reasons of his own. Any warm feelings she had for Alec would only sneak back to ambush her. It was better to keep her distance. "I certainly hope no one sees me dressed like this," Meg said, pleased with the haughty note of disdain in her voice.

He pulled a dark gray coat from a branch of the oak. "If they did, it might start a fashion trend."

She smoothed back a tendril of hair the wind had blown across her cheek. "Very amusing."

He moved toward her, easing into the close-fitting riding coat. "I remember when you used to wear Colin's old breeches. But you never filled them out as well as you do those."

Meg shook her head, dismissing his flattery. It was only meant to keep his prisoner docile, she reminded herself. Only a fool would get all warm and syrupy inside at the possibility this man actually found her attractive even in trousers. Only a complete idiot would tremble from merely being near him. Yet here she was, trembling like the leaves overhead. She smoothed her hand over her hair, working at the tangles with her fingers. Without a comb or brush her tangled mane was untamable. She must look a sight.

As though Alec could read her thoughts, he withdrew a tortoiseshell comb from a leather case near the base of the tree. "Here, you look as though you could use this."

In other words, she looked wretched. "Thank you."

Meg turned away from him, putting several feet between them before pausing near an ash tree by the side of the stream. It was hard to think of Alec as the enemy. She had spent too many years thinking of him in an entirely different light. Alec had always been her hero. Her ideal. The knight who would one day return to claim her. And so he had. To bring her back to her father. If it weren't so humiliating she might actually have found some humor in the irony of the situation.

Meg tugged the makeshift ribbon from her hair and stuffed the crumpled cravat into a pocket of her coat. The breeze ruffled her unbound hair. In ten years, Alec had never come to see her. Not once. She slashed at her hair with the comb. There was no reason to imagine he had spared her even a single thought in all those years. It made it all the more humiliating to admit that her infatuation with him had haunted her, like a besotted idiot. The comb twisted in a tangle, sparking pain in her scalp. She muttered a curse, disgusted with the heavy mane.

"I can see you don't have much experience with getting out tangles," Alec said.

Meg glanced at him, watching him move toward her with a fluid grace born of power. "I'm seldom in a position to have my hair tied into knots."

"Let me." Alec lifted a handful of her hair.

The soft touch of his hand on her hair tugged on her somewhere deep inside. In spite of the warmth seeping into her blood, she managed a cool smile. "I've never had an abigail who wore trousers," she said, handing him the comb.

"Abigail? Humm, that position could be interesting." His grin turned devilish. "I'll wager you never had a maid who could scrub your back as well as I could."

Meg glanced away from him, staring at the water as it tumbled over the rocky stream bed, ignoring the wickedly appealing images his teasing had conjured in her brain. "You shall have to keep your bet, MacLaren. Since I have no intention of discovering what skills you may have in a dressing room."

Alec laughed, the soft rumble coaxing her lips into a reluctant smile. "Pity. I think I could learn to like this position."

So could she. The warmth of him radiated against her back, tempting her. In another time and place, a world where dreams came true, she could lean back against his hard chest, feel his arms close around her, hear his words of devotion. Yet this was not a time when wishes and dreams came true. The sooner she got that through her head, the better.

He eased the tangles from her hair, dividing the tangled mane into sections, starting near the bottom, working his way upward, slow and gentle. The soft, rhythmic tugs on her hair relaxed her. Meg closed her eyes, surrendering to the pleasure of having his long fingers slide through her hair.

Alec slid the comb through her hair, watching sunlight ripple through the shiny filaments, finding sparks of red in the golden strands. Hidden fire. Like the fire hidden in the woman.

When all the tangles dissolved, Alec kept combing, sliding the silky strands through his fingers. The breeze lifted her hair, brushing the strands against his chest. His muscles tightened. His skin tingled beneath the soft cambric of his shirt. For a moment he wished he hadn't donned his shirt. He wanted to feel the brush of silky strands against his skin. But the scars of war were hardly a fit sight for a lady. He didn't want to contemplate how repulsive Meg had found him. The look of shock he had glimpsed on her face told him far too much.

"You always had such pretty hair." Alec lifted a handful of gold, brushing the silky strands against his cheek, breathing in the scent of vanilla and spice. "I remember when you were a little girl, you were all hair and eyes, your braids thicker than your arms."

Meg tilted her head, frowning at him over her shoulder. "Are you implying I was spindly?"

Alec grinned at her. "Aye. You were that."

"I was slender."

"As a blade."

Her soft mouth pulled into a hard line. "You may find my figure negligible, MacLaren, but I can assure you there are gentlemen who believe it is more than adequate."

"I suppose you can find men who appreciate a slender figure," he said, teasing her. He had always preferred a trim figure over one well padded.

Meg lifted one light brown brow, giving him a smug smile. "More than a few."

An unexpected emotion sank its teeth into his belly at the thought of other men admiring her slender curves. Alec wasn't well acquainted with jealousy. Yet he had a sneaking suspicion that was what had nipped him. He drew the comb down the length of her hair, brushing her back through the curtain of gold, thinking of the curves hidden from his sight. Why would the idea of Meg with another man disturb him? "I suppose you have had more than a few admirers over the years."

"I haven't expired from lack of attention, if that is what you mean."

Alec drew the comb through her hair, watching the way the silky strands clung to his hand. "It's funny, I never really thought you were the type to enjoy all that nonsense in London."

Meg glanced at him. "What nonsense?"

"Flitting from one party to another. Sharing the latest *on dit* with all the gossips. Flirting. Playing the role of coquette."

She turned to face him, a single line etched between her finely arched brows. The breeze brushed a lock of hair across her cheek. "You make it sound as though I were an outrageous flirt."

He smoothed the curl back from her cheek and tucked the silky strands behind her ear, the warmth of her skin bathing his hand. "Do you think you would have flirted with me if we had ever met at one of those parties?"

Meg smiled sweetly. "Only if I had suddenly lost my wits."

Alec pressed his thumb against her soft lower lip. The warmth of her startled sigh seeped into his blood, where it spiraled through him, gathering low in his belly. He slid the pad of his thumb over her bottom lip, remembering the shape and taste of her lips beneath his. "I wonder."

Meg stared up at him, her eyes wide and wary. "What?"

Alec felt the slight trembling in her body, recognized the flicker of flame in her eyes. She might not like him, but she was attracted to him. He had more than enough experience to recognize desire when he saw it in a woman's eyes. "I wonder what might have happened if we had met again at a ball? Instead of the way we did last night. I wonder if you would have danced with me. I wonder if we would have become . . . friends again."

"We'll never know," Meg said, her voice a soft brush of breath against his hand.

Alec cupped her cheek in his hand. Desire coiled around him, tugging on him drawing him toward her. "I was hoping we might start all over."

Meg turned her face away from him, lowering her eyes, hiding any emotions he might search for in the green depths. "I doubt you and I could ever be friends again."

Alec turned, watching her march away from him. She was so proud and defiant. Meg clutched her anger like a shield. Yet he had glimpsed the woman hidden behind all those icy defenses, the Scottish lass imprisoned by English bars. That woman just might be worth a fight to free. He took a moment to tuck his shirt into his trousers before following the lady.

What was wrong with her? Meg wondered. The man touched her and her mind melted to mush. Another moment standing that close to him, and she would have done something dreadful. Wouldn't Alec find it amusing to have her throwing herself at him. She tied her hair back with his rumpled cravat, silently chiding herself for being a fool. She would not be manipulated by Alec MacLaren. She would not play the fool for any man. He would soon see she was far too sophisticated to succumb to his blatant masculinity.

Alec caught up with her, falling into step beside her. As she walked with him back to camp, she couldn't dismiss the irony of the situation. She was with the only man she had ever imagined in terms of happily ever after, and it was for all the wrong reasons.

Alec didn't care for her, at least not in the way she had always hoped he would care for her. He hadn't planned this lovely picnic for the sake of romance. This picnic was to keep his prisoner out of sight. She really must keep that in mind. It was too easy to think of other things when she was near Alec. It was too easy to look into his eyes and imagine she saw everything she had ever wanted in the stunning blue depths.

Alec held her chair, his arm brushing hers as he seated her at the small linen-draped table. Heat shimmered with the brief touch. He took his place across from her and gave her a warm smile. He was so very good at this, making a woman feel precious and protected, even when she didn't have a special place in his life. He had a way of looking at her that made her feel beautiful, even when she knew she looked like a homeless waif. Alec was . . . dangerous. He could steal her heart, strip her bare, leave her nothing to hide behind.

While the servants brought around scones, sausages, wedges of plum cake, and slices of cold beef, she wondered if Alec made a habit of entertaining ladies at elegant picnics. Was there someone special in his life? Somehow, through all the years since Meg had last seen him, she had never imagined Alec with another woman. Until now.

The piece of scone she was buttering crumbled beneath her knife, raining upon her plate, pinging softly against the ivory china. Wonderful. Now the man would think her a clumsy ninny. Meg glanced at him and found him smiling, in that warmer-than-summer way he had, his eyes sparkling with humor.

"Better the scone than me," Alec said softly.

Meg twisted the knife in a misty ray of sunlight spilling through the branches swaying overhead, and smiled at him. "I couldn't do nearly enough damage with something as paltry as this."

Alec lifted his black brows. "I never underestimate an angry woman."

"And do you have much experience with angry women?" she asked, keeping her voice level and composed, revealing nothing.

He shrugged. "Enough."

Meg spooned a lump of strawberry preserves onto a piece of scone, and tried not to dwell on Alec's experiences with other women. With his looks and his easy charm, women no doubt had an unfortunate propensity for casting themselves at his feet. She popped the sweetened morsel into her mouth. It might as well have been sawdust, for all she noticed.

She caught herself watching Alec. The movement of his lips as he ate. The slick sheen left on his lips from a bite of sausage. The way he dabbed away the oil with a brush of his napkin. Small, incidental things made fascinating when performed by this man.

Meg nibbled a forkful of plum cake, trying not to stare at the man. Alec had neglected to wear a neckcloth. The first few buttons of his shirt were unfastened, allowing the soft cambric to spill open at his neck. Strange, how the sight of something as innocent as his neck could twist her insides into knots.

Foolish woman.

Alec MacLaren had probably left a string of broken hearts across the peninsula. France and Belgium were no doubt littered with his castoffs. Silly women. Besotted idiots. Foolish enough to surrender their hearts to a species who remained alien to the concept of monogamy.

Men were amusing creatures, as long as a woman did not try to regard one in a serious light. Meg had long ago dissected the motives of the breed. A man wanted marriage to a respectable, preferably wealthy woman who would fill his nursery and look the other way while he kept a string of ladybirds in comfortable little cages.

Meg plunged her knife into a plump sausage. Well, she was having none of it. She would never trust her heart to a man. Especially not a man who was as treacherous as he was handsome. As far as she was concerned Alec MacLaren was the enemy. And enemy he would remain.

Chapter Five

Alec watched Meg slice through a sausage with all the bravado of an Imperial Guard ripping through a regiment of infantry. Even though she maintained that icy facade, the lady simmered with anger. He could see it in the glitter of her eyes, the color high on her cheeks, the tightness of her lips. He suspected the anger served to hide the pain of wounds suffered long ago. He knew from experience the wounds hardest to heal were those carved not into flesh, but into the soul.

"Do you still enjoy fishing?" Alec asked, hoping to ease the tension he sensed stretching inside of her.

Meg glanced at him from behind the walls of her icy defenses. "I haven't gone fishing in years."

"That surprises me. You always liked to go fishing with Colin and me."

Meg glanced down at her plate as she spoke. "Things change."

Too many things had changed. The breeze lifted a

long tendril of hair that had escaped the ribbon she had made of one of his cravats. The silky strands brushed her cheek with gold, teasing him with the memory of her soft skin beneath his fingers. "Would you like to go fishing with me when we get back to Dunleith?"

Meg swept the wayward curl back from her cheek. "I don't plan to stay in Dunleith longer than it takes to tell my father what I think of his high-handed tactics."

Alec studied her a moment, looking into the soft green of her eyes, seeing bitterness where dreams once sparkled. What would it take to put the sparkle back in those beautiful eyes? "Give your father a chance, Meg. You'll have him for only so many years. Don't waste any more of them."

"I wasn't the one who tore my family into shreds."

"No. But you could be the one who helped repair the damage."

"I've thought of that." She glanced away from him, staring down at her plate. "There were times when I would have given anything to bring my parents back together."

"It isn't too late to try."

"Isn't it?" Meg poked her fork into a piece of plum cake. "And what would I do if he betrayed my mother again? How could I live with myself if I knew I had helped cause more humiliation, more pain?"

"Robert said he never betrayed your mother, and I believe him."

Meg jabbed at the cake. "I know what I saw," she said, her voice deceptively composed.

"You saw the machinations of a desperately needy woman."

"I realize you believe you have reasons to be loyal to Sir Robert Drummond." Meg moistened her lips. "Still,

I believe I'm the better judge of what happened that night."

Alec leaned back in his chair, recognizing the stubborn set of her chin. Her father had the same stubborn streak. Once Robert Drummond set his mind to something, nothing could sway his course. "What about you? Can't you give him a chance to be your father again?"

"I've seen my father six times in the past nine years. Two of those times came since he returned from the war. He came to see me because he was anxious about his estates." Meg rested her fork across her plate. "That is hardly the behavior of a man who wants to be a father to his daughter."

"Perhaps it's the behavior of a man who doesn't feel welcome." Alec smiled, hoping to ease the sharp edge of his words. "Did you ever make him feel you wanted to be his daughter?"

Meg stood and dropped her napkin on the table by her plate. "Please excuse me. I have a few things I wish to attend to before we get back on the road."

Meg turned away from him, but not before Alec caught a glimpse of the vulnerable little girl hidden beneath all the English ice. The young lass he had known was still there, trapped beneath layers of pain and pride. Since she was as stubborn as most of the Drummond clan, he knew she wouldn't surrender her defenses without a battle.

Alec watched her walk away from him, her head held high, her shoulders thrown back, proud and defiant in her fury and pain. He watched her, admiring the shapely curves of her long legs beneath buff-colored wool, the sway of thick golden waves against her back. He watched her until Meg disappeared down the path leading toward the stream. He stared long after she had vanished from sight, listening to the soft rustle of leaves in the breeze, wondering if anyone could ease past her pain.

And the pain was there. No matter how hard Meg tried to hide her pain beneath ice, it was still there. Alec could sense it.

Gordon Murray lifted Meg's plate from the table. "I canna speak fer her nature, but she's a bonnie lassie."

Alec glanced up at Gordon's grinning face. Short and stocky, with hair the color of graying ginger, Gordon had been a servant at Dunleith Castle since before Alec was born. He had followed Alec to war, and acted as his personal servant all through the bloody years of fighting. "That she is, Gordon. And she's every bit as stubborn as she is beautiful."

Gordon chuckled softly. "I could see she weren't lappin' up the cream like most. That's one lassie not easily charmed."

Alec shook his head. "This woman is different."

"I was thinkin' as much." Gordon grinned when Alec cast him a questioning look. "It shows when ye look at 'er."

Alec laughed softly. "Something tells me she'll be the death of me."

"I'm thinkin' she'll tak' more care than most of the lassies ye've known."

"Aye. A great deal more care."

Gordon smiled down at his master. "I'll be bettin' on ye, sir," he said, before leaving Alec alone with his thoughts.

Although Meg presented the world a carefully composed mask of indifference, she was fragile beneath that facade. In a very real sense, she had lost her father as well as her brother. Alec knew what it meant to lose a family. Only, for him, the loss was irreconcilable. His parents and his brother were forever beyond his reach.

Strange, Alec had never imagined he would be the

one to survive while they perished. In the past few months, he caught himself time and time again thinking of the years he had wasted in his search for glory. Years he might have spent with his family. Now he wished he had a few days from all those years. Just a few more days to spend with them, to kiss his mother's cheek, to see his father's smile, to hear his brother's laughter.

Alec drew in his breath, easing the tightening in his chest, drawing the clean, cool air into his lungs. There were mornings, in that misty space where sleep gives way to waking, when his dream-drenched mind altered the reality of his life. In those brief moments, his world was whole again. For a few fleeting moments his parents and his brother still lived. For a few moments. Only moments, before he remembered the truth. Could he make Meg realize how precious those few moments could be? He had to try, not only for Robert, but for the girl who had once given him her innocent affection.

When Meg returned to the carriage she had her icy mantle wrapped tightly around her. For the remainder of the day, aside from a few concise replies, she managed to deflect his attempts at conversation. The next day found her just as remote. By the time evening arrived, Alec felt like a man who had been throwing himself against a stone wall for two solid days. They would reach Dunleith tomorrow morning, and he hadn't made any progress in melting her defenses. He was beginning to wonder if there was any Scottish fire left in her.

Now Meg sat across from him in the darkened coach, as stiff and unyielding as carved marble. She stared out the window, ignoring him as she had managed to ignore him the past two days. Safe behind her wall. A beautiful princess, locked away, high in her castle tower, where no man could penetrate.

Moonlight streamed through the glass windowpane, touching her face, sliding through her hair. Alec studied her profile, tracing the slant of her brow, the upward tilt of her slim nose, the pouty curve of her lips. There he lingered, memory distracting him.

Meg had felt good in his arms. Warm and supple and willing. She had tasted like rain, sweet spring rain falling softly upon a Highland glen. She had smelled of vanilla and a sweet, spicy scent that was uniquely hers. Alec drew in his breath, trying to catch the scent of her skin in the small compartment. But he was too far away to sample the delicate fragrance.

Alec thought of sitting beside her, of slipping his arms around her, of pulling her across his lap and tasting her lips. And he thought of other things. For the first time in months, he realized it had been a long time since he had tasted the pleasure of a woman's body.

The last time he had bedded a woman was the night of June 15, 1815. The night of the Duchess of Richmond's ball in Brussels. The night before the gates of hell had opened. That night, rumors of the advancing French and the possibility of battle had circulated through the ballroom, tantalizing the guests. Shortly after midnight, when Wellington arrived at the ball, rumors had turned to fact. The army would march to meet the French at Quatre Bras in the morning.

Soon after Wellington's arrival at the ball, Alec had left with Lady Pamela Elkington. The beautiful widow had wanted to make what might be his last day on earth memorable. Strange, although Alec remembered thinking she was beautiful, he could scarcely remember her face. He suspected if Lady Pamela were sitting here this evening, instead of Meg, the blood would not be pumping low and hard in his belly from merely looking at her.

Meg turned her head. A frown creased her smooth brow when she caught him staring at her. She touched her hair, tested the cravat to make certain her thick golden mane was under control. "I hope there are a few of my mother's dresses still at Penross House. I would hate to return to London dressed like this."

Alec smiled, in spite of the uncomfortable ache in his groin. "I'm certain Robert will find something for you to wear."

Meg glanced away from him, staring for a few moments into the moonlight. "Tell me something," she said, in that clear, direct, give-no-quarter way she had.

"What do you want to know?"

"You said you wouldn't be alive today if not for Robert Drummond." Meg fixed him in a steady gaze. "What happened? How did he save your life?"

The war wasn't a subject he cared to discuss. Some memories a man wanted to forget. Especially those that came back to haunt him in the middle of the night. Yet there was more at stake here than his own comfort. Meg was curious about her father. He couldn't allow the opportunity to pass. She needed to know about Robert Drummond, for more than a few reasons. She needed to understand the kind of man her father was.

"You probably know I was wounded at Waterloo," Alec said, keeping his voice washed of emotion.

"Your name was included in the casualty list published in the *Times*," she said, in a matter-of-fact tone of voice.

Alec nodded, thinking of the mess the surgeon who had reported him dead had made of things. He wondered what Meg had thought when she had read his name listed in that long roll call of death. Had she felt a moment's pause, a single regret over the loss of an old friend? He would like to think she had. The lass he had known would have mourned him. This Englishwoman might not have wasted a moment's thought. "The Ministry declared me dead. At the time, it wasn't much of an exaggeration."

Meg glanced at his chest, an unconscious lowering of her eyes that told him more than Alec wanted to know. Heat prickled his cheeks when he thought of the disfigurement she had glimpsed. The scars. The flesh that was still raw from wounds that had nearly killed him. The ugly reminders of war. He turned away from her. He stared out the window, watching moonlight flow like water across a rolling meadow.

"After the battle, your father found me. He carried me to a farmhouse that had been converted into a hospital." Memories shifted inside of him, rising from the dark corners of his soul, spreading a chill through his blood. "When the surgeon told him I was too far gone to take up his time, Robert tended me. He stayed with me, cleansing my wounds, forcing broth down my throat, ordering me to live. If not for him, I'd be buried in a Belgium grave."

Alec could see Meg from the corner of his eye, watching him, as though looking for answers to questions she wasn't certain she wanted to ask. "Father said you and Colin were together at the end. What happened that day?"

Alec hadn't discussed that last day with anyone. If he spoke of it, he wasn't certain he could keep the ghosts at bay. Ghosts that haunted him still. Deep inside he perceived a shaking, where memories battered him like angry waves smashing the shore. His muscles tensed with the strain of keeping his emotions under close rein.

"If you don't want to discuss it, I'll understand." Meg glanced down at her hands. "Perhaps I shouldn't have asked. It's just difficult. Not knowing."

Alec recognized her need to understand Colin's loss.

In a very real sense they shared the same pain. And in some strange way he didn't quite understand, he needed to share his memories of that last day with her. "We were ordered to stop a wave of calvary coming in close behind French infantry. We cut our way through. Then the recall was sounded, but no one turned. I was in command. I tried to get them to turn back, but I couldn't. Everyone was too caught up in the moment, drugged by a sense of glory. Perhaps they thought that one bold charge would end the battle. It didn't."

Alec drew in a slow breath, willing away the trembling deep inside of him. He couldn't contain the memories. Screams of men and horses echoed in his brain. The strange humming sound of a saber slicing air, thudding as it collided with flesh. Artillery an infernal carillon, pounding, pounding, pounding. Once again, he could taste black powder upon his tongue mingled with the strange sweet smell of blood. The savagery of it all remained with him. He suspected it always would.

"Colin's horse had been killed; he was on foot. I went to help him. But the numbers were against us. We both went down," Alec said, his voice washed of emotion.

"Father said Colin was killed by a Prussian soldier after the battle."

Alec tried to swallow, but his mouth was as dry as parchment. "There are always looters after a battle. Men from both sides who strip the dead of everything they have. Peasants who flock like scavengers, moving from one body to the next, slaughtering their prey if he happens to struggle."

"And there is no one to protect them?" Meg said, her voice soft with shock.

Alec shook his head, keeping his face turned toward the window, his reflection glowing like a ghost in the glass. The air in the coach had grown warm, so warm and thick he could scarcely draw a breath. Yet his skin was cold and damp beneath his clothes. "After a battle of that size, it's almost impossible to remove all the dead and wounded from the field. They try, but there are too many wounded, too many dead."

"You and Colin were left behind."

"I awakened on the field that night after the battle had ended. It was quiet, except for a few voices, whispers in the night. Men calling for help, feeble supplications for water, for mercy." He would never forget the soft, pleading sounds. No matter how hard he tried. "There were men all around me, slumped in odd positions against the ground. For a while you wonder if they are only sleeping. Then you notice the moonlight reflecting on the wounds. You realize you're surrounded by dead men. All alone. It's an odd feeling."

"I imagine it's horribly frightening," she said, her voice a soft caress in the shadows.

Alec nodded, taking a moment to compose his voice before he spoke. "Then I heard Colin, calling my name. He was no more than ten feet away. It was a comfort, hearing him, knowing we'd both cheated death that day. At least for a little while."

Alec rubbed his hands together, appalled at the dampness of his palms. "We lay there, on the damp ground, talking, both of us too badly done in to move. We talked about how good it would be to get back home. How much we wanted to see our families. He wanted to see your mother and you."

Meg glanced down at her hands. "He always came to see us when he was home on leave. Even if it was for only a few hours. He always came."

"He loved you both."

Meg kept her eyes focused on her hands. "You were there when he died."

"Aye. I heard him cry out; I tried to move but I couldn't. There was a dead officer of the Imperial

Guard across my legs. My arms were . . . I couldn't move. I couldn't help."

From the corner of his eye he saw her. She was sitting very still, as though she were afraid any movement might shatter her composure. "The Prussian was coming for me when your father found us. Robert killed the bastard. But it was too late to save Colin. Robert had been searching for us since the battle ended. And it took a moment too long."

"Strange, isn't it." Meg smoothed her fingertip over the buff-colored wool covering her knee. "How the difference in a few moments can mean the difference in life or death."

Alec often thought of what might have happened if that Prussian had come for him first. Colin would have been the one to come home. "If your father hadn't come searching for us, I would have died that night."

Meg sat quietly, staring at her tightly clasped hands for a moment. "I understand why you are so loyal to him."

"I hope you might understand he is the type of man who deserves loyalty. Not only from the men who fought beside him. But from his wife and daughter."

Meg looked up at him, tears glistening in eyes that shimmered with pain and bitterness. "He had my loyalty."

Alec wanted to draw her into his arms. And he realized it was more than a need to give her comfort. He needed to feel her warmth radiate against him. Maybe then he could ease the memories carved across his soul. Alec touched her hand.

Meg drew back, as though she were afraid he might slap her. "Don't," she whispered. "Please don't touch me."

Alec fell back against his seat. He felt drained, as weak as he did when he awakened from a nightmare.

81

His chest ached with the dull throb of old wounds, his heart with the fresh cut of her rejection. He studied the woman sitting across from him, seeing his fate in the stubborn set of her chin. Meg had retreated once more to her tower. Deep in his Celtic blood, he knew what lay before them. The battle was yet to begin.

Meg huddled in the corner of the coach, feeling like a fawn trapped in a lion's den. If he touched her, all the walls she had carefully constructed around her emotions would shatter. She would tumble into his arms, dissolve into a fit of weeping like a lost child. She would hold him, tell him how much she gave thanks he had come home alive, let him hear the pitiful ranting of a woman who had never outgrown her childish infatuation with him. She would humiliate herself.

Meg drew in a breath, easing air into her constricted lungs, watching him. Alec turned his head on the back of the seat and closed his eyes. He seemed exhausted, as though reliving the events at Waterloo had drained the reserves of his strength. A thick lock of hair had tumbled over his brow. He looked so young. So vulnerable. It took every ounce of her willpower to keep from touching him.

She had never in her life wanted to hold someone as much as she wanted to hold Alec. If she were not very careful she would commit some horrible error in judgment, allow emotion to counter logic, jeopardize her pride as well as her heart.

Affection was such a treacherous emotion. It threatened her from all directions. She had thought her affection for Alec carefully buried. Yet the grave was too shallow. Being near him, glimpsing his pain beneath his carefully composed features, had nearly been her demise. The need to comfort, to give comfort in return, tugged on her heart like a tether. It drew her toward him, dragging her toward the edge of a cliff where destruction awaited her. Alec was a Scottish male. A Highlander. Loyal to Robert Drummond. He was certainly not a man she could trust with her heart.

Meg had to maintain some distance between them. It was the only way she would survive this war with her heart and her sanity intact.

Chapter Six

Joanna stared out the coach window, the rolling hills of green pasture a blur in her vision. Her thoughts were turned inward to a place of pain and doubts. What would she say to him? How could she protect herself from the man? She hadn't spent more than a handful of time in Robert Drummond's company in the last nine years. The last time they had actually shared more than a few chilly civilities was the day he had tried to convince her of his innocence.

Hermione fidgeted on the blue velvet cushions across from Joanna. "Have you ever slept on a more uncomfortable bed? I swear I'm bruised. Bruised from head to toe. And those sheets."

Her mother's voice was a low drone in her ears, drowned by a flood of memories. The look in Robert's eyes when she had refused to believe his lies. It was as though she had plunged a knife into his heart. All the warmth died in his beautiful brown eyes. In a space of moments, the man who had so passionately stated his love for her had frozen into a cold stranger. He had looked at her as though she were the one who had betrayed their vows. Now, in a few short days, she would be facing the scoundrel in a place that had once been her home.

"Now you can see why I insist on bringing my own linen when I travel," Hermione said. "Pity I couldn't bring my own bed. But it doesn't work. I ended up spilling feathers from Somerset to Amesbury the last time I tried."

She could retain a tight rein on her emotions, Joanna assured herself. She had become an expert at containing her feelings. She certainly would not reveal how much she still hurt from what had happened. No, she wouldn't show Robert Drummond a glimpse of her pain. She would remain composed. She would get her daughter out of this mess without giving Robert Drummond the satisfaction of knowing she was still in love with him.

"Joanna," Hermione said, her crisp voice breaking into Joanna's thoughts.

Joanna glanced at her mother. "What?"

Hermione pursed her lips. "You haven't heard a word I've been saying."

Joanna rubbed her arms, feeling chilled. "I'm a little distracted."

"Yes. I can well understand." Hermione studied her daughter a moment, a frown etching a line between her white brows. "I've been thinking of something, and though I hate to paint a picture blacker than need be, I was wondering where Margaret and that man might be staying each evening. Do you suppose he has been taking her to inns? And if he has, has someone seen her? My goodness, I don't want to imagine what would happen if someone saw her."

Debra Dier

"Margaret is wise enough not to draw attention to herself." She only prayed Alec was wise enough to keep her daughter well hidden. "I wouldn't be surprised if Alec drives straight through, stopping only when necessary."

"Traveling alone with a man." Hermione clicked her tongue against her teeth. "What could Drummond have been thinking by sending that man to kidnap my little girl? Doesn't he realize the position he has placed her in?"

Joanna turned her face to the window. Clouds were gathering, blocking out the sun, turning the countryside gray and cold. "Robert knows precisely what position he has placed her in. I'm certain he plans to use it to his advantage."

"You don't mean . . . He wouldn't. . . . To his own daughter?"

Joanna glanced at her mother. "Would you really put it beyond him?"

"Good gad! He would do such a thing. He would. Oh my." Hermione rocked back and forth on her seat, wringing her hands. "Oh, my goodness. We have to reach her before it's too late."

Joanna clasped her hands in her lap, praying it wasn't already too late.

The soft yellow light of late morning spilled across the gray stones shaping the sprawling wings and gables of Penross House. Sunlight glittered on the sash windows that looked out upon a lush green glen and rocky slopes. Meg stood on the gravel drive, dressed in a pair of buff-colored pantaloons and a dark gray coat, feeling like the lost waif she looked. She had been born in this house. She had lived here the first fifteen years of her life—the happiest she had ever known. Yet she felt like a stranger here.

Alec rested his hand on her shoulder. She glanced up, startled by the gentle touch. "Although I realize I might be risking bodily injury"—he smiled down at her—"I'd like to be the first to welcome you back home."

Meg was certain he must be relieved. His part in this intrigue was over. Soon Alec would walk away without a second thought of her. While she would still be thinking of him on the day she took her last breath. "This isn't my home," she said, appalled at the shaky sound of her voice.

Alec lifted one black brow. "Are you sure of that?"

"Quite." Meg's heart pounded like a fist against her ribs as she climbed the stone steps leading to a huge oak door. The quicker she got this confrontation over, the better.

The butler opened the door as Meg reached the top step. He stood for a moment in the threshold, smiling at her. "It's good to see you again, Miss Margaret."

Meg smiled at the tall, thin man with the smiling gray eyes. "It's nice to see you again, Carlton."

A short, plump woman wearing a dark gray dress swept past Carlton. She paused on the threshold, smiling at Meg, looking her over from her head to her emerald satin slippers. "Och, but it's good to see ye again, Miss Meggie. And look at ye, dressed up just as ye always were when chasin' after yer brother and this handsome laird 'ere."

"Dorrie!" Meg threw her arms around the little housekeeper. The sweet scent of ginger and cloves swirled around her with Dorrie's plump arms.

Dorrie hugged her so tightly, Meg could scarcely breathe. "Ye've bin a long time in comin' home, lass."

Home. Meg closed her eyes against the sting of tears. If only things had been different, she thought. If only . . .

"You made good time, Alec. I wasn't expecting you until this evening."

Meg froze at the sound of her father's deep voice. She pulled back from Dorrie, staring at her father over the crisp white cap Dorrie wore upon her gray curls. Robert Drummond was watching her, his brown eyes filled with a certain wariness in spite of his smile. Once upon a time she had imagined this man would always be there for her, with a wise word, a warm smile, a gentle touch. She reined in the emotions threatening to overwhelm her.

A pair of Irish red setters trotted from her father's side to greet Meg. She bent, petting the animals, ruffling their long ears. She had once owned a beautiful red setter. But she had been compelled to leave him behind when she had gone to live with her grandmother. It was only one of the blows she had suffered because of Robert Drummond.

Meg straightened, fighting the tears that stung her eyes unexpectedly and threatened her dignity. She would not allow this place or these people to break her composure. She fixed her father with a cool look. "It would seem you wanted to see me, sir."

"We have a great deal to discuss," Robert said.

Meg held his steady look, relying on years of practice to maintain her mask of indifference. "That, sir, is a matter of opinion."

Robert frowned. "Dorrie, show Meg to her room. I'm sure she'll want to freshen up after such a long ride."

Meg wanted to get back in that coach and ride straight back to London. She needed to get away from this house and these people. It hurt too much, being here.

"Ye'll never get into yer old clothes. Ye've grown so tall." Dorrie patted Meg's arm. "Lady Joanna left a fair number of dresses and such. I'll bring ye some fresh clothes and have a nice warm bath prepared fer ye."

Meg smiled at the little housekeeper. "Later, Dorrie. I've traveled a great distance to hear what my father has to say. I see no reason to wait."

Robert studied her a moment, his expression growing grim. He looked to Alec. "It would seem my daughter is anxious to have a word with me. I think you should hear what she has to say."

Meg glanced from her father's grim expression to Alec's equally somber face. "I see no reason why the MacLaren should be included in our discussion."

"I do." Robert headed down the wide central hall, with the setters trotting close on his heels. "Come along. No sense in postponing this."

He might have been commanding one of his dogs, Meg thought. She hesitated. For the first time she noticed her father was using a cane, limping as though he had injured his left leg. He had been fine two weeks ago. What had caused . . .

Meg flinched when Alec touched her shoulder. She glanced up at him, stunned by the sadness in his eyes.

"Give him a chance, Meg," Alec said softly.

Meg pulled away from the gentle pressure of his hand on her shoulder. "This doesn't concern you, MacLaren."

Alec released his breath in a long sigh. "I'm afraid it does."

Meg stared up at him, an uneasy sense of disaster prickling the base of her spine. Her father might have saved his life, but that didn't give Alec the right to interfere in her private affairs.

Robert paused when he reached an adjoining hallway. He glanced at her, his face drawn into the stern lines of a general facing his command. "Have you changed your mind?"

"No. I haven't." Meg hadn't changed her mind about

her father, or the scoundrel who stood beside her. She forced starch into her spine and marched to war.

Robert limped into the library, resenting the cane he needed for balance. He had made it through the long bloody war with nothing more than scratches. And here he was, crippled on his own land, brought down by a poacher's bullet.

He sank into a leather wing-back chair near the stone hearth and eased his aching leg onto a leather footstool. The dull throb of pain in his leg was nothing compared to the open wound carved across his heart. His dogs flopped on the carpet on either side of his chair, giving quiet support for the ordeal that would come.

Robert watched his daughter march into the room, her head held high, twin flags of dusky rose flying in her cheeks. The last place she wanted to be was here, in her own home, with her father. Lord, it was hard looking truth straight in the eye.

There was a time when his little girl would come running into this room, anxious to see him. Robert remembered the days Meg would crawl up onto his lap and listen as he told her a story. She would fall asleep with her head nestled against his chest, so sweet and trusting. Later, when she was older, they would sit here, his wife, his daughter, his son, sharing events of the day, thoughts of tomorrow, hopes for the future. He had never thought his future would be so empty.

Memories etched a ragged path through his heart. Emotion tightened his throat. A man could not go back and change the past, he reminded himself. He could only do his best in making the present worth living.

Alec closed the door, the soft click of the latch a gunshot in the quiet room.

Robert gripped his cane, staring at the girl who stood

before him, stiff and proud and angry. Lord help him, he had commanded a division of men into battle time and time again. Yet he felt over his head dealing with this one slip of a girl.

"I must say I resent your tactics, sir." Meg folded her hands at her waist, staring at him like a governess scolding a wayward charge.

"Not any more than I resent the need to use them."

Meg glanced at Alec, who had taken a position near the hearth, then turned her angry glare back to her father. "What kind of father sends a man to kidnap his daughter from her bedchamber?"

Robert flinched inwardly at the sharp tone in her low voice. "A father with a daughter who has forgotten what it means to show him respect."

Meg stiffened, squeezing her hands together until her knuckles blanched white. "Respect must be earned, sir."

Robert smoothed his thumb over the polished gold handle of his cane, holding her angry look, keeping his own emotions under tight rein. "I thought I'd earned your respect, Meg. I thought I'd earned your trust. But I discovered I was wrong."

"How can you expect me to respect you, to trust you, after what you did to Mother?"

"I never betrayed your mother."

"I saw you and that woman," Meg said, her voice breaking with emotion.

Robert looked straight into her eyes, as green as Joanna's, they were. And just as angry and accusing. "Drusilla Buchanan wanted to be my mistress. I told her I had no need for another woman. She came to the town house that night, without an invitation from me."

A single tear slipped down Meg's cheek. "She was undressed. In your bedchamber."

"I didn't invite her," Robert said, forcing his voice to

91

remain calm, when he wanted to scream. "I didn't know she was in the house until I slipped into bed and found her there. I was trying to make her leave, when you and your mother arrived home."

"She simply planted herself in your bed, without encouragement." Meg slashed at her damp cheek. "It's difficult to believe, sir."

"Not so difficult, if you trust a man. If you knew he had never lied to you." Robert swallowed hard, forcing back the tight knot in his throat. "If you knew he loved you with all his heart. I'm thinking it wouldna be so hard to believe him."

Meg turned away from him. He watched as she crossed the room; she paused by his desk, resting her hands on the edge of the smooth mahogany top. She stood there for a moment, with her stiff back to him, composing herself. Silently he prayed she would finally believe him. Yet, when she turned to face him, all hope of that miracle withered beneath her icy glare.

"I would like to return to London as soon as possible," Meg said, her voice dripping frost.

"Stay with me, Meg," Robert said, his voice soft with the yearning he couldn't hide. "Give us a chance to find a way through the storm."

Meg shook her head. "My life here ended a long time ago."

Robert held her icy look, feeling his options slipping away like water through a sieve. "I can't let you marry Wildon Fethersham."

Meg set her jaw. "You have no right to tell me who I can or cannot marry."

Robert squeezed the handle of his cane. "I'm your father."

"How convenient of you to have remembered."

"And what is that to mean?"

"If Colin had lived, you certainly wouldn't be concerned about my plans to marry anyone. You're only concerned now because you're afraid your precious land will fall into the hands of an Englishman."

"Aye, I'm afraid the English dandy will do here what he did to MacLaren land. Clear away the crofters, as though they were rubbish, to make room for sheep." Robert stared into the polished gold handle of his cane. "I've seen what the clearances have done. Chieftains turning their backs on their people. English marrying Scottish heiresses to get their hands on Scottish land. Men who fought long and hard for the Crown, returning to find their families gone, sent away for the sake of gold." He looked at her. "And I swear it won't happen on Drummond land."

"You might think you can order me about as though I were one of your soldiers, but you're mistaken. I shall marry as I see fit." Meg pivoted and marched across the room.

Robert watched her leave, realizing there was only one way to end this war. It certainly wouldn't win him the girl's affection. But he couldn't allow her to destroy her life. He only hoped Alec would agree to his plan.

Alec watched Meg march out of the room. The solid thud of the door closing behind her ripped through him like artillery fire. He felt as though he had just stumbled back from a battle, bruised and bloody, sick with the sense of loss.

Robert sat frowning at his cane. "Now that you've seen how she feels about me, what do you suppose my chances are of convincing Meg to change her mind?"

Alec stirred the fire with a poker, watching sparks scatter from the glowing chunks of peat. "I'd have to give you worse odds than Napoleon had after Waterloo."

"I'd have to agree." Robert shook his head. "The girl

93

has a stubborn streak deeper than the North Sea."

Alec grinned, in spite of the tension coiling in his stomach. "I can't think of where Meg might have gotten it."

Robert was quiet, studying the handle of his cane as though answers could be found in the polished gold. "I can't have her marrying Wildon Fethersham, Alec."

Alec felt an odd twist in his chest when he thought of Meg marrying Wildon. He settled the poker in the brass holder on the hearth. "He isn't the man for her."

Robert tapped the tip of his cane on the carpet. "I have to do something to stop her from going back to London."

"Aye. You do." Alec drew in his breath, dragging the smoky scent of burning peat across his tongue. The air settled heavily in his lungs, as though a weight were pressing against his chest. Silently he cursed the lingering weakness from wounds barely healed. He had a feeling he was going to need every scrap of his strength to deal with one stubborn Englishwoman.

"I won't rest easy until Meg is properly wed to a man I can trust." Robert turned his head, fixing Alec in a steady gaze. "I'm going to ask you again if you'll marry her. This time I hope you realize there are no alternatives. There isn't any time for getting acquainted or thinking about changing her mind."

Even though Alec had expected this, the reality of the decision awaiting him settled over his shoulders like an iron yoke. "I know."

"Even though she's stubborn, she's a lovely lass," Robert said softly. "Wouldn't you say?"

Alec smiled, thinking of the way early morning sunlight touched her face. "Aye. Fair as a spring morning."

"I think you and Meg would make a fine match."

Alec lifted his brows. "A boxing match is more like

it. And I have an uneasy feeling I'd be the one to take it on the chin."

Robert shrugged. "As I recall, you always had a way of charming the ladies."

Meg was different from the women who had drifted in and out of his life. There was something about her that touched him deep inside, in places he had thought too scarred to feel. "Meg won't be forced into marriage without a fight."

"I'm her father." Robert came to his feet. Using his cane to steady his injured leg, he limped to his desk. "My word should mean something to her."

Alec curled his hand into a fist against the carved oak mantel. "She can't see past the bitterness and pain."

"I know." Robert leaned against the desk. "But I won't allow her to ruin her life. No matter what Meg thinks of me, I canna allow her to marry that English bastard."

Alec rubbed his neck, trying to ease his taut muscles. Meg and Wildon—he couldn't allow it to happen. The man would destroy her. Still, an arranged marriage to a woman who was more English than Scottish. Lord, he didn't care much for the prospect.

"If you won't agree to marry her, I'll find someone who will."

Alec recognized the determination in Robert's eyes. Nothing would change his mind.

"Will you do it?" Robert asked.

Alec had never imagined forcing a woman to be his bride. In fact, most of his adult life, he had avoided the snares of women who wanted to drag him to the altar. Still, he wouldn't be here today if not for Robert. And he had to admit, when he thought of Meg in another man's bed, something curious coiled in his chest, an emotion he hardly recognized: jealousy. He stared into the fire on the hearth for a long moment before he spoke. "If I agree, how the devil will you convince her to speak her vows? I'm not exactly high on her list of favorite people."

Robert gave him a grim smile. "She'll speak her vows. I'll make certain of it."

Chapter Seven

The man had no right to tell her who she could and couldn't marry. Meg followed Dorrie down the hall leading to her bedchamber. She was still shaking from the confrontation that had taken place in the library. It didn't matter that she had no intention of marrying Wildon Fethersham. It was the principle that mattered. Robert Drummond had given up his rights as a father the day he had betrayed her mother. If he thought she was going to marry that fool Fethersham, so much the better. Let him suffer worrying about his precious lands. Still, in spite of her anger, somehow he had managed to plant doubts where there had once been only certainty.

Could her father be innocent? Was he telling the truth? She had spent so many years believing in his guilt. It was hard to imagine the past in a different light. Yet . . .

He couldn't be innocent. Meg had seen him with that

woman. Meg had seen the way Drusilla had stood in the hall, half-naked, beside her father, both of them facing the woman they had betrayed. She shivered with the memory.

But Meg couldn't dismiss the doubts her father had planted inside of her. She couldn't ignore everything Alec had said about the man who had sired her.

Had her father truly been so dishonorable? Could it have been as he said? Today there had been a look in her father's eyes . . . could he have been telling the truth?

"Yer room is just the way ye left it." Dorrie threw open the door to Meg's bedchamber and marched inside. "All these years, the laird had us dustin' it and keepin' it ready, just in case ye ever found ye're way home."

Meg remained on the threshold, watching Dorrie open the pale yellow silk brocade drapes shrouding the windows. Sunlight streamed into the room, spilling across the intricate design of the yellow and ivory Savonnerie carpet. Carved rosewood pillars suspended an ivory lace canopy over the bed, lush swags of ivory lace cascading from each corner. A porcelain doll with auburn curls sat on the table near the bed, dressed in the same emerald silk gown she had always worn.

Meg curled her hands into balls at her sides, trying to contain the shaking. Inside she lifted a shield against the memories. Yet they slipped past her defenses. She forced her legs to move, her feet to carry her into the room. The scent of lavender and heather lingered, the fragrance drawing her back in time. She glanced toward the vanity, where fresh potpourri filled an ivory porcelain bowl. It was as though she had never left.

Dorrie tugged open the drapes at the window directly across from the bed, brass rings sliding against a brass rod. "I'll bring ye some fresh clothes and have a nice warm bath prepared. . . ." She hesitated when she turned to face Meg. "Are ye all right, lass? Ye're as pale as a ghost."

Meg felt like a ghost, back to haunt the place where she had died. She managed a smile. "It was a difficult journey."

"Aye." Dorrie patted Meg's arm. "Once ye've had a nice warm bath and some of Cook's gingerbread, ye'll feel better."

Meg watched Dorrie leave. She suspected it would take a great deal more than a bath and warm gingerbread to make her feel better. She lifted her doll from the round rosewood table by the bed. Her father had given it to her when she was twelve, a present from one of his business trips to Edinburgh. At the time, she hadn't realized what he did on his trips to Edinburgh.

A gift for my little princess.

Meg smoothed the auburn curls, fighting the tears burning her eyes. She wouldn't cry. She had cried enough to learn tears couldn't change anything. Still, she realized her faith in her father's treachery wasn't built on stone. She wanted to believe him; that was why she was so confused, Meg assured herself. If he were innocent, then all of these years . . .

Was she wrong to leave? Should she stay and give him a chance to make her believe in him again? Dare she trust him?

Once Meg allowed the doubts to enter, they remained, growing like vines, lashing around her heart. A warm bath didn't help her mood. The gingerbread had no flavor. Meg scarcely found the intelligence to respond to Dorrie's cheerful chatter as the little housekeeper helped her dress in a pale blue muslin gown that had been Joanna's. She sat like a statue in front of her vanity as Dorrie fussed with her hair, coaxing the heavy mass of waves into graceful curls suspended at the back of her head.

"Ye're as lovely as yer mother." Dorrie smiled at Meg in the mirror. "How is it such a bonnie lassie never married?"

Meg lowered her eyes, afraid she might betray something in the mirror. She traced a leaf she had long ago crafted in the embroidered lace scarf covering the top of the vanity, trying not to think of Alec and all the reasons she couldn't forget him. "I wanted to be certain, I suppose."

"And 'ere I was thinkin' ye never found a man in England as handsome as one of our Highland lads."

Meg lifted her chin, meeting Dorrie's humor-filled eyes in the mirror. "I assure you, I haven't spent the past ten years pining for any Highland lad."

"Maybe not." Dorrie rested her hands on Meg's shoulders. "But there's a handsome young laird waitin' fer ye in yer sittin' room."

Excitement surged through Meg, tingling every nerve. "MacLaren is in my sitting room?"

Dorrie grinned. "Aye. Anxious to have a few words with ye, he is."

Meg pursed her lips, hoping to disguise her feelings behind a cool mask. Still, she couldn't do anything with the color that had risen in her cheeks. "I doubt I shall care to hear anything he has to say."

"Now, Miss Meggie, give the man a chance. The MacLaren certainly would make a fine husband."

"I'm afraid I have to disagree with you, Dorrie. Alec MacLaren is hardly the type of man a woman could trust."

"Keep him happy at home, and he wouldna stray. He's a good man. Now be nice to him." Dorrie patted Meg's shoulder before leaving her alone with her doubts.

Her mother had kept Robert Drummond happy at home. And the man had still managed to take a mistress. Or had he? Was he innocent? Had he been as much a victim as her mother had?

Meg stood and smoothed the soft skirt of her dress. She wasn't certain of Robert Drummond's guilt or innocence. She wasn't even certain if she should attempt to make amends, or if it was even possible to repair the damage done to their relationship. Yet, in spite of the doubts, she did know she needed to stay, at least for a few days. She needed a chance to know more about her father. And she had to admit, Alec MacLaren had more than a little to do with her decision to stay awhile.

Meg intended to show the infuriating beast she was a desirable woman who no longer possessed an idiotic fascination for him. Now if she could only keep from shaking at the mention of his name, she would be just fine. She paused at the door of her sitting room. She took a deep breath, composed her features into what she hoped was a calm expression, before opening the door.

Alec was standing by the windows, staring out at the west gardens. He turned when Meg entered. Sunlight touched his face and slipped golden fingers into the thick black hair that tumbled over the back of his white collar in luxuriant waves. Framed by burgundy silk brocade drapes, he stood tall and elegant in a close-fitting dark gray coat and buff-colored trousers, so handsome her heart did a slow tumble in her chest.

Alec smiled at her, a warmth kindling in his stunning blue eyes. Heat unfurled inside of her like a banner in a gathering breeze, stealing the breath from her lungs. She forced her feet to carry her into the room. He couldn't see her legs shaking, she assured herself. He couldn't know her heart was thudding against the wall of her chest. Could he?

His smile tipped into a devilish grin, telling her he knew exactly how he could set the blood pumping in her veins. The infuriating Highlander!

"You look lovely, Meg. Though I was becoming real fond of seeing you in my pantaloons."

Meg ignored the thrill tingling along her nerves. The man would see she was no longer an impressionable child head over heels in love with him. "I outgrew the inclination to run about in male attire a long time ago."

"Did you now?" Alec asked, moving toward her.

"Yes. Along with most other childish notions."

"I wonder." Alec invaded the safe cushion of air between them, stepping so close the warmth of his body brushed against her.

The warm scent of sandalwood curled around her. Her skin tingled. For one horrible moment Meg feared she might do something foolish. She stepped back, putting a respectable distance between them. Yet the distance couldn't ease the frantic pounding of her heart.

"What do you wonder?" she asked, appalled at the breathy sound of her voice.

Alec closed the distance, each movement filled with the sleek grace of a man certain of his prowess. "If you really have abandoned all your youthful notions."

Meg stepped back, her heel colliding with the closed door. She lifted her head, assuming a haughty pose in spite of the trembling in her limbs. "I can assure you, I have."

Alec smoothed his fingers over her cheek, spreading warmth across her skin. "You told me once you would never love another man the way you loved me."

Meg swallowed past the tight knot in her throat. "Children say the most outrageous things."

"Children do."

Alec traced the curve of her left eyebrow with his fingertips. The simple touch sizzled along her nerves, sending sparks scattering in all directions, setting fires in their wake. Heat swirled through her, simmering low in her belly. She should break away from this man. Yet she couldn't convince her muscles to move. They were melting in the same heat threatening to turn her brain to mush. She snatched at her retreating wits. "If you think for one moment that I still . . ."

Alec nuzzled the sensitive skin beneath her ear. Meg tried to form a protest, but her brain wasn't functioning. Her muscles shifted without thought, her body melting against him. Sensation swirled across her breasts as they nestled against his hard chest.

"I need to know something," he whispered, sliding his hand into the curls at her nape, cradling her head in his big palm.

Meg stared up into his eyes, mesmerized by the flames simmering in the celestial depths. "What?" she asked, her voice sounding strange to her own ears.

"This." Alec lowered his lips to hers.

Meg sighed with the exquisite pleasure of his lips sliding against hers. Somewhere in the back of her mind she realized she shouldn't be cooperating with this. She should protest. Now. She should pull away, make him see she wasn't still under his spell. Yet the spell he had cast long ago had altered in the last few days. His masculine magic had grown stronger with the passing years, while her ability to resist had weakened.

His warmth, his taste, his scent intoxicated her. Meg slipped her arms around his neck, surrendering to the need to hold him close against her. She buried her fingers in the soft waves at his nape, grateful she wasn't wearing gloves. Black strands slid against her skin, cool and smooth as silk.

Meg snuggled against Alec, parting her lips, welcoming the sleek slide of his tongue into her mouth. Plunge and retreat, plunge and retreat, he teased her until she followed his lead, gliding in an intriguing rhythm that whispered to a secret place deep inside of her, where her body was growing warm and liquid.

An image of him standing half-naked in the sunlight blossomed in her mind. Meg wanted to unbutton his shirt and slide her hands over the dark curls and golden skin stretched tautly over sharply defined muscles. She wanted to trace the horrible scars with her fingertips, assure herself he was healed, celebrate his triumph over death.

Alec lifted his head, breaking the kiss. He stared down at her, his eyes reflecting the same turmoil roiling through her. His breath, tinged with the scent of the coffee she had tasted on his tongue, fell warm and soft against her lips, tempting her to press her lips against his. "I think we'll do fine together, Meg."

His words tore the delicate fabric of fantasy Alec had slipped around her, allowing reality to creep through. "We'll do fine? At what?"

Alec kissed the tip of her nose. "At being husband and wife."

It took a moment for the words to sink through the haze shrouding her brain. A moment of stunned silence before his meaning hit her, like a fist to the jaw. The room tilted; her vision blurred. She gripped his shoulders to keep her balance. "Are you asking me to marry you?"

"Aye." Alec slid his hands upward along the curves of her back, the warmth of his palms soaking through the soft muslin of her gown. "Will you be my bride, Margaret Drummond?"

"Oh!" Meg stumbled back and smacked the door. Pain flickered in the back of her head. The jolt assured her she wasn't dreaming. She stared at him, afraid to believe in her dreams, sensing there was more here than the fulfillment of her fondest wish. "Why? Why have you suddenly decided you want to marry me?"

Alec studied her a moment, his expression growing serious. "I could lie to you, Meg. But I've never been one for choosing a lie over the truth."

The serious tone of his voice poured over her. Ice trickled into her blood. It took every ounce of her willpower to keep her voice steady. "You're doing this because of my father."

"There are things you need to know," he said, his voice low and soft.

"Such as?" Meg leaned back against the door, watching him move to a lyre-back armchair by the white marble hearth. He didn't sit, but stood staring at the chair, a frown digging lines between his black brows. She tried to gather her defenses around her, only to find them badly damaged. She wanted to turn and run, but she needed to hear what this man had to say.

Alec slanted her a glance. "Your father is concerned about your plans to marry my cousin."

"If I hadn't become his heir, my father wouldn't care if I married a cobbler."

"That's not true, Meg. You were always in his thoughts."

Meg wished she could believe him. She wanted to believe her father had thought of her at times during the last nine years.

"Robert is determined you won't marry without his permission."

Meg pressed back against the door, needing the solid support. "I'm hardly a minor. I do not require my father's permission to marry anyone. I shall marry as I see fit."

"Wildon Fethersham is not the man for you," Alec said, his voice a soft contrast to the hard glitter in his eyes.

Meg forced her spine to straighten. "I don't remember giving you leave to determine my decisions," she said, pleased with the icy tone of her voice.

"I've seen what Fethersham's idea of land improvement is, Meg. I've seen the ruins of cottages where families had lived for generations. He has no respect for the crofters. He cares only for his own pleasure and comfort." Alec returned to the windows. He stared out at the mountains rising in the distance, where gray clouds were gathering over the rugged crests. Sunlight flickered, brushing his face as though needing to touch him one last time before succumbing to the clouds seeking to smother it. "I'll be willing to bet he started paying court to you the day after he discovered you would inherit Drummond land. Don't you see, lass, he wants your inheritance."

Meg knew exactly what type of man Fethersham was. Still, she didn't care to hear Alec imply the only reason a man might want to marry her was for her fortune. "I don't believe this is any of your concern."

Alec glanced at her, his face drawn into grim lines. "Your father has made it my concern."

Her father had asked Alec to marry her. Meg was certain of it. He had humiliated her in the past, but this cut deeper than she had ever imagined. "He asked you to take me off his hands, didn't he?"

Alec frowned. "He gave me the honor of trusting me with his daughter."

Alec certainly didn't look like a man pleased with the prospect of marriage. In fact, he looked like a man about to be marched to the gallows. Meg didn't have to ask him to know why Alec had agreed to marry her. Loyalty to her father. A sense of duty. Responsibility. Oh, she wanted to scream! Yet she was afraid if she started she wouldn't be able to stop. "You're willing to go to great lengths to satisfy a debt of honor. Marrying a woman you don't love."

Alec gave her a gentle smile. "I care for you, Meg. If I didn't, I wouldn't have agreed to marry you."

Alec had *agreed* to marry her. *Agreed!* As though he had agreed to buy one of her father's cows. Meg curled her hands into tight fists at her sides, struggling to control her emotions. "I hope you will understand if I don't accept your very generous offer."

Alec released his breath in a long sigh. "No one can force you to speak your vows."

"No. They can't." Meg turned away from him.

"But you need to know your father is a determined man. He intends to keep you from marrying Blandford. At all costs."

Meg paused with her hand on the brass door handle, Alec's words brushing like frost across the base of her spine. "He can't force me to marry you."

"No. But he will cause a scandal if you decide not to marry me."

Meg pivoted to face him. "What scandal?"

Alec remained quiet, allowing the moment to stretch until Meg thought she would scream. "You traveled with me all the way from London. Without a chaperon. Your reputation would be blown to perdition if anyone should discover the truth."

Meg held Alec's steady gaze, hoping he wouldn't see her fear. If anyone found out about the last few days, her life would be ruined. "No one saw me. No one need ever know."

"If you decide to disobey him, Robert will make certain all of London knows."

Her heart crept upward in her chest, until each beat pounded at the base of her throat. "He would actually destroy his own daughter?"

"If it's the only way to keep you from making the mistake of marrying that fortune-hunting jackass, then yes, he would destroy your reputation. Better your reputation be destroyed, than you find yourself shackled for the rest of your life to that blackguard. Even Fethersham would hesitate to marry a woman who has become a social liabilty. He likes his parties too much."

Any doubt Meg might have had about her father's innocence died in that instant of realization. A man capable of ruining his own daughter was capable of breaking his marriage vows. She leaned back against the door, her strength dissolving with her hopes. She never imagined her father could betray her this way. And Alec . . . her very own hero. How could he do this?

Through a blur of tears Meg watched Alec move toward her, tall and powerful, a woman's dream. Only her dream had turned into a nightmare. She wanted to turn and run, escape the humiliation. Yet there was no refuge. No place to hide. She drew in her breath, straightened her shoulders, and willed the tears not to fall. From experience, she knew if she stared straight ahead and didn't blink, they wouldn't fall.

Alec paused before her. "I'm sorry it has to be this way, Meg," he said, his voice a dark caress.

Meg was certain he was sorry. The last thing he wanted to do was marry her. Her chest ached from the strain of holding back her emotions. "No more sorry than I am."

Alec smoothed his fingertips over her cheek, the gentleness of the touch shredding her pride. The last thing she wanted from this man was pity. She looked up into his eyes, those incredible blue eyes that had haunted her dreams for so many years. What emotions did she see in those stunning blue depths? Sadness. Wariness. Regret?

If she weren't careful she would wallow in regret. Still, she couldn't stop thinking of what might have been. If only things were different. If only Alec loved her.

His full lips drew into a generous smile. "We'll make the best of it, lass. I promise we will."

Make the best of it. She felt as though she was going to be ill.

Alec stared down into her misty green eyes. A man could get lost in those eyes, tumble into the green pools and drown. "What do you say? Will you marry me, Meg?"

Meg stared up at him, all the sadness in her tear-filled eyes shifting into a grim determination. In that instant he realized how good this woman was at cloaking her feelings. And he wondered how deeply the softer emotions were buried.

Meg pulled away from him. Alec stood near the door, watching her move toward a pedestal table near the windows, soft blue muslin rippling around her legs. She stared down at a vase filled with dried flowers, where the dusty fragrance of roses and lilies suspended in time spilled into the air.

Alec told himself it didn't matter if Meg agreed to be his wife. If she refused to marry him, he could walk away with a clear conscience. In the end, Robert would make her see reason. Robert would marry her off to another man, someone he could trust. Alec would keep his freedom. The land would be safe. And Meg would be another man's wife. His chest tightened with that thought.

Alec watched and waited, his stomach curling with the same icy dread he had experienced each time he had ridden into battle. "Meg, there is nothing you can say to your father to change his mind."

"It would seem my father has left me no choice." Meg glanced over her shoulder, fixing him in a cool green gaze. "Since I have no desire to live the rest of my life as an outcast, nor do I wish to humiliate my mother further by causing another scandal, I shall do as my father dictates."

Alec released the breath he hadn't realized he had been holding. "There is a minister waiting in the drawing room."

Meg lifted her chin. "Father was quite certain of victory, wasn't he?"

"He suspected you would see there was only one course of action."

She marched to the door, her skirts brushing his leg as she passed him. "Let's get this farce over with."

A farce. Alec followed his future bride, wondering what twist of fate had brought him to this moment in time. He had always imagined he would marry one day. The woman would be beautiful, intelligent, warm and loving. He would be as much in love with her as she with him. His marriage would be as ideal as his parents' union.

How did reality compare to that ideal? His future bride possessed beauty. Meg was definitely intelligent. Warm and loving? Now there was the problem. Although she presented the world a facade carved from ice, Alec had glimpsed the fire hidden deep within her. A fire that could consume a man. A spark from that fire had sizzled in his blood. He wanted more.

Alec took her arm as they reached the stairs. Meg didn't glance at him. She stood proud and defiant, as English as the Tower of London. On the outside only, he assured himself. A Scottish lass still dwelled in that icy prison.

It wasn't going to be easy to melt the ice. Nothing worth having ever was. Since he wasn't a man who would settle for a lie, he needed to chip away all the bitterness, free the woman hidden beneath the ice. Because deep in his blood, he knew it was the only chance they would have of turning this farce into a real marriage. And he wouldn't settle for anything less.

Chapter Eight

Alec stared at Dunleith Castle from the window of his coach. Gray clouds were gathering in the sky above the gray stone turrets and spires. High on the brow of a rocky cliff rising from the north bank of Loch Laren, the gray stones of the castle had been shaped to withstand battle. Dunleith Castle had stood its ground since 1372. Since the time of the original square fortress, his ancestors had each left a mark on the castle, but none so complete as his grandfather, Lord Duncan Mac-Laren, the ninth earl.

Lord Duncan had employed Robert Adam to civilize the ancient pile. Two symmetrical wings had been added, the turrets and towers had been enlarged, new ones added, turning the once homely collection of stones into a romantic vision.

From this approach, the blackened stones of the east wing were hidden from sight, but not from his thoughts. Alec wondered what his parents would have thought of their son this day. He doubted they would approve of his tactics. Still, he thought they would approve of his bride. His parents had always cared for Meg. Regret fisted around his heart when he realized his parents and his brother would never have the pleasure of knowing his bride. They would never look upon his children, except from a place in heaven.

The air was growing cold with the approaching storm. Yet not as cold as the atmosphere within the coach. Alec looked at the woman sitting across from him. *My bride.* Strange, how easy it was to get accustomed to the idea of having Meg for his wife. Natural. As though he had simply taken the next step along a path that had been mapped out for him all of his life.

Unfortunately, the lady wasn't accepting the situation with such equanimity. The seven miles from Penross House had seemed like seven hundred. Meg hadn't spoken a word since she had spoken her vows. She sat staring out the window, as stiff and unyielding as a carved piece of flawless white marble. A proper English princess. Cold. Aloof. Untouchable.

Alec could understand her anger at the situation. A woman with a stubborn streak as wide as the Atlantic couldn't be forced into anything without feeling a wee bit piqued. Having something as important as marriage thrust upon her would naturally bring on a substantial fit of fury.

The anger would pass, Alec assured himself. Her anger didn't bother him half as much as his doubts about the other feelings Meg might have. He wasn't certain the lady would ever reconcile herself to making this a real marriage. And that uncertainty had latched onto his vitals, gnawing away at his insides. He wasn't certain how she felt about him. He only knew he couldn't settle for a chilly marriage of convenience. Not with Meg.

When the footman opened the door, Alec left the coach and offered his wife his hand. Meg didn't spare him a glance. She swept out of the coach and marched toward the entrance as though he were a ghost, invisible in the realm of the living.

Alec drew in his breath, an uncomfortable heaviness settling in his lungs. He gathered his strength and followed Meg into the huge entrance hall. Her footsteps tapped briskly against white and black marble squares, then stopped. Meg stood rigid, glancing up at a scene from Greek mythology that spread across the ceiling, where Vulcan fell from Olympus, tossed by his father's hand. She stared at the wide winding staircase rising gracefully at one end of the great hall. She glanced around the huge hall, a woman who had suddenly lost her way.

Meg seemed so small in the cavernous oak-paneled room. So fragile. The great entrance hall had welcomed every Countess of Dunleith for the past four hundred years. Yet Meg looked as though she had stepped into hell.

Alec gave his coat to the butler, Ogilvey. Earlier he had sent a message alerting the servants to prepare for their arrival. Now he decided his lady's introductions to her staff could wait until he had a few words alone with his bride.

Alec touched Meg's arm. Her muscles tensed beneath his palm, yet she didn't pull away from him. She glanced up at him, her expression reminding him of the dazed looks of men who had lived through their first artillery bombardment.

"We need to talk," Alec said, helping her remove her mantle.

Meg moistened her lips. "Yes. I'm afraid we do."

Alec handed her coat to the butler, then took her arm. As he led her toward an adjoining hallway, the clatter of paws on marble drew him up short.

Alec turned to find his two-year-old Irish red setter galloping toward them from the direction of the staircase. Always filled with more good-natured enthusiasm than good sense, Seamus had yet to learn the improvidence of charging full-out on a slick surface.

"Look out!" Alec said, stepping forward to protect Meg from his charging canine.

Seamus set his paws in an attempt to stop. His front feet slipped in opposite directions. His chin hit the marble. Yet he kept going, barreling forward, straight into Alec.

Alec gasped with the impact of six stone of dog plowing into his legs. His feet skidded out from beneath him. He fell back, thumping the marble with a dull thwack.

Seamus recovered before Alec. The setter planted both front paws on his master's chest and peered down at Alec, brown eyes bright with excitement, pink tongue lolling from the corner of his mouth, smiling in a canine expression of affection.

Alec rubbed the dog's long, silky ears. "Lord love you, Seamus. One of these days you're going to kill me with affection."

A strangled giggle brought Alec's attention from the dog perched on his chest to the woman standing nearby. Meg pressed her fingers to her lips in a futile attempt to contain her giggles. Laughter escaped her tight control, the soft giggles pealing like bells in the cavernous hall. It was amazing how a smile could transform her face, Alec thought. A simple smile altered stern beauty into a warm, captivating loveliness. It was almost worth an injured bottom and bruised dignity to see her smile.

Alec cocked one brow, giving her a look of mock severity. "Let me guess, you find public hangings amusing, don't you lass?"

"I can think of one hanging I might find amusing." Meg clapped her hands, coaxing the dog's attention from his master. Seamus trotted over to her, trampling Alec's chest on his way.

"I'm terribly sorry, my lord," Ogilvey said, rushing to his master's side. "Given the dog's problems with smooth floors and all, I told Henry to keep Seamus occupied until you were out of the hall. You can be certain I'll have a talk with the lad."

"It's all right, Ogilvey." Alec rose to his feet and straightened his coat. "Seamus has a mind of his own. It might not be a sound mind, but it's a determined one."

Ogilvey's lips twitched. "Aye, sir. That it is."

Alec turned to his bride, watching Meg as she knelt on one knee and stroked Seamus's smooth head. Seamus was sitting in a regal pose with his head high, his chest out. Meg was smiling at the dog, softly praising him for his beauty and his sweetness.

Alec saw a glimmer of the girl he had known in her unguarded countenance, a glimpse of the woman he hoped to discover. "He likes you."

"I suspect he likes most people." She glanced up at Alec. "He looks a great deal like my dog Wallace."

"He's one of Wallace's sons," Alec said.

Meg turned her attention back to the big red setter, her smile fading. "Father told me Wallace died last year."

"Aye. But he had a good long life."

Meg scratched Seamus under the chin. The dog leaned forward, his eyelids drooping. "When we left Penross House that last day, I wanted Wallace to come with me, but Grandmama wouldn't have a dog that size in her house. And I couldn't ask Wallace to start sleeping in the stable. It wouldn't have been fair. That last day, Wallace stood on the drive watching me as I climbed into the coach. He watched until the coach drew out of sight. I don't think he ever understood why I left him."

There was a softness in her voice that betrayed the hurt she still felt over leaving her friend. "Robert took Wallace along with him everywhere. You can be sure the dog was well cared for."

Meg rose to her feet. She smoothed her hand over the front of her gown, and he could almost see her drawing her armor around her. "My father has a way of taking care of things, doesn't he."

Alec sensed the pain within this woman, the bitterness that had festered over the years. How could he mend the wounds that hadn't healed? He didn't have the answer. But he knew he had to try. Alec took her arm and led her down an adjoining hallway, into the large drawing room.

Warmth radiated from a fire on the white marble hearth, chasing the chill from the air, spilling the pungent fragrance of burning peat into the room. The pale blue silk drapes had been opened. Gray light flowed into the room, spilling across the intricate floral design of blue and ivory in the carpet, the Empire sofas, the giltwood chairs, all upholstered in pale blue silk brocade.

Memories stirred inside of him. Alec, his parents, and Patrick had often gathered in the crimson drawing room in the evening, a place that no longer existed. Alec thought of the possibility of a family of his own, his wife and children, enjoying each other's company. The images kindled a warmth deep inside of him.

Meg drifted to the hearth, as though seeking the warmth of the fire. Seamus followed her, trotting to his favorite place near the fire, where he flopped onto his side on the carpet.

Alec stood near the door watching Meg, searching through his experience for help in dealing with her. Since he had never in his wildest dreams imagined forcing a woman to be his bride, circumstances had him feeling as though he had taken a plunge into a loch, with his hands tied behind his back.

He pulled open the door of a cabinet across from the windows and poured two glasses of brandy. He was hardly a schoolboy. He had charmed more than a few women over the years. How difficult would it really be to melt one icy female? Meg glanced up at him as he offered her the brandy. He smiled, hoping for a glimmer of warmth in return. "It will help take the chill away."

"Thank you," Meg said, as cool and cordial as a princess with one of her court.

Alec rested his arm against the smooth marble mantel. Firelight played against her face, a warm flicker of golden light against skin as smooth and pale as cream-colored satin. He smoothed his fingers over the bevels cut deeply into the crystal snifter, resisting the urge to touch her. He sensed Meg would pull away from him if he touched her just now. And the last thing he wanted was her to run away from him.

Meg lifted the brandy snifter, her thick dark lashes lowering as she inhaled the fragrance before taking a sip. The brandy left a sheen on her lips, and Alec caught himself wanting to lick the brandy from that sweet mouth. He watched the quick slide of her tongue across her lips, warmth licking across his skin.

My wife. The thought conjured images in his brain: Meg lying bare in his bed, sleek and supple, her long legs sliding against smooth silk sheets, her thick golden hair spilling across his pillow, her slim arms sliding around him, drawing him into her warmth. Blood gathered low in his belly, where a tight fist of desire pounded.

He sipped his brandy, the amber liquid warming his throat, the way Meg warmed another part of his anatomy. It had been a long time since a woman had triggered such an instant response in him. He thought of all the nights he would hold her in his arms. All the years he would have to savor this woman. If he could only break through the castle defenses.

"I would like to leave for London as soon as possible," she said, staring into the flames lapping over the black peat logs.

Alec stared at her a moment, refusing to believe the meaning behind her words. "I hadn't planned to spend the autumn in London, but we could stay a few weeks if you'd like."

A muscle in her cheek tightened with the setting of her jaw. "I would like to return to my home, MacLaren. Alone."

"This is your home now, Meg," he said softly.

"No. It isn't."

"Meg," Alec said, resting his hand on her arm, "if you would just look past—"

Meg turned to face him, her eyes flashing fury. "You and my father have what you want. Drummond estates are safe from the English invaders. Now I would like to go home."

"We're married, lass."

"In name only, MacLaren."

Alec held her angry gaze, searching for ways to ease past the barriers she had erected between them. "Is that how you would have our marriage, Meg? A sham? Me living here, while you continue your life as it was before you spoke your vows?"

"Don't speak to me of shams," she said, her voice low

119

and strained from her tight control over her emotions. "And don't you dare try to throw my vows into my face. You and Father brought this about, not I. And I shall not be held to vows that mean nothing."

Disturbing images flickered in his mind: Lady Margaret Drummond MacLaren, Countess of Dunleith, flitting from one party to the next, flirting with one randy buck after another, each sniffing after her skirts, salivating like hungry hounds. Would she teach her husband a lesson by taking a lover? Would she fill his nursery with bastards? An unexpected tide of red-hot anger surged inside of him. It was all he could manage to keep his voice level as he spoke. "It doesn't matter what brought us together, Meg. The fact is you are my wife. You belong here, with me. And here you'll stay."

"You can go to blazes! I will not be trapped here with you, pretending to be your wife."

"You are my wife. Make no mistake about it." He leaned toward her as he spoke, until his nose was an inch from hers. "And you can be sure I will not have you roaming London, taking one lover after another so you can take your revenge on me."

Meg stepped back, her lips parting on a sharp gasp. For a moment she stared at him, as though he had suddenly sprouted an extra head. "You think I would . . . Oh!" She tossed the contents of her glass into his face.

The brandy hit him like an open palm across the face. Alec blinked, the amber liquid stinging his eyes.

"Brute! How dare you imply I would behave in such a dishonorable fashion?"

Alec had always prided himself on his ability to remain calm under fire. A quick temper gained nothing in battle. And here he was, flying off in a rage at the mere thought of another man touching Meg. Damnation, but the woman was more provoking than a regiment of French cuirassiers.

"I apologize." Alec pulled his handkerchief from his pocket and mopped the sticky liquid from his face. Meg was a high-strung thoroughbred. She needed a gentle hand. Not a brute ramming the bit. "I didn't mean to question your honor."

Meg lifted her chin. "I am not in the habit of taking men to my bed."

Alec took the glass from her tight fingers and placed it with his on the white marble mantel. "Circumstances have changed, Meg. There is one man I hope you will accept in your bed."

She backed away from him, her eyes growing wide and wary. "That isn't going to happen, MacLaren."

"Ah, lass," he said, smiling at his wary bride, "I'm your husband."

She lifted one brow. "Only because I had no choice in the matter."

"I know things haven't gone the way you would have planned. I can tell you truly, I never expected to find myself in this position." Alec moved toward her. "But here we are."

Meg lifted her chin. "I won't be staying."

"There is a spark between us, lass. You can't deny you feel something when I hold you in my arms."

Meg took a step back, then dug in her heels. "Nothing I feel for you is worth mentioning."

Alec touched her cheek, sliding his fingers over her smooth skin, feeling her jaw tighten beneath his touch. "Give us a chance, Meg."

She stiffened. "I will not be manipulated by you or any man. You will soon see—"

Alec wrapped one arm around her and pulled her close against him, lifting her until her toes brushed the

121

floor. Before she could utter more than a startled "Oh," he covered her mouth with his.

He slid his lips over hers, tasting the brandy in her startled sigh. A bolt of heat sliced through him, setting fire to his blood. He lifted his head, startled by the sudden blaze of hunger inside of him. Meg blinked up at him, bemused and utterly charming in her bewilderment. "Stay with me, lass. Be my bride. Let me hold you this night. Let me coax that spark between us into a flame."

Meg tottered back a step, straight into the arm of one of the sofas. She jumped, then cast him an embarrassed glance before turning away from him. But Alec had caught a glimpse of uncertainty in her eyes. He had tasted desire in her kiss. It was enough to give him hope.

Meg marched to the windows, her back stiff with injured pride. She stood there, staring at the dark canes of dormant roses in his mother's garden for a long moment before she spoke. "Your attempts at seduction are pointless, MacLaren. I assure you, I want nothing you have to offer."

Alec studied her a moment, sensing the pain behind the cool mask. He wanted to hold her, to draw the ache of bitterness from her wounds. And he wanted more. Looking at her, seeing the gray light of an approaching storm touch her face, he realized he needed her in ways he was only just beginning to understand.

Chapter Nine

From the corner of her eye, Meg saw Alec move toward her, his strides slow and contained, a hunter approaching a wary doe. He paused behind her, touching her only with his warmth. The heat of his body soaked through the pale blue muslin of her gown, drenching her skin, tempting her to lean back against him.

"Have you ever thought you might like to have children, Meg?" he asked, his deep voice a gentle caress.

Meg hugged her arms to her waist, fighting the weakness inside of her. "I wouldn't want to bring children into a house where their parents were living a lie."

"No. Neither would I."

"Then you can see there is no reason for me to stay here." She drew in her breath, hoping to steady herself. Yet her breath was colored by sandalwood and man, the scent simmering through her like an exotic spice.

He rested his hands on her shoulders. She tensed beneath his touch, like a dove trapped in a hawk's talons. "There is no reason to be frightened of me, lass. I would never harm you."

She forced starch into her spine. "I'm certainly not frightened of you."

Alec rubbed his thumbs against the stiff muscles in her shoulders. "We can build a home together, Meg. I know we can. Give me a chance to be a good husband to you."

Good heavens, he was so good at this. He had a way of penetrating her defenses, touching her in all those places where she had hidden her dreams. She curled her shoulders away from him. "I was quite satisfied with my life before you kidnapped me, MacLaren. All I want is to return to that life."

"Things can never be the way they were, lass." He slid his hands down her arms, warming her through the long muslin sleeves. "Sometimes we take a turn from the life we thought we would lead. And there is nothing for us to do, except make the best of this new course."

She couldn't live like this, with this man, knowing he was only making the best of a dreadful situation. "I intend to make the best of this situation by returning to London and doing my best to forget you ever existed."

He drew his hands upward, along her arms. "It won't work, Meg. I do exist. I am your husband. And I'm going to find a way to show you there are some advantages to marriage."

"No doubt you're accustomed to women swooning from your blatant masculinity. Fortunately, I do not count myself among their number."

His hands paused against her shoulders. In the window glass, she could see the reflection of his handsome face, and the confidence in his smile. "Completely immune to my dubious charm, are you?"

She set her jaw. "You will find I am not easily seduced."

"You will find I seldom give up on something I want." He tugged on her shoulders, turning her until she faced him. "And I want you."

She curled her hands into fists at her sides, snatching for the anger that would keep her safe. "I know what you want and why you want it."

He lifted his brows. "Do you?"

"You want to add me to your list of conquests." She forced her lips into an aloof smile. "Your pride will not allow you to accept the fact that I want nothing to do with you."

He released his breath on a soft sigh that touched her face with the warm scent of brandy. "You don't know me very well. If you did, you would know I've never set about to conquer a woman."

"I know you as well as I want to," she said, hoping he wouldn't see her fear. "Your efforts at seduction shall be for naught, MacLaren."

He toyed with the ivory ribbon dangling from the small bow at the neck of her high-waisted gown, his hand brushing the gathered muslin between her breasts, scattering sensation across her skin. "Sure of that, are you?"

"Completely." She snatched the ribbon from his long fingers. "I can assure you, I do not appreciate your attempts at seduction. In fact, I find your tactics rather distasteful."

A smile tipped one corner of his lips. "Do you now?"

She swallowed hard. "Yes."

He traced the curve of her jaw with one fingertip, the soft caress sending tingles sprinting across her nerve endings. "My touch leaves you cold?"

She squeezed her hands into tight balls at her sides. "As cold as ice."

He rested his hand on her shoulder, the warmth of his palm seeping through the soft blue muslin of her gown. "And I suppose my kisses fail to move you."

She stared up into the pure blue of his eyes and tried desperately to marshal her troops. "Not one bit."

He slid his fingers into the hair at the back of her head. "Then you have nothing to fear from my clumsy attempts to win your heart."

She pressed her hands against his chest, intending to push him away. Yet her fingers curled against his shirt, sliding against firm muscles, absorbing the heat of his skin through soft white cambric. "I'm certainly not afraid of you."

Alec held her captive with his look, eyes as blue as a summer sky stripping away her defenses, baring her secrets. "You're trembling."

Meg stepped back. "You're most vexing."

Alec closed the distance, slipping his arm around her waist when she tried to escape. "Not nearly as vexing as you are, my bonnie lass."

She watched as he lowered his head, his sensual lips parting, warm breath spilling across her cheek. "I really must insist you—"

Alec drank the words of protest from her lips. A sigh rose and quivered within her at the warmth of his lips sliding over hers. She fought the shifting within her, the inescapable desire simmering in her veins. She would show him she was unmoved by him. Demonstrate her resolve. Earn her freedom. She would be ice in his arms.

He slid his other arm around her and pulled her close against him. Her breasts snuggled against his hard chest and sensation splintered through her, like shards of light through crystal. Oh dear, she felt like ice in his arms, ice that had been left in the bright rays of the sun until it liquified, until it turned to steam and rose in misty swirls toward that blessed, golden heat.

He lifted his head, his breath warm against her lips as he spoke. "Feel a flicker of warmth, Meg?"

She drew a shaky breath. "Not at all," she said, her voice far too thin.

"Hummm." He brushed his lips over her chin. "Let's try again."

Oh no, she wasn't certain she could withstand another direct assault. "Take your hands off of me."

He held her close, smiling down at her in that devilish way he had of melting her heart. "You feel good in my arms, Meg."

"I can't say the same." She tried to pull away from his maddening embrace. Yet he held her, his arms tensing around her, drawing her closer to the heat and power of his body. Allowing this intimacy did not suit her purpose. No, she definitely should not allow this behavior. Yet the intelligence of her purpose was drowning in her own need. Common sense withered in the fiery storm of his embrace.

He opened his mouth over hers, kissing her as though he were starving and she his only hope for sustenance. She should remain impassive in his arms. Protect herself at all costs. Yet her defenses were crumbling beneath his sensual assault. Her own need was too powerful to hope for the strength to reject his scorching kisses. He touched the seam of her lips with the tip of his tongue, and she opened to him, surrendering to her own blazing need for this man.

She moved as one drugged with dreams, sliding her arms around his broad shoulders. She slipped her fingers into the soft hair at his nape—strands of silk sliding against her fingers, cool near the ends, warm as she drew close to his scalp.

"You set fire to my blood, Meg," he whispered, sliding his hands over the curves of her bottom. He crushed her lips beneath his as he lifted her, pressing her against the intimate heat of his body.

She gasped against his lips, shocked by the thrust of his aroused flesh pulsing against her through the layers of their clothing. As shocking as it was, it was mild compared to the stunned realization of how much she craved the feel of his flesh against hers.

Wicked she might be. Wanton perhaps. Foolish definitely. But she wanted to strip away the barriers of wool and cotton and muslin, feel the brush of warm skin against skin. What would it be like, she wondered, to abandon herself completely to this man?

In the back of her mind a voice screamed in protest. She couldn't allow this. She couldn't give herself so completely to this man. Yet the protest tangled in the muddle he had made of her brain.

"Meg." He kissed her cheek, her jaw, her neck, warm lips moving softly against her skin, like the kiss of a flame. He slipped his hand down her back, his long fingers grazing the fastenings of her gown. "My own bonnie Meg."

Before her befuddled mind could comprehend his intention, he was peeling the gown from her shoulders, pushing the garment and the shift beneath it down over her breasts. She gasped as the cool air touched her heated flesh. A flicker of reason returned with the shock.

"Alec, I—" Her words dissolved into a startled gasp at the first touch of his lips against her breast.

He drew one rosy tip into his mouth, suckling her with the exquisite care of a master of seduction. Sensation shot from the captured nipple, a flaming spark sizzling through her, igniting fires in all directions. She gripped his shoulders, clinging to him like a drowning woman clutching a lifeline. Good heavens, this was all getting out of hand.

"Do you have any idea how much I want you?" he whispered, sweeping her up into his arms.

He gave her no chance to answer, covering her lips with his, fanning the flames he had kindled inside of her until they rose and shimmered through her, until they threatened to consume her. Cambric warm from his body brushed against her breast with the sensual shift of powerful muscles. She snuggled against him, pressing her aching breasts into his hard chest. Cool silk touched her bared back as he laid her down upon the nearest sofa.

He lifted his head, his breath falling warm and soft against her face. "My own bonnie Meg. Lord in heaven, I never realized you'd grow up to be so beautiful."

Triumph glittered in his eyes, and with that triumph came her own humiliation. Reality swept down upon her, as cold and brutal as a north wind. She turned her head when he lowered his lips toward hers. "Don't."

He drew back, a frown marring his brow. "What is it, sweetheart?"

She crossed her arms over her bare breasts, feeling more foolish than she had ever felt in her life. "You would seduce me, here, in the middle of the afternoon?"

"Afternoon, morning, evening. Any time is ripe for feeding this hunger." He brushed his lips against her bare shoulder, touched her skin with the tip of his tongue. "We'll go to my chamber."

Desire shivered through her, trembling along her every nerve. "You're very good at this, seducing women. It must come from a great deal of practice."

He smoothed his hand over her hair. "I haven't lived the life of a monk, Meg. But I can honestly say I've never taken advantage of a woman's innocence."

Until now, she thought. She struggled to draw her

gown back over her breasts. "You must be pleased with yourself, degrading me this way."

"Degrading you?" He drew the soft muslin of her gown over her shoulders, covering her breasts. "Sweet lady, this had nothing at all to do with degradation."

"You wanted to prove I wasn't immune to your masculine wiles."

He sat with one hand braced against the curved back of the sofa, scowling at her. "I wanted to prove there was a spark between us. And I did. Whether you want to admit it or not."

She struggled to fasten the ties at the back of her gown. "This changes nothing. I have no desire to stay here as your wife."

He released his breath in a frustrated sigh. "Turn around. I'll fasten the blasted gown."

She obliged, presenting him her stiff back.

"You have a stubborn streak wider than the North Sea, and just as bitter." Alec tugged on the ties, fastening the gown. "You're all twisted by something you think your father did to your mother. And now I'm left to pay the price for it."

She lifted her chin. "I didn't ask you to marry me."

"But you did marry me." He gripped her shoulder and forced her to face him. "And I have some strange notions about marriage, my bonnie bride. I believe in living together, in enjoying all that comes between a man and a woman. I believe in making a home where children can live and laugh."

"Then you should have married a woman who wanted to be your wife, MacLaren."

Alec studied her a moment in that penetrating way he had of making her feel he could read every thought in her befuddled brain. "Why don't you rest a bit. The past few days have been difficult. After you rest, and we have dinner, we'll talk."

Meg kept her gaze on the fire burning in the hearth. "I won't change my mind."

"We'll see, lass." Alec smiled at her frozen profile. "We'll see if I can change your mind."

Meg set her jaw against the weakness inside of her, the treacherous instincts coaxing her to surrender to Alec. She caught herself slipping into a pool of regret—if only things were different, if only Alec truly wanted her.

She stared at the flames lapping over plump black logs, marshaling her defenses. The rogue would not manipulate her. She would not allow him the opportunity to humiliate her again. She couldn't surrender to her own blasted need.

In the corner of her eye, she watched Alec walk away from her, with Seamus trailing after him. If she weren't careful she would be trailing after Alec like a besotted puppy. All of her life she had dreamed of becoming this man's wife. But this dream had taken a nasty turn. She had been content as a spinster, she assured herself. Safe. The door closed with a soft click behind Alec.

Alone for the first time since her hasty marriage, Meg released the tenuous hold she held on her emotions. Tears burned her eyes as she stared into the fire. She felt ill, her stomach twisted into a tight mass.

Never in her life had she felt so completely alone. With one stroke fate had robbed her of every illusion she still maintained about romance. And now she was in danger of losing every grain of her self-respect. Alec proved that this afternoon. He could shatter her restraint with a touch of his hand.

Everything had happened so quickly and so brutally. She kept thinking she would awaken and this would all be some horrible dream. Yet she knew this was real. The realm of dreams did not allow for such a complete feeling of desolation.

131

She swiped at her damp cheeks. Tears would win her nothing but sore eyes. She had learned that lesson a long time ago. Nothing could be accomplished by feeling sorry for herself. She must think of a plan. An escape from this travesty. Before Alec destroyed her.

Chapter Ten

"You mean to tell me you're married." Alec's cousin, Niall Fergusson, sat in a leather armchair near the hearth in Alec's library, staring at his cousin. "This day. To Margaret Drummond."

"Aye. We were married at Penross House this morning." Alec handed Niall a snifter of brandy. He was glad Meg was still resting in her chamber. It gave him an excuse to avoid disturbing her. Although he hated to admit it, he was hiding his bride. He didn't care to think of what she might say to anyone about their hasty marriage. Meg had a way of making him feel like a villain, in spite of Alec's attempts to justify his actions.

Niall stared at his cousin, his dark gray eyes wide, his expression revealing his astonishment. "I saw Miss Drummond at a party in London last week. Since neither the lady nor you mentioned your upcoming marriage, I'm surprised, to say the least."

Alec sank into a leather armchair across from Niall. Where his father's eldest sister, Georgianna, had produced a pompous, self-centered blackguard for her firstborn and only son, seven and twenty years ago Douglas MacLaren's youngest sister, Christina, had managed to deliver into the world a good-natured, handsome lad. Of course, Christina had made a better choice of husbands by marrying a member of the Scottish gentry, rather than an English viscount, Alec thought. English and Scottish blood did not settle together easily.

Niall resembled his father. He was tall and slender and had the dark chestnut brown hair of his sire. And, like his sire, Niall had a way of piercing to the heart of the matter with a look. "I assume Sir Robert arranged the match."

Alec and Niall had always been as close as brothers. Alec saw no sense in dancing around the truth. Yet he sought to couch his reply in a way that would salvage his wife's dignity. "Robert was concerned about Meg's future. I assured him I would take proper care of her."

"I thought as much." Niall sipped his brandy, his expression growing thoughtful. "Robert must have heard about our cousin's plans to marry the lady."

"Aye. Robert had a fairly good notion Meg was going to marry Blandford to spite him. He thought I might alter the situation."

"You always did have a way of charming the ladies." Niall grinned. "There will be more than a few gentlemen cursing your name when they discover you've made off with the Snow Queen."

"The Snow Queen?" Alec asked.

"Your lady. It's said she can freeze a man with a single glance of those beautiful green eyes, which of course made her an even more tempting challenge to the gentlemen of the ton. Every Season for the past five years, London has been littered with the frozen corpses of all the men who have tried to win the icy hand of the Snow Queen."

The Snow Queen. It suited Meg. Alec stared into the brandy in his glass, where flames from the hearth reflected in the amber liquid. He had glimpsed fire deep inside his beautiful bride. And somehow he would find a way to melt the ice, he assured himself.

"If you glance in the betting books of any club in London, you'll find wagers placed on who shall coax the Snow Queen to the altar. In fact the last time I saw our cousin Blandford, he was entering his name into the book at White's." Niall laughed softly. "Old Blandford won't be happy to learn of your coup."

"No. I suspect he will want to see me on the gallows."

Niall nodded. "He still thinks you returned from the grave just to spite him."

Alec sipped his brandy, the heady fragrance flooding his nostrils as the potent liquid warmed his throat. In some circuitous way, Alec was responsible for casting his cousin Wildon into dun territory. If Alec hadn't returned from the grave, Wildon would have had more than enough blunt to cover his extravagant expenditures during his short tenure as Earl of Dunleith. Still, considering the damage Wildon had wreaked upon the tenants of Dunleith, Alec found it difficult to conjure any sympathy for the blackguard. It was a pity Niall wasn't the next in line for the title, instead of standing behind Blandford. Niall would never have evicted the crofters.

Niall cocked one dark brow. "I wish I'd known your intentions toward Miss Drummond. I could have made a small fortune if I had bet on you."

Seamus rested his chin on the arm of Alec's chair, seeking attention. "Did you have a candidate in mind who you thought might coax the lady to the altar?" Alec asked, smoothing his hand over the setter's sleek head.

"From what I've observed, the lady has never shown a partiality to any gentleman, including Blandford." Niall settled his brandy snifter on the pedestal table beside his chair. "Of course, most ladies have this uncanny ability to deceive a man. A fool is a man who thinks he has figured out all the intricate workings of a female mind."

The bitterness in his cousin's voice caught Alec by surprise. "Can I surmise by this that things are not going well with you and the Carnwath chit?"

Niall released his breath in an exaggerated sigh. "It seems the lady's mama has her heart set on marrying her daughter to a peer. Without a title, I don't have a chance of winning the lovely Miss Carnwath."

Alec frowned. "If the chit feels that way, she probably isn't worth your time."

Niall shrugged. "I'm beginning to convince myself of that. Still, I've had moments when I wondered what might have happened if I had inherited Dunleith after your 'death,' instead of Blandford. I might have married the lovely Miss Carnwath before you returned from the grave."

"It sounds to me as though you had a close call, my friend. There are better ladies out there for you."

"Aye." Niall smiled at Alec. "And I intend to enjoy myself while I'm looking."

Alec sensed the disillusionment behind Niall's smile. A woman could wreak havoc with a man. He was becoming well acquainted with that fact. Each day with Meg, he realized more and more how much she meant to him. If he couldn't melt his icy lady, he had an uncomfortable feeling she would walk away with his heart.

Alec came to his feet when Niall rose to leave. At any other time, he would have enjoyed Niall's company.

Now he had Meg to consider. Just how would his reluctant bride behave toward her husband in front of a guest? "Will you stay for dinner?"

Niall grinned at him. "No. I shall leave you to your wedded bliss."

Wedded bliss. Alec rubbed the back of his neck, trying to ease the tension in his taut muscles as Niall left the room. This was his wedding day. He should be looking forward to the activities that would come this evening. Instead, he was faced with the daunting prospect of winning the heart of a stubborn woman who insisted she wanted nothing to do with him.

He glanced up at the painting hanging on the mahogany paneling between a set of gilt-trimmed bookcases built into the wall. The portrait of his parents had been painted in the rose garden of Dunleith the year of their wedding. Dressed in pale blue, his mother sat on a stone bench, sunlight glinting on her light brown hair, humor sparkling in her gray eyes. Tall and dark, wearing the MacLaren tartan, his father stood beside her, his hand resting on her shoulder, his blue eyes filled with the contentment of a man who had all he wanted from life. The artist had captured the hint of mischief simmering between them, the spark that glowed when they were near each other.

Alec had never seen any two people more in love. It was as if each day was a glorious adventure, simply because they were together. He had always imagined finding that special kind of affection. An image rose in his mind, a woman with golden hair and eyes the color of a Highland glen. Deep in his Celtic blood, he had a suspicion that what he was looking for was close at hand. Hidden beneath a crusty slab of ice.

Meg leaned against the white bark of a birch tree and slipped off her right shoe. A pebble tumbled from the slim blue slipper to the moss-covered ground. Stones and bracken had scraped and sliced the soft kid leather of the shoe. The other shoe hadn't fared any better. She wasn't exactly dressed for a hike through the woods, but she didn't have a choice. The road would be too dangerous. Once MacLaren discovered she was gone, he would set the hounds after her.

Meg clutched her mantle to her neck, shivering, wishing she had a heavier coat, something that could withstand the drizzle seeping through the sparse, golden leaves overhead. If the storm would hold off just a little while, she could make it to Penross House without getting drenched.

She stared across the loch, trying to gain her bearing. Heavy gray wreaths hung around the mountain summits, mist curled along the craggy slopes, harbingers of the coming storm. Penross House couldn't be more than three more miles, Meg assured herself. She could make it before the storm swept down from the mountains. She only hoped she could convince Dorrie to help her once she reached it. If not, she would simply find another way to escape. She would not stay and act as a brood mare for the man who had aided her father in savaging her life.

Meg trudged along the bank of the loch, hugging her arms to her waist in an attempt to stay warm. In time, the drizzle gathered into rain. Wind swept the rain against her, fingers of cold penetrating her wool mantle. She huddled against the slender trunk of a birch, taking what little shelter the tree offered. She had no choice but to continue. There was nothing between here and Penross House except trees and stones.

It wasn't far now. Another mile. Perhaps two. She could endure the cold and the wet, she assured herself. What she couldn't endure was humiliation at the hands of Alec MacLaren. The man wouldn't be satisfied until she had betrayed every wretched feeling she had for the infuriating beast. She wouldn't live that way. She couldn't live with him, knowing he was only making the best of a horrible situation.

I can tell you truly, I never expected to find myself in this position. His words echoed in her brain, taunting her.

Alec had never expected to marry her, while most of her life she had dreamed of becoming his wife. *Demented fool!* Well, she refused to surrender her pride or her freedom. Once she was back in England, she would manage a nice quiet annulment. When she was back with her mother and grandmother, they would find a way to deflect any attempts her father might make to ruin her reputation. She would show both Drummond and MacLaren she wouldn't be manipulated or controlled.

Wool and muslin tangled around her legs, her sodden mantle and dress chilling her skin. Meg clenched her jaw and forged ahead, bending against the wind that swept sheets of rain against her. Through the steady howl of the wind and hiss of the rain, she heard a rumble. Thunder? she wondered, glancing up at the gray sky. No. The sound was closer than thunder, a rumble coming from behind her.

Meg glanced over her shoulder. Through the gray curtain of rain she saw a rider atop a huge silvery gray horse emerge from the woods. She knew the man at a glance. Her heart pounded with the same ferocity as the horseshoes thumping the ground. She froze beside the loch with rain pouring down her face.

Alec rode directly for her, a warrior bearing down on the enemy. For one horrible moment Meg wondered if he meant to trample her, free himself from this distasteful union. She stumbled back as he pulled up beside her, horseshoes scattering stones.

Alec dismounted in one fluid move. Two long strides brought him face-to-face with her. Rain streamed from the brim of his dark gray hat. Through the rain Meg stared up into a pair of furious blue eyes.

"What the bloody hell do you think you're doing?" Alec shouted.

"Leaving you!"

"Damnation! You'll catch your death out here dressed like that."

Meg fought to keep from shivering as she watched him unfasten the buttons lining the front of his great-coat. "Go away, MacLaren. I don't want your help."

"Stubborn little . . ." Alec shrugged out of his coat and whipped it around her shoulders. The warmth of his skin lingered in the blue silk lining the dark gray wool, warming her, the heavy folds falling to the ground around her feet. "You haven't the sense you were born with," he said, grabbing her upper arm.

Meg dug in her heels, struggling when Alec tried to drag her toward the horse. "I'm not going anywhere with you. If you think I shall be your brood mare, you're mistaken."

"Brood mare?" Alec stared at her a moment, rain pelting the dark blue wool of his riding coat. "We'll talk later."

Meg tugged against his hand. "I'm not going."

Alec released her arm, only to wrap one arm around her shoulders, the other beneath her knees. She gasped as he swept her up into his arms. "Put me down!"

Alec obliged by setting her atop his horse. The huge gray stallion tossed its head, whinnying with the sudden weight. Before Meg could lose her balance, Alec swung up behind her and grabbed the reins, imprisoning her between his arms. He slipped his feet into the stirrups, one muscular thigh coming up beneath her thighs.

Meg sat sideways in the saddle, braced against his solid chest, her bottom nestled intimately against his loins. The spark of contact penetrated the heavy wool between them and shivered through her blood. She leaned forward, trying to avoid touching him. "If you take me back I'll find some way to escape you."

Alec dropped his flat-crowned beaver hat upon her head. "Choose a sunny day next time you try."

Alec urged the horse into a canter, the sudden movement thrusting her back against his chest. Each powerful surge of the horse rocked her against the man holding her cradled against his body. After a few moments, Meg abandoned her attempts to keep some distance between them. She settled back against Alec's chest, willing herself to ignore him.

Impossible.

The heat of him wrapped around her. In spite of her best intentions, Meg couldn't dismiss the warmth kindling inside of her. Alec was so large, so powerful, so completely male, he made her feel delicate and protected. Wrapped in his coat and hat, sheltered in his arms, she barely noticed the cold. But he did. She could feel his muscles tense with the lash of the wind, his body shiver against hers.

Still, Alec didn't request the return of his hat or coat. Her conscience pricked her. Meg ignored it. She hadn't asked for his help. Indeed, she didn't want it. If the man insisted on playing the chivalrous knight, then she would let him. Until she figured a way to escape the handsome brute.

Chapter Eleven

Alec sat near the hearth in his library, watching flames lick over the peat logs piled on the polished andirons. He had changed out of his sodden clothes, but he couldn't shake the chill that had penetrated his bones.

Iona Macpherson shoved a pewter mug under his nose. "This will warm ye, milord."

Alec took the mug, the pewter warm against his cold hands. The scent of coffee liberally laced with whiskey filled his nostrils. He took a sip and welcomed the warmth into his tight chest. He smiled up at the small, gray-haired woman. "Thank you."

Iona pursed her thin lips. The little sparrow of a woman had once been Alec's nurse. Now she was the housekeeper, but she had never abandoned her tendency to look after him like a worried hen. "Beggin' yer pardon, milord, but I wish ye wouldna go runnin' about without a coat. Ye'll catch yer death, ye will. And ye so soon out of the sickbed."

Alec resisted the urge to lean toward the fire. He didn't want Iona to realize he was chilled straight through to his marrow. The little woman was worried enough about him. "I had a coat when I left."

"Aye. And I wish ye would 'ave kept it. Ye look tired, milord. Ye should take better care. Ye should lie down a bit before dinner. Ye need rest."

"I'm fine, Iona."

"But ye—"

He raised his hand, cutting off her lecture. "Have you seen to my lady's comfort?"

Iona's expression turned sour. "Aye. I've told Fenella to look after 'er needs."

Alec smiled up into her disapproving gray eyes. "Lady Margaret has suffered more than a few shocks in the past few days, Iona. I would appreciate it if you and the staff would make her feel welcome."

Iona nodded, her expression revealing her sentiments about the new Countess of Dunleith. "I'll do me best, milord," she said, before quitting the room.

Alec rested his elbows on his knees and held the cup between his palms, while he leaned toward the fire. A chill shivered through his muscles, making his hands shake. He gripped the mug, wanting nothing more than to curl up in his bed and sleep for a month. The past few days had taken a toll on him, physically as well as mentally. He needed time to catch his breath. Yet he couldn't retreat to his room. Not yet. Not until he dealt with his reluctant bride. The question remained: What the devil was he going to do with her?

Seamus poked his cold nose against Alec's hand, as though asking what was wrong with him. Alec smiled into the dog's innocent eyes while he scratched the soft fur behind Seamus's right ear. "There are times when I envy you, my friend. Life can become far too complicated when you walk about on two feet."

Seamus tilted his head back and forth, as though trying to understand Alec's every word. The dog had spent the past two years of his life traveling with Alec from one army camp to the next. Still, it hadn't taken much for the animal to grow accustomed to the soft life at Dunleith. Alec only wished he found it so easy to fit into this new life.

Steam sweet with the scent of coffee and whiskey bathed Alec's face. He sipped the strong, hot brew, hoping to ease the shaking deep inside of him. This afternoon, when he had discovered Meg had run away from him . . . Lord, he had never before felt such a violent surge of emotions. Anger and hurt and a chilling fear. What if he hadn't found her?

The damn stubborn wench. She could have gotten herself killed in her attempt to leave him. Slipped and fallen off a cliff. Caught her death in the freezing rain. Because she couldn't abide the notion of being his bride. Lord help him, he was married to a bloody Englishwoman.

What the devil am I going to do with you, Meg? He stared down into his coffee, the candlelight reflected in the black liquid. His wife of less than a day would rather plunge into a storm than live with him. The truth wasn't exactly easy to swallow. Still, he realized he had pushed her too far, frightened her with a taste of her own desire. She needed time to adjust to the situation. In time he could convince her this marriage wasn't the biggest mistake either of them had ever made he assured himself.

Alec sensed the moment Meg entered the room. The air altered, crackled and thrummed with a sensual energy he felt whenever she was near. He turned his head and watched as she approached, her head held high, her expression cool and remote. His beautiful, untouchable Snow Queen. Seamus trotted over to her. In spite of her icy demeanor, she paused to greet the dog, smiling at him, ruffling his long ears, stroking his head.

"Your housekeeper said I might find you here," Meg said, keeping her attention focused on Seamus.

Alec dragged air into his lungs, a vise squeezing his chest until he could scarcely draw a breath. Not now, he thought. He couldn't fall ill now, when he had a maiden to claim. "Have you everything you need?"

Meg looked up from Seamus. "Everything except my freedom."

Alec glanced away from her angry expression. He stared into the fire and gathered his strength, while searching for words amid the fog clouding his brain. "I've been sitting here, trying to ascertain how I might convince you there is no reason to be frightened of me."

"Frightened?" Meg marched to the hearth in front of Alec. "I can assure you I'm certainly not frightened of you."

Alec glanced up at her. "Yet you ran away like a frightened child."

Meg stared down her slim nose at him. "I told you I had no intention of remaining here, pretending to be your wife."

Seamus sat beside Alec's chair, looking at Meg as though he were trying to understand the anger radiating from her. Alec rolled the mug between his palms, absorbing the warmth radiating through the pewter. "You would run off to London, pretend you never spoke your vows, rather than stay and try to make something of this marriage."

She rested her hand on the mantel and stared down into the flames. "I would rather forget I ever saw you."

Alec studied her a moment, watching the firelight flicker against her skin, golden light exposing the bitterness beneath her calm mask. "Are you certain you aren't afraid of me, Meg?"

She tilted her head and fixed him in a chilling glare. "Why would I be frightened of you, MacLaren? Do you plan to do me some injury?"

Although her voice remained cold and hard, he sensed a flicker of doubt behind the confidence. "No, lass. I would never harm you."

"Then why would I be frightened of you?"

"Perhaps you're afraid I might break through those thick walls you've built around your heart. Perhaps you think I might find a way to touch you, to make you care for me. Perhaps you're afraid of making this marriage into something more than empty vows."

Her hand curled into a fist against the white marble mantel. "Perhaps you're a little too confident of your prowess with women."

Heat crept across his skin, chasing chills. "What have you got to lose, Meg? If you stay here and try to make a real marriage with me. What do you lose?"

A real marriage. If it weren't so horribly sad Meg might have laughed. For years she had dreamed of a real marriage with this man. Now she possessed his name, but not his love. What did she lose if she tried to make a real marriage out of this bitter farce? Her pride. Her dignity. Her ability to face herself in a mirror.

Alec didn't love her. He needed her to provide legitimate heirs. When she was breeding he would no doubt pick up his life where he had left it. Men could not be trusted. And Alec was worse than an ordinary man—he was a Highlander.

Memories flickered in her brain, her mother facing the man she loved and the harlot who had warmed his bed. Meg would find herself in the same position if she were not careful. A man who didn't claim love or devotion for his bride would have no qualms in betraying her.

The truth was a bitter draft, Meg thought. But it was better to swallow it now, instead of hiding it away where it could grow more potent in the shadows, until it fermented into a poison that would destroy her. "I gain nothing by staying."

"Are you so certain, Meg?" Alec asked, his voice a soft brush against her back. "Do you truly believe you could find nothing of importance here?"

"I told you once before, I left nothing in the Highlands." She fixed her features in a haughty mask before she turned to face him. "I want nothing here."

He set his mug on a small table beside his chair. He stood, rising slowly. "I can't let you leave, lass."

Meg frowned as she watched him walk toward her, each step far too controlled, as though he were stepping along the edge of a cliff. "Will you keep me a prisoner?"

Alec paused beside her, resting his arm against the mantel. "If you turn me into a jailer, that's what I'll be. It's not a role I'd choose, but I can't let you go. I won't allow you to return to England and annul our vows."

She stared at him, stunned by the easy way he had of discerning her intentions. "I'll find a way to escape you, MacLaren. I'll find a way to make certain you and Father regret your treachery."

Alec touched her cheek, his fingers strangely cool against her skin. The sweet scent of whiskey-flavored coffee brushed against her face with the warmth of his breath. "Don't force my hand, lass. I pledged to keep Drummond land safe from men like my cousin Blandford. And I intend to keep my promise. Even if it means taking measures that might seem a bit harsh."

Meg stepped back from him. "What measures?"

"There is one way I can be certain you won't be able

147

to end this marriage." Alec was quiet a moment, staring down into the fire, a frown digging twin furrows between his black brows. "Once we've consummated the vows, you would have to do more than seek a simple annulment, Meg. You would have to get a divorce. And there is no way you could keep that quiet."

She stared at him. "You would force yourself on me?"

"It's not something I would care to do." Alec fixed her in a cool gaze, the expression in his beautiful eyes hard and unyielding. "But I'll do what is necessary."

She turned away from him, unwilling to allow him to see the hurt in her eyes. "You are a true Highlander, MacLaren. As brutal and base as any of your ancestors who wielded a mace. Kidnapping women. Raping. Pillaging."

"Aye. I'm a Highlander," he said, his voice a soft contrast to his words. "I honor my vows, no matter how unpleasant the task becomes. Unlike the woman I married."

His words lashed her like the sting of a whip. She set her jaw and steeled herself against the pain. "So it seems you can commit rape in the name of honor."

"I'm your husband. You gave me the right to make love to you when you spoke your vows."

"I didn't give you the right to take me by force."

Alec moved up behind her and rested his hands on her shoulders, the warmth of his hands soaking through the ice blue silk of her gown. "After this afternoon, do you really imagine I would have to force you, Meg?"

Meg swallowed past the tight band of emotion squeezing her throat. "Since I don't want you, MacLaren, what else would you call it?"

"A gentle taming. A sweet seduction." Alec brushed his lips across the top of her ear, sending shivers skimming down her neck. "You might not like me, but your body trembles when I touch you."

Meg curled her shoulders, trying to escape his touch. "Revulsion."

He laughed, a deep, masculine sound that rumbled from low in his chest. "You're a stubborn wench. But I know the difference between revulsion and desire. Even if you don't."

Meg pulled away, putting three feet of air between them before turning to face him. "You can try to justify your intent from now until Judgment Day, MacLaren. But the truth is, if you take me against my will, I will hate you until the day I die."

Alec studied her a moment. "I wouldn't want that to happen."

"Then let me go."

"I can't." He smiled, a gentle curving of his lips that warmed the depths of his eyes and set a vise around her heart. "Let me be your husband, Meg. Not your jailer."

"I don't want you as my husband," she said, forcing her voice to remain level as she spoke the lie.

A muscle flickered in his cheek with the clenching of his jaw. In a few beats of her heart, the warmth in his expression cooled. Where hope had flickered in his eyes, regret mingled with an icy resolve. "I've given my word to your father that I would take care of you and keep the land safe. I can't let you go."

That was all she was to this man—a promise to be kept. "Oh, how I wish you had never come home from Waterloo! You should have been the one that Prussian murdered."

Alec flinched at her words, as though she had struck him hard across the face. She pressed her fingers to her lips, immediately regretting the careless words. Still, she could find no way to retrieve them.

Alec held her gaze, his emotions stripped bare, leaving him raw and vulnerable. For one shattering moment she glimpsed his pain, his sadness. In spite of her anger, she ached for this man. It took all of her will to keep from touching him.

The silence stretched between them, filled with the crackle of the fire, the steady rattle of rain against the windowpanes. Alec turned away from her and braced his hands on the mantel. He stared into the flames for a long moment before he spoke. "Promise me you won't try to run away. Promise me you'll give us a chance to get to know each other again. And I will promise I won't make love to you until you're ready."

Make love. What a beguiling term. Implying something wonderful. "I'll never be ready."

Alec turned his head. Firelight flickered against his face, illuminating the grim lines of his expression. "Give me your word you won't try to escape me, Meg. Or I swear, I'll take you right here, right now."

He would do it. He would throw her on the floor, toss her gown around her waist, and proceed to consummate their vows. Meg caught herself growing warm in spite of her anger and indignation. "It would seem you have left me no choice."

"There is a choice. You could work at building something between us, instead of running from the possibility like a spoiled child."

Meg clenched her hands into fists at her sides, resisting the urge to scream. This horrible situation was not of her making. Yet the man would cast her as the villain. "I want nothing between us, except perhaps an ocean."

Alec didn't blink. "Will you agree to the terms?"

Meg glared at him. "Yes."

He studied her a moment, an icy determination in

his blue eyes. "I hope you're a woman who keeps her word."

She bristled with the jab to her integrity. "I am not in the habit of breaking my word."

He nodded. "I'm glad to hear it. Because if you change your mind, know this. I'll track you down, Meg. I'll find you and haul you back here. And there will be no room for negotiation. Do you understand me?"

"I understand you perfectly." In that instant she lowered her affection for him along with her hopes and dreams into a casket, the weight of their remains tugging on her heart. The hollow sound of a lid closing echoed through her. If only things could be—No. She wouldn't drive herself insane with wishes and regrets. This was war. And she would not end up a casualty.

Honor was a two-edged sword. Alec had learned that fact a long time ago, but never had it cut as deeply as it had today. He had never thought to find himself in a position to threaten a woman the way he had threatened Meg. The fact that she had left him no choice provided little solace.

Alec glanced down the long length of the dining room table to where his wife sat. Meg looked elegant in a gown of pale blue silk, her hair falling in lush curls over one shoulder. Light from a silver candelabra glowed golden against her face, revealing a deceptively calm expression. It was as though she had packed up all of her emotions, leaving him to face a cool indifference. The icy English Snow Queen.

Seamus lay beside his chair, looking up at him with liquid brown eyes. Alec handed the setter a piece of salmon. Seamus swallowed the chunk in one bite, then looked up, hoping for more.

The room was quiet, so quiet Alec was aware of the long case clock marking time in one corner of the room. Beyond the pale green silk brocade drapes, rain pounded against the windowpanes, mocking the silence. Four footmen stood like statues across the room, their emerald green livery plastered against the pale green walls, as they observed the silent repast.

Alec couldn't sit here without thinking of other nights he had spent in this room. His mother had always sat beside his father at dinner. He and Patrick would sit across from each other. When his parents and brother were alive, this room was never quiet at any meal.

When the MacLarens gathered to share a meal, they had always shared conversation and laughter. Lord, how he missed them. Even though he had spent most of his life during the past ten years away from them, his family had always been here, the rock on which he had based his life. Now he was the last of the Dunleith MacLarens. He sipped his wine, forcing the claret past his dry throat, the fragrant bouquet flooding his senses.

Alec stirred a piece of salmon through a buttery herb sauce on his plate and tried to find an appetite. The pounding in his head was growing worse. Yet his physical complaints paled in comparison to the ragged state of his emotions. Meg had a way of penetrating his guard, piercing more than flesh. All in all, he would have to say it had not been a good day. Especially considering it was his wedding day.

He watched Meg sip her wine, trying not to think of how her lips would taste, sweetened by the claret. What would it take to win his reluctant bride? How long before he could hold her in his arms again? When would she release the grip she held on bitterness and anger? *What am I going to do with you, Meg?*

Alec sipped his wine and contemplated his own battle strategy. One day this room would sparkle again with conversation. One day he would hold his children, hear their laughter. One day he would find a way past the lady's defenses. He would turn this icy imitation of marriage into something warm and real.

From the pounding mess of his brain, he retrieved the memory of Meg, warm and supple in his arms. He would taste her passion again. A woman with as much fire in her as Meg couldn't maintain her icy facade forever. One day soon, he would set a fire warm enough to melt the English ice. Or—he smiled into his wine— he would die trying.

Chapter Twelve

She couldn't face him. Not this morning. Not after the dreams that had haunted her last night. Meg stood by a window in her bedchamber, staring out at Loch Laren. Morning sunlight glinted on the rolling waves. Across the water, mist still shrouded the peak of Ben Lyon like a filmy silk scarf. When she was a girl she had dreamed of living in this beautiful place, as Alec's wife. Strange how dreams could turn into nightmares.

It had taken her hours to fall asleep last night, her wedding night. When at last she had managed to drift into slumber, Alec had invaded her dreams, stripping her clothes, taking her into his arms, exercising his connubial rights in ways that shocked her waking mind. What was worse than recognizing the dark side of her dreams was the horrible truth she had to face: She had participated in those carnal acts with wanton abandon. She had awakened hugging her pillow, restless with a horrible feeling of emptiness. Would it ever go away? Could she ever rid herself of this terrible need? This shameful longing for a man who could easily destroy her?

"Good morning."

Meg pivoted at the sound of Alec's voice. Heart hammering against the wall of her chest, she faced the man standing in the doorway that connected her chamber with his. "What are you doing here?"

"I came to walk with you to breakfast," Alec said, moving toward her, keeping his right hand hidden behind his back. His dark gray riding coat hugged the breadth of his shoulders. Buff-colored leather breeches hugged the muscular curves of his legs before plunging into a pair of shiny black boots. Power and grace. With his impeccable white shirt and cravat, he managed to blend elegance with his own heady brand of dangerous masculinity.

"I don't recall inviting you to enter my chamber."

"I knocked, but you didn't hear me." He stepped into the column of sunlight spilling through the window, so close she could smell the tang of sandalwood on his skin. He drew his hand out from behind his back. "I picked these for you this morning."

Her breath caught at the sight of the simple bouquet of purple heather. She took the bouquet from his fingers, appalled at the sudden trembling of her hand. The ivory satin ribbon he had used to tie the stems brushed the inside of her wrist.

"I remember you used to like the smell of heather."

She remembered far too much—dreams and hopes and memories of a gallant Scottish lad. She breathed in the delicate fragrance, recalling the first time he had brought her a bouquet of heather. She had been a young girl, too ill to attend a fair. Alec had been her hero. "You needn't pretend this marriage is anything more than it is, MacLaren."

155

He slipped his hand beneath her chin and tilted back her head. The warmth of his smile caressed her. The longing in his eyes whispered to a hidden part of her. "Did you have trouble sleeping last night, lass?"

She turned toward the window, afraid he might see too much in her eyes. "No. I always sleep well after I've been kidnapped and forced into marriage."

"I couldn't sleep. Not for a long while." He rested his shoulder against the window casement. From the corner of her eye she could see him watching her. "I kept thinking of you in here. I kept thinking it wasn't the way things should be between a man and his bride."

She squeezed the stems of heather. "I've never understood why it is termed a marriage of convenience, when it is anything but."

He brushed the backs of his fingers over her cheek, the gentle caress gliding over the pool of longing deep inside of her. "Meg, I hope in time . . ."

She pulled away from him, unwilling to listen to another lie. They were all so appealing, so very tempting. "I thought you had come here to escort me to breakfast."

He released his breath in a soft sigh. "As you wish, my lady."

He didn't say another word as they walked the miles and miles of corridors leading to the dining room. He simply walked beside her, so close she could feel the warmth of him radiate against her side. At breakfast, Meg sat at the foot of a long table in the cavernous dining room, thinking the twenty-foot length of polished mahogany was not nearly long enough. She nibbled her food and tried valiantly to control the headlong rush of her heart each time she looked at Alec.

Soon after breakfast, she set out to explore the rambling expanse of her prison, requiring some distance from her maddening Highlander, determined to gain control of her emotions. It was lust, she assured herself. Nothing more. She couldn't love Alec. Not again. She would never give her love to that Highland barbarian. *Never!* In time, she was certain she could quell this irritating attraction she had for the brute.

Meg threw a heavy oak door open at the end of the corridor and stepped into a long gallery. Sunlight streamed through the arched French doors running along one side of the room, illuminating smooth white plaster walls stripped bare of adornments. Two gold-and-crystal chandeliers hung from the ornate ceiling. Clusters of musical instruments and cherubs spread across the richly gilded plaster ceiling. Although the room was crafted for elegant entertaining, with a commanding view of the loch and the mountains, it was bare. She suspected no one had entertained here in a long time.

Meg stared at the door at the far end of the room, her heart thudding against her ribs. Although she couldn't be certain, since for the past few hours she had been rambling through corridors and rooms until her sense of direction was baffled, she believed the door at the end of the room led to the east wing of the castle. For a moment, she considered turning around and retracing her steps. Yet an unsettling curiosity drew her toward that door.

Her footsteps tapped against bare oak parquet as she crossed the room. Her image drifted like a ghost through the gilt-trimmed mirror above the white marble fireplace. She pulled her cashmere shawl close around her, fighting the chill in the room. Near the end of the room, the floor was warped, as if it had been exposed to heat or water, or both. The oak-paneled door looked new. She hesitated a moment, then gripped the brass handle and tugged. It was locked.

She should turn around and explore another part of the castle. Yet she couldn't dismiss the need to see what remained in the aftermath of the horrible fire that had taken the lives of Alec's parents and his older brother. She drifted toward the nearest French door.

The French doors opened to a stone terrace running along the side of the house on the cliff above the loch. A chilly breeze, sweet with the scent of meadow grass and heather, brushed her cheeks and rippled the skirt of her pale green muslin gown as she stepped onto the terrace. She paused beside the low stone wall rising at the edge of the terrace, drawing her shawl close around her, gazing out at the countryside.

The waters of Loch Laren lapped against the rocky shore a hundred feet below. Across the wide, rippling expanse of blue-green water, white birch trees arched graceful limbs along the shore, green meadows stretched toward the gently rising slopes of Ben Lyon, where heather painted the rugged gray-green mountain shades of purple. She had almost forgotten how beautiful this country was.

"Exploring?"

Meg jumped at the sound of Alec's deep voice. She turned, frowning as she watched him step onto the terrace with Seamus trailing close behind him. "Must you sneak up on me like that?"

Alec grinned. "I didn't realize I was sneaking up on you."

Meg was far too aware of the heavy thudding of her heart. The headlong race of that normally dependable organ had little to do with her surprise and everything to do with the man who had surprised her. Seamus trotted over to her, stepping on her toes in his enthusiasm to get close. Wallace had always been just as clumsy with his large feet. Her throat tightened with emotion when she thought of her poor, sweet dog. She

158

had cried for days when she had learned she must give him up forever. It was just another of the things her father's infidelity had taken from her.

"Have you come searching for me to make certain I haven't found a way to escape my prison?" Meg asked, stroking the dog's silky ears.

"Since you gave your word not to try to escape, why would there be a need to look for a way out?" Alec leaned against the stone wall near her, resting his forearm along the wide top, his fingers brushing her arm.

Meg smiled up into his handsome face, ignoring the shivers the slight touch had scattered across her skin. He was a man. Merely a man. Even if he was one of the most attractive she had ever met. She could defy his treacherous male charm, she assured herself. "You shouldn't grow too complacent, MacLaren. I haven't abandoned all hope of facilitating your downfall."

The breeze tousled his thick hair, reminding her of how silky those ebony strands had felt against her fingers. "Planning my demise?"

"Murder? Hmmm." Meg traced the rough perimeter of a square-cut stone set in the top of the wall, fixing a thoughtful expression on her face. "Although it's tempting, I shouldn't think I would need to go that far."

"That's comforting."

"I do hate public displays, and I'm afraid hanging for your murder would make an atrocious spectacle."

He smiled. "I applaud your reasoning."

She tilted her head, smiling, feeling rather smug. "I have another idea."

Alec lifted one black brow. "I'm almost afraid to ask what it might be."

"It's simple, really." She turned and drifted along the terrace, forcing him to follow her if he wished to hear her thoughts. Seamus dashed ahead, barking at an osprey that had landed on the wall at the far end of the terrace. The hawk spread its large brown wings and soared off the wall with a shrill cry.

"What do you have cooking in that beautiful head of yours?" Alec asked, joining her, walking so close the warmth of his body brushed against her side.

Meg tried to ignore the thrill tingling along her nerves. "In a short while, all of London will be aware of our marriage."

He frowned. "There is no reason to keep it quiet."

She cast him a chilly look. "I can think of several. But I'm of a practical nature. I realize there shall be no annulment. Since I would rather not plunge my mother into another scandal, I shall not try to divorce you. Which means you and Father shall make certain I remain locked in this dreadful union."

Alec smoothed the tousled waves back from his brow. "Your warmth toward our marriage leaves me humbled."

Meg smiled at his sarcasm. "Since I will not be able to obtain an annulment, there really isn't any reason to keep me here."

Alec gripped her upper arm, bringing her to a halt. "I can think of one or two reasons."

She stared up into his stunning blue eyes and tried not to notice the warmth of his hand radiating through her shawl, or the heat seeping into her blood. "Such as?"

"Companionship. Someone to share my days." He wiggled his black eyebrows. "And my nights."

His words conjured beguiling images in her mind. Heat slithered low in her belly, a tempting serpent of desire. She ignored it. "It's only a matter of time before you realize there shall never be anything between us except the barest of civilities," she said, keeping her voice cool and composed, while she simmered inside.

GET YOUR 4 FREE BOOKS NOW— A $21.96 Value!

Mail the Free Book Certificate Today!

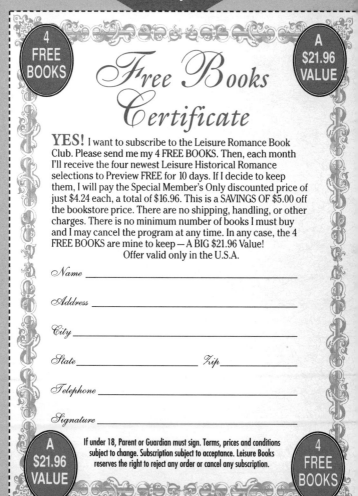

4 FREE BOOKS

A $21.96 VALUE

Free Books Certificate

YES! I want to subscribe to the Leisure Romance Book Club. Please send me my 4 FREE BOOKS. Then, each month I'll receive the four newest Leisure Historical Romance selections to Preview FREE for 10 days. If I decide to keep them, I will pay the Special Member's Only discounted price of just $4.24 each, a total of $16.96. This is a SAVINGS OF $5.00 off the bookstore price. There are no shipping, handling, or other charges. There is no minimum number of books I must buy and I may cancel the program at any time. In any case, the 4 FREE BOOKS are mine to keep—A BIG $21.96 Value!

Offer valid only in the U.S.A.

Name _____

Address _____

City _____

State _____ *Zip* _____

Telephone _____

Signature _____

If under 18, Parent or Guardian must sign. Terms, prices and conditions subject to change. Subscription subject to acceptance. Leisure Books reserves the right to reject any order or cancel any subscription.

A $21.96 VALUE

4 FREE BOOKS

Get Four Books Totally FREE — A $21.96 Value!

PLEASE RUSH
MY FOUR FREE
BOOKS TO ME
RIGHT AWAY!

Leisure Romance Book Club
P.O. Box 6613
Edison, NJ 08818-6613

AFFIX
STAMP
HERE

"When that happens, you shall realize it is pointless to keep me here against my will."

"What about children?"

"Ah, yes." She shrugged, trying to look indifferent, as though the thought of having Alec's children had not occurred to her at least ten thousand times. "Under the circumstances, I don't feel obligated to provide you heirs."

"And I suppose you have no desire for children."

She glanced down at the water, where sunlight skipped over the rippling waves, hiding her true feelings behind a smile. "Not for yours."

"Since I shall not be able to have any of the benefits of marriage with you, I might as well send you packing. Is that the plan?"

The breeze rippled her skirt, brushing the soft muslin against his legs. "Once you realize I shall not change my mind, you will soon grow tired of trying to make this marriage more than the travesty it is."

Alec brushed his fingers over her cheek, a smile curving his lips, an unnatural heat shimmering from his hand—the contrast between her cold cheek and his warm hand, she reasoned. "It'll take a lifetime to convince me to give up on you, Meg. We're married. And I take marriage seriously."

She pulled away from him, annoyed by the trembling deep inside of her. "You gave your word not to force me to be your wife in more than name only."

"True." Alec leaned against the low wall, smiling at her. "But I can try to convince you."

And he could be very convincing. When Alec looked at her, warmth shimmered through her. When he touched her, she trembled. When he kissed her, she melted into a besotted idiot. What was worse, a part of her wanted him to touch her, to kiss her, to do . . . more. The man was dangerous. She curled her hands into fists at her sides, fighting the treacherous weakness deep within her. "You shall fail."

His smile tipped into a devilish grin. "Are you so certain of that?"

"Yes." She pivoted on her heel, marching along the terrace, needing to put some distance between them. She was so caught up in her turmoil, it took several moments before she realized the change in her surroundings. A faint scent of ashes brought her to a halt. She turned, staring at the gray stones of the castle, which rose four stories above the terrace. This was the east wing. Flames and smoke had sketched a black stain above the arched windows on each floor. The glass was gone, leaving gaping holes, like the eyes of a skeleton.

She peered through the windows across from her, emotion squeezing her throat until she could scarcely draw a breath. Sunlight spilled through the skeletal remains of the roof and upper floors, tumbling into the blackened shell of what had once been a proud room. Timber and debris had been cleared. Nothing remained except charcoal streaks on stone walls, and the blackened squares of stones on the floor. It was a charred reminder of a tragedy.

Alec paused beside Meg, so close he could feel a whisper of her warmth against his side. The soft brush of heat drove home just how cold he felt, chilled from an emptiness inside of him, aching with a loneliness he hadn't recognized until the day an icy lady had plowed into his life.

Alec stared into the scarred remains of the crimson drawing room, resisting the need to hold the woman who shunned his every attempt to touch her. Last night Meg had haunted him, slipping into his dreams. Warm and willing, she had filled the evening with a beguiling range of fantasies that had vanished in the light of morning.

Aside from waking with an uncomfortable ache in his loins, he had discovered a night of restless slumber hadn't dulled the throbbing in his temples or eased the heaviness in his lungs. His muscles ached. His throat burned. He felt flushed one moment, cold the next.

Meg glanced up at him, mist filling her eyes. "How did it happen?"

"They think a candle was left burning in the chapel," he said, his voice barely rising above the whisper of the waves against the shore below.

"I'm sorry. They were fine people."

"Aye. They were."

She rested her hand against his arm, the gentle touch tugging on his heart. "Are you going to rebuild?"

"I don't know. A part of me wants to close it up and never look at it again." Alec closed his eyes, recalling the warmth he had always found here with his family: evenings spent sitting around the hearth, sharing conversation and laughter. Then he looked into blackened ruins. "And another part of me wants to put it all back the way it was."

Meg was quiet a moment, staring into the blackened shell of the once-elegant drawing room. "Your parents were not the type of people who would want a blackened shell as a memorial."

"No. They weren't. I have a feeling my parents would never want any part of their home to lie in ruins." Alec smiled into her lovely face. "Will you help me rebuild, Meg?"

She stepped back, her expression revealing a flicker of uncertainty. "I doubt I shall be here long enough to see this part of the castle rebuilt."

He wanted to rebuild more than stone and wood, and she knew it. "I almost forgot about your plan to make my life with you so miserable that I send you packing."

She pursed her lips. "I didn't say I would make your life miserable. I simply intend to show you how futile it is to hope I shall ever be a true wife to you."

He smiled. "You know, I think my parents had always hoped you would marry into the family."

"I suppose Patrick would have made a suitable husband," she said, drawing her shawl close around her.

He laughed. "Not for you."

Meg stared up at him, a picture of righteous indignation. "And what is that supposed to mean?"

"Patrick was a gentle soul. His passion was improving the land, finding better ways of using the soil, helping the crofters raise better crops." Alec smiled, remembering the man who had been his friend as well as his brother. "He wouldn't have dealt well with a stubborn lass who also had a bitter temper."

Meg's eyes narrowed. "I do not have a temper. And I am certainly not stubborn."

He rolled his eyes toward heaven. "And Scotland has had a peaceful history."

She lifted her chin. The breeze fluttered the tiny curls framing her face with shimmering gold. "I wouldn't expect you to see the difference between being obstinate and simply being determined."

"I can see you're determined to be obstinate," he said, smiling at her.

Her lips twitched, as if there was a smile there, trying to break free of her tight control. "You, sir, have more than a passing acquaintance with the characteristic of obstinacy."

"Aye. Which makes us well suited, I think."

She lifted her brows. "I don't share your opinion."

He nodded. "Which makes it necessary for me to alter your opinion. Since mine, of course, is the right one."

She smiled. "Spoken like a true barbarian."

"I suspect it will take a barbarian to turn a spoiled Englishwoman with—"

Meg gasped. "Spoiled Englishwoman!"

". . . with ice in her veins into a suitable wife." Alec shrugged as if resigning himself to the inevitable. "Although I'd prefer to be married to a fine Scottish lass with a bit of fire in her, I'm willing to try to make this marriage work."

She stared up at him, her lips parted, her eyes wide with fury. "Why you . . . you . . . Oh, you are the most odious . . ."

Alec grinned into her outraged face. "You see, already some fine Scottish fire is burning its way through all the English ice."

"Of all the . . . Ooooo!" Meg marched back toward the doors leading to the gallery.

Alec jogged to catch up with her, the swift movement setting the blood pounding in his temples. "I thought we might go riding this afternoon."

"You thought wrong," she said, without sparing him a glance. "I don't intend to spend any more time than necessary in your company."

"Afraid of me?" he asked, goading her.

She halted. "Don't be ridiculous."

"You're afraid if you spend time with me, I just might be able to make you want to stay. Admit it."

"Nonsense." She tilted her head at a regal angle. "I could spend from now until Judgment Day with you and not change my mind."

"Then you have no reason not to come for a ride with me." Alec opened the French door, ignoring the pounding in his temples. "I'll have the horses saddled while you change."

Meg stared up at him, and he could almost hear the debate raging in her beautiful head: Go and risk exposure to her enemy, stay and be branded a coward.

"What's it going to be, Meg? Are you going to hide from me like a frightened child, or face the challenge head-on?"

Meg patted his chest, smiling up at him, a hard glitter of determination in her eyes. "I'll be ready in twenty minutes."

Alec stepped aside as she swept past him, the scent of spicy vanilla flooding his senses. He held the brass door handle, steadying himself against a wave of dizziness as he watched her march away from him. Silently he cursed the illness. He had plans this afternoon. And he didn't intend to allow an annoying cold to get in the way.

It wasn't the first time he had gone to battle without feeling his best, he reminded himself. He chose not to dwell on the consequences of losing this war. Alec called for Seamus and closed the door after the dog trotted into the room. The setter quickly set off after Meg, his paws tapping against the oak floor.

Alec followed them, gritting his teeth against the pain in his head, matching Meg's quick strides as she left the room. Ogilvey met them in the corridor leading to the central block of the castle and informed them visitors were waiting in the blue drawing room for Alec and his lady.

The only thing that surprised Alec about the visit was the fact that his aunt had waited until this afternoon, instead of descending upon them last night after Niall had returned home with the news. Although Alec usually enjoyed seeing his Aunt Christina, this afternoon he wished her anywhere but here. He instructed Ogilvey to serve refreshments and inform his aunt and cousin they would join them directly.

"I'm not certain you remember her, but my Aunt Christina is my father's youngest sister," Alec said, once Ogilvey had left. "You probably remember Niall. He and Colin and I were inseparable as boys."

Although Meg cast him a chilly look, he glimpsed a flicker of anxiety in the green depths of her eyes. "I'm well acquainted with Mrs. Fergusson and her son. In case you weren't aware, they spend every Season in London. She is quite a notable hostess, as are her two daughters."

"Aunt Christina has always had a passion for town life. Unfortunately, with all that time in London, both her daughters ended up married to Englishmen," he said, trying to tease her out of her anxiety.

Her lips flattened. "A fate worse than death, in your eyes."

Alec gave her a devilish grin. "As luck would have it, both Mary and Frances managed to find Englishmen who were worthy of their fine Scottish fire. A rare occurrence."

"Indeed." Meg closed her eyes on a frustrated sigh. "Do they know about us?"

"Niall was here yesterday afternoon, while you were planning your escape."

The color drained from her cheeks. "Then I suppose you told him all about the circumstances surrounding our marriage. How very humiliating."

Alec slipped his fingers under her chin and tilted her head back, coaxing her to meet his gaze. He saw the ghost of old wounds lingering in Meg's eyes, and a stern determination to face her fate with as much dignity as she possessed. "As far as anyone need know, we married because it was what we both wanted."

Her eyes narrowed. "And so you expect me to go about pretending to be your devoted wife."

He grinned. "I would rather it be more than an act."

She scowled. "You really must pardon me if I don't swoon at your feet, MacLaren. I am, after all, an *icy* Englishwoman. We tend to be quite discriminating in our taste. Brutish louts have never appealed to me."

He grimaced. "That hurt."

One corner of her mouth twitched with a smile she managed to suppress. "I have no intention of allowing anyone to believe I'm enthralled with your primitive male charm."

"I see. You would rather have them think you're some poor woebegone creature, forced into a disagreeable marriage." Alec lifted his brows. "I suppose I understand why you want them to pity you."

Meg's lips parted on a startled gasp. "I realize I am not the first woman to find herself in a disagreeable *marriage de convenance*. And I can assure you I am quite capable of handling this situation without asking for *pity* from anyone."

Alec watched her march away from him, her head held high, her shoulders thrust back, proud and determined. He had learned a long time ago how to find an enemy's weakness and exploit it. Meg's pride was a weakness. Her pride wouldn't allow her to parade her discontent to the world. She would rather die than have anyone pity her. Alec followed, trying to ignore the pounding in his head, and the ever-increasing tightening in his chest. He didn't have the time or patience to be ill. He had a battle to fight. A war to win.

Chapter Thirteen

"Wicked man!" Christina MacLaren Fergusson rose from a sofa near the hearth in the blue drawing room. The curls framing her heart-shaped face were still as black as ebony, her figure as trim as that of a young lass in a gown of black sarcenet. Although she had received numerous offers of marriage in the past twelve years since her husband had died, she preferred to keep the company of many rather than relinquish her reins to one. "How dare you go running off and get married without even telling your favorite aunt?"

"I would have told you if I had planned the event. But you see, I had no choice in the matter." In the corner of his eye, Alec could see Meg tense beside him.

Christina glanced from Alec to Meg and back again, a serious expression chasing the humor from her violet eyes. "Alec, I'm certain you don't mean to say that."

"The truth is, I was forced to marry Meg." Alec ignored his aunt's shocked expression. He took Christina's slender hands and kissed her fingertips, allowing Meg to stew a moment in a broth seasoned with her own bitter determination to keep this a *mariage de convenance*.

"Alec, you surprise me," Christina said softly, obviously stunned by what she took as brutal honesty.

Alec turned his head and smiled into Meg's stricken expression. "I had to marry Meg, before someone snatched her away from me."

Meg's lips parted on a soft exhale. A quiver full of emotions flickered across her face, relief followed swiftly by a slap of realization of how he had teased her. Her eyes narrowed, her lips tipping into a smile that spoke of vengeance. "Indeed, one might say Alec kidnapped me."

Alec winked at his bride. Meg lifted her brows, her lips tipping into a smug little smile that told him she knew exactly what he was doing.

Christina looked from Alec to Meg, the anxiety draining from her lovely face. "I'm certainly glad to see you've managed to find someone so well suited for you, Alec."

"There is no other woman I would rather have as my bride," Alec said, intending only to strengthen the masquerade. Yet the words rang with an unexpected quality of truth within him.

"I'm surprised you could sweep Miss Drummond away so easily." Niall smiled at his cousin, mischief filling his dark gray eyes. He kissed Meg's hand. "You have succeeded where so many before you have failed."

"All it took was the right man to coax her to the altar. Meg couldn't resist my charm." Alec slipped his arm around his wife's slender waist. Although he felt her stiffen, Meg smiled at him, far too sweetly. The back of his neck prickled.

"Alec swept me off my feet," Meg said.

Alec flinched with a sudden pinch on the toes of his left foot from a dainty little shoe grinding down upon his black boot.

"Are you all right, Alec?" Christina asked, a frown crinkling her brow. "You're a bit flushed."

Alec tugged on Meg's waist, pulling her off of his toes in what appeared to be a lovers' embrace. "It happens when I'm near my bride."

Meg smiled up at him, her eyes glittering with fury. "Your regard can be so overwhelming, *dearest*."

"Are you certain you're feeling well, Alec?" Christina asked. "You really are in high color."

Alec smiled in spite of the throbbing in his temples. "It's all the excitement of finding myself a married man."

Christina smiled, a flicker of doubt remaining in her eyes. "I can imagine. My head is still whirling from the news. I never had an inkling of what you had planned."

Alec led Meg toward a chair near the hearth. "I've never been one for long engagements. The time was right to take a wife. And start a family. Fortunately, I found Meg."

Meg sank to the blue silk brocade seat, pointedly ignoring him. Alec sat on the arm of her chair and slipped his arm around her shoulders. Meg flashed him a pointed glance. He smiled, daring her to pull away and expose their little sham. As he expected, her pride wouldn't allow it. She remained steady beneath his light embrace, stiff and cold. He brushed his fingertips over the nape of her neck. She stiffened, yet he felt a tremor beneath the ice.

Alec watched his bride as she served tea to their guests, admiring the grace and ease of Meg's movements. Meg filled the role of hostess to perfection, maintaining light conversation, and displaying a surprising sense of humor. At times he had to remind himself it was all an act for the sake of her pride.

"I'm afraid Mrs. Carnwath shall be terribly disappointed to hear of your marriage." Christina smiled at Alec over the rim of her cup, a cat purring over a pot of cream. "I shall make a point of stopping by this afternoon to deliver the news personally."

Alec frowned, glancing at Niall. His cousin was staring down into his cup of tea as though the creamy liquid could whisper of destiny. "Why the devil should Mrs. Carnwath be disappointed over my marriage?"

"Mrs. Carnwath is a woman of high ambition." Christina sipped her tea. "She plans to marry her daughter Lillith to a title, and she had her sights set on yours. Not that she cares who wears the title. While Blandford was Earl of Dunleith, she was intent on ensnaring him. Although I suspect she much preferred to trap you for the lovely Miss Carnwath."

Meg stiffened beside him. Alec glanced down at his bride. Was the sudden tension he saw in her expression due to her own feelings toward his cousin? That possibility brushed against his neck like frost against a windowpane.

During the space of their visit, which lasted a little more than an hour, Alec took advantage of every opportunity to demonstrate husbandly affection for his bride. He knew he was teasing Meg unmercifully. Still, it was strange to discover how pleasant it was to assume the role of devoted husband to this woman. Unfortunately, the moment Christina and Niall left, the illusion of a happy home vanished.

"I suppose you found that amusing." Meg stood near the windows, with her hands firmly planted on her slim hips.

Alec rested his hand against the smooth white marble mantel. In spite of the heat radiating from the fire on the hearth, chills whispered across his skin, leaving

him damp and cold beneath his clothes. *Bloody hell.*
He wasn't about to succumb to a blasted cold now. "I
always enjoy visiting with my Aunt Christina and
Niall."

Meg folded her arms over her chest. "And do you
always enjoy taking advantage of a woman?"

Alec grinned at her. "My bonnie Meg, you can't
blame a man for showing some warmth for his bride."

She lifted her chin. "Such vulgar displays are not acceptable."

Alec drew in his breath, trying to clear his head. The
scent of burning peat stung his nostrils. He couldn't
seem to pull enough air into his lungs. A weight rested
on his chest, pressing down against his lungs. "Vulgar
displays?"

"You know exactly what I mean." Meg fidgeted, as
though she were uncomfortable in her skin. "You kept
. . . touching me."

"I like touching you," he said softly, surprised at how
much truth was in the words.

She rubbed her arms. "You like annoying me. I really
could not believe it when you kissed my temple in front
of everyone."

Alec knew women well enough to recognize the difference between revulsion and pleasure. The woman
was attracted to him. Even if she refused to admit it.
"You've been around too many married English couples. My father often kissed my mother, and he didn't
care who was around to see it."

"Your father and mother are not my concern. I must
insist you refrain from such base behavior."

Alec stepped away from the fireplace, relinquishing
the support of the mantel. He was appalled to find his
legs trembling with each step he took toward her. "I'm
surprised to discover how much I enjoyed playing the
role of devoted husband."

Meg huffed. "You will pardon me if I don't applaud your performance. I found it quite annoying."

"I really think, with some practice, we might both get accustomed to this business of being husband and wife."

She tilted her head and fixed him in an icy glare. "I don't plan ever to grow accustomed to this deplorable situation."

Blood pounded in his temples. His lungs felt heavy. He couldn't get enough air. "Pity. The role suits you."

"I'm afraid I disagree."

"I'll have to change your mind," he said, brushing the backs of his fingers over her smooth cheek.

"Your hand . . . you're very warm." Meg frowned as she studied him a moment. "Are you ill?"

Her voice seemed to come from a distance, as though she stood at the long end of a tunnel. The room darkened. His vision blurred.

"Alec, what is it?"

He tried to focus on her face. "Nothing. I'm . . . fine."

Meg gripped his arm. "And horses can fly."

"I've known a few horses who . . ." Darkness closed in around him. He swayed on wobbly legs.

"You should sit." She tugged on his arm.

Alec tried to follow her lead, but the room was spinning too wildly. He felt Meg's hand tense against his arm as his legs dissolved into water beneath him. Still, she couldn't keep him steady. He crumpled to the floor.

"Alec!" Meg knelt on the carpet beside him. She rested her hand against his cheek. "Good heavens, you're on fire."

Alec swallowed hard against the tight band closing around his throat. "Open the windows. Need . . . air."

"Why the devil didn't you say you were feeling ill?" she demanded, the soft touch of her hand sliding against his brow a sharp contrast to her scolding tone.

174

He closed his eyes against the pounding in his head. "I'll be fine. Just need . . . a little rest."

"You stay right here. Do you hear me? Don't you dare try to move. I'll get help."

Meg's voice echoed with the blood pounding in his ears. He couldn't let her leave him. He lifted his hand toward her, but she was already out of his reach. Through a blur he saw her running from the room, pale green muslin flaring around her legs.

"Meg," he whispered, struggling to stand. The effort drained the last dregs of his strength. With a moan, he fell back against the hard cushion of the carpet.

Something wet stroked his cheek. He opened his eyes to the sight of Seamus standing over him. "It's all right, boy. I'm . . ." His words dissolved as he tumbled into a blessed dark pool, far away from the pain.

Joanna smoothed her fingertip over a Chelsea figure that stood on the white marble mantel in the green drawing room of Penross House. Robert had bought the delicate piece of porcelain for her more than twenty years ago. It was a present for no particular reason except that the figure of a chestnut-haired lady standing on a windy hill had reminded Robert of his wife. Emotion gripped her throat, threatening to block her breath. Regret. Bitterness. Pain. She couldn't escape them here.

Nothing had changed. The room looked exactly as it had nine years ago, when she had entertained morning visitors here. It was as though she had stepped through the front door of Penross House and stepped back in time. Nothing had changed. Except her entire world had crumbled.

"The audacity of Drummond." Hermione sat on a Sheraton sofa near the hearth, flicking her fan under her chin. "How dare he keep us waiting here like this!"

175

Joanna forced air past her tight throat. "I doubt he is anxious to see us."

"And well he should dread seeing us. I intend to tell him exactly what . . ." Hermione hesitated as the door opened.

Robert Drummond crossed the threshold. He looked from Joanna to Hermione and back again, his features carved into an expression that revealed nothing. He might have been greeting his steward or the vicar or anyone of casual significance to him. Calm, composed, remote, he fixed Joanna in a cool gaze.

Joanna fought to keep her own expression composed, while her heart sprinted into a furious pace, and her legs shivered into a steady tremble. She had promised herself she would not be moved by the sight of this man. She had assured her poor heart it would be safe. She had pledged she would remain cool and unaffected by this man. Yet all the promises she had made to herself were crumbling inside of her. This tall, golden-haired Highlander still had the power to annihilate her senses as well as her sensibilities.

"Where is my granddaughter?" Hermione rose from the sofa. "I demand you take me to her immediately."

Robert lifted one golden brow. "I see the trip has not improved your disposition, Hermione."

Hermione narrowed her eyes. "I'll see you behind bars, Robert Drummond. I'll see you—"

"Mother. I would like to speak with Robert alone."

Hermione stared at her daughter as though Joanna had taken leave of her senses. "Alone? You want to speak to Drummond alone?"

"Yes."

"But I—" Hermione started.

"I think it would be best." Joanna crossed the room, meeting Robert's curious look with cool resolve. "As I recall, the library is just down the hall."

His lips tipped into a slight smile. "I'm surprised you remember."

Joanna remembered too many things, such as the way those finely molded lips had felt against her skin. For years she had tortured herself with doubts about her own worth as a woman. She was sick to death of it. Yet coming here had opened all the old wounds. What had she done to cause her husband to break his vows? Why had he turned to another woman? What was she lacking?

"Shall we?" Joanna asked, keeping her voice low and composed, completely washed of the turmoil churning inside of her.

Robert lifted his hand toward the door. "After you."

Her skirt brushed his legs as she passed him, the casual contact whispering along her skin. Joanna marched down the hall and stepped into the library, trying not to think of how everything had gone so terribly wrong. They had spent so many evenings here, in this room, with Meg and Colin. They had shared so much. Now it was all gone.

A pair of red setters trotted over to greet Robert as he entered the room. After greeting their master, the dogs turned their attention to the stranger in their midst, bounding over to her with their tails wagging. The dogs slipped beneath her anger, pricking her sentiments. It seemed a lifetime ago when she and Robert had brought home their first red setter from a trip to Ireland. Robert had chosen the dog because the color of his coat had reminded him of her hair. And now these dogs greeted her as a stranger in her own home.

Robert walked to a leather armchair near the hearth. His favorite chair. She frowned as she noticed he was limping, using a cane to support his weight. He sank to the chair without waiting for her to take a seat. The

177

dogs trotted to their master and flopped on the carpet on either side of his chair.

"You're injured," Joanna said, managing to keep the concern from her voice.

Robert rubbed the cane against his thigh. "A stray bullet from a poacher."

She suppressed the urge to question him about the extent of the injury. His welfare was no longer her concern, she reminded herself. She was here to rescue her daughter. "Where is Margaret?"

Robert lifted one golden brow. "Meg is at Dunleith Castle. With her husband."

The words struck her like a closed fist. A wave of white-hot anger washed over her. It was everything she could do to keep from throwing something at the brute. "How could you do this?"

Robert twisted the tip of his cane against the floor. "I only did what I thought was best for the girl."

"You had her kidnapped."

He shrugged. "She wouldn't come home on her own."

Joanna moved toward him. "You forced her to marry against her will."

"It's a good match."

She paused in front of him, glaring down at his handsome face. "Blast you, Robert Drummond. You weren't content with ruining my life; you have to ruin our daughter's as well."

"I couldn't sit back and watch her marry that fortune-hunting imbecile, Blandford. *That* would be ruining her life."

"You had no right to interfere in her life!"

His eyes narrowed to dark slits. "I'm her father."

"You haven't been a father to her in nine years."

"How the devil was I to be a father to her, when she treats me like a leper?"

"She has reasons."

"None of them justified."

"Aren't they?"

"No. They aren't."

Joanna turned away from him, appalled by the shaking in her limbs. She stared into the hearth, where flames licked black peat logs, burning hotter than any fire from English wood. "You aren't going to tell me you're innocent again, are you?"

Robert was quiet a moment. "No."

The single word pierced her defenses, inflicting a sharp stab of pain as it hit her heart. What had she expected? Had she really thought he would find some magical way to erase all the pain? Still, she realized there was a small part of her that wanted to believe in his innocence. Even after all these years.

"I realized a long time ago you didn't have enough faith in me to believe me."

Joanna cast him a sharp glance. "How dare you imply this was all my fault?"

Robert held her angry glare, his expression washed of emotion. Yet his dark eyes betrayed a lingering pain from wounds that had never healed. "I once believed our love was strong enough to endure any storm. I once believed you trusted me. I once believed you would stay with me for all our days. You showed me how wrong I could be."

Tears burned her eyes. A scream rose in her throat. She choked it, fighting to remain in control of her emotions. It was all so unfair. She hadn't destroyed their life together. She hadn't betrayed their love. "You expect me to believe you didn't invite her to the town house that night."

"Only a fool would invite a woman into his bed knowing his wife would arrive any minute."

"You weren't expecting me until morning."

179

Robert shook his head. "I never invited her into my bed, Jo."

"You cared for that woman. You paid her every attention. You visited her every day."

"She was the widow of a dear friend. Malcolm asked me to look after Drusilla with his dying breath. What was I to do? Turn my back on her?"

"You weren't supposed to carry your concern for her needs to the extent of servicing her in bed."

Robert looked straight into her eyes. "I didn't."

Joanna glanced away, unable to hold his steady gaze. "I saw you. If I hadn't, if someone had told me, I never would have believed it."

"I never realized how needy Drusilla was until that night. I never realized how far she would go to get what she wanted."

Joanna stared into the fire, fighting the doubts threatening to tear her to shreds. "You were the innocent victim, I suppose."

"If I had wanted Drusilla Buchanan, I would have taken her as my mistress after you left me. I certainly never would have gone off to join the bloody army."

The logic of his words trickled over her like icy rain, seeping into her blood, chilling her. She braced her hand against the smooth mantel. "I've often wondered why you did take a commission."

"After you left, there was nothing for me here. I had lost my wife, my daughter; all I had left was my son. I wanted to be with him." Robert was quiet a moment, and when he spoke his deep voice betrayed a dark sorrow. "I only wish I could have kept him safe."

Through a fine mist of tears, Joanna stared at the portrait hanging on a polished mahogany panel across from the hearth. A young man with light chestnut brown hair and dark eyes smiled at her from the confines of a gilt-trimmed frame. Colin. Pain as finely honed as a saber twisted in her heart, opening wounds that would never truly heal. A mother was not meant to outlive her children. Yet her little boy was gone.

She turned away from the portrait, fighting the tears that burned her eyes and threatened her dignity. After all of this time, all of the pain, she still caught herself wishing she could feel Robert's strong arms around her. He was the only one who could truly understand her pain. Yet he had taken away from her the comfort she had always found in his arms, the love that had always given her such strength. His treachery had stolen her friend, her lover, her husband.

"I didn't come here to open old wounds," she said, appalled by the tremor in her voice.

Robert released his breath on a long sigh. "No. You came here to take my daughter back to England, so she could marry that blackguard."

Joanna pivoted to face him. "I came here to rescue my daughter from a loveless match."

"*My* daughter doesn't need rescuing. She is married to a fine young man. The same young man she has adored since she was a wee lass."

Joanna waved aside his words. "A child's infatuation."

Robert shrugged. "Where there was once a spark, a flame can blossom."

"And what of Alec? You can't mean to tell me he is in love with Margaret."

Robert stared into the gold handle of his cane. "I think he cares for the girl. Eventually that feeling could grow."

"And if not, you have managed to trap Meg in a marriage with a man who has no true affection for her. What will prevent him from betraying her the first time he sees a woman who catches his fancy?"

Robert looked at her, his dark eyes filled with a granite hard certainty. "Alec is a fine man. Honest. Loyal. He won't be breaking his vows."

She had once believed the same of Robert Drummond. "I'm afraid I find your opinion less than comforting."

He lifted one golden brow. "What you think is really not important. They are married. And married they will stay."

Joanna planted her hands on her hips. "Robert Drummond, if you think for one moment I shall stand by and watch you destroy my daughter's life, you had better think again."

Robert studied her a moment, but before he could reply someone knocked on the door. At Robert's command, the butler entered.

Carlton glanced at Joanna, then fixed his gaze on the laird. "A footman from Dunleith Castle arrived a few moments ago with a message for you, sir. The earl is gravely ill."

Chapter Fourteen

Meg stood near the white marble hearth in Alec's sitting room, staring at the door leading to his bedchamber. Alec had looked so ill this afternoon, so terribly ill. Seamus sat beside Meg, leaning against her leg, as though he sensed her anxiety and sought to comfort her. Absently she smoothed her hand over his head, his fur warm and silky against her skin.

Perhaps it wasn't nearly as grave as it appeared, Meg assured herself. The surgeon was with Alec now. No doubt he would soon come to tell her everything would be fine. It was a cold, or some other trifling illness. Nothing serious. No reason to fear Alec might die. Oh, Lord, he couldn't die. *Please don't let him die!*

Robert paced the length of the room, limping from the windows to where Meg stood near the hearth. "For heaven's sake, Meg. You're married to the man for two days and he ends up in a sickbed. What the devil did you do to him?"

In spite of the guilt nibbling at her heart, Meg lifted her chin and met her father's accusing stare with defiance. She certainly had not asked Alec to chase after her in the storm yesterday. And she certainly had not asked him to give her his coat and hat. "I am hardly to blame for MacLaren's illness."

"How the devil did he take ill?" Robert demanded.

"I'm not altogether certain." Heat flickered in her cheeks under her father's intense glare. "I suppose he could have caught a chill when he came after me yesterday. In the storm."

"When he came after you yesterday." Robert frowned, his lips pulling into a tight line. "Do you mean to say you ran away from your husband?"

Meg clasped her hands at her waist. "Under the circumstances I believe it isn't so difficult to understand why I might not care to stay here."

Joanna moved to her daughter's side. "I can certainly understand Margaret's motives."

Robert nodded. "Aye. You would support the girl's cowardice."

Meg stepped back, feeling as though he had slapped her. "Cowardice?"

Robert nodded. "Aye."

Joanna glared at her husband. "And just exactly what is that to mean?"

"It means at the first sign of trouble you turn tail and run, like a frightened little rabbit." Robert leaned on his cane, staring down into Joanna's face. "And it seems your daughter has inherited that same streak of cowardice."

Joanna's lips parted, but not a single word escaped. She turned away from him. She marched to the windows, where she stood staring out at the craggy slopes of Ben Lyon. "You have no right to condemn me."

"You've managed to take away all my other rights as

a husband." Robert sank into a lyre-back armchair near the hearth. "I'm thinking I'll keep the right to my opinion."

Meg stood near the hearth, staring down at the garlands of gold and blue and ivory in the carpet. The fire in the hearth radiated against her side. Yet the warmth of the fire couldn't touch the cold places deep inside of her. She felt as though she were standing on the side of a road, staring at the broken remains of a carriage accident, where no one had survived.

There was a time when her parents had glowed with the warmth of affection. No two people could have been happier with one another. It seemed they had been destined to meet and love. There was a time when Meg had wished for a marriage just like the one her parents shared. She nearly laughed. It seemed a fairy with a twisted sense of humor had granted her wish.

Meg glanced up as the surgeon entered the room. Short and plump, with dark brown hair swept back from a high brow, Dr. James Addison surveyed the room with keen brown eyes, his gaze touching each of the three occupants in a cool, appraising way.

Meg drew in her breath, the acrid taste of burning peat streaking her tongue. "Is he all right?"

"How is he?" Robert asked, rising to his feet.

"Will he recover?" Joanna asked.

Dr. Addison plumped out his lower lip. "I believe it's a lung fever."

Meg's heart crept upward, until each beat throbbed at the base of her neck. "That sounds serious."

Dr. Addison nodded. "It can be."

"He is going to be all right," Robert said.

"I've had patients come out of it in a few days, and others . . . who didn't come out of it at all."

Meg stared at the doctor, unwilling to accept his

185

meaning. "Certainly a man as strong as the MacLaren will overcome this illness."

Dr. Addison smoothed his hand over his chin. "I have to be honest with you, Lady Dunleith. The earl was injured very badly in the war. He has only recently regained some measure of his strength, but he is by no means completely recovered. He might not be strong enough to pull through the illness."

The blood drained from her limbs. Meg gripped the back of the chair her father had abandoned to steady herself. "There must be something you can do."

"I've cupped him," Addison said. "And given him some medicine. I'm afraid there is little else to do, except try to make him as comfortable as possible while the illness runs its course. In a few days we'll know."

Meg squeezed the back of the chair, her fingers sliding against polished rosewood. Alec could die. The realization slammed into her with the force of a charging stallion.

"There is nothing more I can do. I'll be back this evening to see if there is any change." Addison left them alone with the grim news.

Meg didn't dare look at her father. She couldn't abide the accusation she was certain she would see in his eyes. Yet she couldn't avoid the guilt lurking inside of her.

Joanna touched her arm. She met Meg's tortured gaze with a gentle smile. "I'm going back to Penross House for your grandmother. I won't be gone long."

Meg nodded, her throat too tight to allow her words to pass.

"I'll be coming back as well, Meg," Robert said. "I'll be staying here until the lad is out of danger."

Joanna looked at her husband, her expression revealing her surprise. "You're going to stay here?"

Robert frowned. "Don't worry, Jo. It's a big house.

You won't have to put up with my company any more than is necessary."

Joanna lifted her chin, pinning Robert with an icy glare. Yet Meg knew the pain behind the haughty mask. She watched her parents leave, wondering if one of them might murder the other on the way back to what had once been their home together. It certainly didn't seem there was any way they might forgive the past. Even after all that had happened, Meg still caught herself wishing there was a way to end the war between her parents. She thought of her own marriage, and realized there was just as much hope of ever ending her own war. *If* Alec lived.

Tears burned her eyes. She resisted the urge to sink into the chair and dissolve into a fit of weeping. "Tears are a useless thing, Seamus," she said, patting the dog's head.

Meg walked toward Alec's bedchamber, summoning all of her will. Alec needed her. She was not about to dissolve into a simpering idiot. Not now, at any rate. She opened the door to Alec's bedchamber and paused on the threshold, stunned by the sight that greeted her.

Where was he? Alec's body burned, as though he were staked out naked in the sun. His arm throbbed. The devil's own blacksmith had set up shop in his head. Memories of a hospital in Brussels floated through the fog clouding his brain. Yet things didn't fit. Instead of the stench of stale blood and infection burning his nostrils, each breath delivered the clean fragrance of linen dried in the sun. The mattress beneath him was far too soft to be a hospital cot.

Alec pried open his throbbing eyes. Gold dragons flew through a burgundy sky above him. He closed his eyes, swallowed hard, then once again risked a peek.

He blinked, until his blurry eyes focused on a familiar canopy.

Alec turned his head, frowning at the closed windows. The room was stifling. He needed air. Yet there was a weight on his chest. He couldn't draw enough air into his lungs.

Memories crept into his mind, cutting like sunlight through the fog. He was home. For an instant the thought filled him with a sense of peace. And then he remembered—nothing was as he had left it. His parents were gone. His brother. And there was more . . . something else that he couldn't quite place . . .

Meg!

The thought of his wife ripped through him like a shot. Where was she? How long had he been lying here? He tossed back the covers and struggled into a sitting position. Meg was probably halfway back to London. He slid his legs over the edge of the bed.

The blood swirled before his eyes. Sweat broke out beneath the white linen nightshirt he wore. For a moment he sat clutching the edge of the mattress with eyes closed, while he fought his way through a wave of dizziness. He had to stop her. He had to bring her home. He wouldn't have his wife making a fool of him.

Gathering every ounce of his strength, Alec forced his legs to stand. The room wobbled. He swayed. He clutched a post at the foot of the bed, struggling for balance. He had to find Meg.

"What the devil are you doing?"

A feminine voice dragged his gaze toward the door. Through a haze Alec saw a woman marching toward him, with Seamus trotting along beside her. She stepped into the dying sunlight streaming through the windows. Golden light slipped into the luxurious curls spilling over her shoulder, igniting hidden fire. She paused beside him, staring up at him, her green eyes glinting displeasure.

"Meg," he whispered, managing a smile.

"You're insane." Meg grabbed his arm. "What maggot crawled into your head?"

Alec frowned, trying to decipher her anger with a brain that refused any attempt at dissembling.

"Get back into that bed." Meg tugged on his arm. "This instant."

Alec was only too happy to oblige. He released his hold on the bedpost and tried his best to stay on his feet. He stared down into her beautiful, frowning face, and tried not to notice the way the room was spinning slowly out of focus.

"Alec!" She slipped her arms around his waist. "Don't you dare faint. Do you hear me?"

He tried. He really did. But his legs weren't taking orders. He crumpled against her.

"Oh my . . ." She squeaked as his weight knocked her back against the bed.

He fell across the mattress, settling against the soft eiderdown beside her, his arms slung around her slender shoulders, his face pressed against her soft fragrant hair. Her breasts snuggled against his chest. Her long legs tangled with his. Her scent penetrated his senses. A swift heat flooded his blood, and this time it had nothing at all to do with his illness.

He forgot the pain in his arm, the throbbing in his temples, the heaviness in his lungs. He reveled in the feel of her pressed against his body, soft and yielding. He had never imagined a woman could move him this way, with a desire powerful enough to penetrate fever and pain.

"Alec," she whispered, her soft voice edged with anxiety. She pressed her cool hand against his hot cheek.

Alec opened his eyes and sank straight into the pure

green of spring. A man could get accustomed to awakening to this sight. Perhaps he already had.

"What were you thinking?" she demanded. "Getting out of bed in your condition, you must be addled."

"Had to find you," he said, his throat tight around the words.

Meg frowned, a line marring the smooth skin between her light brown brows. "Find me?"

"Can't let you leave." He slipped his hand into the soft curls at her nape and cradled her head with his palm. "You belong with me."

Her lips plumped into a beguiling pout. "I gave you my word, MacLaren. I told you I wasn't going to run away."

"Aye." Alec lowered his lips toward that tempting pout. Her startled sigh brushed damp heat against his lips. He slid his lips over hers, tasting lips as sweet and pure as spring rain. Her soft lips fluttered beneath his, parting, clinging to his. He tasted her need, the poignant nectar simmering through his veins. And then she was pulling away from him.

Meg stared at him, her wide eyes filled with confusion, her breath agitated puffs against his lips. "What the devil do you think you're doing?"

He smiled. "Kissing my bride."

She shook her head. "How can you think about trying to seduce me when you're burning up with fever?"

Alec smoothed his fingertip over the frown marring her forehead. "Aye, I have a fever. That's what you've done to me. You've set fire to my blood, lass."

"Oh." She clutched his nightshirt, her fingers curling against his back. "This is foolish. You must get back into bed. You must rest."

Alec held her when she tried to pull away from him. "I like the feel of you in my arms. Come to bed with me, Meg."

Meg closed her eyes, her lips moving on a silent oath. "You're incorrigible."

He kissed the tip of her nose. "You're bewitching."

She struggled out of his grasp and scrambled from the bed. She smoothed the front of her pale green muslin gown, as though she were trying to soothe the ruffled edges of her composure. "I would wager you would still be trying to seduce women if you were on your deathbed." Her hand stilled against her gown, her expression betraying a sudden consternation. "Not that you are on your deathbed, of course."

Alec rolled to his back, the effort sending a wave of blood rushing before his eyes. "There is only one woman in my life now. My beautiful, untouchable bride."

Meg planted her hands on her slender hips. "There is only one woman for *now*."

The woman had so little trust in him, so little trust in his sex as a whole. "One woman, for the rest of my life."

She shook her head, dismissing his words. "Save your strength, MacLaren. You're going to need it."

"To win my bride."

"To regain your health." She grabbed his ankles, slim, cool fingers curling around his hot skin.

He stifled a moan as she hoisted his legs back across the bed. Fires of the damned raged over his body. The blacksmith pounding in his head seemed intent on pulverizing what was left of his brain. And Meg was covering him with a blanket, of all things.

"Too hot," he muttered, trying to push aside the covers. "You'll roast me alive."

Meg tossed aside the blanket, but drew the sheet up to his chin. "You mustn't catch a chill."

Alec lay for a moment, trying to draw breath into lungs that felt like lead. Lord, he had an uneasy feeling he was a good deal more ill than he first thought. "Has the surgeon been here?"

"Dr. Addison left a few minutes before I came in and found you trying to savage your health even more than you have already managed."

Alec swallowed hard, pushing bitter bile back down his throat. He was tired, weary to the bone. "That explains the reason I feel as though someone has rammed a hot poker up my arm. The surgeon wielded his knife."

"He cupped you, if that is what you mean."

"I've seen too many men die after a surgeon has drained them dry. When next I see him, I'll be sure to tell Addison I won't have him going about cutting open my veins."

Meg smoothed the hair back from his forehead, her touch a cool brush against his hot skin. "I'm certain he knows what is best to treat a lung fever."

"Lung fever?" He blinked, trying to bring her features into focus.

Meg nodded. "He thinks you might have an infection of the lungs."

Bloody hell! Alec tried to moisten his lips, but all the moisture had simmered from his mouth. "I'm thirsty. Would you . . . mind . . . giving me a glass . . ."

Before he finished, Meg was already filling a glass full of water from a pitcher that had been placed on the bedside table. She slipped her arm around his shoulders, supporting him while she pressed the glass against his lips.

Water flooded his mouth and spilled down his chin. Alec swallowed in self-defense.

"Sorry," she said, righting the glass.

He smiled up at her contrite expression. "It's all right. The water feels nice and cool on my neck."

Meg tipped the glass up to his lips, this time taking

care not to drown him. Alec drank deeply, draining the glass dry.

"Do you want more?" she asked, easing him back against the pillows.

"No. Thank you." He managed a grin. "I suppose this means we'll have to postpone our ride? And I was going to have Cook prepare a nice picnic lunch for us."

"You really must take more care," Meg said, setting the glass on the table. She swiped her fingers across his wet chin, brushing away water. "You're far too ill even to imagine getting out of bed."

"If I didn't know better, I would say you're concerned about me. Is there someone watching? Is that why you're still acting the role of devoted bride?"

Her soft mouth tightened. "I don't want to see you die, MacLaren. Don't make my concern any more than what it is."

Her voice seemed to come from far away. Her image swam before his blurry eyes. "It's encouraging. Knowing my bride isn't anxious to become a widow."

She smoothed her hand over his hair. "That doesn't mean I'm anxious to be your wife."

"Beautiful Snow Queen. One day you'll be mine."

Her hand stilled against his hair. "I've never cared for being called that."

"It suits you. So beautiful. Cold. Untouchable." Darkness crept toward him. He gripped the sheet, fighting to retain his tenuous hold on consciousness.

Her slender fingers slid through his hair, her fingertips brushing his scalp. "You should rest."

"Will you ever warm for me, my bonnie Meg?"

She frowned. "Close your eyes, Alec. Rest a while. You mustn't waste your strength."

The gentle caress of her hand against his hair eased the tension in his body. "My bonnie lass, one day I'll melt the ice. One day . . ." His words dissolved as he succumbed to oblivion.

Chapter Fifteen

"Margaret, I think you should stay away from him."
Hermione stood near the door in Alec's bedchamber,
wringing her hands. "You'll catch something dreadful."

Meg set a bowl of ice and water on the table by Alec's
bed. "Dr. Addison said there was only a small chance
for contagion."

Hermione huffed. "And just who do you think shall
give you better advice? Some Scottish physician, or
me?"

"I believe it's too late to consider possible contami-
nation for me, Grandmama. But it certainly isn't too
late for you." Meg glanced to where her mother stood
near the windows, silently pleading for Joanna's assis-
tance. Her grandmother had been in high dudgeon
since arriving from Penross House before dinner.

"Mother, perhaps you should retire for the evening.
It's been a rather long day," Joanna said.

"How could I sleep when our little girl is tending to

194

this . . . this Scottish barbarian!" Hermione pressed her hand to her heart. "Margaret, how could you have gone through with this? Married! You've married a Scottish barbarian."

Meg sat on the edge of Alec's bed. Even though she wasn't touching him, she could feel the heat of him radiating against her. "I didn't have much choice in the matter."

"You could have refused," Hermione said.

Meg smoothed the waves back from Alec's forehead, damp strands of ebony curling around her fingers. He turned his head toward her, a moan escaping his lips, the soft sound tugging at her heart. "Father threatened to create a scandal if I didn't marry Alec. He intended to let it be known I had spent several days alone in the company of a young unmarried man."

"That blackguard! He would ruin his own daughter." Hermione pressed the back of her hand to her brow. "I do believe I shall faint from the strain."

"Mother, do stand a little closer to the chaise lounge by the fireplace," Joanna said, her voice soft and calm. "It will cushion your fall."

Hermione sent her daughter a dark look. Meg glanced away from her grandmother, wishing Hermione would seek some solitude in her room. Although she knew her grandmother meant well, Meg's nerves were stretched so tightly, she was afraid she might snap and say something regrettable.

Meg rested her hand on Alec's brow. Light from the wall sconce beside the bed fell golden upon Alec's face. An unhealthy color rode high on his cheeks. "The medicine doesn't seem to have helped at all. Alec is still burning up."

Joanna rested her hand on Meg's shoulder. "The doctor said it might take a few days. I'm certain it's only a matter of time before he will be up and about."

"Of course," Meg said, feeling far less than confident. "He will be fine."

"Perhaps the young barbarian shall die," Hermione said from her perch near the door, her voice filled with righteous scorn.

Meg glanced at her grandmother. "You almost sound as though you wish he would."

Hermione shrugged, her plump shoulders lifting beneath black bombazine. "Of course I don't mean it literally. Although it would serve him right."

"Mother, really," Joanna said. "No matter what has happened, we certainly hope Alec gets well. Soon."

Hermione frowned, her expression growing indignant. "Yes. Of course we do."

Meg dipped a cloth in the bowl of ice water. Alec had to get well, she thought, wringing out the excess water. She couldn't imagine a world without Alec MacLaren. He had been a part of her existence from the time she first took a breath. He had filled her days with wistful imagining, her nights with romantic dreams. She smoothed the cloth over his brow.

"It's late. You've been tending him for hours," Joanna said. "Why don't you go to bed? I'll sit with Alec."

Meg watched the slow rise of Alec's chest. His breathing was labored, each inhale a fight for air, each exhalation wheezing past his lips, his entire chest contracting with the effort. "I want to stay with him."

Joanna squeezed her shoulder. "All right. I'll see you in the morning. Come along, Mother."

"You can't mean to leave the child alone with that monster?" Hermione said.

Joanna took her mother's arm and ushered her toward the door. "Margaret is hardly a child."

"All the more reason to stay and protect her," Hermione said.

Joanna ushered her mother into the hall. "Alec is hardly in any condition to do her harm."

"Well, I must say—" Hermione's words were clipped by the closing of the door.

Meg turned back to Alec after her mother and grandmother left the room. After dampening the cloth in the cold water, she slipped the cool white cotton down his neck, parting the folds of his sweat-dampened nightshirt, hoping in some small way to ease his suffering. Soft white linen spilled open across his chest. Beneath the hollow of his neck, damp black curls glistened in the candlelight.

She stared at him, unable to look away, while something tightened inside of her. She traced the curve of his lower lip with her fingertip, memories of his kisses creeping back to taunt her. As ill as he was, he had left his bed to find her. He had held her, kissed her, teased her. Of course, she could place no greater importance on his actions than the proprietary notions of a male who believed he must take possession of the female in his midst. She was his wife; therefore he would conquer her. There was no affection between them, she reminded herself. Their marriage was built on far less romantic soil.

Meg pressed the damp cloth against his neck, trying not to imagine touching him under different circumstances. It wouldn't do to become hopelessly entangled with this man. Still, it was impossible not to wonder about the more intimate aspects of marriage. Especially when her husband was as handsome and infuriatingly masculine as Alec MacLaren. Especially when that man had always been her hero.

"I remember the time you came to see me when I was ill with a cold. I was thirteen, and so upset about missing the fair at Dunleith." She smoothed her fingertips over one of his thick black eyebrows. "You brought me a bouquet of heather, just as you did this morning. I suppose you would find it amusing to know that I still have a sprig of that old heather. Pressed between the pages of a volume of Shakespeare's sonnets."

Alec turned his head on the pillow. Meg clenched her jaw at the labored sound of his breath. "You might be a terrible brute for marrying me the way you did, but I didn't want this to happen, Alec. I would never want to see you hurt. Never."

He shifted restlessly, a moan rising from low in his chest. His hands tugged at the sheet at his sides. Thick black lashes fluttered against his flushed cheeks.

"Can you hear me, Alec?"

His only response was a low shudder of breath. Meg slid her fingers down his neck and ventured into the soft hair shading his chest. A single white scar peeked from beneath a fold of his nightshirt, a hint of the damage wreaked upon this man. She traced the raised flesh of the scar with her fingertip, and in her mind rose images of this man standing shirtless in the sunlight, the legacy of war carved boldly across his body. The wounds were scarcely healed. Was he strong enough to pull through this illness?

She cupped his hot cheeks in her hands. "Alec, you have to get well. Do you understand?"

He dragged air past his parched lips. Being near him was like standing too close to a fire. The heat of his fevered skin soaked through her gown, searing her skin. "Think of how terrible it would be if you died. Why, all of Dunleith would fall into my hands."

She pressed her lips to his fevered brow, her throat tightening with fear. "You have to fight, Alec MacLaren. You have to gather all your strength and fight this horrible fever. Do you understand me? You have to get well. I couldn't bear it if anything happened to you."

"He's a strong man, milady."

Meg jumped at the sound of Iona's voice. She glanced over her shoulder to find the small house-keeper standing near the door. Iona moved toward her, a smile curving her thin lips.

Meg stiffened, appalled to realize this woman had witnessed her pathetic confession. "Did you want something, Iona?"

Iona paused beside the bed. "I brought the stone, milady."

Meg frowned as Iona held out a smooth ball of crystal suspended in a gold filigree holder. "The stone?"

"Aye. The *Clach Bhuaidh.*"

Meg remembered enough of her Gaelic to translate the words: *Clach Bhuaidh*, the Stone of Virtue. As a child she had heard the stories of the magic stone of clan MacLaren. At the time she believed in magic, as she believed in all the other Celtic nonsense: the legends of Fionn, fairies with their stone rings and ancient mounds, and magical crystals with healing powers. Yet she had left all that foolishness behind a long time ago.

"The laird MacLaren or his lady must stir the stone through water, three times sun-wise." Iona placed the stone near the pitcher on the table by the bed. "He'll be better soon after he drinks from the water."

"I appreciate your concern, Iona, but I'm afraid I don't place much store in magical stones."

Iona pursed her lips, a familiar look of displeasure replacing the warmth that had filled her gray eyes a few moments ago. "The stone was found on the eve of Bannockburn, when the laird MacLaren was on the road to join Robert the Bruce. When his men stopped for the night they hoisted the MacLaren standard. The next morning, when it was drawn from the ground it bore the *Clach Bhuaidh*. Since then, the stone has brought healing powers to the laird or his lady."

Meg shook her head. "Superstition. It has no place in a modern society."

Iona lifted the stone from the gold holder and held it out for Meg to take. "If the stone grows dim or damp, it is a sign the laird is close to death."

Meg's chest tightened at the unsettling thought. She allowed Iona to place the stone in her palm. A curious tingle rippled along her arm, a remnant of childish beliefs, she assured herself. It fit snugly in her cupped hand, cool and smooth, clear crystal except for a silvery shading within the stone. She tested the weight of it in her hand, appreciating the stone for the relic it was. She studied the ancient talisman a moment, fascinated by the way the silver shading resembled the head of a wolf.

"It's clear and dry, Iona." Meg glanced up at the small woman. "Which, according to legend, is a good sign."

Iona stared down at Meg, a plea in her gray eyes. "Use the stone, milady. You're the only one who can help him. Have faith in the healing power."

Meg carefully placed the stone back in the filigree holder on the table. "I'm sorry. I don't believe in superstitions. I believe in medicine and science."

Iona released her breath in a long sigh. "I pray you see the light, milady. Before it's too late."

Meg watched Iona leave, an uneasy sensation of anxiety coiling in her stomach. Seamus left his place beside the hearth, trotting over to Meg. He sat beside the bed and rested his chin on her knee.

She stroked the dog's sleek head and tried to dismiss the uneasiness inside of her. "It's all nonsense."

Seamus lifted his head, regarding her with solemn brown eyes.

"Well, it is. Magical stones," she whispered, turning back to Alec. She smoothed her hand over his damp hair. "It's nothing more than Highland nonsense. No respectable Englishwoman would resort to anything so pagan."

Robert paused beside Meg's chair. Morning sunlight flowed through the square panes of the windows in Alec's bedchamber, touching his daughter's lovely face. She showed no sign of heeding the sun's gentle prodding. Exhaustion had claimed her. Even in sleep her face revealed the strain of the past two days. Dark smudges marred the skin below her eyes. Her skin was pale.

For the past two days Meg had maintained a constant vigil over her husband. Day and night Robert had found her here, bathing Alec's brow with cold water, spooning broth into his mouth when he roused enough to swallow, feeding him medicine. Still, all her efforts seemed in vain. Alec was not improving.

Robert lifted the blanket that had tumbled around the base of her chair. He drew the soft ivory wool over her lap, then hesitated a moment, looking at her sleeping face, remembering all the times he had tucked her into bed when she was a wee lass. Carefully, he pressed his lips to her brow, his throat tightening with regret. If she were awake she wouldn't allow him even this simple gesture of affection.

Seamus lay beside Meg's chair, regarding Robert expectantly. The dog thumped his tail on the floor when Robert bent to stroke his smooth head. Robert knew how much leaving Wallace behind had hurt his daughter. He hoped in some way Seamus could make up for that loss. And he hoped for a great deal more. Although Meg wouldn't believe it, Robert hoped for his daughter's happiness. He truly believed she could find it with Alec.

Robert turned from the sleeping girl, to the man who lay in the bed beside her. Sunlight flowed over Alec, revealing the pallor of his skin, the unnatural color high on his cheeks. Through the night his restless slumber had tangled the bedclothes around his legs. Robert eased the sheet from around his thighs and smoothed the covers over Alec's chest. Alec didn't respond to Robert's ministrations. He lay with his face turned toward Meg, his eyes closed, his lips parted, his chest rising and falling with each hard-won breath.

"I'm sorry, lad. I never should have involved you in my problems. I should have known better. You weren't even healed, and here I was, sending you back out to do battle." Robert smoothed the damp black waves back from Alec's heated brow. "I just couldn't imagine entrusting my daughter to any other man. I knew you'd be good to her. I knew you'd care for her. Protect her. You would keep her safe."

Robert closed his eyes, silently praying for help from above. He drew in his breath, easing the tension in his chest. "You must get well, lad. I've seen you come through when everyone had given you up for dead. You fight this, Alec MacLaren. You come back to us."

When he turned from the bed, Robert found Joanna standing just inside the door. She was watching him, her expression unguarded for a moment, revealing her own concern, a glimmer of her pain. Deep inside a familiar need clenched his vitals. Through the years, through all the bitterness, the woman still had the power to set a torch to his blood.

Joanna stepped into the hall. He followed her, hating the awkwardness of it all. He watched the soft black muslin of her gown swirl around her ankles with each step she took. No matter how hard he tried, he couldn't keep from imagining the long, shapely legs hidden beneath that gown. Although it was more than foolish to recall the way those long legs had slid around his hips, he couldn't prevent the memories, or the heat they brought to his blood.

Blood pounded like a clenched fist low in his loins. He knew every inch of her body. The taste of her. The scent of her. There were times when the need for her sank so deeply into his bones, he felt he might go mad for the want of her.

Damnation! The woman was his wife. He had every right to grab her and kiss her and do any of the more intimate things they had so often enjoyed. Except, of course, she had turned her back on their vows. Distrust had destroyed any chance they might have had at forever. The woman who had told him she would give him her love for all time, had failed to give him her trust. He might desire her. That he couldn't deny. Yet he would hang by his thumbs over the fires of Hades before he let the sanctimonious little she-devil know how much he still loved her.

Joanna paused a few feet away from Alec's bedchamber. "He is going to die, isn't he?"

Robert shook his head, refusing to surrender his hope. "He's a strong lad. He won't allow a fever to get the best of him."

"He is so ill." Joanna leaned against the oak-paneled wall. She looked tired. And so very melancholy. For all the world, Robert wished he could take her in his arms and hold her.

"I've seen Alec in worse condition," Robert said. "And he pulled through."

Joanna rubbed the back of her neck, thick chestnut curls brushing her arm. "Meg loves him. I can see it each time she looks at him."

"Aye. She loves the lad. She always has."

"How could you do this?" Joanna asked, her voice a harsh whisper. "How could you put her in this position?"

If he lived to be a hundred, he would never understand women. "I've arranged for Meg to marry the man she loves. Why is that so wrong?"

"Alec isn't in love with her. How do you think she must feel? Living with a man she cares deeply about, knowing he married her out of an obligation to you."

Robert frowned. "He cares for her. Love will come in time."

"And if it doesn't?"

"Alec will make her a good husband, Jo."

Joanna drew away from the wall. She stared at him, her back as straight and stiff as a lamppost. "I won't allow her to be hurt. When Alec recovers, I'm going to take my daughter away from here."

Robert clenched his jaw. "Run away. That's your answer to everything. Isn't it?"

She stepped toward him. "I had reasons to leave."

"I thought you had reasons to stay."

Joanna paused, so close her skirts brushed his legs. "You took away those reasons."

"No. I didn't." The sweet scent of lavender rose with the heat of her skin, teasing his senses, taunting his memory. So many times he had watched her smooth the sweet lavender water over her pale skin, anointing the delicate skin beneath her ears, the soft territory behind her knees. So many times he had pressed his lips against that silky skin, and breathed the scent of woman and lavender deep into his blood. The memories stirred him. "Unfortunately, you didn't have the courage to fight the woman intent on taking your man away from you. You ran away like a frightened child."

Her eyes flashed emerald fire. "Why would I stay and fight for a man who would betray me?"

"I never betrayed you," he said, keeping his voice soft when he wanted to shout his innocence.

Joanna lifted one finely arched brow. "Do you mean

to tell me you haven't been with another woman since I left?"

Lord help him, he wanted to drag her up against him and kiss that sweet, taunting mouth. And it was only a small part of what he wanted from this woman. Robert gripped the handle of his cane. He wouldn't allow this woman to control him. Never again. "You gave up the right to ask me that question when you turned your back on our vows."

"Go to blazes! I am not the one who caused all the trouble between us."

"No, lass. You aren't. But did you ever consider, if you had stayed instead of running away, we might have found a way to mend the breach?"

Joanna stepped back, her expression betraying her doubts. She held his gaze for a long moment before she spoke, her voice barely rising above a whisper. "I thought you loved me."

"I thought you trusted me."

"I did."

He released his breath in a long sigh. "Not enough."

She shook her head, as though she were dismissing some internal argument. "This isn't about us."

"No. Our time has past."

She glanced up at him, her eyes betraying the pain he had shared all these years. "Yes, it has."

Something painful twisted inside of him at the finality in her voice. Through all the years, he still found it hard to face the truth, to acknowledge that his marriage was dead and buried. He had loved this woman since the first time he had glimpsed her at a ball in London when he was still a lad. For over thirty years he had loved her. And he still couldn't find the way to let go of that love, or the pain.

"I won't have my daughter humiliated," Joanna said. "You have to give Meg a chance, Jo. You have to let her stay and work through the difficulties. It's the only way she'll ever have a chance at a real marriage."

"A real marriage. Out of this travesty?" Joanna glared at him. "A real marriage with a man who didn't even want to marry her?"

"She's a beautiful, intelligent woman. If Meg put her mind to it, she could have Alec in the palm of her hand."

Joanna frowned. "You expect her to risk a great deal."

"What does she risk if she runs away? Do you really want her to spend the rest of her life alone? Or do you want her to take lovers, break her marriage vows?"

"Of course not."

"Then what choice does she have, if not to stay and make this marriage into something real? It might be her only chance at finding happiness."

"This is impossible." Joanna turned away from him. She marched a few feet down the hall before pausing beneath the portrait of a long-dead MacLaren laird. She stood with her back rigid, her hands curled into fists at her sides. After a few moments she turned to face him with her chin tilted at a defiant angle. "All right. I won't try to take Meg back to England with me. Not yet. But I intend to stay here and keep an eye on things until I'm certain there is a chance they can make this marriage acceptable."

He held her angry glare. "You won't be regretting this, Jo."

She rolled her eyes toward heaven. "I'll believe that when I see it, Robert Drummond."

Chapter Sixteen

An angel had come for him. Through the blaze of hell-fire raging over his body, the fever that dulled his vision, Alec could see her. She stood by the windows near his bed, a beautiful angel suspended in a column of sunlight. A soft white gown draped her slender figure. A golden nimbus shimmered around her head, thick golden waves tumbling to her waist.

A beautiful angel, here to take him to his family. His parents, his brother, were waiting for him. Yet he wasn't ready to leave. There were so many things left to do. Someone who . . . needed him.

Alec searched through his throbbing head, seeking answers to the bits of memory floating through his mind like froth on a roiling sea. "Too soon," he whispered. "I can't go with you. Not now. Please, not now."

The angel turned at his soft plea. She floated toward him, her long hair swirling around her shoulders.

"Alec," she whispered, pressing a cool hand to his brow.

He stared up into her face, recognizing the features he had glimpsed in a dream. "Meg?"

"Yes, Alec." She smoothed her hand over his brow. "It's Meg."

"My own bonnie Meg." He lifted his hand, wanting to touch her face. But he hadn't the strength. His hand fell back to the bed before he could reach her. "I thought you were an angel, come to take me."

Meg slipped her hand around his. "There will be no angels for you, Alec MacLaren. You're going to get well."

Alec smiled as she lifted his hand to her soft cheek. "I'm thinking you'll have your freedom . . . soon. No more wicked Highland barbarian to . . . plague you."

Meg's jaw tightened beneath his hand. "Is that any way for a Highland warrior to talk? There's a battle to be fought, Alec MacLaren. You can't give up now."

"Ah, lass." He brushed his fingertips against her cheek. "I'm so tired of fighting. So tired. All I want . . . some peace."

"You have to get well, Alec." Her eyes glittered with sparkling stars. Something cool and moist fell against his cheek. "It's going to take a fight. It's going to take every ounce of your will. But you have to get well."

Lord, he didn't want to leave her. Meg needed him, even if she didn't know it. She needed a home and family. And he wanted a home with Meg. He wanted to see his children. *Home. Family.* He wanted these things more than anything in the world. Yet he wondered if these things were ever meant to be. He was so tired, he didn't have the strength to keep his eyes open. "Kiss me, lass. Kiss me just once more."

Meg squeezed his hand, as though she were trying

to drag him back from the brink of hell. "Alec, you have to fight!"

"So tired." His eyes slid closed, his strength slipping away from him. He felt the soft brush of her lips against his. So cool. Like the touch of spring rain against his parched lips.

"Fight Alec. Fight to get well."

"Meg," he whispered, before the darkness claimed him.

"Alec!" Meg smoothed her hand over his hair. "Don't you dare give up this fight. Do you hear me!"

His only reply was a soft exhalation of air that touched her face with a moist heat.

"Alec?" For one horrible moment she thought he had breathed his last. Then she heard a thready inhalation. She pressed her hand against his chest above his heart. Only when she felt the steady beat of life beneath her palm did she breathe again.

Meg sat back on the bed beside him and scrubbed the tears from her cheeks with her handkerchief. Tears would accomplish nothing. Still, she had never in her life felt more helpless. There must be something she could do. Anything to help Alec.

Sparks of light glinted against her face. She looked toward the table by the bedside, her gaze fixing on the crystal mounted on a gold holder. Sunlight played in the round stone, sparking glints of color that drew her. Without conscious thought she lifted the *Clach Bhuaidh* from the holder.

Was it her imagination, or had the stone grown dim? Meg turned the small sphere in the late-afternoon sunlight, staring at the silvery shading held within the crystal. The image of the wolf was just as clear as yesterday, she assured herself. Wasn't it? Or was it just a little cloudy?

If the stone grows dim or damp, it is a sign the laird is close to death.

Superstitious nonsense. Meg smoothed her thumb over the crystal, assuring herself it was dry. No one could be healed by simple faith. Could they?

Meg's gaze turned from the stone to the man lying on the bed beside her. Thick black lashes rested on his cheeks, veiling the pure beauty of his eyes. She rested her hand against his cheek. Even though his valet had bathed and shaved Alec this morning, his beard was already shadowing his cheeks, teasing her palm with the masculine bristle. For several moments, she listened to the labored sound of his breath flowing in and out of his lungs. Two days, and the medicine hadn't helped. Alec was still feverish. And she had the dreadful feeling he was growing weaker.

Meg smoothed her fingers over his cheek, wondering if she would ever feel free enough to touch him this way when he recovered. *If* he recovered, she thought, her throat tightening with emotion. Dear Lord, he had to recover.

"Is he improved at all?" Joanna asked, as she entered the room.

Meg shook her head. "I'm afraid he hasn't."

Joanna paused near the foot of the bed, taking a moment to rub Seamus's ears before moving to Meg's side. She stared down at Alec as she spoke. "I suppose all he needs is time to heal."

Meg glanced up at her mother. "You do think he is going to get well, don't you?"

The spicy scent of lavender settled around her as Joanna rested her hand on Meg's shoulder. "We can only hope and pray for his recovery, my darling."

Meg squeezed the crystal in her palm, Iona's words echoing in her mind. *You're the only one who can help him. Have faith in the healing power.*

"This came for Alec this afternoon," Joanna said, handing Meg a letter.

Meg smoothed her thumb over the expensive ivory parchment, frowning at the writing. The elegant, flowing script looked decidedly feminine. And she doubted any male would anoint a letter with the sweet floral scent she detected wafting from the missive. Heat crept into her cheeks while an emotion much too akin to jealousy sank claws into her heart. She turned the letter over, stared at the tulip emblazoned in the middle of the burgundy red seal, and wondered about the woman who had sent it. Who was she? More important, what was she to Alec? A friend? A relative? A lover?

"What is that you have?" Joanna asked.

Distracted by the brutal emotions assaulting her from gazing at a simple letter, Meg stared at her mother. "What?"

Joanna frowned. "The crystal you're holding."

"Oh. It's the *Clach Bhuaidh*." Meg offered Joanna the crystal. "The Stone of Virtue."

"I've seen this before." Joanna lifted the crystal from her daughter's palm. She held it up to the sunlight, studying it a moment before she continued. "Isobel showed it to me once. She said there were people who still made application to use it."

"Iona places great store in its healing prowess." Meg set the letter on the bedside table. She clasped her hands tightly in her lap, setting aside her thoughts about the woman who had sent her husband a letter. It didn't matter who the female might be, she assured herself. The important thing right now was to get Alec well again.

"Magic," Joanna whispered. "They say this is an ancient talisman given by the fairy folk."

"It's all nonsense, of course." It was foolish even to

211

imagine a piece of stone could heal a fever, Meg thought. Wasn't it?

Joanna turned the stone in the sunlight, scattering the sparks of colored light that splintered from the crystal. "The Highlands are filled with Celtic superstition."

"Yes." Still, Meg couldn't dismiss her doubts. There was a great deal in heaven and earth that no one could truly explain or even try to understand.

"A great many ancient beliefs are carried on to this day." Joanna handed Meg the stone. "There are those who still hold Beltane ceremonies on the first of May. Many who still believe Fionn and his soldiers are living in a cave on Skye. Silly really," she said, a flicker of doubt coloring her voice.

Meg glanced at Alec's pale face. "I suppose it comes from a lack of education."

"I suppose it does," Joanna said slowly.

Meg turned the crystal in her hand, watching sunlight ripple though the silver shading deep inside, while she wrestled with her own nagging superstitions.

"Although, as I recall, Isobel had mentioned that a herd of cattle had been healed by using that stone," Joanna said. "Eighteen years ago, actually. Not so very long ago."

Meg glanced up at her mother, seeing the uncertainty in Joanna's eyes. "A herd of cattle?"

"Yes." Joanna gave Meg a sheepish smile. "I suppose it was merely coincidence."

Meg rubbed her fingers over the smooth stone, her heart thudding against the wall of her chest. "I suppose."

Joanna shifted on her feet, her gaze fixed on the crystal. "What exactly did Iona tell you should be done with that stone?"

"She said I should stir it three times in water, in a

sun-wise direction. Then Alec should drink of the water."

"I see." Joanna glanced at the pitcher on the table by the bed. "It's a rather simple request, isn't it?"

Meg rose from the bed. "Do you suppose . . ."

"I do." Joanna lifted the pitcher. "I'm afraid I lived long enough in the Highlands to conclude there is more to this world than what we can see."

"If anyone ever found out about this . . ."

"We would be labeled superstitious fools. Ridiculed behind our backs." Joanna looked at her daughter, a question in her eyes. "Still, if there is a chance it might help him . . ."

"Then we should." Meg hesitated a moment before she slipped the crystal into the water. She held her breath, clenching the crystal, while she stirred her hand three times through the water.

"Joanna! Margaret! Look who has arrived," Hermione said, sweeping into the room.

Meg jumped at the sound of her grandmother's voice. She glanced toward the door, her hand still inside the pitcher. Hermione stood a few feet into the room, beside Wildon Fethersham. Since Alec had taken ill, this was as far as Hermione would venture into the room.

"Wonderful," Joanna muttered under her breath.

"What are you doing here?" Meg gasped, unable to keep the panic from her voice.

"I wrote a note to dear Lord Blandford before we left London, telling him we would be visiting your father for a few days. He decided it would be an excellent opportunity to visit his cousin." Hermione tilted her head. "Why do you have your hand in a pitcher?"

Meg snatched her hand from the pitcher, flicking water into her mother's face. "Terribly sorry."

"It's nothing, dear." Joanna lifted her brows, and

lowered her gaze with purpose to the crystal. "Nothing at all."

Meg closed her hand around the crystal. The last thing she needed was for anyone, especially her grandmother and Blandford, to know she had been performing a Celtic healing ceremony. They would think she was ready for Bedlam.

Seamus trotted over to greet the new arrivals, wagging his long tail. Hermione crinkled her nose and flicked her hand at the dog. "Go away."

Seamus sniffed at Blandford, garnering a raised eyebrow from the viscount. Meg caught herself wishing the animal would growl, bare his teeth, send both her grandmother and Blandford running from the room. Instead, the dog turned and sauntered to his favorite place by the fireplace, as though he found nothing interesting in the new arrivals.

"Margaret, why did you have that stone in the pitcher?" Hermione asked.

Meg shoved her hand into the folds of her skirt. "Stone?"

Hermione frowned. "Yes. That stone you're holding."

"Oh, I, was . . ." Meg glanced at her mother, seeking support. "I was . . ."

Joanna's eyes widened. "She was, ah . . ."

"Cleaning it." Meg forced her lips into a smile.

Hermione blinked. "You were cleaning a stone in the water pitcher?"

"Yes. I only just realized it was dusty." Meg set the stone back in the gold filigree holder on the bedside table. "There, now it sparkles the way it ought."

Hermione stared at her a moment before turning her bewildered gaze on Wildon. "Margaret has been under a strain lately."

"Yes, I can understand." Wildon moved toward Meg, offering his hand.

Meg turned her hand palm up. "Wet, I'm afraid."

Wildon pulled his handkerchief from his pocket and laid the crisp white linen over her palm. "My dear Miss Drummond, Lady Hermione has told me all about your terrible ordeal at the hands of my cousin."

Meg cringed inwardly. She wasn't at all happy with the role of damsel in distress. "Has she?"

Wildon glanced at the bed, his cheek bunching with the clenching of his jaw. "I never imagined my cousin could sink to such depths."

Meg experienced an unexpected surge of protectiveness toward her wicked Highlander. "Alec was repaying a debt of honor to my father. We really mustn't place the blame on his shoulders."

Wildon closed his hand around hers when she tried to return his handkerchief. "Had I but known what mischief he was planning, I would have saved you from this, my dear lady."

Meg eased her hand from his grasp. "I appreciate your concern."

Wildon looked down at his cousin, contempt etched across his delicate features. "It appears he is quite ill. Lady Hermione said there is a chance he won't survive."

Meg stiffened. "I'm certain he will be fine."

"He does, however, need rest." Joanna took Wildon's arm and led him toward the door. She snagged her mother's arm on the way. "Mother, I trust you can entertain Lord Blandford until Lord Dunleith is well enough to see to his cousin."

Hermione scampered to keep up with Joanna's quick strides. "I'm certain Margaret would like to see to her guest."

Meg clenched her hands at her waist, watching her mother deftly usher Wildon and Hermione through the door.

"Mother dear, I'm certain you can see Meg is more than a little busy caring for her husband," Joanna said.

"But I'm—" Hermione started.

"I know you are more than happy to act as hostess in Meg's place," Joanna said. "We shall see you both at dinner."

Hermione stared at her daughter a moment. "Very well, my dear. I shall make certain Lord Blandford is made quite comfortable. Come, my dear young man."

Joanna watched them walk down the hall, then closed the door. "I had no idea Mother let Blandford know where we had gone," she whispered.

Meg rubbed her throbbing temples. "What must she have been thinking?"

"You should know by now, Mother seldom takes the time to think."

"I'm certain she meant well, but I do wish she hadn't brought Blandford down upon us. And at such a time."

Joanna came away from the door. "I must say I never would have come up with such a remarkable explanation for what we were doing."

Meg lifted her hands at her sides. "I couldn't very well tell them what I was really doing, could I?"

Joanna grimaced. "Good heavens, no. They would have packed us off to Bedlam."

"Perhaps I should be sent to Bedlam." Meg glanced at the crystal sitting on the table. "I must be insane."

"Not insane." Joanna patted Meg's arm. "Concerned. Desperate. You see someone you care about struggling for his life, and you want to help him."

Meg sank to the edge of the bed. "It's not that I'm in love with him, you understand."

"It isn't?" Joanna asked softly.

Meg touched Alec's hot cheek. She could keep a tether on her emotions, she assured herself. Once Alec was well, she would show him just how resistible she found him. "Under the circumstances it would be foolish to fall in love with him."

"I rather suspect intelligence and common sense never have a great deal to do with falling in love."

"Well, I am *not* in love with him. I admit I cared for him when I was a child, but I've outgrown that unfortunate attraction." Meg smoothed her hand over Alec's shoulder, easing a crease from the damp white linen of his nightshirt.

"Have you?" Joanna asked.

"Yes." Meg thought her mother looked less than convinced. "Oh, I'm concerned about him. Simply because . . . well, I've known him such a long time. And he was such a close friend of Colin's."

"Meg, have you thought of what your future would be if you don't stay here and try to make this marriage into something real?"

Meg had thought of it, over and over and over again. Still, she had no choice. She couldn't stay with Alec. She couldn't take the chance of giving him her heart. "Since I never planned to marry, I shall be quite content to return to London and resume my life as it was."

"And Alec? Does it bother you to know he will more than likely take a mistress if you leave him?"

A proprietary urge stirred within Meg, sinking claws into her heart. Something much too akin to jealousy nipped at her vitals. She quickly crushed the feelings. "That is likely to happen whether I stay and act the devoted wife, or I leave. The only difference is that I shall not be around to be humiliated."

Joanna sighed. "Alec might choose to honor his marriage vows."

Meg rolled her eyes to heaven. "And I might become queen of England. Believe me, it will be better for all concerned if I leave. All I need do is convince MacLaren there shall never be anything between us, and he will cease to be amused by keeping me here."

"Are you convinced there shall never be anything between you?" Joanna asked.

Meg frowned. "Mother, you can't actually think I would choose to stay here, with a man who agreed to marry me because of a sense of duty? You can't imagine I would ever be able to trust him."

Joanna's smile held more sadness than hope. "I understand how you feel. Even under the best of circumstances, marriage is difficult."

Meg squeezed her mother's hand. "You shall see; when Alec is well I will soon convince him it will be better for both of us to live our separate lives."

Joanna cupped Meg's cheek in her warm palm. "I hope things work out for the best, my darling."

"They will," Meg said, sounding more confident than she felt.

"Shall we see if Highland magic really does work?" Joanna lifted a glass from the tray beside the bed and filled it from the pitcher.

Meg accepted the glass from her mother. "Do you think I'm being foolish?"

Joanna smiled. "My darling, there are times when we all need a little magic in our lives. And I believe that young man deserves any chance we can give him."

Meg eased her arm beneath Alec's shoulders. A soft moan slipped from his parched lips as she lifted him against her. His head nestled against her breast. Tingles spiraled through her, setting the glass shivering with her trembling hand. She bumped the rim of the glass against his parted lips, spilling water down his chin. If she weren't careful, she would drown him in her feeble attempts to cure him.

Meg spilled a little water between his lips and

watched as instinct forced him to swallow. Highland magic. She truly must be insane. Yet deep inside she prayed the magic would touch the man who lay cradled as helpless as a babe in her arms.

Chapter Seventeen

Threads of smoke coiled upward from chunks of glowing peat, like serpents escaping an inferno. Meg lay on the Grecian chaise lounge in Alec's bedchamber, staring at the embers smoldering on the hearth. Although she was tired, she couldn't sleep. She couldn't set aside her fear for Alec, or other equally depressing thoughts.

She drew her hand over Seamus's head. The dog lay beside her, his chin resting on one of his paws. A horrible feeling of loneliness lurked deep inside of her. An empty, terribly hollow feeling, as though some vital part of her had been ripped away.

For the past few years she had convinced herself a contented woman was one who lived free of the shackles of marriage. Men, on the whole, could not be trusted. Although she hadn't changed her mind about the male of the species, being near Alec was enough to make her doubt her ability to remain aloof. Alec had a way of penetrating her defenses with a smile.

She hugged the pillow she had taken from Alec's bed, breathing in his musky scent. Beneath the prim white cotton of her nightgown, her skin tingled. She smoothed her fingertip over her lips, remembering the touch of his lips against hers. Heat whispered across her skin as she recalled the feel of his arms around her.

Until Alec, she had never realized the true extent of her own femininity. She had never truly grasped the potent reality of lust. It was lust, she assured herself. It could be nothing more. She would be lost if her feelings for that maddening Highlander solidified into something impossible to dismiss. She would be a fool if she ever gave Alec that kind of power over her.

The door opened with a soft click. Seamus lifted his head. Meg glanced over her shoulder, watching as a man entered the darkened room. At first, she assumed it was Gordon Murray, Alec's valet. When he stepped into the moonlight flowing through the windowpanes, Meg recognized the slim figure and smooth features of Wildon Fethersham. What was he doing here in the middle of the night?

Wildon paused beside the bed, his back to Meg. He stood staring down at the unconscious man, his hands curled into fists at his sides. She lifted her dressing gown from the curved arm of the chaise lounge, and slipped into the soft emerald velvet.

"Lord Blandford," she said, rising to her feet.

Wildon jumped, an audible gasp escaping his lips. He pivoted, pressing his hand to his heart when he saw her. "Miss Drummond, I didn't realize you were still here."

Meg tugged the belt of her dressing gown close around her waist as she moved toward the startled viscount, with Seamus close at her side. "I must confess, I'm surprised to see you here at this hour."

Wildon smoothed the silk lapels of his shiny, dark

purple dressing gown. He glanced at the dog as though the animal made him uneasy. "I couldn't sleep. So I decided to look in on my cousin. It appears as though there has been no improvement in his condition."

Wildon sounded a little too pleased to find his cousin's condition as grave as ever. Meg turned her attention to the man lying quietly in the bed. In the moonlight that spilled across the bed, Alec's face looked as smooth and cool as finely sculpted marble. Silvery light tangled in the thick black waves tumbling over his brow, mining sapphire highlights in the silky mane. She smoothed the ebony waves back from his feverish brow. "I thought the fever would have broken by now."

"I have to say, I admire you greatly for what you are doing," Wildon said.

Meg glanced up at him. "I'm not certain what you mean."

Wildon lifted one arched brow. "Under the circumstances, few ladies would be sitting at my cousin's bedside, tending to him as though he were a cherished husband."

Meg turned away from Wildon, afraid of betraying her feelings. She walked to the windows, where she stared out at Loch Laren. Moonlight poured over the dark surface of the water, shaping mirrors that glittered like polished silver before shattering with the next wave. "I've known Alec all of my life. Regardless of the circumstances, I would do everything in my power to help him recover."

Wildon joined her at the window. "Your compassion is only one of your more charming qualities."

Meg smiled. "You're far too kind."

"No, dear lady. It is you who are far too kind." Wildon glanced at Alec, the corners of his mouth turning downward. "I don't have to tell you how much I regret what has happened. I think you realize I had hoped, in time, we might have married." He released his breath in an exaggerated sigh. "I suppose it's too late to imagine what might have happened, if fate had not been so unkind."

Meg refrained from informing the young man she had never had the slightest inclination to marry him. "Only bitterness can come of looking back with regret, Lord Blandford."

"Yet I find it difficult not to look back with regret at all I have lost at the hands of my cousin."

Although his voice remained light, and his manner composed, the bitterness was there, veiled by a polite veneer. "I'm certain Alec had no intention of ruining your prospects, Lord Blandford. As I mentioned earlier, he was only repaying a debt of honor to my father."

Wildon turned his face to the moonlight. He looked out at the loch for a long moment before he continued. "I always thought this was one of the most beautiful homes I had ever seen. When I was a boy, and my mother would come here to visit my uncle, I used to walk along the parapets and imagine I was a king of legend, surveying his kingdom."

It was easy to imagine fairy tales and legends in this place, Meg thought. Especially when moonlight glowed upon the clouds on a night like this, spinning a silvery wreath around the top of Ben Lyon. On a night like tonight, she could almost believe this was a place where Celtic fairies dwelled.

"I made great strides in improving the land, in the few short months I was earl." Wildon lifted his chin at a proud angle. "Sheep is the answer, you know. The land was meant for sheep, not farming. When I was Earl of Dunleith, I brought Dunleith into the modern world. Cleared the land of dirt-digging peasants."

Meg bristled at his casual disregard for the people of Dunleith. "There have been crofters on this land for generations."

Wildon smiled at her as though she were a naive child. "Yes, scratching out the meanest of livings. They are far better off emigrating to Canada, or finding work in the mills."

"There are those who would disagree with you, Lord Blandford," she said, keeping the annoyance from her voice.

"Yes." Wildon glanced back at Alec, his expression growing hard. "There are those too steeped in tradition to see the modern way of things."

Meg looked at her husband. Alec had grown restless, as though his cousin's voice disturbed him. Seamus stood beside the bed, watching his master. Alec lay twisting the sheet in his hands, tossing his head back and forth against his pillow, soft, inarticulate sounds slipping from his lips.

Meg moved toward the bed, drawn to Alec. She rested her hand on his shoulder, despair closing around her. There was nothing she could do, except watch and pray Alec would fight his way back to her.

"You should try to get some rest." Wildon touched her arm. "There is nothing you can do here."

"I'll be fine." She glanced up at Wildon, wishing him anywhere but here. "Good night, Lord Blandford."

Wildon lifted one brow at her thinly veiled dismissal. "Good night. I shall see you in the morning."

Wildon left the room, the door closing with a soft click behind him. If only the man would keep going, Meg thought. But she suspected Wildon intended to remain a guest at Dunleith Castle for quite some time.

Meg dipped a cloth in the basin of cool water on the bedside table. She sat on the edge of the bed and draped the cool cloth over Alec's brow.

A low moan escaped his lips. He muttered beneath his breath, turning his head so violently the cloth slid from his brow.

"Alec," she whispered, smoothing her hand over his cheek. "Rest easy, my darling."

"Turn back!" Alec bolted into a sitting position. "The guns! Turn back, you bloody fools! Turn back!"

"Alec!" She pushed against his broad shoulders in an attempt to quell him. "Lie back. Rest."

"Bloody hell," he muttered, his voice a harsh whisper. "The recall! Can't they hear it? No one turning back. No one . . . The guns!" He fell back, as though the outburst had drained the last reserves of his strength.

She ached for this man, his pain as palpable as her own. "Alec," she whispered, smoothing the damp waves back from his brow.

Thick black lashes fluttered against his cheeks and lifted. He stared at her with blue eyes dulled by fever. "Meg?"

Her breath caught in her throat. "Yes, Alec. It's Meg."

He moistened his lips. "Never wanted to hurt you, lass. Never wanted to . . ."

As quickly as the moment of clarity had come, it vanished. Alec slipped away from her, sinking once more into a feverish slumber.

Seamus made a low sound deep in his throat, a whimper, a pitiful plea for his master. Meg patted the dog's head. "He's going to be all right, boy. He just needs a little time," she said, her voice breaking with emotion.

Meg lay on the bed beside Alec and slid her arms around him. Holding him close, she stroked his hair, fear and regret forming a tight band around her chest. She pressed her lips against his heated forehead. "You have to get well, Alec. Do you hear me? You have to fight."

Meg rocked Alec slowly in her arms, whispering encouragement, demanding he get well, until exhaustion claimed her. She fell asleep with her cheek against his soft black hair, her arms around him.

Alec felt as though he were rising from the bottom of a dark loch, swimming upward through layers of darkness, seeking a dim light high above him. Slowly he broke the surface. Sunlight flickered on his closed eyelids. His first conscious impression was of a weight nestled against his shoulder, something silky brushing his chin, a delicious softness pressed to his side. It took no more than a heartbeat to connect the sensations to a familiar source: a woman. He opened his eyes to the sight of a golden head nestled against his shoulder.

Meg.

She lay with her arm slung over his waist, one knee over his thigh. For the first time in he didn't know how many days, his head wasn't pounding, his body wasn't on fire. He felt weak enough to realize the fever had nearly consumed him. But it was gone. And his beautiful bride lay snug against him.

Alec smoothed the silky hair back from her cheek. Meg stirred, rubbing her cheek against his shoulder like a contented kitten, a soft sigh escaping her lips. Memories flickered in his mind, shreds of what had happened since he had taken ill. Every scrap of memory was filled with the woman lying in his bed: her voice piercing his feverish mind, demanding he fight for his life; her face floating in and out of his consciousness—a beautiful angel guiding him back to life.

Meg sighed and stretched, her breasts grazing his chest. Heat seeped into his blood, a far different fever from the one that had nearly killed him.

When she opened her eyes, he smiled at her. "Good morning."

Meg blinked, her expression revealing her surprise. "Alec?"

He gave her a devilish grin. "Have you forgotten me so soon?"

"The fever . . ." Meg pressed her hand to his brow, her slender fingers cool against his skin. Mist glittered in his eyes, a silent testament to the relief she couldn't hide. She drew her fingertips down his cheek, touching him as though she were a blind woman learning the shape of his face, the texture of his skin. That gentle touch told him more than a thousand words could ever have whispered. "Thank heaven. The fever has past."

"No, lass, it hasn't. The truth is, I think it's grown stronger."

A frown creased her brow while a sudden concern filled her eyes. She cupped his cheek in her hand. "But you feel cool. Your eyes are clear. I'm quite certain the fever must have broken."

"Still, I feel warm inside, as though a fever were burning in my blood. It must be from awakening with a beautiful woman in my bed." Alec turned his head and pressed his lips against her palm. "I could get used to this, Meg."

"Oh!" Her eyes grew wide, as though she suddenly realized where she was and who she was with. She scrambled from the bed in a flurry of white cotton and green velvet. In her haste, she tripped. She smacked her hip against the bedside table. Everything on top of the polished mahogany table wobbled. She grabbed the pitcher. Snatched the glass. Still, he heard a loud thump against the carpet, followed by a sheepish, "Oh, dear."

He coughed, covering his laughter. She cast him a dark look, obviously seeing straight through his valiant attempt to spare her dignity. He grinned at her. "While you have the pitcher and glass, I wonder if you might pour me a drink. My mouth feels like parchment."

"It would seem you are feeling much improved this morning," Meg said, splashing water into the glass.

Alec gave her a devilish grin. Although he still felt as weak as a newly foaled colt, he couldn't resist teasing her. "Come back to bed, and I'll show you just how good I feel."

Meg thrust the glass under his nose. "You surprise me, MacLaren. I didn't think you cared for icy Englishwomen."

"I don't." He slipped his hand around the glass, imprisoning her slender fingers beneath his. "But I find I have a real strong desire for the beautiful lass who stayed by my side day and night."

"I did nothing out of the ordinary." Meg jerked her hand from beneath his.

The glass plunged from his grip. It plunked against his chest. Water splashed his face, his neck, his chest. He flinched as the cool flood soaked through his nightshirt. "Careful, lass; you'll drown me," he said, snatching the glass before it could roll off his chest.

Meg folded her hands at her waist, the proper English Snow Queen. Except that the blush high on her cheeks and the fiery fury in her eyes spoiled the aloof pose. "You deserve a good soaking, MacLaren. Preferably in boiling oil."

Alec plucked at the sodden nightshirt. "Now is that any way to talk to a man who has just been dragged through Hades?"

Meg gave him a smug little smile as she plucked the empty glass from his hand. "I hope you took a good look around, MacLaren. I'm certain one day you'll be taking up permanent residence there."

Seamus jumped up, plopping his front paws on the bed beside Alec. He gazed down at Alec, pink tongue lolling to the side of his mouth, brown eyes bright and happy.

"Oh, I've already spent a great deal of time in Hades, Meg," Alec said, stroking the dog's head. Content all was now right with the world, Seamus dropped to the floor and curled into a ball near the foot of the bed. "The afterlife can't be much worse than the army."

A frown etched a line between Meg's brows. "If you felt that way, why didn't you leave?"

"I had reasons for staying." Alec thought of the time he had wasted in his search for glory, the precious years he could have spent with his family. "Though now that I look back, none of them were really that important."

Meg studied him a moment, her eyes filled with questions he wasn't certain he wanted to answer. Yet she didn't voice them. Instead, she scolded him. "You should get out of that wet nightshirt before you catch a chill."

Alec pulled the sodden linen away from his chest, then hesitated. Although he wanted to take off the wet nightshirt, he didn't want to expose Meg to the ugliness hidden beneath the white linen.

"Go ahead. I'll fetch you a fresh one."

He grinned at her, hiding his uncertainty behind a roguish mask. "Why, Meg, I never realized you were so anxious to get me undressed."

She pursed her lips. "I'm anxious not to have an invalid in the house. There were moments in the past few days when I wasn't certain if you would pull through. Poor Seamus was fraught with worry."

"Well, I wouldn't want to upset Seamus." Alec glanced to where his dog was lying beside the bed. He took some comfort that the animal hadn't been the only one worried about him. He had a feeling the lady cared more than she wanted to admit. He glanced at the glass Meg still held. "I could use a sip of water."

Meg filled the glass from the pitcher and handed it to him. Alec sipped from the glass, relishing the cool rush of water across his tongue and down his throat. He watched her as she bent to retrieve something from the floor. "You surprise me, Meg."

She frowned as she straightened. "And how did I manage to do that?"

"Every time I opened my eyes, you were here. Scolding me to get well. If I didn't know better, I would think you actually cared for me, just a wee bit."

Meg lowered her eyes, hiding the expression in the green depths. Sunlight poured through the windowpanes behind her, slipping into her unbound waves. "I didn't do anything exceptional."

Alec knew better. The woman had stayed beside him day and night. "Tending a sick man isn't exactly what I'd expect from a spoiled Englishwoman."

She glanced at him, fury flashing in her emerald eyes. "I am not spoiled."

"Maybe not." He grinned at her. "And maybe you're not as English as I thought."

Meg lifted her chin. "I assure you, MacLaren, I managed to purge myself of any unfortunate Scottish tendencies I might have had a long time ago."

"Have you now?"

"Yes."

Alec looked up into her beautiful, haughty face, searching for some trace of the Scottish lass he had known. There was fire beneath the ice, he assured himself. He was certain of it.

Meg ignored his regard. She turned her attention to the object she had retrieved from the floor, holding it up to the sunlight, as though she were studying it for any damage. Sparks splintered from the round stone she held, capturing Alec's attention.

"The *Clach Bhuaidh*," he whispered, staring at the ancient talisman. "What are you doing with that?"

Meg glanced up from the stone, her eyes wide, her lips parted, looking as guilty as a sinner caught on Judgment Day. "This?"

His instincts pricked. "Aye. Did Iona decide I needed a dose of the ancient cure?"

"I'm afraid she is very superstitious."

"After I came back from the war, I was still very ill. Iona is convinced the stone was what saved my life."

Meg rolled the stone from one hand to the other. "You used it?"

"Aye. I've seen it work in the past."

She glanced down at the stone. "Do you actually believe a stone can work magic?"

"I believe there is more to this world than what we can see or hear or feel. Some call it magic."

"There is no such thing as magic." In spite of her icy tone, Meg handled the ancient crystal as though it were made of delicate porcelain as she slipped the stone into the gold holder on the bedside table.

So the lady had purged herself of all her Scottish tendencies. He wondered if that was true. "According to legend, only the laird or his lady can coax magic from the stone."

"Yes, Iona said as much." Meg fluttered her hands in a gesture of dismissal. "Silly, really."

"So you didn't use it?"

She fiddled with a curl that had tumbled over her shoulder. "Me?"

"Aye. You're the lady of Dunleith now."

"Medicine is what helped cure your illness, MacLaren. Not Highland magic."

His months working as a spy had honed his skills for recognizing when someone was hiding something. "You really don't believe in magic?"

"Of course not."

Alec shivered, the cool air of the room chilling his wet nightshirt. "There was a time when you did."

She folded her hands at her waist in that proper governess pose of hers. "I'm no longer a child."

He grinned. "I noticed."

Her soft mouth tightened. "You really must take off that sodden shirt before you catch cold."

If the lady could believe in Highland magic, she could learn to shed all that English ice. "I remember my father used the *Clach Bhuaidh* more than once. He believed in it. So did my mother. As did I."

"Superstitious nonsense." Meg snatched a letter from the bedside table. "This came for you while you were ill."

Alec suspected the lady wanted to divert his attention. He set the letter aside with little more than a glance at it. "Were you even tempted to use the stone, Meg?"

Meg pivoted and marched to the tall mahogany armoire that stood against the far wall. "I believe your nightshirts are kept in here."

Alec set his glass on the bedside table. He watched her rummage through the drawers of his armoire in her search for a nightshirt. Since he wore nightshirts only when he was ill, they were stacked in a bottom drawer. Still, he wondered if he would now have to make a practice of donning a nightshirt before retiring to bed—that is, after he convinced his wife to share his bed.

When Meg turned to face him with a fresh nightshirt draped over her arm, he still hadn't removed the one he wore. Strange, there was a time when he wouldn't hesitate to strip bare with a woman he scarcely knew. Now he was with the woman he had married, and he was loath to expose her to the sight of his bare flesh.

She already thought him a monster. And he had seen the shock on her face from only a glimpse of his bare chest. He didn't want to shock her more, or see the revulsion he knew she would show at the sight of his disfigured flesh.

Meg frowned as she marched toward him. "Do you need help getting out of it?"

"No, thank you." Still he hesitated.

She lifted one finely arched brow. "I never realized you were so modest."

"You should know I haven't a stitch on under this thing," he said, teasing her, knowing he was only delaying the inevitable.

She tugged at the sheet. "You have the sheet to preserve your modesty and my delicate sensibilities."

It was only a matter of time before he would have to expose her to the ugly scars, he thought. He really didn't plan to spend the rest of his life making love to his wife while dressed in a nightshirt or hidden by darkness. Still, he had hoped this moment would come at a time when he had warmed her a bit. A little affection might blind her to the horrible sight of him.

Chapter Eighteen

Meg watched Alec, sensing his uncertainty. She thought of that morning by the stream when she had intruded on his privacy. She remembered the haunted look in his eyes when he had realized she had glimpsed his scars. And she realized in some way his masculine pride had been damaged. He was ashamed to expose her to the devastated flesh.

"I won't swoon if you take off your nightshirt, MacLaren. If you recall, I've already seen all your masculine glory and survived quite nicely," she said, keeping her tone light and mocking.

Alec glanced up at her, his blue eyes filled with a certain wariness in spite of his smile. "Now, lass, you haven't seen *all* my masculine glory."

"I have seen Italian sculptures without going into the vapors. I doubt I should swoon if I should happen to glimpse a little male flesh. Now take off that blasted shirt."

His brows lifted in mock shock. "Yes, sir."

Meg felt her lips twitch with a smile. She quickly pulled them down into a scowl, refusing to encourage the rogue. There really wasn't any need for her to stay, she thought. She could, and should, inform the others that Alec was better. Her father was terribly worried, as were Christina and Niall Fergusson. They had come every day to see Alec and should arrive soon. She should see to her own toilette. Gordon Murray could handle the task of getting Alec into a fresh nightshirt. Yet something perverse inside of her dictated that she stay. Something soft and vulnerable within her insisted she show this man she wasn't frightened of a few scars.

Alec struggled into a sitting position. The effort cost him dearly. He leaned forward, bracing his arms on his knees, breathing hard. In spite of his earlier teasing, she suspected the illness had left him terribly drained of strength.

Meg laid the fresh nightshirt over the foot of the bed. "Here. Let me help you."

He smiled at her. "Your help would be welcome, lass."

She tugged the nightshirt out from under the sheet and tried not to think of all those Italian statues of Greek and Roman gods she had studied. "Lift your arms."

Alec complied, lifting his arms while she tugged the wet nightshirt up over his head. The warmth of his skin bathed her cheek. She tried to ignore the warm reminder that this was flesh and blood, not cold, hard marble sculpted into an illusion of muscle and bone. Yet she couldn't ignore the flicker of heat low in her belly.

When she pulled the nightshirt away, the sheet settled low over Alec's lap. For one heart-pounding moment, she stared at the smooth curve of his bare hip before she turned away from the bed. Her insides tightened with what could only be lust, she assured herself. Dear heaven, this was a mistake, she thought. She should have left him to Gordon Murray's care. Yet even now, with the familiar excitement tingling through her veins, she couldn't convince herself to leave Alec.

The warmth of his naked flesh remained in the white linen of his nightshirt. A musky scent lingered on the garment, a spicy masculine fragrance that tempted her to press her face into the soft white linen. She couldn't do anything so absurdly primitive, she assured herself. Still, after she rolled the garment, she hesitated a moment, rubbing her fingers against the warm linen, before setting it on the floor beside Seamus near the foot of the bed.

Meg turned toward the bed and froze. Alec was lying back against the pillows with the sheet tumbled around his waist. The sight of him lying there, in that big bed, with nothing but a sheet covering him from his waist down, stole the breath from her lungs. Her gaze traveled over him; she couldn't help it. The scars were there, of course, wicked reminders of war. Yet they ceased to shock her this time. This time she feasted on the sight of him.

Golden skin against white linen. Broad shoulders. Wide chest tapering to a lean waist. Black hair shading his forearms, his chest, narrowing to a thin line that disappeared beneath the sheet and dragged her imagination with it. She stared at the white linen draped over his slim hips, the long length of his legs, trying not to imagine lifting away the veil. For one horrible moment, while the blood pounded in her veins, she thought she might do something shocking. His own brand of potent masculinity had never been more powerful.

Alec's hand fisted in the sheet beside his thigh. For

an instant she thought he meant to tug the sheet over his chest, but he didn't. Instead he lay there, exposed to her hungry gaze, eyes as blue as a summer sky filled with anxiety and a silent hope for acceptance.

Meg lifted the nightshirt from the foot of the bed and walked to his side. "I understand most men are quite proud of their war injuries. I really must say, I find nothing exceptional in a few scars."

Alec studied her a moment, as though looking for answers in her eyes. "So my scars don't impress you," he said, a whisper of wariness beneath the light tone.

"I'm afraid not." He looked so young, so vulnerable, lying there with his black hair tousled around his face. She smothered the urge to smooth the thick black waves back from his brow. The illness had passed, and so had her time for easy displays of affection.

"A few scars are hardly something to parade about as though they were badges of honor." With the tip of her forefinger she traced the smooth white scar that plunged diagonally from his left shoulder to a point somewhere below his waist. The scar continued beneath the sheet. She didn't. She had meant only to show him she had no aversion to the horrible scars that marred the perfection of his chest and arms. She hadn't expected his muscles to shift beneath her touch, or the soft exhale of his breath. She hadn't expected the tightening deep inside of her that came with a thrilling excitement.

Meg curled her fingers into her palm and sought composure. "Quite unexceptional," she said, her voice far too breathy.

"I'm afraid I disagree, lass."

She met his gaze. The warmth in his eyes mirrored the gentleness she had heard in his dark voice. He was looking at her as though he were seeing her for the first time, and the sight surprised him.

"I'd say you're more than exceptional, Meg. You're a very special lady."

The soft tone of his voice curled around her, teasing the longing that dwelled deep within. Gratitude. She mustn't see affection where there wasn't any. It was frightening to realize how easily this man could wrap her around his little finger. "I'm certain you would like to bathe before you change."

Alec gave her a devilish grin. "I'd love a bath, especially at the hands of my beautiful wife."

Meg didn't want to think about all the women who might have obliged the rogue. Still, she couldn't prevent a sharp stab of jealousy from jabbing her. She molded her lips into a smile. "I'm afraid you'll have to settle for Gordon's hands, MacLaren. I'll tell him you're ready."

"Wait." Alec grabbed her wrist.

Meg froze in his grasp, feeling trapped by more than the gentle hold of his hand. "What is it?"

"Would you stay for a while and . . ." He glanced around as though looking for something. He lifted the letter from the sheet beside him. "Read this to me."

Meg turned her gaze on the letter. The parchment looked delicate in his long, sun-darkened fingers. Her muscles tensed when she thought of those elegantly tapered fingers against the pale skin of the woman who had sent that letter. "I really should—"

"I find I'm not feeling very well. Please stay and read the letter to me."

Jealousy was not an emotion she could well afford, Meg reminded herself. It wasn't a question of *if* the man would be unfaithful to his marriage vows, but *when*. No matter what he might say to get her into his bed, she knew Alec would take a mistress as soon as he was certain she was breeding. Meg had no doubt of it. She certainly didn't intend to allow him to trample her heart or her pride. The only defense she had against the man was to keep her heart well guarded.

Meg plucked the letter from his fingers. "You should cover up before you savage your health," she said, keeping her voice cool and composed.

Alec pulled the sheet over his chest. "Your concern warms me."

In response, Meg rolled her eyes to heaven. Still, she wasn't satisfied. The sheet was hardly thick enough to help her ignore what lay beneath. She pulled the burgundy coverlet splashed with gold dragons up to his chin, then sank to the chair beside the bed. With studied determination to maintain her composure, she broke the seal on the letter and unfolded the ivory paper.

"My darling Alec." Heat prickled her neck. "Although it has scarcely been two months since we parted, it seems years since I last saw your handsome face."

Alec muttered something under his breath. Meg glanced up at him. "Pardon me?"

His grin looked sheepish. "I doubt there is much of interest in that letter."

"It's not very long. It will only take a short time to finish it." Meg squeezed the paper, in an attempt to keep her hands from trembling. She intended to see this through to the end. "I recently returned to London from a delightful holiday in Italy. Yet I couldn't help think how much more delightful the trip would have been with you. Pity you were still so ill. Town is dreadfully dull without you. I hope you shall soon condescend to grace the ladies of London with your charming smile. As for one lady in particular . . ."

Meg hesitated over the words that followed. The woman was obviously his mistress. Perhaps one of many. She eased air past the knot forming in her throat. It didn't matter, she assured herself. If she didn't allow Alec to conquer her heart, she could handle anything that happened. "As for one lady in particular, I hope you know she would very much like to taste once more the delights you shared with her in Brussels. The nights are growing colder. She craves your warmth and hopes to see you soon. Do take care, darling. Affectionately . . . Pamela."

In the periphery of her vision she could see Alec. He was watching her, his expression quiet and searching. No doubt he was judging her every reaction. She would show him the letter meant nothing to her. She carefully folded the letter and placed it on the bedside table. He could take a hundred mistresses, she thought. A thousand. It didn't matter. She would walk away now. Without a mention of the letter. No, she certainly wouldn't mention Pamela. "It would seem your mistress is in need of your services."

Alec frowned. "She isn't my mistress."

She rose from her chair and did her best to contain the trembling in her limbs. "Oh, I suppose the intimate nature of the letter confused my feeble mind."

"Meg, I won't deny I've been intimate with other women. But I've never asked any woman to be my mistress."

She managed a smile she hoped reflected some measure of composure. "I see. You simply prefer to bed a woman and move on to the next."

A muscle in his cheek flickered with the clenching of his jaw. "I've never been dishonest with any woman. I've never told any woman I loved her. I've never seduced an innocent female. And I've never in my life promised more than I was willing to give."

It was true enough, she thought. Alec had never spoken of love to the woman he had married out of a sense of duty. In some twisted way she could applaud his honesty, except at the moment it hurt too much. "As far as I'm concerned, MacLaren, I don't give one whit how you conduct your liaisons. You can take as many mistresses as you want, as long as you don't expect me to live with you, and pretend to be your devoted wife."

He grabbed her wrist when she started to leave. "I take marriage seriously, Meg. I intend to honor every vow I pledged to you."

Meg remained rigid in his hold. "But your natural male tendencies will soon lead you astray," she said, managing a mocking tone in her voice when all she wanted to do was scream.

Alec smoothed the pad of his thumb over the smooth skin at the inside of her wrist. "Not all men are scoundrels, Meg. There are those of my sex capable of loyalty. Capable of honoring their marriage vows. I know. I've seen it. My father never once betrayed the love he and my mother shared."

Love. Perhaps if Alec loved her . . . A hard hand twisted around her heart. If Alec loved her, would she be able to trust him? Meg had once thought love would make a difference in marriage. Yet her father had shattered that illusion.

A woman couldn't trust a man, even if he pretended to love her. And without the illusion of that elusive emotion, a woman could be certain nothing would keep a man from betraying her heart. "I've seen the type of marriage my parents shared, the wonderful illusion of devotion. I've seen the pain a man can inflict on an unsuspecting woman when she is foolish enough to trust him. And I can assure you, I shall never give you that power over me."

Alec held her sullen gaze for a long moment before he spoke. "I'll have to find some way of making you see there's no reason to fear me. All I want is a home and family. I have no desire for more than one woman in my life."

She lifted her brows. "Is that one woman at a time?"

"It's one woman, for the rest of my life."

"Hmmm, pleasant sentiment."

He slid his fingers around her hand. "I don't want a mistress. What can I do to convince you, I want only to make this marriage into something real?"

His words whispered deep inside of her, rippling over the pool of longing hidden there, like a breeze across a quiet loch. "I don't trust you," she whispered.

"I know." His long lashes lowered as he brought her tightly clenched fist to his lips. Warm breath brushed her skin. Soft lips caressed her hand. She felt herself melting beneath the gentle touch, warmth sliding through her limbs, weakening her resolve. "Somehow I'll change your mind, lass."

She shook her head, afraid to use her voice, knowing it would betray her weakness.

Alec smiled, as though he were satisfied by what he saw in her eyes. "You can't deny the spark that glows when we're together. And one of these days that spark will ignite into a flame, Meg. You'll see."

She pulled her hand from his grasp. Yet she felt as though a part of her were left behind, in his keeping. Oh dear, she really had to get away from this maddening Highlander. "If you'll excuse me, there are a few people in the house who will be pleased to see you are out of danger."

Meg pivoted and marched toward the door. The man would not manipulate her, she assured herself. He would not seduce her. She knew better than to allow a man to slither under her defenses. But oh, how she wanted to believe him. She couldn't possibly trust him. Could she? It was foolish to imagine he would ever remain loyal to her. Yet she couldn't prevent her foolish heart from coddling a dangerous infant of hope.

*   *   *

Discipline was an officer's responsibility. Alec had learned long ago to maintain his own composure in the face of battle—it was the only way to maintain control over his men. In turn he had learned to control anger, fear, frustration, any emotion that would get in the way of duty. Yet, at the moment, as he lay against his pillows and watched Wildon Fethersham pace the length of his bedchamber, Alec found it difficult to control the urge to throttle the man.

"You must be quite pleased with yourself." Wildon paused beside Alec's bed, glaring down at his cousin. "And pray, do not tell me you weren't aware of my intentions toward Miss Drummond before you kidnapped her."

Alec's head was pounding. As much as he hated to admit it, he needed rest—a commodity in short supply. Although he had enjoyed his earlier visits from Robert, and later Niall and Christina, this was one visitor Alec could well do without. "I knew precisely what your intentions were toward Meg."

Wildon lifted his chin. "Good gad! You knew I intended to make Margaret my wife, and you went ahead with this despicable course of action?"

"Is it the lady you lament losing, Blandford? Or her inheritance?"

Color rose to stain Wildon's smooth cheeks. "Confound you. Isn't it enough that you returned to take away my inheritance? Now you interfere with my marriage plans. It is too much, Dunleith."

"Yes, terribly inconvenient of me to survive the war," Alec smiled at his cousin. "Would you like to call me out, Blandford? We could settle this over pistols at dawn."

"Very amusing." Wildon stepped back from the bed. "I'm not fool enough to meet you, cousin. It's not a secret you are a crack shot. I don't intend to give you the chance to murder me. And you would dearly like to murder me, wouldn't you?"

"You overrate yourself, Blandford. I may wish to live my life without seeing you again, but I certainly wouldn't take the effort to murder you. Unless, of course, you insist."

Wildon drew in his breath, his slender shoulders rising beneath the bottle green wool of his close-fitting coat. "You may think you've managed to take everything away from me, Dunleith, but there is one thing you don't have—Margaret's affection. The lady was going to marry me of her own free will."

Alec held Wildon's triumphant gaze, hiding his doubts concerning his lady. "The lady married me. And I intend to make certain she has no reason to regret her choice."

Wildon's lips tipped into a smug smile. "The lady wasn't exactly given a choice, was she?"

His cousin's artillery shot had hit Alec squarely in the chest. As much as he wanted to deny it, Alec couldn't stop wondering if Meg had really cared for Blandford.

"I hope you have been giving your cousin a proper set-down," Hermione said, as she swept into the room in a cloud of red satin, red ostrich feathers fluttering in her hair.

Alec stifled a groan as he watched Hermione march toward him. Why the devil hadn't he told Gordon to lock the door to his bedchamber? Joanna Drummond followed her mother, entering at a much more sedate pace, tall and elegant in somber black muslin.

Hermione paused beside Wildon. "Have you by any chance called him out, Lord Blandford?"

Wildon glanced from Hermione to Alec and back again. "I'm afraid it wouldn't be prudent."

"If I were a man, I would take great pleasure in meeting you on the field of honor." Hermione glared at Alec as she spoke. "You, sir, are not a gentleman. When I think of what you have done to my poor granddaughter . . . Kidnapping her!" She pressed the back of her hand to her brow. "Oh my, I feel faint."

Wildon's eyes grew wide as the plump little lady swayed toward him. "Lady Hermione!" he said, grabbing her arm.

"Mother, I do hope you don't intend to faint on top of Lord Dunleith." Joanna stood at the foot of the bed, smiling at her mother. "I'm afraid you might do yourself some injury. Not to mention what damage you might inflict upon the earl."

Hermione pursed her lips. "I can think of any manner of injury I should like to serve the earl."

"I understand." Joanna cast Alec a pointed look before turning her attention back to her mother and the viscount. "Lord Blandford, I believe my mother could use a nice cup of tea. Would you mind escorting her to her sitting room and seeing to it?"

"Yes, of course," Wildon said.

"Tea?" Hermione lifted her chin, her expression growing mulish. "I have a few things I intend to tell this young man."

"I'm quite certain Lord Dunleith is aware of your sentiments on this matter, Mother." Joanna took her mother's arm and ushered her toward the door. "And there are a few things I would like to discuss with him. Alone."

Hermione threw up her hands in surrender. "Very well. But I expect you to be quite harsh. Come along, my dear Lord Blandford."

Alec leaned back against his pillows, watching as his cousin and Lady Hermione left the room. Although he was grateful to Lady Joanna for getting rid of his unwanted guests, he wasn't at all easy with what the lady might have to say to him.

Joanna walked toward him, her expression washed of emotion. "Thank you for sending me that note informing me of my daughter's whereabouts."

Alec released the breath he had been holding. "I didn't want you to worry about her."

Joanna paused beside the bed and folded her hands at her waist, assuming a pose he had often seen Meg take. "I want you to know, I am quite prepared to take my daughter away from here."

"Your daughter is my wife," he said, keeping his voice low and contained. "Her place is here with me."

Joanna studied him a moment. "Can you give me one good reason why I should allow my daughter to stay with a man who kidnapped her and subsequently forced her into marriage?"

Alec smiled, hoping to melt a little English ice. "I wouldn't have married Meg if I didn't think we would suit each other. I think we can have a fine life together, if she ever decides to trust me."

Joanna lifted one brow. "Why should she trust you?"

"Because I believe in honoring my vows." He smoothed his fingers over the silk coverlet at his side. "Because I want a home, a family. I want Meg as my wife, and I'm determined to make her see this is where she belongs. With me."

Joanna stood beside the bed, a judge deliberating her sentence. He held her appraising stare, knowing his life would be twice complicated if he couldn't convince this beautiful, headstrong woman to fight on his side of this war.

Joanna walked into the abandoned music room of Dunleith Castle. This isolated part of the house was the only place left to search for her daughter. Meg had disappeared several hours ago, shortly after delivering the good news about Alec's recovery. Through the square panes of the last pair of French doors she could see her daughter, standing on the terrace overlooking Loch Laren—a solitary figure in black, lost in quiet reflection.

Joanna hesitated a moment, wondering if she should intrude. Yet the sadness that reflected from the girl drew her. Deep inside she knew Meg needed her.

She crossed the room, her footsteps echoing against the bare oak parquet, stroking a desolate chord within her. She glanced around at the smooth white plaster walls, the empty floor, remembering when this room had shimmered with elegance. It seemed a lifetime since she had been in this room. She had attended musicales here, shared conversation and laughter with Isobel and Douglas—a lifetime ago, when life was filled with simple pleasures. Now Isobel and Douglas were gone, as lost as the life Joanna had known.

A cool breeze penetrated the black muslin of her gown and rippled the hem of her paisley shawl as Joanna stepped onto the terrace. Meg turned at the sound of the door opening, her expression betraying a flicker of expectancy before easing into a smile.

"Here you are," Joanna said, closing the door behind her. "I was wondering where you might be hiding."

Meg tugged her black cashmere shawl close around her. "I'm not hiding."

Joanna paused beside her. "Aren't you?"

Meg sighed. "I suppose I am, just a little. It was easier being near Alec when he was ill. He can be quite vexing when he is awake."

Joanna understood exactly what had driven Meg into hiding—her attraction to a dangerous male. The wind swept over the heather that spread across the rocky slopes of Ben Lyon, brushing her face with the soft, damp fragrance. Dark gray clouds shrouded the peak of the mountain, promising a storm. "Strange, isn't it, how the Highlands can be so beautiful even on a day like this. The dark, brooding weather makes the mountains seem all the more mysterious."

"You miss living here," Meg said, without question.

Joanna wondered if Meg could even imagine how much she missed the life she once led. "This country has a way of getting into your blood, especially here in the Highlands."

Meg looked out across the loch. "According to some people, I've had all the Scottish drained out of me. Replaced with English ice water."

"Speaking of 'some people.'" Joanna shivered in the damp breeze that whipped across the loch and frosted the rolling waves. "A short while ago, I had a long conversation with Alec. He assured me he wanted nothing more than to make this marriage a success."

Meg drew her shawl closer around her neck. "It's a convenient thing to say, especially to you."

"He seemed very sincere."

Meg rubbed her fingertip against the ridge of a stone set in the top of the wall. "He has a purpose. He wants legitimate heirs. He needs my cooperation for that."

Joanna stared down into the blue-gray waves crashing against the rocky shore a hundred feet below. There were things she had never shared with Meg, things she had kept close to her heart. Things Meg needed to consider. "When I left your father, I thought I was doing the right thing. My pride wouldn't allow me to stay and try to mend the breach. Yet there have been moments when I've wondered if I should have stayed. If I should have fought for what was mine, rather than run away."

"You were justified in what you did," Meg said, her voice filled with steely determination. "No woman should be expected to live with a man as his devoted wife after he has betrayed his vows. How could you ever trust him again?"

Joanna looked at her daughter and saw her own bitterness reflected in Meg's green eyes. She thought of what Robert had said about Meg having a chance for happiness. And she wondered if her daughter's chance rested with Alec. "There is a loneliness that cannot be filled, except by the man you love. It's too late for me to know what might have been if I had stayed. I only hope you shall not come to mourn the bridges you might burn behind you. I wonder . . . perhaps you should give Alec a chance."

Meg shivered in the damp breeze. "Father was in love with you, and he still betrayed you. Can I really hope to trust Alec?"

Joanna looked into her daughter's eyes and knew she didn't have the answers to the questions she saw burning there. "I honestly don't know."

Meg rubbed her brow. "No matter how many times and how many ways I examine the situation, the answer never looks terribly bright. To hope for a man's faithfulness when he has pledged devotion is a risk, at best. To nurture that hope when he doesn't even pretend affection is foolish."

Joanna stared at her daughter, stunned by words that might have fallen from her own lips. "I never realized what happened to me would so dramatically alter your thinking toward marriage."

Meg smiled, her eyes reflecting a bitter resolve. "It opened my eyes."

Joanna held her daughter's steady regard. Had she nurtured this stubborn streak of anger in her daughter? Was all the bitterness justified? Or would holding on to the past destroy any chance Meg might have for the future? Joanna didn't have the answers. All she could offer were doubts. "There are some marriages that do succeed."

"Are you saying I should surrender myself to that man?" Meg asked, her voice a harsh whisper.

Joanna leaned back against the wall. Meg had no reason to trust the man she had married, and Joanna could find no argument that could defeat all the doubts they both shared. "I keep wondering if Alec might just make you happy."

Meg rested her hands on the wall. She stared at the waves crashing against the rocky shore below for several moments before she spoke. "Although I hate to admit it, I'm frightened of him. I'm frightened of this power he holds over me. When I'm near the man, I can't think with any clarity."

Joanna slipped her arm around her daughter's waist. "I wish I had the answers that would ease your mind. I don't. I just have this feeling that you need to give Alec a chance to make things right."

Meg stared down at the water. "If I did, I would also be giving him the chance to destroy me."

Joanna patted Meg's arm. "You have to look at what your life would be without Alec compared to what it might be with him. And you have to decide if a life with Alec is worth the risk."

Meg nodded. "I know."

"There you are!" Hermione said, as she swept onto the terrace, with Wildon Fethersham trailing close behind. "I've been looking for you everywhere."

Joanna suppressed a sigh. There were times when she dearly wished her mother would return to London, and take Lord Blandford with her.

Hermione's gown of cherry-colored satin rippled in the breeze as she marched toward Joanna and Meg. Red ostrich feathers fluttered in her hair. Much to Joanna's displeasure, Hermione had abandoned mourning etiquette after they left England, stating how black did forever remind you of the dear one you had lost. Here in the wilds of Scotland Hermione felt certain there was no harm in wearing something more cheerful.

"It's dreadful out here. You both must come in before you catch your death. And you, my dear," Hermione said, taking Meg's arm, "must come entertain Lord Blandford with a game of chess."

Meg frowned. "Chess?"

"I told him how delightfully you play." Hermione ushered her granddaughter toward the viscount. "And now that you've finally emerged from the sickroom, it's time you tend to your guest."

Wildon took Meg's hand. "I've been looking forward to playing chess with you all afternoon."

"I'm afraid I haven't played in a while." Meg glanced back at Joanna, obviously searching for help in extricating herself from Hermione's snare.

"I'm certain you will find her play poor sport indeed, Lord Blandford," Joanna said. "I fear you'll be terribly put out."

"Never." Wildon tucked Meg's arm through his. "I could never find a moment in Miss Drummond's company a bore."

"It is Lady Dunleith now." Joanna cast her mother a glance full of meaning. "I suggest we all remember that."

Hermione lifted her brows.

Wildon's mouth tightened. "Of course." He turned to Meg. "Now, dear lady, please tell me you shall honor me with a game."

Meg's smile was less than enthusiastic. "I would be delighted."

"Now run along," Hermione said, fluttering her hands. "Have a pleasant game."

Joanna walked beside her mother as they followed Meg and Wildon into the music room. She grabbed her mother's arm, halting their progress near the hearth. After Meg and Wildon had left the room, she closed the door and turned on Hermione. "What are you about, Mother?"

Hermione's eyes grew wide, her expression pure innocence. "Whatever do you mean?"

"You know exactly what I mean," Joanna said. "Meg is married. Why are you still trying to throw her into Blandford's path?"

Hermione huffed. "I'm quite certain I can have this dreadful marriage annulled. The child was forced into it, after all."

"I'm not at all certain having this marriage annulled is a sound idea."

Hermione waved away her words with a pudgy hand. "There is a chance of scandal, of course, but Lord Blandford doesn't care. After he marries Meg, all the difficulties shall soon pass. With the combined power of the Blandfords and Chadburnes, we shall weather the storm."

Joanna stared at her mother. "In case you have forgotten, let me remind you: Meg doesn't want to marry Blandford. She never did."

Hermione lifted her chin. "Not now. Still, I'm certain once Lord Blandford rescues her from the evil clutches of that vile Scottish barbarian, Margaret shall be overjoyed to marry him."

Joanna shook her head. "Mother, I do not want you to interfere with Meg's marriage."

"You expect me to stand by and watch my granddaughter destroyed the way you were destroyed?"

The jab connected, as it always did. Joanna clenched her jaw. "This has nothing to do with my situation. I believe we need to give Meg and Alec a chance to make this marriage succeed. It might be her only chance at finding true happiness."

"But she—"

"Mother, I want you to promise me."

Hermione pursed her lips. "Very well. I shall not interfere with Margaret's chance at happiness."

The stiff declaration left Joanna with doubts. Joanna stood by the hearth and watched her mother march from the room. She felt as empty as the room in which she stood. And more confused than she had felt in a very long time.

Chapter Nineteen

Meg resisted the pull of morning, clinging to the soft, hazy space between dreams and reality. There were days when reality was much too unpleasant to face, days when she longed to stay in the realm of dreams. In dreams Alec came to her; he held her and kissed her and told her how much he adored her. She trusted the realm of dreams. She was safe there. Contented there.

A moist heat drifted across her cheek. Something warm brushed her lips in a soft, gentle slide. Warmth radiated against her, with an intriguing scent that teased her nostrils. Her senses tingled, tugging her from slumber. With a sigh, she opened her eyes and stared straight up into Alec's smiling face.

"Good morning, sweetheart," Alec said.

Meg blinked, her body jolting with the sudden reality of Alec. In spite of her best intentions, she caught herself devouring the sight of him. Early morning sunlight spilled through the windows, embracing him, slipping golden fingers into his thick black hair. The dark smudges beneath his incredible eyes were gone. The pallor of his skin had dissolved into a fine, healthy glow. He looked better than he had in days. "What are you doing here?"

The bed dipped as he sat beside her, his hip brushing against her hip. He rested his hand on the blue silk coverlet on the other side of her, his hand grazing her waist as he leaned over her "Wishing my bride a pleasant morning."

Meg tugged the covers up to her chin. "I don't recall giving you leave to come as you please."

He smoothed his fingertips over her temple. "You probably didn't know this, but a husband has the right to visit his wife's bedchamber."

A husband had a right to do other things as well, things that haunted her dreams. "I thought we had an agreement."

"My darling Meg. You can rest easy." He dropped a kiss on the tip of her nose. "I didn't come here to have my wicked way with you."

Perhaps he didn't intend to force himself on her. But she knew how terribly convincing the man could be when he set his mind to seduction. She clenched the covers. "Why did you come? And at this time of the day. It can't be much past dawn."

"I've come to whisk you away before your grandmother or my cousin can take the notion to tag along. I want some time alone with you."

Meg hadn't been alone with Alec since the morning his fever had broken. She had arranged it that way, making certain she always had a chaperon when in the company of her husband. It wasn't that she was frightened of him. She knew he would never force himself on her. The truth was, she was frightened of her own feelings toward him. If she were never alone with him, then she couldn't possibly make a complete fool of herself over the man.

His smile kindled warmth deep in the depths of his blue eyes. "I've had Cook pack us something for breakfast. I thought we could take a walk to the old fort and have a picnic."

"It's too chilly for you to be out."

"It's a fine, gentle morning."

She drew a shaky breath, catching the scent of sandalwood and a spice all his own. The intriguing aroma shimmered through her, sparking along her nerves. "It's much too soon for you to be walking about the countryside."

He smoothed his hand over her hair, as though he loved the feel of the unbound tresses beneath his palm. "I'm not an invalid."

No, he wasn't. Which made him all the more dangerous. "You're not completely healed."

He slipped his hands around hers. "Come with me, Meg."

The warmth of his hands radiated against hers, seeping into her blood. She shouldn't spend time alone in his company. It was contrary to her plans, not to mention dangerous to her own tenuous hold on her resolve. Yet she couldn't deny the doubts inside of her, doubts that had only grown stronger at her mother's gentle urging to give Alec and this marriage a chance. "I suppose you shall bother me until I agree to go with you."

"Aye." Alec gave her a devilish grin, mischief glinting in his eyes. "But if you're thinking you would rather stay here and while away the day, I'll be content to keep you company."

Meg forced her lips into a scowl, though she wanted very much to smile. "Go away. Give me a chance to dress. I'll be ready in twenty minutes."

He lifted her hands and pressed a soft kiss to each in turn. "I'll be waiting."

Meg watched him leave, admiring his long, graceful strides. The man could set her heart racing with a glance. How the devil was she going to resist the wicked Highlander? More to the point, should she even try?

An hour later, Meg sat beside her husband in a place she hadn't visited since she was a child. Alec had spread a thick patchwork quilt of multicolored chintz across the moss-covered ground within the tumbled remains of an ancient circular fort. Over the low remains of one of the stone walls, she could see sunlight rippling across the rolling waves of Loch Laren. The walls of Dunleith Castle less than a mile south rose like a vision from a fairy tale.

Strange, how she could come to think of this place as home in such a short space of time. Dangerous, really. Yet she couldn't prevent the warm feeling of belonging she had here, just as she couldn't crush the emotions that stirred in her at the mere thought of Alec. She glanced at the man sitting across from her, watching as he ate a thick slice of crusty bread and cold ham. How the devil could she find the simple act of watching him eat so utterly fascinating? She couldn't deny the truth any longer: She was painfully besotted with the man.

During their meal, Alec maintained a proper distance, keeping to his side of the quilt. Yet it didn't prevent her from thinking of how it might be to sit beside him, with his arm around her shoulders, snuggled close against his warmth. She was foolish to want such things. But she couldn't suppress the longing. Although the food was delicious, Meg could scarcely find an appetite for the crusty, fresh bread, thick slices of juicy pink ham, wedges of cheese, and flaky apple tarts.

After breakfast, Seamus lost interest in his human companions when they packed the remaining food away in a wicker basket. He trotted away from them, disappearing into the tall grass and fading heather that spread out across the rolling hills behind the fort. Although the blood of great bird-hunters flowed through the dog's veins, Seamus preferred chasing rabbits. "If you don't soon train Seamus to hunt birds, he will never be a good bird dog."

"He can chase what he likes. I've lost my taste for hunting." Alec rested his wrist on his raised knee and turned his face into the breeze whispering across the loch.

The shrill cry of an osprey pierced the quiet morning. Meg watched the hawk glide over the surface of the loch, brown wings spread wide in its hunt for prey. She supposed Alec's years in the army had spoiled any love he might have had in killing for sport.

Alec breathed in the cold morning air, as though he were savoring an expensive perfume. "I haven't been here in years."

Meg brushed pastry crumbs from the front of her black wool mantle. "I remember when you and Colin and Niall would come here and play."

"Aye. We were the bravest of Fionn's soldiers, holding off the marauders from the south." Alec stared across the loch, his expression growing thoughtful. "Wee lads, playing at war. Not really understanding what war was really all about."

Alec had come to know all about war, Meg thought. The knowledge had nearly cost him his life. She shivered in a cold breeze that swept across the loch and penetrated the heavy dark cashmere of her mantle. She frowned at Alec. "I doubt Dr. Addison would approve of what you're doing."

Alec gave her a devilish grin. "I've been in and out of enough hospitals in the past nine years to know the only way to get stronger is to get up and move about."

"If you aren't careful, you shall savage your health." She noted the ruddy color the wind had painted on his cheeks. She rose and clasped her hands at her waist. "You've been out long enough. We should go back to the house before you catch a chill."

Alec tilted his head, grinning up at her in that way he had of tripping her heart. "I've never known a woman who could manage to be so bewitching while she was scolding me."

Bewitching. Her pulse danced to a quicker beat. Did he really find her in the least way bewitching? "No doubt you've given many women abundant reasons to scold you."

He rose in one fluid movement. "I never tried to give any woman reason to be angry with me."

Meg lifted one brow as he closed the distance between them, hoping she looked aloof in spite of the trembling in her limbs. "I suppose you think kidnapping isn't an offense that might make a woman angry."

He grimaced. "I suppose it might. Yet I'm hoping the woman I kidnapped might find it in her heart to forgive me. You see, I never worried much about what a woman might think of me." He drew his hand down her arm, from her elbow to her wrist. The soft black wool covering her arm wasn't protection against a touch that spread a tingling warmth in his wake. "Until now."

Meg stared into the pure blue of his eyes and imagined she saw longing there. It must be only her own emotions reflected in the pale blue depths, she assured herself, her own need. This tingling excitement was certainly not justified. Was it?

"I care very much what you think of me."

259

"I think you are a fool if you don't guard your health. If you're not careful, you shall soon find yourself back in bed."

Alec wiggled his eyebrows. "I wouldn't mind finding myself back in bed, if you would join me."

She arched one brow, hoping he wouldn't see the excitement behind her cool facade. "You should be thinking about mending your health, instead of . . . other, more base notions."

He traced the curve of her jaw with his fingertips, his bare skin chilled by the breeze. "When you're around, I can't help but think of those *base* notions."

She dismissed his teasing with a shake of her head. Dismissing her own base notions was much more difficult. Lust was a powerful emotion, especially when coupled with affection. "Let's go back. You shouldn't take a chill. And put on your gloves."

He took her hands, holding her when she started to leave. "Let's stay just a little while longer."

Alec tugged on her hands and she followed, like a mare on a tether. "You're very stubborn."

He drew her close until her mantle pressed against his legs, and her pulse pounded against the gathered cashmere collar. "Aye, it's one of the qualities that makes me the ideal mate for a stubborn lady like you."

"Very amusing." She smiled up at him. "I suppose I shouldn't mind if you savage your health. You shall leave me quite the wealthy widow should you die."

"My own bonnie Meg, I intend to plague you for a long time to come."

Something warm unfurled inside of her at the casual way he called her his own. Something dangerous and compelling all at once—hope. "Then I suggest you start taking better care of your health. Instead of running about in storms without a coat and hat, like a proper muttonheaded dolt. And now standing out here in the cold without a hat."

He pressed her hands against his heart. "Ah, how your loving words warm my heart."

She smiled, hoping her expression was haughty enough to disguise her attraction for him. "Save your wicked Highland charm."

"Only for you." He lifted her hands and pressed his lips against her right wrist, above her black glove—his kiss so warm, so soft, like the graze of rose petals warmed by the sun. "Do you realize I haven't had a moment alone with you in days? I think your grandmother is afraid I'll force my wicked way with you if she isn't there to protect you."

She should pull away from him. Yet she couldn't convince herself to step away from his inviting heat. "I can't imagine why my grandmother doesn't approve of you. But then, she has never approved of any sort of brigand. So I wouldn't feel as though she has singled only you out for her displeasure."

He grinned. "She certainly approves of Blandford. My cousin always seems to be sniffing at your skirts, with your grandmother's approval."

Alec had noticed Blandford's attendance on her. It was a normal reaction for a male who believes he owns a female, she assured herself. No need to think he was jealous. Or that he cared. Or any of the other foolish notions flitting through her besotted brain. "Given your low opinion of Lord Blandford, I'm surprised you haven't asked him to leave."

"I couldn't do that. I wouldn't like to give Blandford the satisfaction of knowing how jealous I am of the attention he pays you."

Jealous? She managed to crush the sudden surge of excitement inside of her at the intriguing thought of this man being jealous of her. "I suppose jealousy is a normal emotion for a male to feel when he has proprietary notions for a female."

"Proprietary notions?" He slid his arms around her waist. "Is that what I have for you, Meg?"

A tremor rippled through her as his arms closed around her. He was so close, she could see the faint lines time had carved into the skin at the corners of his beautiful eyes. So close she could feel the warm brush of his breath against her cheek, sweet with the cider he had imbibed at breakfast. So close, all she need do was lift up a bit, raise up onto her toes, and she could kiss his smiling lips.

She stepped back from him before she did something foolish, disengaging herself from his light embrace, hoping he hadn't felt her treacherous response to him. "We're married, which means you have some thought of ownership. Which in turn spurs your natural male tendency toward jealousy when another male intrudes into your territory."

He lifted one black brow, humor sparkling in his eyes. "I see you've made a science of studying the male of the human species."

Meg walked away from him, pausing at one of the ruined walls, which still stood five feet high. "It's important to understand one's opponent in any situation."

"Opponent?" Alec joined her at the wall, leaning his hip against the ancient stones. He studied her a moment, as though she were some rare species he had never come upon before. "That implies we have different goals in mind."

She slanted him a glance. "That's obvious, isn't it?"

"I wonder." He glanced out across the loch, turning his face into the breeze that tousled his thick black waves. "Are the things we want from life so very different?"

Were they? Dare she imagine they might make a life together? It was such a dangerous notion. Yet one she couldn't dismiss. No matter how hard she tried. Every day with Alec made her wonder if she could ever leave him and walk away with her heart.

Alec studied the woman standing beside him. Meg was staring out across the loch, as though she were searching for answers to mysteries scrawled across the rocky face of Ben Lyon. He sensed the uncertainty in her, saw the tension etched upon her beautiful face. In this case, where there was doubt, there was hope. He turned, leaning back against the wall, smiling at her. "Did you ever miss the Highlands when you lived in England, Meg?"

She shrugged. "I grew up here. It's only natural to miss the place where you were born and bred."

The Highlands were in her blood. Even if she wished they weren't. "I always carried a sprig of heather with me all the while I was away from here. In some small way it made me feel close to home, no matter where I was."

She looked up at him, a fine line etched between her light brown brows. "Why did you leave?"

"I've often asked myself that question." He tilted his head back and drew a deep breath into his lungs. A soft trace of heather remained on the cold, damp air, the last breath of dying blossoms. "I suppose I wasn't satisfied being the Earl of Dunleith's second son."

"But certainly there would always have been a place for you here."

"Aye. I could have taken control of the Sterling estate. Father had planned on it. But it wasn't enough for me. I had a need in me. I had to make my own way. I guess I wanted glory." He laughed at his own foolishness. "Whatever that is."

Meg pulled her mantle close around her, as though

she were suddenly cold. "I'm afraid Colin had the same appetite for glory. I remember Father was set against him purchasing a commission. But nothing could change my brother's mind when he had it set on something."

"There are times when I wonder if Colin would have purchased a commission if not for me and all my raving about adventure."

Meg looked up into his eyes, and he felt in that moment she could see the pain carved across his soul. "You can't blame yourself for Colin's decisions. He was a strong-willed man."

"Aye." Alec grinned at her. "Stubborn. It runs in your clan."

She lifted her chin. "There is nothing wrong with keeping firm convictions."

"No, there isn't." He slipped his arms around her waist and tugged her close, smiling into her startled expression. "I have a few firm convictions of my own."

Meg pushed against his chest in a halfhearted attempt to escape his embrace. "We should go back. You really shouldn't push yourself so hard. You'll end up ill again."

"Careful, Meg." He smoothed a wayward strand of hair back from her cold cheek and carefully tucked it behind her ear. "You'll have me thinking you care what happens to me."

She glanced away from him, hiding the expression in her eyes. "Your illness was quite a nuisance. I would rather not go through it again."

And she would rather boil in oil before she told him she cared for him. "My darling Meg. I don't know what I'd do without your sweet, wifely affection."

A smile escaped her tight control, a warm flicker that lasted a moment before she forced it back into hiding. Yet that glimpse of warmth was enough to set his blood pounding. "Spend a great deal of time seducing other women, I suspect."

"There's a woman I'd dearly love to seduce." He pressed his lips against her brow. "A bonnie lass with eyes as green as a summer glen."

She curled her fingers against the black wool of his coat. "Until another lass catches your Highland fancy."

"There's only one woman for me now." He brushed aside the black satin ribbon from her bonnet and nuzzled the warm skin beneath her ear, soft golden curls tickling his nose, the lush scent of vanilla swirling through his senses. "And you can't know how much I want to . . . taste her."

"Oh," Meg whispered, her body tensing with surprise.

"I want to slide my lips over her pale skin, explore all her lovely curves, lush valleys."

"MacLaren, I really must insist you—"

"I want to lick her, taste every delicate inch of her." He touched the tip of his tongue to her skin, tasting her.

She trembled, a soft gasp escaping her lips. "Alec, this is hardly—"

"My own bonnie Meg, you can't know how much I want to make love to you."

She clutched the front of his coat, staring up at him, her eyes filled with a horrible turmoil. "If you aren't in love with me, how can you imagine making love to me? Is it lust, Alec? Or is it simply some need in you to bend me to your will?"

Alec hadn't given his feelings for her much consideration. He cared for her. He wanted her. That was really all he had taken time to acknowledge. The pounding desire that hammered at him each time she was near tended to wash away any attempts at rational thought.

Yet now, looking into her eyes, seeing her fear, her longing, he acknowledged her need. She needed more from him than the simple pleasures that could be found in a lusty tumble. She needed more than the reassurance he wouldn't betray their marriage vows. She needed more than friendship, loyalty, and lust. More than a home filled with children. And for the first time he wondered if he could give her everything she needed.

He smoothed his hand over her cold cheek. "I don't want to bend your will, Meg. I only want the chance to be your husband, in every way."

She lowered her eyes, veiling any emotion he might find there. "Is lust enough to make a marriage, Alec?"

He frowned, disturbed by the matter-of-fact way she had of labeling the spark that burned between them. "It's a beginning."

She looked up at him, her expression carefully scrubbed of emotion. "And what happens when the fires of lust crumble into ashes? What happens to this marriage?"

"What makes you think the fire will die, Meg?"

"The fire dies, MacLaren." She eased out of his embrace and walked away from him, putting several feet of cold morning air between them before she turned to face him. "My father loved my mother, and he still managed to betray her. How do you suppose that made her feel?"

Alec held her determined stare. "Probably as horrible as your father felt when your mother betrayed him."

Meg's lips parted on a startled gasp. "How dare you! My mother never betrayed my father."

"Perhaps not with another man. But your mother betrayed your father by not having faith in him."

"How can you expect her to have faith in him after what happened? How could she ever trust him again?"

"It's only when our faith is shaken, our trust tested, that we see how strong they really are."

She hugged her arms to her waist and lifted her face into the breeze, the satin ribbon of her small black velvet bonnet fluttering beneath her chin. "Once trust is broken it can never be repaired."

"I know you refuse to believe in your father's innocence, which means it will only be more difficult to convince you to trust me." He released his breath in a long sigh that turned to steam on the cold air. "The truth is, I don't know what I can do to make you trust me."

Meg slanted him a glance. "I find trusting you a rather dangerous prospect."

"Is it a more appealing prospect to go back to living with your mother and grandmother, pretending I don't exist?"

"It's safer."

"I care for you, Meg." He moved toward her. "I want this marriage to succeed."

She closed her eyes when he touched her cheek. "You want children."

"Aye. I want children. I want a home." He smoothed his fingertips over the curve of her tightly clenched jaw. "I want you in my life."

She tilted her head, a sad smile curving her lips. "You want me in your bed."

"Aye." He grinned at her, hoping to lighten her mood. He rested his hands on her shoulders and turned her until she faced him. "I want you so much I ache."

She frowned. "Do you?"

He squeezed her slender shoulders beneath the soft black wool. "I wake up in the morning wanting you. I go to bed at night wanting you. And sleep is no hiding place from you. You haunt me. Day. Night. Waking. Sleeping."

She brushed her fingers over his coat, above the place where his heart was thudding against the wall of his chest. "You do have a way about you, Alec Mac-Laren. A way of making a woman think of dangerous things. Wicked notions. Wanton desires. It's almost enough to make a sane woman do something rather foolish."

He slid his arms around her and pulled her close against him. Through the layers of their clothes he felt only a hint of firm breasts against his chest, enough to twist his vitals into a tight knot of longing. "Be my wife, Meg."

Meg twisted her hand in his coat. "I don't know if—"

"Earl of Dunleith, stand away from the woman," a man shouted from the far wall of the fort. "Prepare t'meet yer maker."

Chapter Twenty

Meg jumped, startled by the rough-looking intruder. He stood no more than twenty feet away from them, a slender, dark-haired man of average height, dressed in shabby dark clothes. The rims of his gray eyes were unnaturally dark, giving his thin face a strange owlish look. He stared at Alec with a raw hatred that made her certain he had every intention of using the pistol he held in his hand.

"Alec," she whispered, squeezing the sleeve of his coat.

Alec stepped forward, easing Meg behind him, shielding her from the intruder. "Who the devil are you?"

"Diarmid Hensen. And I'm here t'send ye t'hell, where ye belong." A loud click ripped the quiet morning, the stark sound of a pistol being cocked. "Say yer prayers, Dunleith."

"No!" Meg scrambled from behind Alec and plastered herself back against her husband's chest. She stared at Hensen and the pistol he held, her heart pounding against the wall of her chest.

"Out of the way, woman!" Hensen shouted.

"Why are you doing this?" Meg demanded.

"Meg." Alec gripped her shoulders. "Get behind me."

Meg dug in her heels, resisting as Alec tried to force her out of danger. "He wants to shoot you!"

"I'm goin' t'kill the bastard!" Hensen said. "Now out of me way."

"No." Meg pressed back against Alec. "I won't let you do this."

"Damnation!" Alec gripped her waist with both hands and lifted her off the ground. He pivoted and plunked her down on the ground near the wall. "Stay put."

Meg turned and stared up into his furious blue eyes. "Can't you see? He's going to shoot you."

"Not if I can help it," he said, his voice a harsh whisper. "Now stay out of the way before you get hurt."

Meg gestured toward the man with the pistol. "But . . ."

Alec squeezed her shoulders. "I don't need to be worrying about you right now, sweetheart. Stay out of my way. If he shoots, run toward the house, as fast as you can."

"I'll do no such—"

He shook her gently. "Do as I say."

"Stubborn brute," Meg muttered, watching Alec walk away from her. *Dear lord, please save the scoundrel!* she prayed silently.

Diarmid Hensen was not accustomed to pistols, Alec decided from the awkward way the man was holding the weapon. He doubted the man was much of a marksman, but at this range he didn't need to be. He had to get the man turned, get Meg out of the line of fire, before he made his move.

"Stand steady!" Hensen shouted, turning, keeping the pistol trained on Alec.

Alec kept moving in slow, steady strides, putting more distance between the pistol and Meg, keeping Hensen off balance. From the shabby state of his clothes, he wasn't a very good thief. If he was a thief at all. The man looked as though he hadn't had a decent meal in a month. In fact, from the look of his eyes, and the coal dust under his nails, Alec would wager Hensen was a collier. "If you're after money, I haven't any with me."

"I dunna want yer money." Hensen steadied the pistol with his other hand. "I want t' see ye pay fer what ye did te me family."

Alec hesitated, staring at the man. "What the devil do you mean?"

"Ye who killed me wife, me wee bairn," Hensen said, his voice breaking with emotion. "Now ye'll pay fer it."

Alec raised his hand. "Before you murder an unarmed man, you'll tell me exactly how I managed to kill your family, when I've never seen you before in my life."

" 'Twas ye who sent me Selina back underground. Ye who put the weight on her back and forced her to work like an animal." Tears spilled down Hensen's cheeks. "The babe come too soon. They both died. Both of 'em. And it's on yer head."

Alec lifted his hands to his sides. "I honestly don't have any idea of what you're talking about. But I'm willing to listen, if you'll put down the pistol."

Hensen swiped the back of his hand across his cheek. "We mean so little to such a big, fine . . ." His words dissolved in a grunt.

Alec frowned, watching as the man buckled at the

271

knees and crumpled against the ground. The pistol spilled from his limp hand, discharging with the impact. The bullet plowed into the wall a foot to Alec's left.

Meg stood behind the crumpled man, clutching a rock in her hand. "Should I hit him again?"

Alec stared at her, stunned by her actions. "Why the devil didn't you do as I ordered?"

Meg's eyes narrowed. "As you ordered?"

"I told you to stay out of the way."

Meg tilted her chin at a defiant angle. "I had some ridiculous notion of saving your worthless life."

"You could have gotten yourself killed." Alec knelt on one knee beside Hensen. "If he had heard you coming up behind him, he could easily have shot you."

"In case you didn't notice, he was far too concerned with shooting *you*."

"I had the situation in hand," Alec said, pressing his fingers against the pulse point in Hensen's neck.

Seamus chose that moment to come investigate the commotion. He emerged from the tall grass, trotted into the fort, and sniffed at the man who lay still against the ground.

"Now you come to our rescue." Meg tossed the rock to the ground, where it fell against the moss with a dull thump. She frowned at Alec. "I didn't . . . kill him. Did I?"

"No." Alec lifted the pistol and stood. "I suspect you've only given him a headache."

Meg clasped her hands at her waist. "What did he mean when he said you had killed his family?"

Alec rubbed the taut muscles at the nape of his neck. "I don't know, but I intend to find out."

Alec sat on the edge of his desk, listening as Diarmid Hensen told of the circumstances leading up to his attempt to murder him. As Hensen's story unfolded, Alec realized the man had good reason to want to see the Earl of Dunleith dead.

Diarmid Hensen sat on a Sheraton armchair beside the desk, with a snifter of brandy clutched between his trembling hands. "We had no choice. The manager would've sent me to debtors' prison if we had refused te do as he said. And so me wife went t'work underground. All day long she'd haul coal, a hundred and a half weight upon her back, until she was weepin' from the pain of it."

Alec clenched his hand into a fist on his thigh, fighting to keep his composure as Hensen told of the conditions his wife had been forced to endure.

"She lost the bairn. And a day later, she died." Hensen stared up at Alec, bitter tears glittering in his eyes. "It wanna supposed t'be like that. We thought the changes would stay, but the old earl died, and with him went all the changes he'd made."

Alec held Hensen's accusing stare. "I knew of my father's mines at Culross. I never knew he had one at Tranent."

"The earl bought the mine at Tranent last year. How is it you dinna know about it?"

"I was in the army. I didn't return until after my father had died."

"Yer father was a fine mon, he was. He come t'see us all, he did. Told us he was goin' te make changes that had been in place at his other mines. He told us he was hopin', in time, the other mine owners would see they could still make a profit and not have women and children underground. Then he died." Diarmid lifted the snifter with both hands. After taking a long drink, he swiped the back of his hand across his lips. "The next we knew, there was a new manager, and with him all the old ways."

Alec fixed Diarmid in a steady gaze, the weight of his responsibilities pressing against his chest. "I didn't know anything about the mine, or my father's reforms."

"But we were told 'twas ye who hired the new manager. The new earl who wanted more profit."

Alec thought of Blandford, and how very much he would like to strangle the man. "My cousin assumed the title after my father died."

Diarmid frowned. "Yer cousin?"

"Aye. It's complicated. For a time I was legally dead."

Diarmid shook his head, as though trying to understand how a man sitting before him could be legally dead. "Then it's yer cousin who is responsible fer Selina," he said, his voice growing dark with rage.

"Nothing can come of further violence." No matter how appealing it might seem, Alec thought. "Although I realize nothing I can do will bring back your wife and child, I can assure you, I shall make certain my father's reforms are reestablished."

"I believe ye, sir." Diarmid rubbed the back of his head. "And I'm dreadful sorry fer almost killin' ye this mornin'."

"I'm glad you came to me, Diarmid. I'm glad you told me about the mine."

"I'm sure now that ye know what's 'appening, ye'll make a difference, sir."

Alec glanced at the portrait of his parents hanging on the wall across from his desk. They would not be proud of him. He had never thought to shoulder the responsibilities of Dunleith. And, it seemed, he was making a complete mess of things.

After Diarmid had been shown to the room where he would stay the night, Alec went searching for his cousin. He found Blandford in the blue drawing room with Meg and her grandmother. Something dangerous turned over inside of him when he saw Blandford sitting beside Meg on one of the sofas. It took all of his will to rein in his anger as he walked toward his wife.

Meg rose and met him halfway across the room. "Is he gone?"

Alec smiled at his brave lady. When he thought of how she had risked her life to protect him, he wanted to grab and shake her almost as much as he wanted to hold her and kiss her. Lord, she had scared the life out of him. "He'll be staying the night."

Meg lifted her brows, her eyes glittering with curiosity. "He must have had something interesting to tell you."

Alec nodded. "Most interesting."

Blandford picked a piece of lint from the sleeve of his claret-colored coat. "You have an interesting way of dealing with criminals, cousin. I never would have invited one to stay the evening."

"I can't understand how you could allow that murderer into this house." Hermione pressed her hand to her heart. "What shall keep him from murdering us all in the night? When I think of it, I could faint."

"Dear lady." Blandford rushed to Hermione's side. He took her pudgy hand and patted it gently while he gave Alec a reproachful look. "You can be assured I shall let no harm come to you or the other ladies."

"A murderer!" Hermione pressed the back of her hand to her brow. "You have exposed us all to danger, Dunleith."

"Diarmid Hensen isn't a murderer." Alec looked at Blandford. "Although he had reason to want to see the Earl of Dunleith dead."

Hermione huffed. "I imagine there are more than a few who would like to see the Earl of Dunleith dead. You seem to have that effect on people."

Alec ignored the barb. He fixed his cousin in a steady

stare. "Apparently you didn't care to keep the reforms my father initiated at Tranent, cousin. The manager you hired to run the mine has managed to overset everything my father had in place."

"Tranent?" Blandford tapped his forefinger against his lower lip. "Oh yes, I recall. Several of the other mine owners came to see me. They pointed out the profit I could make if I were to initiate a few changes in the mine. One of them recommended a man to run the operation. Profits went up the first month. I should think you would be more than satisfied with the results."

Alec took a step toward his cousin, then caught himself. It wouldn't do to strangle the man. No matter how tempting it might seem. "The changes your manager made involved sending women and children into the mines to haul coal. Diarmid Hensen's wife and unborn child died as a result of those changes."

Wildon stiffened. "I'm certain the manager employed the same methods all the other mine owners are using."

"That's exactly what my father was trying to change. That's the reason he purchased the mine at Tranent, to introduce the same reforms that have been employed in the west since the turn of the century."

Meg stared at Wildon. "You allowed women and children to work in the mines?"

Wildon tugged on a lace-trimmed cuff of his shirt, color rising in his pale cheeks. "You must understand, I never realized anything so vile would come of hiring the man."

"Of course you didn't," Hermione said, smiling at the viscount. "You did what you thought was best."

Wildon's lips curved into a grateful smile. "You have a kind and understanding heart, dear lady."

"Excuse me, I have a great deal of work to do." Alec

left the room, before his control could snap and he tossed his cousin and Lady Hermione Chadburne out the door. Still, it was his own hand in this tragedy that cut deeper than his anger at Blandford.

Meg froze on the threshold of the library. It was past midnight. She had come here hoping to find a book to ease her restlessness. Instead she found the cause of her vexation, sitting in a leather wing-back chair near the fireplace. Alec had sequestered himself in the library this afternoon and had failed to emerge even for dinner. Apparently the demons that had driven him into seclusion still remained.

"I'm sorry, I didn't expect you to still be here," she said. "I didn't mean to disturb you."

Alec rested his chin on the steeple of his fingers, regarding her while a smile shaped the sensual curves of his lips. "You've been disturbing me since that first night in London."

Heat rose across her breasts. "Have I?"

"Day and night."

Goodness, the man had a way of making her feel as though she were the most desirable woman on the face of the earth. He was definitely dangerous. Seamus left his place beside Alec to greet her. After extricating her foot from beneath his big paw, she ruffled the dog's silky ears and praised him softly, all the while wondering if Alec would prefer to be left alone. Although she knew she should leave—it was the wise and infinitely more cautious decision—she also acknowledged a need deep inside of her: She had been alone far too long.

Alec leaned forward in his chair, powerful muscles shifting beneath the tight-fitting pale gray wool of his trousers. He had removed his coat and neckcloth, opened the first few buttons of his shirt—a lion relaxing in his lair. "You couldn't sleep?"

"No." She stood on the threshold, contemplating the wisdom of staying in this place alone with this man. "It's been a difficult day."

"Aye." He rubbed the back of his neck, and she caught herself wondering what it might be like really to be this man's wife. To massage the taut muscles of his neck when he had a vexing day. To fall asleep in his arms. To awaken to the sight of his smile. Foolish notions that were impossible to prevent.

"I spent the better part of the afternoon and evening reading my father's journals." He stared into the fire as he spoke. "I keep thinking, if I had known about the conditions at Tranent months ago, I might have prevented that poor woman's death."

She ached for this man, sensing his pain as sharply as if it were her own. "You can't blame yourself for what happened."

He released his breath in a long sigh. "I'm afraid I can. I should have known about the mine."

She should leave. It was the safe thing to do. Alec had a way of muddling her thoughts, until all she could do was feel. She should definitely leave. Now. Instead she stepped inside, defying her own best judgment concerning Alec MacLaren. She closed the door, blew out the flame of her taper, and set the brass holder on a table near the door. Although the wall sconces had been extinguished, the fire on the hearth cast a golden light across the brass and mahogany bookcases.

"Your father's steward or man of affairs should have told you all you needed to know," Meg said.

"I wish he could have. Unfortunately, the old gentleman is dead. He died three weeks after Blandford discharged him."

"I'm sorry."

"So am I." Alec came to his feet, pacing the short distance to the fireplace, where he rested his arm against the mantel. "Aside from the land and tenants, there are so many investments. Textiles, shipping, banking, mining operations. It's hard to get my arms around it all. The man I hired as steward hasn't had time to acquaint himself with everything."

Her heart pounded against the wall of her chest as she approached Alec. There was no help for it, she supposed, no chance to control this alarming excitement he ignited in her when he was near. She had to face it, just as she had to face the longing for him, the treacherous need to be with him. Seamus trotted over to the hearth and flopped against the carpet near Alec. She understood why the animal sought his master.

"If your steward hasn't been able to learn everything about your father's investments, why do you think you should have been able to do it?"

"Patrick would have known." Firelight flickered against the taut lines of Alec's face. "My brother was the one meant to take over the reins from my father. He wouldn't have made a mess of things the way I have."

She rested her hand on his arm, absorbing the warmth of his skin through the soft white cambric. "I'm certain you're just as capable of filling the role as Patrick was."

He glanced at her, his blue eyes filled with doubts of his own worth. "I wish I could be that certain."

A thick lock of hair had tumbled over his brow. She hesitated only an instant before smoothing the silky strands back from his brow. "I have a feeling you can accomplish anything you set your mind to."

Alec smiled, warmth kindling in the depths of his eyes along with a hundred questions. He slid his hand down her arm, the heat of his palm soaking through the emerald velvet of her dressing gown, the white linen beneath. "Anything?"

Meg realized what lay beneath the soft question. A prudent woman would turn and leave, retreat before it was too late. Yet a part of her realized it had been too late the night he had swept her away from London. "Anything," she said, her voice a soft whisper.

He slid his fingers into the thick, unbound waves at her nape, his long fingers cradling the back of her head. He stepped closer, while coaxing her toward him with a soft pressure on her nape. "Why did you step between me and that pistol this morning?"

She rested her hand on his chest. Beneath the white cambric warm from his body, she felt the solid thud of his heart, beating to the same frantic rhythm as her own. "I was afraid he would shoot you. I thought he might hesitate to shoot a woman."

"My brave lady." He slid his arm around her waist, drawing her closer. "You scared fifteen years off my life. All I could think about was a bullet ripping into you."

The dark concern in his voice warmed her. "In that case you wouldn't have an icy Englishwoman to plague your life."

"Meg," he whispered, nuzzling the sensitive skin beneath her right ear. She leaned against him, melting in his warmth. He pressed his lips against her temple, rested his cheek against her hair. "I want you as my wife, in every way."

His deep voice brushed against her, heavy with the same longing that dwelled inside of her. "Do you, Alec?"

Chapter Twenty-one

"Be my wife, Meg," Alec whispered, desire flickering like flame in his blue eyes. "Let me hold you this night, and all our nights to come."

Meg found no resistance inside of her. No thought to pull away from him. For too many years she had dreamed of this moment. For too many nights she had longed for his kisses, for the touch of his hands against her skin, for the mysteries he could share with her. For all the reasons she should protect her heart, she needed this more.

He lowered his head. She rose onto her toes, meeting his kiss, welcoming the tantalizing slide of his tongue into her mouth. He tasted of brandy and a spice that was unidentifiable, a taste she would forever think of as Alec.

He closed his arms around her, drawing her up against him. She slid her arms around his neck, holding him as she had dreamed of holding him most of her life. A tingling sensation spiraled from the tips of her breasts, coaxing her to brush against him. A deep growl emanated from low in his throat, the primitive sound whispering to the wanton he had awakened deep inside of her.

Alec kissed her as though the world could crumble into ashes around them and he wouldn't notice or stop or care. He slid his hands over the curves of her bottom, lifting her into the heat of his loins, allowing her to feel the hard thrust of his aroused flesh through the layers of their clothes. Shocking. Tantalizing. Tempting. A pulse flared deep in the core of her most private region, a bittersweet ache, a drizzle of liquid heat.

She tried to think of all the reasons she shouldn't be doing this. Yet she couldn't scrape together enough fear or anger to strengthen her crumbling resolve. She might be insane, but she wanted him.

A soft sound came from deep inside of her, a primitive plea to strip away the barriers between them. She needed to feel his skin against hers. She needed his hands upon her bare flesh, his lips, his tongue, all the things he had promised, and more.

He slipped his hand between them, as though he understood her plea without words, as though he needed her as much as she needed him. And that was what she allowed herself to believe. She clung to the need she tasted in his kiss, the desire she felt in the fine trembling of his powerful muscles, the hope inside of her that one day lust would deepen into love.

He tugged open the sash of her dressing gown, flicked open the pearl buttons lining the front of her gown, tearing the soft white lawn in his haste. Yet she was beyond caring. She wanted only to rip away the barriers, to lie with him, to know him as she had longed to know him these past few days while lying in her lonely bed.

It seemed inevitable, the final chapter in a book that had been written long ago. She belonged in Alec's arms. She always had. She always would.

He slid his hands inside of her nightgown, warm fingers grazing her skin, rough palms sliding over her shoulders, stripping away her nightgown and dressing gown. The garments slid over her skin, brushing her, tingling flesh more sensitive than she had ever imagined. Her clothes tumbled around her ankles in a soft sigh of surrender. She stood trembling, bathed in firelight, touched by the warmth of Alec. He slid his hands over her arms, from her shoulders to her wrists, warming her as his gaze traveled over her, warmer than the breath of fire from the hearth.

"Lord, you're beautiful," he said, lowering his lips to the joining of her neck her shoulder.

Meg caught her breath as he drew her skin between his teeth. He slid his hands down her back, spreading warmth across her skin. She slid her hands over the soft cambric covering his shoulders. Yet it wasn't cloth she wanted against her skin. She wanted to feel the brush of his skin against hers. She fumbled with the buttons lining the front of his shirt, unfastening three before he lowered his head to her breast and she lost any hope for directing her trembling fingers.

Sensation chased sensation as he tugged and suckled and drove every thought from her mind. He slid his palm down, over her belly, sliding lower and lower until his fingers trailed in the soft curls between her thighs. He touched her, sliding his long fingers along the soft feminine folds made slick with her need for him. He drew his damp fingers upward, parting her, finding a secret bud nestled beneath the soft petals. Good heavens, she had never felt anything so . . . startling.

"What are you . . ." Her words tangled with a sharp

stab of pleasure, shredding her thoughts. "Oh my, that's very . . . I never . . . Oh!"

He slipped one long finger inside her feminine passage. "Blessed heaven, you feel good," he whispered.

He flicked his tongue over the tip of her breast, took the tight tip into his mouth while he stroked that secret place where sensation sparked and shot in all directions. Slowly he eased his finger in and out of her. She gripped his shoulders, clinging to him, certain her legs would buckle from the exquisite sensations streaking through her. Pleasure rose inside of her, swift and sharp, catching her unaware. She tipped back her head, allowing the sound to rise inside of her, to crest and flow with the sparkling rush of passion.

"That's it, my own, sing your pleasure for me." Alec lifted her trembling body in his arms and laid her down upon the crumpled linen and velvet of her nightclothes. He covered her, his warmth radiating through the layers of his clothes.

She lay beneath him, trembling with need. The soft wool of his trousers brushed the insides of her thighs. The cool air whispered across her damp nipples, sending shivers through her. With each breath her breasts lifted in quiet invitation. Yet he remained out of reach, touching her breasts with nothing more than the heat of his body. Firelight flickered golden against his face, illuminating his smile.

"Tell me you want me, Meg," he whispered, drawing one fingertip down the center of her chest, the heat of his hand grazing her breasts.

"I want you, Alec," she whispered, her heart in her words.

"Meg," he whispered, lowering his head toward her.

She slid her arms around his shoulders, drawing him against her, his clothes rough against her, stimulating her bare skin. He crushed her lips beneath his, opening his mouth over hers, devouring her as though he were as hungry for her as she was for him.

His fingers grazed her belly as he unfastened his trouser buttons. She felt the heat of him through the soft white cotton of his drawers. Instinctively she lifted her hips, brushing her aching flesh against him, seeking the mystery only he could reveal. He passed his hand between their bodies, unfastening his drawers. She gasped against his lips, stunned by the feel of his hard shaft pulsing hotly against her thigh.

"Don't be afraid of me, angel," he whispered, lifting to look down into her eyes. "Never be afraid of me."

She smiled up into his handsome face. "I'm not afraid of you, Alec."

"Meg," he whispered, lowering his smiling lips toward hers. "My own bonnie Meg."

He kissed her, long and deep, dipping his tongue into her mouth, withdrawing, until she followed his lead, teasing him with the same plunge and retreat he played. He shifted his hips, pressing his aroused flesh against her moist entrance, while he passed his hand between their bodies and touched her. He slid his fingers over her nether lips, finding once more that tiny bud that ignited sensation, torturing her with pleasure, until she trembled beneath him, until she arched her hips, until she begged for what lay just beyond her grasp.

With one sharp thrust he came into her, plunging past her virginal barrier, altering her body for the rest of her days. She cried out with the sudden pain, twisting her fingers in the soft white cambric covering his back. She held him, praying she wouldn't do something unforgivably gauche—such as faint.

"There's no easy way around it," he whispered, nuzzling the sensitive skin beneath her ear. "The worst is over."

285

She drew in her breath. "You obviously aren't observing from my angle."

He smiled against her neck. "Trust me."

Trust me—many a woman had been led to ruin by following that advice when given by a man. She closed her eyes and clenched her jaw, determined to endure to the finish with dignity. It was utterly amazing how something that had promised to be so exquisite could turn out to be such a debacle. Yet she should have known better. Her experience with men should have warned her.

Alec brushed his lips across hers, the warmth of his breath brushing her cheek. He cupped her bottom in his hands, lifted her away from the floor, and pulled her close against him. "Relax."

Relax! Only a man would say such a ridiculous thing at a time like this.

He shifted his hips, withdrawing until he nearly left her, then easing into her again, all the while kissing her, caressing her, sliding his hands over her breasts, her belly and lower, teasing that secret little bud of sensation. He drew the pain away with the slow ebb and flow of his body into hers. Coaxed pleasure with the touch of his hands, his lips, his tongue.

Although the pressure remained, that odd sensation of his length and breadth inside of her triggered an entirely new response. Involuntarily, her muscles clenched, trying to hold him each time he withdrew. Her body adjusted to his rhythm, moving in time with him, arching her hips, seeking the unexpected pleasure that shimmered on the horizon, like the sun rising slowly in the morning sky.

Pleasure rose inside of her, warming her, hotter than the sun. She lifted to meet the pleasure, to greet it, to exalt in it. She gripped his shirt, pulling hard, as her body lifted into his, and he sank deep into her. She felt the hot stream of his essence pump inside of her, heard his soft growl of release, while her world did a lazy spin out of control.

He eased against her, settling into her embrace. She lay with her arms around his shoulders, her cheek pressed against his neck, breathing in the exhilarating musk of his skin. She pressed her lips to Alec's damp neck, flicked her tongue against his skin, tasting him. She savored the weight of him, pressing her down into the soft cushion of her clothes, his arms tight around her, cradling her as though he never intended to let her go.

Never would she have imagined it was possible to rise from such pain into such blinding pleasure. Yet she knew with a certainty that came from the deepest part of her soul that it would only feel this way with Alec. From the time she was a child she had always felt a connection to this man. This moment of sublime pleasure was simply a physical completion to all the years she had dreamed of him.

Something cold poked her shoulder. She glanced up, straight into Seamus's curious expression. "Good heavens."

"Go," Alec said, waving his hand at the dog.

Seamus tilted his head, giving the humans one last curious look, then turned and trotted over to his place by the hearth.

Meg watched Seamus, realizing for the first time since Alec had touched her exactly where they were. She had coupled with her husband on the floor of the library. Consummated their marriage on the floor! With the acknowledgment of how completely depraved she had behaved came the realization of how totally she had exposed herself to this man. "The library," she whispered. "I've completely lost my mind."

Alec lifted away from her, far enough to look down

into her face, a devilish grin curving his lips. "I had intended to make you my wife in my bed. I'm afraid things got a wee bit out of control."

"So it seems." Meg lay beneath him—with the smooth wool of his trousers bunched against her thighs, his open shirt brushing her breasts—wondering how to salvage some measure of her pride. Considering the circumstances, it was ludicrous to claim indifference to his masculine wiles.

"I touch you, and my brain stops functioning." Alec cupped her cheek in his palm, touching her as though she were delicate porcelain, his face alight with masculine pride. "You burn like a fever in my blood."

"It would seem the fever is contagious." Intellect had no chance when faced with primitive need—she was proof of that. She couldn't deny the truth of her own weakness. She would do this again. There was no hope for it; one taste of this dangerous forbidden fruit would not be enough. Yet, for her, it was more than lust. She had surrendered more than her body this night. Alec owned her heart. In spite of her resolve to face this surrender with dignity, she was frightened.

"I've never touched such innocence before." He smoothed his fingertips over her temple, as though he couldn't keep from touching her. "Innocence and passion. Lord in heaven, you take my breath away, Meg."

Part of her wanted desperately to believe they could build this marriage into a fortress strong enough to withstand the natural male tendency to stray. Still, she was of a practical nature. It was only a matter of time before Alec's fancy would turn to another woman. It didn't matter how beautiful a wife might be, how intelligent, how worthy—her mother was proof of that. Men like Alec simply did not possess the necessities for maintaining their loyalty. No, any woman who betrayed her love for a man like Alec would soon find her pride trampled right along with her heart.

"Are you all right?" He smoothed his hand over her hair. "I didn't want to hurt you. I just didn't know of any way to ease the first time."

"I'm fine." Except she felt as though she had stepped out onto a very narrow ledge. She smoothed her hand over his thick black waves. "You were right, my wicked Highlander."

He lifted one black brow. "You don't mean to say you actually think I was right about something?"

"On one account, perhaps." She slipped her fingers into the thick, silky waves at his nape and tugged the dark tresses. Lust was a safe emotion. A shield against surrendering her pride to this man. Lust was a haven from all the other, more troubling emotions she felt for him. "I find, as you once advised, a few 'base notions' can be most enjoyable. I never realized lust could wield such power."

Lust. Her matter-of-fact way of categorizing what they had just shared as lust struck a discordant chord inside of Alec. Perhaps this marriage hadn't been based on love. Yet, lately, he couldn't think of Meg without a certain warmth creeping around his heart. And tonight, when he had claimed his reluctant bride, he had found more than he had ever imagined in their joining. It had never been this way with another woman—so complete, as though he had found a long-lost piece of himself in this one lovely woman.

He smoothed his hand over the rumpled silk of her hair. Certainly it was more than lust. He knew lust. Understood it. Felt comfortable and secure with it. Love was another matter.

Although he had no experience in tangles of the heart, he had an uncomfortable suspicion he was already caught in his wife's delicate web. Did she really view this connection they shared as nothing more than the gratification of some animal need? The spark that glowed between them nothing but lust?

She curled a lock of his hair around her finger. "You're a master at seduction."

He frowned in the light of her smile. "Are you going to say I forced you into this?"

"No." She drew in her breath, her breasts lifting to brush his bare chest through the parting of his shirt. The soft brush sent a shot of sensation straight to his loins. "I find carnal desire to be a powerful influence."

"Carnal desire? Lust?" His voice sharpened with his rising anger. The damn woman made him feel like a cheap whore. "Is that what you think this is?"

Her eyes narrowed. "What were you hoping for, MacLaren?" She ran the tip of her finger over a scar that showed through the opening of his shirt. "Were you expecting me to pledge my undying devotion for you? Did you expect me to fall on my knees before you?"

Infuriating witch! The woman was a confounded mystery. His Snow Queen melted well enough when he touched her. She enjoyed the more intimate physical aspects of marriage. Yet she was holding herself back from him. She would give him her body, not her heart.

Damn! His icy English wife had managed to sear her way into his heart. Never in his life had he ever once wondered what a lady's intentions might be toward him. Never in his life had he actually cared. Until now.

He pulled away from her, leaving the warm haven of her body, feeling as though he had left a part of himself behind. He rose and straightened his clothes, aware of the soft sounds of her dressing behind him. It took him several minutes to calm his anger and his voice. "You don't know me very well if you think for one moment I want you on your knees before me."

"Perhaps not," she said, her voice cool and composed. "But you do expect me to pledge my love, my loyalty, my devotion. You expect nothing less from your wife."

He pivoted to face her. She stood with her hands clasped at her waist, pressing against the emerald velvet of her dressing gown, her chin lifted in that proud, defiant way she had. He could find no trace of the fiery temptress he had held in his arms in this cold statue of a woman. "Aye. I want your affection. Your loyalty. Your trust. Is it so wrong to want these things from my wife?"

"And in exchange for my devotion, you will give me what?" she asked, as though asking a shopkeeper the price of a new bonnet.

"My affection." He moved toward her as he spoke. "My loyalty. My trust."

She shrugged and glanced away from him, hiding the expression in her eyes. "I've discovered words mean very little when there is no substance behind them."

He caught her chin on the edge of his hand and coaxed her to look at him. "How can I convince you that you have no reason to be afraid of me?"

Her eyes narrowed. "I proved tonight that I wasn't afraid of you."

"No, lass. Tonight you showed me how very much afraid you really are. You keep thinking I'll go off and betray you, and so you're determined to keep me locked outside the castle gates, tossing me scraps, until I do go away and find a warm place to rest." He smoothed his thumb over the lush curve of her lower lip. "You won't be content until your bleak prophesy comes true."

She lifted her chin. "I didn't exactly keep you locked outside the castle gates this evening. Did I?"

He smoothed his knuckles over the heated softness

of her cheek. "What do you suppose you're doing now?"

She turned away from him, the velvet hem of her dressing gown brushing his legs. She stalked the few feet to the hearth, where she stood and stared at the flames lapping over thick peat logs. Seamus thumped his tail against the carpet, anticipating her attention. Yet she didn't respond. "You said you wanted me in your bed, Alec. And now you have me, for I shall certainly not pretend an indifference to you in this regard. Why isn't it enough for you?"

In the past he had asked nothing more from the women who drifted into his life. Pleasure found in unbridled coupling was all the satisfaction he needed or wanted. Now, looking at this woman, seeing her tension in the taut lines of her slender back, remembering the feel of her virginal sheath tight around his hardened shaft, he knew possessing only her body would never be enough for him. He had to believe there was a chance to make something wonderful out of this union. "Is it really enough for you, Meg?"

She hugged her arms to her waist. "It is more than I expected from this marriage."

He closed the distance between them, no longer able to be near her without touching her. He wrapped his arms around her waist, and drew her back against him. She stiffened but didn't try to escape. "Perhaps you don't expect enough from this marriage."

"Perhaps you want too much." She plucked at the sleeve of his shirt. "Perhaps you want more than I can give you."

"No, lass." He rested his cheek against her hair, breathed in the spicy vanilla scent clinging to the soft tresses. "You have all I need hidden deep inside of you. I know it. Affection and trust, locked away, safe and sound. And one day you'll share it all with me."

She tilted her head and frowned up at him. "You're very confident."

"I'm hopeful." He stroked her cheek with the backs of his fingers, where firelight flickered golden upon the pale satin of her skin. "And determined. One of these days you're going to open those beautiful green eyes of yours and see I'm not a scoundrel bent on breaking your heart."

"Am I?" she whispered.

"Aye." He turned her in his arms and smiled down into her wary eyes. "One woman is all I need in my life. Be my wife, Meg. Be my lover, my friend. And I'll never give you any reason to regret the trust you place in me."

Meg stood rigid in his embrace, a beautiful statue. Yet her eyes revealed her humanity. Those lovely green eyes were filled with turmoil. "I don't know if I'm capable of trusting you."

"My bonnie Meg." He pressed his lips against her smooth brow. "You need time to heal, lass."

She rested her hands on his chest, and for a moment he thought she meant to push him away. Instead she curled her fingers into the white cambric and held on as though she were afraid of falling from a high ledge.

He held her close, rocking her gently in his arms. It took time to heal, especially from wounds that had been carved into the soul. He knew. "I have business in Tranent. I need to be away from Dunleith for a few days."

She pulled back in his arms, her expression growing wary. "When are you leaving?"

He kissed the tip of her nose. "I thought *we* could leave tomorrow. I plan to stay in Edinburgh and ride over to Tranent. My business won't take but half a day at most. I thought you might enjoy a few days in town. We could shop, take in the theater, anything you want to do."

She lifted one brow. "Frightened I shall run away if you aren't here to guard me?"

"You gave me your word, Meg. And I trust you."

She frowned. "I suppose you want me along to warm your bed."

"Aye. Now that I've had a taste of you, I have a feeling I won't be able to get enough of you." Alec slipped his arm under her knees and lifted her in his arms.

She grabbed his shoulder, as though she were afraid he might drop her. "What are you doing?"

He winked at her as he carried her toward the door. "I'm going to carry you to my bed, lass, and have my wicked way with you. I want you again already."

A smile barely tipped one corner of her lips. "If you carry me all that way, you won't have the strength to ravish me."

"Never underestimate a Highlander, lass. Now that I have you in my arms, the devil himself couldn't keep me from making love to you."

Alec entered his bedchamber through the sitting room, closing the door with his foot, relegating Seamus to the smaller room for the evening. Moonlight spilled through the windows of his bedchamber, casting silvery squares across the carpet and his bed. The bedclothes had been turned down, revealing smooth white sheets glowing in the moonlight.

Heat coiled in his belly when he thought of lying with her in that pale oasis. In spite of Meg's dire warnings of exhaustion, Alec wasn't even breathing hard by the time he set her on the floor by his bed. Yet his heart was pounding from his need for her. No one could be more surprised than he to find his hands trembling as he stripped away her clothes.

My wife, he thought, pride stirring with passion in his blood. He slid his hands over the warmth of her slender shoulders, pushing away emerald velvet and white linen, baring her to the moonlight. Brave and beautiful, proud and passionate, Meg was everything he could want in a wife. And no matter what she said, or how hard she tried to keep him locked outside the castle of her heart, he knew he belonged there, and he would fight to stay.

"My own bonnie Meg." He lifted her trembling body in his arms and laid her down upon the cool linen sheets. The mattress dipped as he climbed onto the bed and straddled her smooth thighs.

"Alec," she whispered, resting her hands on his chest. "Although I haven't any experience with these matters. I suspect you are dreadfully overdressed for the occasion."

Moonlight tangled in the thick golden waves spilled across his pillow, creating a silvery nimbus around the head of an angel. His muscles tensed as he watched her unfasten the buttons of his shirt. In spite of her former bravado at viewing his scars, he still dreaded revealing such ugliness to her.

She parted the shirt and slipped her hands inside. "I know you think I'll have my delicate sensibilities shattered by the sight of your scars, but I've never been the least bit missish."

The feathery soft touch of her hands whispered to the primitive male sequestered low in his belly. "The scars really don't bother you?"

"Not at all." She slid her hands upward, over his chest, across his shoulders, peeling away his shirt.

He felt as though she were stripping away more than his shirt. The woman had a way of plowing through his defenses with all the force of French artillery.

"You're a splendid-looking man, in spite of the scars. Like a sculpture of a Greek deity. Only warm, and supple." She drew her hands over his bare shoulders. "I've wanted to touch you this way for a very long time."

Debra Dier

Heat swirled through his blood at the soft touch of her hands against his skin. "I was under the impression you wanted to boil me in oil."

"The thought crossed my mind." She brushed her fingertips over the puckered scar below his left shoulder. "But lately I've discovered you do have your uses."

He felt his desire rising for her, straining against his trousers, hungry for her. "Does this mean you've finally decided it might not be such a terrible fate to be married to me?"

"There are certain aspects of marriage I find"—she drew her fingertip over his nipple, smiling as his muscles quivered beneath her touch—"intriguing."

He brushed his fingertips over her taut pink nipples, smiling at her soft gasp of pleasure. "I knew there was fine Scottish fire hidden beneath all that English ice."

"Fire? Hummm, yes. When you touch me, I feel as though I'm on fire." She slid her fingertips over the saber scar that slashed diagonally across his chest. "I want your skin against mine," she said, slipping her fingers into the waistband of his trousers.

The soft command sent heat shooting straight to his loins. He climbed from the bed and stripped away his boots and clothes. When he turned toward her, he found her watching him, her gaze sliding up and down over his frame. Moonlight poured over him, brutal in its honesty, sliding across the horrible scars carved into his skin. Yet she didn't look away from him. She lifted her eyes, smiling at him, the softness in her gaze drawing him to her.

"So much pain," she whispered, brushing her fingertips over the smooth white scar that slashed across his upper left thigh. "I don't know how you survived. I only know I'm very glad you did."

He climbed onto the bed. He rested on his side and drew her close against him, until her firm breasts

296

grazed his hard chest. "I'm glad to hear it."

She slipped her hand into the hair at his nape. "I know I've said some dreadful things. I was angry, even though I realized you were only doing what you thought was right. But I never wished you had died in battle."

He pressed his lips to her brow, smiling against her skin. "It's nice to hear you say it."

She was quiet a moment, lying still in his arms. "Did the scars bother Pamela?"

Although her voice remained deceptively calm, he heard the wary undertone in the question. "I haven't been with a woman since before Waterloo. Until tonight."

Meg smiled up at him, her thoughts carefully hidden behind a composed mask. "Little wonder you were so anxious to have me in your bed."

"I would have been sniffing after your skirts if I had just had my fill of a hundred women." He smoothed his hand over her silky hair while his shaft swelled against her smooth thigh. "I've never wanted a woman this way, Meg. Completely."

She smoothed her hands over his back as she shifted against him, brushing her breasts against his bare chest. "I never realized desire could burn so brightly. It blinds the intellect."

"It feeds the soul." He eased her back against the sheet. "Too many nights I lay here, thinking of you, wanting you."

She smiled up at him. "Proprietary notions."

"Aye." He trailed his tongue along the curve of her jaw. "I want to possess you. All of you."

She flexed her hands against his shoulders, her fingers sliding against his skin. "It would seem you have already succeeded in your quest."

"I'm only getting started, my own." For too many

nights he had imagined her lying here, warm and supple and eager for his loving. Now she was his, and he intended to make all those wicked imaginings reality.

He kissed the tip of her nose, brushed his lips against the warm satin of her cheek, savoring the feel of her. Misty memories drifted through his mind—this woman scolding him, demanding he hold on to the tenuous thread of life. She had dragged him back from the brink of death, and he wouldn't rest until she knew how much she had come to mean to him.

He brushed his lips against the hollow of her neck, tasted her skin, drew her fragrance deep into his lungs. He pressed kisses along the delicate line of her collarbone and trailed lower, over the first swell of her breasts. A soft sigh slipped from her lips and curled warmly around his heart. Her breasts rose and fell with each agitated breath she took, lifting to him. He flicked his tongue over one pink nipple, drew the hard little nub into his mouth, suckled hard and long, until her soft sighs grew into a deep-throated sob of pleasure.

She tugged on his shoulders, lifted her hips, the soft curls at the joining of her thighs brushing wantonly against his belly. Yet he forced himself to ignore the silent invitation, to abandon the need pounding like a fist in his loins. He had taken her the first time without allowing himself the time to fully savor her. He lavished her other breast with kisses, tasted her sweet little nipple, then drew his tongue down, over the silken skin of her belly.

She shifted beneath him, her muscles fluttering against his mouth. He brushed his lips over the smooth curve of her hip, drew his tongue over the soft-as-down skin of her thigh, her calf, her slender ankle, and trailed kisses down to her toes.

He knew he could lavish her with words of devotion and she would believe none of them. Words were insignificant compared to actions, especially for a woman as wary as his beautiful bride. And so he would show her how much he adored her.

He brushed his cheek against the warm satin of her inner thigh, savored the soft sighs slipping from her lips, then moved upward. He pressed his lips high against her inner thigh, soft feminine curls brushing his cheek.

"You're as fair as a summer morn," he whispered, trailing his fingers into the damp feminine curls. "So beautiful."

She lifted her hips, moaning softly. He lowered his head, bringing his lips to the womanly warmth of her.

"Wicked, wicked Highlander!" She sank her fingers into his hair. Yet she didn't try to pull him away from her.

Meg was his wife, and no one could claim this was a marriage of convenience. She was all he wanted, every sweet dream come true. He wasn't certain when it had happened—perhaps that first night he had kissed her—he only knew she owned his heart.

Alec savored her, tasting the sweet feminine honey, inhaling her scent, feeling her passion rise. With his lips and tongue he told her of his need for her, his love for her, pleasuring her until her hands fisted in his hair and her body trembled. Her soft song of pleasure filled his ears and his heart. Before the last tremor subsided, he sheathed himself in her trembling warmth.

He kissed her, drinking her soft sighs while he moved inside of her, surrendering to the pounding passion, finding his own release in the haven of her arms.

Chapter Twenty-two

"I'm terribly sorry about this." Joanna paced the length of Meg's bedchamber in Alec's Edinburgh town house. "I did everything I could, but you know your grandmother. Once she has her mind set, nothing can change it. Certainly not a plea to her sensibilities."

"She means well." Meg sat at the rosewood vanity, regarding her reflection with a critical eye. Fortunately, she had something appropriate to wear to the theater tonight. Since Joanna had decided the duration of their stay at Dunleith might be of some length, she had sent for their clothes from London. Still, Meg caught herself wondering if Alec would find her gown of black silk attractive. She wasn't in the habit of caring what any man might think of her appearance. Yet, poor besotted idiot that she was, she couldn't deny she wanted Alec's approval.

"I never truly expected Mother to come along and bring Blandford with her." Joanna paused near the windows and stared out into the gardens behind the house. "I had hoped you and Alec might have some time together without Mother's interference."

Meg recalled the hours she and Alec had spent together last night, and again this morning. Heat rose with the memories, tingling across her belly, her breasts. She dabbed perfume behind her ears, the spicy scent of vanilla curling around her.

She had never realized a husband and wife might enjoy intimate relations in the morning. Of course, she had never truly understood the primitive need that lurked deep inside of her. She must truly be depraved or insane or both. Alec need only look at her—in that dark, sultry way he had of letting her know exactly how much he wanted her—and she was ready to rip the clothes from his back. As much as she wanted to deny it, she had never been happier than when she was with her wicked Highlander. She had also never been more frightened in her life. "Mother, have you ever been frightened to be happy?"

Joanna turned to look at Meg. "Frightened to be happy?"

"It sounds insane, doesn't it?" Meg drew her fingertip over the smooth back of her silver-handled brush. "But then, lately, I've been more and more certain that I've lost my mind entirely."

Joanna crossed the room and paused beside Meg's chair. "Perhaps it's not your mind that you've lost, my darling. Perhaps it's your heart."

"Perhaps it is." Meg looked up at her mother. "The way I feel about Alec . . . it's so powerful. I want to be with him day and night. I can't be near him without wanting to touch him. He is like some virulent disease, and I've caught it."

Joanna rested her hand on Meg's shoulder. "You're in love."

301

Meg released her breath in a long sigh. "I never stood a chance to resist him."

Joanna smiled, her expression revealing a bittersweet pain. "You're happy when you're with him, and you're frightened all that happiness will be taken away."

Meg nodded. "I despise this weakness. Yet I'm not certain what I can do about it."

Joanna held Meg's troubled gaze. "Perhaps you should stop worrying about the inevitable. And start enjoying your time with him."

"Enjoying his company has never been a problem." Meg smiled at her mother. Yet she couldn't quell the doubts that plagued her, sinking claws into her heart. Trust was not something she gave lightly. And without trust, there could be no basis for a future.

Alec stood on the threshold of his drawing room, wondering if anyone would notice if he strangled his cousin. The subject of his murderous imaginings sat in a wing-back chair near the hearth, his feet propped on a footstool, his hand curved around a snifter of brandy—lord of the manor.

Wildon lifted his glass in salute when he noticed Alec enter the room. "You know, one of the things I miss about giving up the title is the excellence of the Dunleith cellars."

Alec walked past his cousin and headed for the crystal decanter sitting open on a cabinet against the far wall. He always tolerated his cousin better after a good strong drink.

"I've been sitting here contemplating the odd nature of fate." Wildon sipped his brandy. "It's strange, isn't it? You never cared about the title and all of this. Yet here you are. With everything."

"I never thought to inherit the title. It isn't that I never cared."

Wildon cradled his glass between his palms, smiling at Alec. "I imagine you must find it all overwhelming. After all, being earl isn't exactly what you were trained for, is it?"

Alec swirled the brandy in his glass. "I appreciate your concern, but I think I can manage."

"Of course." Wildon glanced down into his brandy. "Still, it isn't exactly the same as commanding a regiment, is it? I imagine you must find it all dreadfully dull. And on top of it all, you find yourself married to a woman who doesn't care to be your bride. How dreadful for you."

Alec downed his drink in a single swallow, scarcely tasting the aged brandy. The heat of the liquor warmed his throat and spread like hot butter through his chest. Still, he wasn't certain the potent liquor could keep him from tossing his cousin out on his ear. Seldom had he encountered a more irritating bore. "I'm quite satisfied with my wife. I could want for nothing more."

One corner of Wildon's lips tightened. "Still, to look at Margaret's beautiful face day after day, knowing she would have chosen another as her husband, must be like a blade twisting slowly in your chest."

Alec smiled at his cousin's feeble attempt to wound him. He was certain Meg had only considered marrying a man like Wildon to spite her father. Meg was his, in more than name only. Although she was reluctant to admit there was more to this marriage than the pleasure they shared in bed, he was certain one day he would win her trust. "I think I can manage to keep my lady satisfied."

"You were always so confident of yourself, even as a boy." Wildon's eyes narrowed. "One of these days you will receive exactly what you deserve, cousin. Perhaps sooner than you think."

Alec squeezed his brandy glass, his fingers sliding against the deep bevels cut into the crystal. Instincts honed in battle stirred as he held his cousin's angry gaze. He didn't care for the smug look on his cousin's face. The man was up to something. Yet the arrival of Meg, Joanna, and Hermione prevented Alec from exploring Wildon's provocative statement.

One look at his wife, and Alec forgot his irritation with his cousin. One look and he was ready to snatch Meg up into his arms and carry her to his bed. Her black silk gown bared her creamy shoulders, hugged her rounded breasts, exposing the first pale swells to his hungry gaze. Her golden hair was swept back from her face, pinned high on her head, allowing a few curls to frame her beautiful face. He walked toward her, drawn by the warmth of the smile she shared with him. Yet before he could reach his bride, Wildon was taking Meg's arm.

Alec clenched his jaw, fighting the urge to yank his cousin off the floor and toss him against a wall. He didn't want the blackguard to touch her. He stepped past his cousin and took his wife's free arm, winning a brilliant smile from his lady. Wildon shot him a dark glance over Meg's head, a look that spoke of vengeance. Alec covered Meg's hand with his, dismissing his cousin. Wildon's jealousy was not going to spoil the evening.

Candlelight flickered against the cut crystal of the chandeliers suspended from gold fixtures attached to each slender pillar that separated the boxes in the theater. Golden light flickered on the people flowing into the blue velvet chairs of the three tiers of boxes. Women in gowns that ranged from the palest white silk to the deepest gem tones paraded on the arms of men in elegant evening clothes. Conversation and laughter lifted in the air, drifting past the blue velvet drapes framing the Dunleith box. Yet the low din wasn't enough to drown Hermione's voice.

Meg was beginning to believe her wicked Highlander had the patience of a saint. She sat on a blue velvet chair between her mother and Alec in the elegant Dunleith box, wondering how her husband could manage to mind his temper. Behind her Hermione was chatting with Wildon Fethersham, lamenting about the inferiority of this theater compared to those in London. From this she went on to various other aspects of Scotland and how nothing compared to England, including the gentlemen, which, she asserted, were few and far between in this "barbaric country."

Meg slanted a glance at Alec. He was leaning back in his chair, surveying the people as they flowed into the seats on the lower level, apparently immune to Hermione's venom. She wished she had never employed her grandmother as a chaperon all those days when Alec was recovering from his illness. She had the uneasy feeling the lady now felt she had a free hand in keeping a watchful eye on her granddaughter.

"It is far too long since I have been here. I've always thought this one of the loveliest theaters I have ever attended," Joanna said, lifting her voice above the low hum of conversation in the auditorium, drowning out Hermione's chatter. "It was most kind of you to allow us to join you, Alec."

Alec smiled, a glint of humor filling his eyes. "It's my pleasure to have your company."

Meg glanced at her mother, silently thanking Joanna for providing cordial conversation.

"I have spent many an enjoyable evening here." Joanna looked out across the theater. "I was always particularly fond of . . ." She hesitated, as though something had struck her hard. After a moment, she drew in her breath and continued, her voice oddly strained. "Fond of attending plays."

Even in the soft glow of the chandeliers, Meg could see the color drain from her mother's face. She touched Joanna's arm. "Mother, is something amiss?"

"No." Joanna molded her lips into a smile that failed to touch the haunted look in her eyes. "Nothing is amiss. Everything is fine. I'm looking forward to seeing *The Quaker*. I understand it's quite amusing."

Meg found her mother's quick denial less than convincing. She sat back in her chair and glanced around the theater, wondering what might have disturbed her mother. Her gaze snagged on a dark-haired woman sitting with an attractive dark-haired gentleman in a box across from them. Meg's breath froze in her lungs. It had been nine years since she had glimpsed this woman's face, but Meg recognized her immediately. Drusilla Buchanan had changed little over the years. The harlot was staring at Joanna, a shocked expression on her beautiful face.

A warm hand touched her arm below the short sleeve of her gown. Meg pulled her gaze from the woman who had destroyed her life, to the man who had forced her into marriage.

Alec was frowning, his blue eyes filled with concern. "Are you feeling all right?"

Meg forced air past her tight throat. "I'm fine."

Alec touched her cheek. "Are you?"

"Yes." She clasped her hands in her lap and tried to wash all emotion from her face.

Chimes sounded in the theater. Boys in blue velvet livery moved along each tier, extinguishing candles, releasing thin threads of gray smoke in their wake. A faint smoky scent swirled around Meg. She forced her gaze to the stage, refusing to allow anyone, especially Drusilla Buchanan, to see her turmoil.

From the corner of her eye, she was aware of Alec, watching her. She wished she could turn to him. A pitiful part of her wanted to curl up in his strong arms and pretend all was right with the world. Only, all was not right in her world. She wanted to get out of this place, turn her back on the past and pretend Drusilla Buchanan didn't exist. But the past couldn't be changed, it remained as it was—a painful reminder of the perfidy of the male of the species.

Something was wrong. Alec knew it, even if he didn't know the cause. Something had happened tonight at the theater. Something that had swept across Meg like a December wind off the mountains, freezing the warm woman he had discovered into the icy statue he had known. After preparing for bed, he went to her, determined to break through the fresh defenses she had built between them.

Meg was standing by the windows when Alec entered her bedchamber. Moonlight streamed through the square panes, capturing an angel in the silvery light. Only this angel looked lost and lonely. He recalled that first night in London, when he had stolen into her room and found her this way—a little girl looking for answers in the stars. He should have realized that first night how easily this woman could steal her way into his heart.

She turned when he drew near, her expression cold and distant, as though she had stuffed all of her emotions into a coffin and lowered them into the ground. "I suppose you feel you have the right to enter my chamber when you please."

"I suppose I have some strange notions about marriage. You see I think a husband and wife should feel comfortable with each other; that means having the right to enter the other's bedchamber." He gave her a warm smile, hoping to win one in return. She refused to alter her icy expression. "I think if there is a problem, they should discuss it."

She turned back toward the window. "I am not in the mood for company right now."

He refused to be dismissed so easily. "If I've done something to upset you, tell me what it is."

She hugged her arms to her waist. The defensive gesture caused her nightgown to draw taut across her breasts, defining the soft curves beneath white linen. "There is nothing to discuss."

He rested his hand on her shoulder. "What happened at the theater tonight, Meg? Something upset you and your mother."

"Nothing happened." She curled her shoulder, drawing away from him. "Now kindly leave me alone."

He touched her cheek and coaxed her to look at him with a gentle pressure of his fingers against her skin. "The castle gates are locked, and I'm to go away and stop asking to come in. Is that it, Meg?"

She lifted her chin. "If you're expecting to exercise your husbandly rights tonight, I must tell you I have no inclination to participate."

He looked into her wide, defiant eyes and wondered how they had managed to slide back into this position. He was the enemy. Again. Well, he was having none of it. He swept her up into his arms and started for the bed.

She crossed her arms over her breasts and glared at him. "You told me you would never force me. I see it didn't take long for you to break that pledge."

He swore under his breath. "I'm growing weary of being called a liar."

"And what would you call it when—" Her words collided with a sharp gasp when he dumped her on the bed. She pushed her hair back from her face and glared at him. "Get out!"

"I will not be locked out of my wife's bedchamber." He tugged open the sash of his sapphire silk dressing gown. "Even if she is the most stubborn, addle-brained—"

"I am not stubborn!"

He threw his dressing gown on a chair near the bed. He wore nothing beneath the garment. Her anger couldn't disguise the hunger in her eyes as she raked his naked form with her gaze. In spite of his best intentions, he felt his desire stir, his shaft swell and rise as though answering her siren's song. "You're the most confounded, infuriating little witch I've ever had the misfortune to meet."

Her lips parted on a sharp exhale. "How dare you say such things to me!"

He climbed onto the bed. "Spoiled, stubborn little baggage."

She scrambled to the opposite side of the bed. He lunged for her, snagging her waist with his arm. He pulled her back against his chest and wrapped his other arm around her.

"Let go of me!"

She struggled to free herself, twisting in his arms, rubbing her bottom against his loins. Desire stabbed through him. He clenched his jaw and focused on his purpose. He had no intention of making love to the little witch. At least not until she admitted she wanted him as much as he wanted her.

"Damnation, woman, I'm not going to rape you." He threw his leg over her thighs, quelling her struggles.

"Let me go, you big brute!"

"I won't be turned away like a hungry mongrel looking for a few scraps from your dinner table." He nuzzled aside her hair and pressed his lips against her neck, smiling when he felt a tremor ripple through her.

"Stop that!" She twisted in his hold. "I won't be used like a common courtesan."

"There is nothing common about you." He flicked his tongue against the soft skin beneath her ear.

"Stop it!"

"Tell me what I did to make you angry with me."

"Just go away!"

He traced the curve of her ear with the tip of his tongue. "Ah, Meg. How the devil am I supposed to make amends when you won't tell me what the devil I've done to make you so bloody angry?" he whispered against her ear.

She glared at him over her shoulder. "Why can't you just leave me alone?"

He looked straight into her furious green eyes and confessed a truth that had worked its way upon him over the past few days. "Because I love you."

Her lips parted, then closed, then parted again. "That's a fine tactic, MacLaren. Designed to keep me off balance."

He brushed his lips against her temple. "Don't turn me away. Let me hold you. That's all. Just let me hold you while you sleep."

"You're very stubborn."

"Aye." He grinned at her. "It runs in my clan."

Meg turned away from him, but not before he saw doubts flicker in her eyes. "I suppose you shall keep plaguing me until I agree to let you stay."

"Aye." He dropped a kiss upon her nape. "I shall keep kissing you until you see reason."

"Very well." She drew in her breath, her back brushing his chest. "Pull the covers over yourself. You'll end up ill again."

He drew the sheet and coverlet over them, sealing

out the chill of the night. When he slipped his arm around her waist, she didn't try to pull away. She didn't snuggle against him either. She lay quiet and still as a statue. Except this statue was warm and supple and smelled of spicy vanilla.

Tomorrow, on his way to Tranent, he would try to piece together the sudden change in his wife's temper. For tonight, he would content himself with the singular pleasure of holding her in his arms. He rested his cheek against her hair, closed his eyes, and tried to ignore the pounding in his loins.

He felt heavy, hot, aching, painfully aware of the soft bottom pressed against his aroused sex. Her nightgown had become tangled in the fray. He could feel it bunched around her hips. Below the crumpled white linen, her slim legs rested against his—his thighs braced against hers, his knees nestled into the backs of her knees. Although his brain sorted out all the reasons why he mustn't press her this night, his body refused to abandon the need to possess her.

Trust. The woman would learn to trust him. And this was the first step, he assured himself. No matter how painful it was. He took a deep breath, the spicy vanilla scent of her ambushing his resolve. He clenched his jaw. The woman would see, he wanted more from her than the use of her luscious body. He would show her he could lie with her, hold her, and not seduce her. Even if it killed him.

Meg stared at the smoldering remains of the fire on the hearth, watching the last embers fade to gray. Lying beside a naked man certainly did not provide for peaceful slumber. Especially when that man was as compelling as Alec. Particularly when she could feel the solid ridge of his arousal pressing against her bottom. Tempting her. The man was forever tempting her to do something foolish.

There was little hope for it: She was a fool. She knew she couldn't possibly trust Alec. He was far too handsome. He possessed too much roguish charm. Even though he was married, women would forever be throwing themselves at his feet. And he would eventually succumb to the temptation. Knowing all of this, she still wanted him.

I love you—Alec's words curled warmly in her memory. It was madness to believe him. He was a worldly man, accustomed to easy conquests. He sought only to weaken her defenses against him. Yet she couldn't prevent the longing deep within her, the need to accept all he offered, the desire to give him all she possessed.

A pulse throbbed in the tips of her breasts and low, in that private place only he had ever touched. Her nightgown teased her skin. She felt restless and hot and aching. His hand lay palm-up on the mattress, so close. All she need do was ease forward and she could press her aching breast into the warm cup of his hand.

Foolish. She couldn't surrender to this weakness. Yet . . . she shifted her hips, pressing back against him. His hard shaft slipped between her thighs. She held her breath, waiting for him to move. Yet he didn't. He lay behind her, his chest rising and falling in a slow, steady rhythm against her back, his body fully aroused in slumber.

The echo of her heart pulsed in the flesh pressed against his arousal. She arched her hips, spreading the dew from her feminine petals along the long length of him: soft velvet stretched over solid oak. She reached between them, touching the velvet hardness of his sex, pressing the tip of him against the bud hidden beneath damp feminine curls, the secret place he had shown her. Pleasure stabbed through her, sharp and aching.

"Meg," he whispered, his dark voice thick from slumber.

"I need . . ." She pressed back against him, rubbing along the length of him. "Alec, I can't help it."

He released his breath in a sigh that brushed her nape with warmth. "Take me, lass."

She tipped her hips. With her hand on his length, she guided him into her feminine passage.

"God Almighty." He encircled her waist with his arm and drew her back tight against him. He flicked open the pearl buttons of her nightgown and slipped his hand inside.

Meg tipped back her head, moaning as he caught her nipple between his thumb and forefinger. He squeezed and tugged, coaxing sensation to splinter and spark through her. He slid his hand between her thighs, stroking the place where sensation flared and sparkled while he thrust into her. She pushed back, meeting each hard thrust of his body, the pleasure rising inside of her, bubbling and surging, until it crested, casting her high above the bounds of earth. He thrust once more, hard and deep. His deep-throated growl mingled with her sharp cry.

As her pulse slowed and her breathing eased, she leaned back in the circle of his arms. She wouldn't think of the future. She wouldn't dwell on the past. The present was enough for now. She closed her eyes and found peace, secure in Alec's warm embrace.

Chapter Twenty-three

A sharp noise pierced Meg's slumber. She came awake with a start, a sudden wrenching from slumber that shocked her muscles and set her heart pounding against the wall of her chest. She stared up at her grandmother, who stood beside the bed dressed in a gown of such bright yellow, Meg wondered if the gown alone could have shocked her from sleep. "What is it? Has something happened?"

"It's past ten. Mustn't stay in bed all morning; there are things to do."

Meg glanced to the place beside her where Alec had spent the night. He was gone. A misty memory floated through her mind—Alec kissing her in the hazy light of dawn, whispering he would be back soon. He had left for Tranent this morning.

"You will be delighted to know that barbarian left before I came down for breakfast. That dreadful Scottish butler told me the blackguard wouldn't be back until this afternoon." Hermione smiled, a smug little smile. "We shan't be bothered with Dunleith today."

Meg frowned at her grandmother. "I do wish you wouldn't refer to the MacLaren as a barbarian."

Hermione waved aside Meg's words with one pudgy hand. "But he is a barbarian, my dear."

"Grandmama, you should—"

"Up with you. I have a marvelous outing planned for us."

"Outing?"

Hermione clasped her hands beneath her chin. "I understand there are wonderful Roman ruins just out of town. Lord Blandford and I are setting out to explore them this morning."

Meg shoved her hand through her tangled hair, wondering how she could tactfully avoid going with her grandmother and Blandford. "I didn't know you had an interest in Roman ruins."

"Oh, my dear, I have always had a passion for anything Roman."

That explained the music room in the London town house, Meg thought. "Mother had mentioned she would like to do a little shopping this morning."

"Your mother set off alone this morning, shortly after receiving a note from an old acquaintance. I'm afraid we simply cannot wait for her to return. Now hurry, dear."

Trapped. There was no hope of escaping her grandmother once Hermione had her mind set. "I won't be long."

Her grandmother was in high spirits, Meg thought, taking a bite of cold beef. She sat with Hermione and Wildon at a round table in a private dining room of the Crouching Lion Inn, listening to her grandmother chatter about the deplorable quality of Scottish inns.

Although her grandmother seemed particularly animated today, Wildon Fethersham was quite reticent. He had scarcely said more than a few words all morning. And when Hermione had insisted they stop for a luncheon, he had been most reluctant to postpone their trip to the ruins. His behavior seemed odd, even for a man like Fethersham.

"Are the ruins much farther?" Meg asked, breaking a small piece from the loaf of oat bread by her plate. Although she hated to admit it, she wanted to be at home when Alec returned. She slathered butter on the warm bread. As it was, with his early departure this morning, she suspected he had already returned to Edinburgh.

"The ruins." Hermione smiled at Meg, her gray eyes bright with excitement. "My darling, I believe it is time we share the wonderful news with you."

Meg lowered the bread and knife. "What news?"

Fethersham shot Hermione a look filled with apprehension. "Perhaps we should wait until we reach the ruins."

Hermione waved aside his words. "Darling, we are not on our way to any Roman ruins."

Meg frowned, a prickly sensation creeping across the base of her neck. "If we aren't going to the Roman ruins, where exactly are we going?"

Hermione clasped her hands under her chin. "Home."

Meg squeezed the knife in her hand. "Grandmama, what are you about?"

"Rescuing you!"

"Rescuing me?"

"Yes, dear. Lord Fethersham and I have it all planned. Once we are back in London, I'm quite certain we can have this horrible marriage annulled."

"Annulled?" Meg stared at her grandmother. Her

316

heart pounded so hard, the black satin ribbon that edged the neckline of her black muslin gown and fell between her breasts fluttered. Hermione was offering her an escape. Wasn't that what she wanted? Hadn't she hoped and planned for a way to escape Alec? Now, presented with the opportunity to leave her wicked Highlander, Meg realized it was the last thing in the world she wanted to do. "We cannot annul this marriage."

"Not to worry, my dear. I know you're concerned about a scandal, but once you and Lord Blandford are married, any gossip shall be forgotten."

Meg looked at Wildon, who sat rigid beside Hermione, his lips drawn into a tight line, his eyes revealing his displeasure with his coconspirator. How could any woman imagine Meg would leave a man like Alec MacLaren for this pampered puppy?

"I wish to return to Edinburgh," Meg said, forcing her voice to remain low and composed.

Hermione frowned. "But you don't understand; we are rescuing you from that barbarian."

"I don't want to be rescued!"

Hermione blinked. "Don't want to be rescued?"

"No," Meg said, realizing the full impact of her decision. She wanted to be with Alec, no matter what.

Hermione stared at her a moment, as though she thought Meg had suddenly taken leave of her senses. "It's the strain. You've been under a terrible strain lately. You aren't thinking properly."

Meg rose from the table, her limbs trembling with a terrible anxiety. She had to get back to Alec. Now. If Alec discovered this plot—it could be a disaster. "I insist we return to Edinburgh."

"I know what is best for you." Hermione smiled at Meg. "Now sit, dear, and finish your meal."

"Grandmother, you have stepped too far." Meg pivoted, and marched to the door.

"Where are you going?" Hermione demanded.

Meg grasped the brass door handle. "If you shall not take me home, I shall find a way to get there without you."

Hermione pursed her lips. "I am taking you home. To London."

Meg squeezed the handle. How strange. A few weeks ago she had thought of London as her home. Now she knew the only place she wanted to be was with Alec. "Grandmama, I have no intention of agreeing to an annulment."

"No intention . . . Oh dear." Hermione pressed the back of her hand to her brow. "You have given me the headache."

Meg released the handle. She couldn't leave her grandmother in this state. "Grandmama, please calm yourself."

"What have I done to deserve such treatment? At the hands of my own flesh and blood." Hermione pressed her hand to her heart. "Oh, dear, I do believe I should faint."

"Grandmama, please, don't be upset." Meg crossed the room and took her grandmother's hand. Although she realized her grandmother's flair for the dramatic was in full gallop, she also didn't want to abandon her grandmother to this fit of nerves.

Hermione looked up at Meg. "I only want to see you happy."

"I know." Meg patted her grandmother's hand. "Please try to understand, I—"

"Oh, my goodness!" Hermione clasped her hand to her neck, her eyes wide as she stared past Meg. "The devil himself!"

Meg turned, her breath freezing in her lungs at the

sight of Alec standing in the doorway. One look at his stormy countenance was enough to reveal the extent of his fury. Alec stepped inside and closed the door. The soft click of the latch cracked like thunder through the room.

Wildon rose from his chair and took a step back. "What are you doing here?" he asked, his voice scraped raw by fear.

Alec smiled, and Meg wondered how anyone could manage to look so menacing with a grin. "I believe you've taken something that belongs to me."

Oh, dear! This wouldn't do. In his state, Alec might very well do something he would regret later, such as murder Wildon Fethersham. "Alec," Meg said, starting toward her husband.

"Away with you!" Hermione grabbed Meg's arm, pulling her up short. "You can't have her. Do something, Blandford."

"Grandmama, I realize you're quite set on me seeing the ruins. Not to worry, you and Lord Blandford can continue without me," Meg said, trying to defuse the situation.

"Ruins?" Hermione stared at Meg, her gray eyes wide. "This barbarian is here to kidnap you again, and all you can think about are Roman ruins. You really have been under a strain. But never fear; once we get you home, you'll be fine."

So much for subterfuge, Meg thought. "Grandmama, I'm returning to Edinburgh with my husband," she said, prying Hermione's fingers from her arm.

"Do something, Blandford!" Hermione wailed as Meg pulled away from her. "Defend her from this blackguard."

"Well, cousin?" Alec leaned his shoulder against the door and fixed Wildon in an icy stare. "Shall we say pistols at dawn? Or would you prefer to settle the matter here and now?"

Wildon stepped back. "Don't be absurd."

Meg rushed across the room to her husband. "Alec, please don't make this into a tragedy," she whispered.

Alec turned his icy smile on her. "The man has tried to steal my wife. Allow him to get away with it, who knows what he will try to take next. Perhaps something valuable, such as one of my horses."

Meg ignored the angry barb. She rested her hand on his arm. "Alec, please."

"Stop him, Blandford!" Hermione shouted, pulling a pistol from her reticule. She pointed the pistol at Wildon. "Shoot the blackguard."

"Grandmother!" Meg stepped in front of Alec. "For the love of heaven, will you kindly calm yourself."

Wildon backed away from Hermione, his eyes wide as he stared at the pistol pointed at him. "Lady Hermione, please put that down!"

"Oh, for heaven's sake." Hermione swung the pistol around, pointing it at Meg. "Step aside, Margaret. I shall give the devil his due."

Meg marched toward her grandmother. "Put that pistol away before someone gets hurt!"

"Damnation, woman!" Alec grabbed Meg's arm, pulled her back, and forced her behind him.

Meg grabbed his arm when he started toward her grandmother. "She isn't going to shoot me, Alec. But she might shoot you."

Alec glanced over his shoulder at her, his eyes narrowed into blue slits. "I told you once before never to get between me and a pistol," he said, his voice low and deadly smooth.

She poked her head out from behind the wall of Alec's back and glared at her grandmother. "Grandmama, if you shoot Alec, I shall never speak to you again. I mean it."

Hermione pursed her lips. "I'm only doing what is best for you, dear."

Meg gripped Alec's arm, holding him back when he would have stormed at her grandmother. "Grandmama, put that pistol away."

"Oh, very well." Hermione huffed as she slipped her pistol back into her yellow satin reticule. "But you'll regret this."

Meg's breath flowed out with the sudden release of tension in her body. "Thank you, Grandmama."

Hermione waved aside the words with one pudgy hand. Wildon sagged against the wall, his breath coming fast and shallow.

"Don't for a moment believe this ends the affair, Blandford." Alec glared at his cousin. "I will expect satisfaction for your part in this little plot."

Wildon swallowed so hard, Meg could hear his Adam's apple click. "There was no harm done."

"That is a matter of opinion." Alec took Meg's arm and ushered her out of the room, snatching her mantle from a peg near the door on the way.

"Alec, you really don't plan to . . ." Meg's protest dried into dust under the furious glare Alec gave her. She glanced around the public room of the inn as Alec threw the mantle around her shoulders. This was hardly the time or the place to discuss the delicate matter of preventing a duel between her husband and his cousin. She was quite certain she could convince Alec to see reason on the way back to Edinburgh.

A brisk wind stung Alec's cheeks. He stared past the fluttering manes of a matched pair of his grays, steering his curricle along the road back to Edinburgh, while his wife sat beside him and tried to convince him not to murder Wildon Fethersham. Some of his anger cooled as he listened to his wife's calm rendering of the circumstances leading up to the moment he had found her at the Crouching Lion Inn.

"So you see, it was all a terrible misunderstanding." Meg clasped her gloved hands against the carriage rug lying across her lap.

Alec slanted her a glance. "I won't be made to look a fool, Meg. Not by you. Not by anyone."

The black velvet ribbons of her bonnet fluttered beneath her chin. "I didn't try to make a fool of you, Alec."

Although he had experienced more than a few doubts about his wife's part in the escapade, his instincts told him it was just as Meg had said. Still, his wife had a few things to learn about trust. And this seemed an excellent opportunity to teach her. "What would you call running off with another man?"

She rolled her eyes to heaven. "Haven't you been listening to me? I didn't run away with Blandford. I thought we were going to visit Roman ruins just outside of town."

He resisted the urge to smile. The narrow carriage seat provided little room between them. Meg's hip brushed his with each sway of the curricle. He was aware of her thigh close to his under the carriage rug, warming him through the layers of their clothes, tempting him to pull the carriage to the side of the road, so he might snatch his beautiful wife up onto his lap and kiss her until her eyes filled with that dreamy look she got each time he stirred her passion. Yet there were things to be settled before he succumbed to his weakness for his beautiful bride. "So you're saying I shouldn't believe what I saw, but I should believe what you've said."

Meg's lips parted. She stared at him a long moment before she replied. "Yes."

"You had no idea your grandmother planned to take you to London."

Meg nodded. "That's right."

"She kidnapped you."

"She thought it was for my own good." Meg tilted her chin, her green eyes filled with a challenge. "It's not as though it's the first time someone has kidnapped me with the best intentions in mind."

Alec shrugged. "Still, your story is difficult to believe, Meg. Especially considering you've been wanting to leave me since the day we were married."

"I'm telling you the truth." Meg stiffened away from the black leather seat back. "And although I may have wanted to leave you in the beginning, I have grown accustomed to your wicked Highlander ways."

"Have you?" He said, fighting to conceal the excitement that came with her simple confession.

"Yes. Although at the moment, I am finding it difficult to understand why."

He studied the road a few moments. "Why should I believe you, Meg?"

Her soft lips pulled into a tight line. "Because I do not have a propensity for prevarication."

Alec turned his head and regarded her, allowing his wife to stew a moment while the sound of horseshoes pounding on the macadamized road filled up the silence between them. "Strange, isn't it? How a person can appear guilty, when he or she is telling the truth."

"I am telling the truth."

"So you say." He turned his attention to the road, watching her from the corner of his eye. "Still, I think it will take a measure of trust to believe you. And trust is something not easily given, is it?"

She looked startled, then thoughtful. After a moment she spoke, her voice barely rising against the clatter of the carriage wheels and horseshoes pounding the road. "No. It isn't."

Meg fell silent and Alec saw no reason to interrupt her reverie for the rest of the trip back to Edinburgh. The lady needed to think about the quality of trust. Not only for the sake of their marriage, but for the sake of the father she had shut out of her life.

Chapter Twenty-four

"I felt as though Alec had slapped me across the cheek. I suddenly realized how easy it truly was to appear guilty when one is innocent." Meg paced the length of her sitting room in Alec's Edinburgh town house. She paused near the hearth and faced her mother. "I realized I had never given Alec any reason to believe me. He had no reason at all to trust me."

Joanna sat on an Empire sofa nearby with her hands tightly clasped on her lap, her expression taut with concern. "Do you think Alec finally did believe you had nothing to do with Mother's outrageous scheme?"

"I'm not certain." The smoky scent of burning peat curled around Meg. "I do know it's quite vexing being accused of something you didn't do."

"Yes." Joanna glanced into the fire. "I'm certain it is."

Meg rubbed her throbbing temples. "Mother, forgive me, but all the way back to Edinburgh, I kept thinking of Father. I kept wondering if it had been as he had said all those years ago."

"I've been wondering much the same thing." Joanna released her breath on a long sigh. "This morning I received a missive from Drusilla Buchanan. Or, I should say, Drusilla Grierson. She remarried seven years ago."

Meg sank to the dark blue brocade cushion beside her mother. She felt as though she were stepping across a frozen lake, not quite certain if the ice beneath her was thick enough to save her from a terrible fall. "What did she want?"

"She asked me to come to her house. There were things she needed to tell me. At first I wasn't going to go. And then I realized I wanted to hear what she had to say."

A weight pressed down upon Meg's chest, apprehension so heavy she could scarcely breathe. "What did she have to say?"

"She apologized for what she had done nine years ago." Joanna leaned forward, opening her hands as though seeking the warmth of the fire. "She swore Robert had never encouraged her, had never invited her to his bed. She asked me to understand the state of mind she was in at the time. She had lost her husband, and she was reaching out to Robert in a desperate attempt to feel loved."

Meg felt the ice crack beneath her, a chill creep upward over her limbs. "Do you believe her?"

"For the past few years, I have wondered if I made a mistake that night." Joanna drew a shaky breath. "This morning, as I listened to Drusilla talk about Robert's devotion to me, I realized how very idiotic I was to leave him."

Tears burned Meg's eyes. She stared into the fire, remembering the look on her father's face when she had accused him of being a vile debauchee. All the wasted years. All the terrible pain. All because she hadn't believed in her father. "You were not the only idiot, it would seem."

"He must truly despise me," Joanna whispered, her voice cracking with emotion.

"Mother." Meg slipped her arm around her mother's slender shoulders as Joanna dissolved into tears. Meg's tears also fell—she couldn't prevent them. Through the tempest, she sought some means to console her mother. "At the time, you had reason to believe in his guilt."

"I had reason to believe in his innocence. I should have trusted him. I should have believed him. I should have stayed with him."

Through the pain, Meg saw a glimmer of hope. She snatched at the slender thread, holding it to her heart. "Mother, it's not too late."

Joanna swiped at the tears streaming down her cheeks. "I'm afraid it is."

"You still love him. I know you do."

Joanna laughed, a soft, bitter sound. "I never stopped loving him. I never will."

"Then go to Father. Tell him how you feel."

"Oh, Meg, you make it sound so simple. All I need do is go to him, confess I was a fool, tell him how terribly sorry I am that I put him through nine years of hell. And he will welcome me back with open arms." Joanna gently brushed the tears from Meg's cheeks with her fingertips. "Your father will never want me back, my darling."

Meg refused to relinquish her stranglehold on hope. "You don't know that for certain."

Joanna shook her head. "I'm certain he hasn't lived the life of a monk all of these years. I suspect he long ago buried any feelings he had for me."

"What do you lose if you try to repair the damage?"

"My pride."

It might have been Meg saying those same words in her stubborn insistence to resist making a real marriage with Alec. "Go to him, Mother. Risk your pride for the chance to mend your marriage."

Joanna leaned back against the sofa. "I cannot possibly bare my soul to Robert Drummond now. It's too late. All he would do is laugh at me. And I well deserve his scorn."

Meg looked into the fire on the hearth, anxiety drawing like an iron band around her heart. There was a time when fear had kept her from claiming happiness. That time had past. Alec MacLaren was her husband. And she intended to be his wife in every way. She only hoped she hadn't already destroyed any chance she might have had at making a real marriage with her wicked Highlander.

Alec sat in a wing-back chair near the fireplace in his bedchamber. He stared at the words printed on a page of the novel he was reading, trying to keep his mind off of his wife. Yet his thoughts kept wandering to the woman who slept in the room adjoining his. Meg had been so quiet at dinner, so sad and withdrawn. Should he go to her? Should he lay his heart once more at her feet, hoping she might accept it into her keeping? Or should he give her more time?

He sensed the moment Meg entered his bedchamber. He looked up from his novel to find her standing in the connecting doorway between his bedchamber and hers. Candlelight from the wall sconces flickered upon her face, betraying the uncertainty in her expression. The soft light slipped golden fingers into the unbound waves that tumbled around her shoulders. She looked warm and lovely, and so very vulnerable his chest ached with the need to reassure her.

Meg clasped her hands at her waist. "I have it on good authority that a wife need not knock before entering her husband's bedchamber."

Alec closed his book and set it on the pedestal table beside his chair. "You never need to knock, Meg."

A shy smile touched her lips. The soft burgundy silk of her dressing gown rippled around her long legs as she walked toward him. She paused beside the fireplace, a few feet away from his chair. For a moment she stared into the fire, as though looking for words amid the flames. "How was your trip to Tranent?"

"It went well. I dismissed the manager Blandford hired, and replaced him with Diarmid Hensen."

Meg looked surprised. "Do you think Hensen shall be able to handle the position?"

"I've arranged for one of my men from the mines at Culross to help Diarmid get settled. I think he'll do fine."

Meg smiled. "That was very kind of you."

The warmth in her voice curled around him. "I only wish I had done something months ago."

"You mustn't look to the past, Alec." She glanced into the fire. "We can't alter the past. We can only try to do our best here and now. We can only hope to shape the future into something better than the past."

Alec resisted the urge to go to her. He sensed she needed to take the next few steps at her own pace. And he prayed she had finally decided to tear down the barriers she had constructed between them.

"Last night you asked me the reason I was upset. And I was too stubborn to tell you." She curled her hands into tight balls at her sides. "Last night, at the theater, I saw Drusilla Buchanan, the woman who destroyed my parents' marriage nine years ago."

Alec had suspected something of that nature. "It

must have brought back all the old bitterness."

Meg nodded, keeping her gaze on the flames lapping over black logs. "I'm afraid I haven't had much faith in the male of the species since that night."

Alec smiled. "I've noticed."

She stood quiet and tense, her thoughts plunging into the flames for several moments before she spoke. "Today you made me realize how easy it was to appear guilty when I was innocent. I hope you do believe me when I say I did not plan to run away from you. In fact, I was about to find transportation back to Edinburgh when you found me."

"Were you?"

"Yes. And what's more, I'm certain Blandford was dancing to my grandmother's tune. I really think it would be terrible if you decided to kill him in a duel over me. And I think it would be even more horrible if he by some chance killed you." She looked at him, her face drawn taut with concern. "You aren't going to meet him, are you, Alec?"

Alec smoothed his fingertip over the blue silk brocade covering the arm of his chair. "I doubt anything would be gained by meeting my cousin over pistols at dawn. I suspect he has learned an important lesson."

She nodded, a relieved little smile curving her lips. "I want you to know that even though my grandmother had hoped to wound my father by arranging my marriage to Lord Blandford, I never planned to marry him. I never would have married him. Never."

The nagging doubts he had about his cousin and his wife dissolved like ice in the rays of the sun. "I always thought you were a woman of distinguished intelligence."

"Unfortunately, I don't always show such intelligence. It seems I've done my father a grave injustice.

This afternoon I realized the full extent of my stupidity."

Alec listened quietly as Meg told him about Joanna's meeting with Drusilla Buchanan. Meg hugged her arms to her waist. "I only hope Father can forgive me for all the dreadful things I've said. When I think of the way I've treated him . . . I will understand if he decides he wants nothing to do with me."

"Your father loves you very much. It is his fondest hope that you would one day allow him back into your life."

She drew a deep breath. Firelight glimmered on the single tear that trickled down her smooth cheek. "I hope he will forgive me."

Alec left his chair, unable to keep from touching her. He brushed his fingers over her cheek, smoothing away her tear. "He will."

"Last night you said you loved me," she said, her voice rising softly above the rattle of rain against the windowpanes. "And I was too frightened to believe you."

Alec's breath grew still. "And now?"

"I love you, Alec." She touched his chest, resting her hand above his heart. "I have loved you since I was a child. And I shall love you until I am old and withered and placed into my grave."

Her words flowed into him, filling the empty places deep in his soul. "My own bonnie Meg. I've found everything I'll ever need in you. I ask only to share the rest of my days with you."

She slid her hands upward, over his shirt. "You'll have a devil of a time getting rid of me, my wicked Highlander. I'm very stubborn when I have my mind set on something. And my mind is set on you."

"Thank the Almighty." Alec drew her into his arms. The scent of spicy vanilla swirled through his senses.

Meg slid her arms around his neck, lifting to meet his kiss. Yet the soft mingling of breath and lips was not enough to feed the hunger that raged between them. They tore at each other's clothes, stripping away the barriers until firelight flickered against flesh. Alec lifted his bride into his arms and carried her to his bed. He lay her down upon the soft linen sheet and covered her with his body. She welcomed him, sliding her arms around his neck.

He showed her how much he adored her, celebrating his love for her with his hands, his lips, his tongue, until she was trembling, until her soft feminine song of pleasure filled his ears. Only then did he surrender to his own burning need. He sank into the slick welcoming heat of her, joining his body with hers. She wrapped her long legs around his hips, holding him with her arms, her legs. Holding him as though she wanted to hold him forever. And he realized this was where he had always belonged, here in Meg's arms. If he died tomorrow, he would go to his maker a happy man, grateful for this instant of pure joy.

Her father's pair of red setters bounded across the library at Penross House, greeting Meg with wagging tails and bobbing tongues. She took a moment to pet each dog, avoiding the inevitable confrontation with the man sitting by the fireplace. "Are they Wallace's progeny?"

"The male is," Robert said. "The female is out of MacDonald's line."

Meg drifted toward her father. "Are you going to breed them?"

"Aye."

Meg paused a few feet in front of her father's chair. "What have you named them?"

"The female is Antigone. The male is Achilles."

Antigone. The Greek heroine who shared her doomed father's wanderings. A bright, shining example of a daughter devoted to her father—loyal, trusting, loving. Everything Meg had not been.

Robert rested his chin on the steeple of his fingers, watching her with wary eyes. "Did you come here today to talk about my dogs?"

To the point. Her father was not one to ramble around an issue. She stood before him, feeling like a little girl caught stealing apples. Only what she had done was far more serious. "I came here today to . . ." Where to begin? "In the past few weeks . . . Ah . . . Lately I've come to see things with a great deal more clarity than I have in the past." She squeezed her trembling hands at her waist, frightened to continue. She didn't know what she would do if her father turned away from her, the way she had turned away from him.

Robert lifted one golden brow, his dark eyes filling with curiosity. "Sit, girl. Tell me what's on your mind."

Meg took the chair across from her father, clasped her hands on her lap, and tried to find the courage to confess. Achilles rested his chin on the arm of her chair, regarding her with solemn brown eyes. Antigone resumed her place by Robert's chair. "Three days ago, while Alec and I were in Edinburgh, Grandmother insisted I accompany her to see Roman ruins. Only she didn't really plan to go to the ruins; she planned to take me back to London. You see, she thought I wanted to have my marriage annulled."

"I'm not surprised to hear your grandmother tried to help you escape from your husband." Robert rubbed his chin. "But your reaction does surprise me. Am I to take it that you don't want your marriage annulled?"

Meg smoothed her hand over Achilles's sleek head. "You'll be pleased to know I've come to my senses and realized how fortunate I am to have Alec as my husband. I love him very much."

A small smile tipped Robert's lips. "I'm glad to hear it. He'll make you a fine husband."

"Yes." She glanced down at Achilles as she scratched behind one of his long, silky ears. "Alec found us at the inn where Grandmama had stopped to eat. I'm afraid at first it appeared as though I was running away from him. I realized then how simple it was to appear guilty when you had no part in the mischief."

Robert glanced away from her, staring into the fire. "I take it Alec believed you when you told him what really happened."

"Yes. He had more faith in me than I deserved." Emotion tightened around her throat. She had to swallow hard before she could continue. "I only wish I had shown you the same kind of faith nine years ago."

Robert looked at her, his expression revealing his surprise. "Do you, Meg?"

"I'm so sorry for not believing you." Meg rose, her legs trembling with the tight rein she held on her emotions. "Father, can you forgive me?"

Robert closed his eyes, and for one horrible moment Meg thought he would send her away. When he opened his eyes, there were tears glistening there. "Come to me, Meg," he said, opening his arms.

Meg ran to her father and sank onto his lap, taking comfort in his strong embrace. A warm, leathery scent curled around her, tugging memories from the grave where she had buried them. Her father had always been there for her, to soothe a bruised knee, to tell her a story, to make her feel as though she were the prettiest and wisest and best lass in the whole of Scotland. Tears welled and flowed, ignoring her every attempt to quell them. Robert held her close, rubbing her back, rocking her gently, as if she were a wee lass again.

When the storm had passed, she climbed off his lap and took a seat on his leather footstool.

"I'm sorry," she whispered, using his handkerchief to wipe away her tears. "I didn't want to cry. I don't usually cry. Lately I've become this horrible watering pot. I must look terrible. Is my nose red?"

"Aye." Robert grinned at her. "But you look bonnie fair to me, child."

She smiled. "I wasn't certain you could ever forgive me. I said such horrible things."

"When I look back at it, I can see how guilty I must have looked." Robert rested his head against the back of his chair. "I suppose it was a great deal to ask to want you to believe me."

"I should have believed you."

He patted her arm. "There were nights when I would look up at our special star and wonder if my little girl was thinking of me."

"I was." Meg knew she wasn't the only one who had been thinking of Robert Drummond through all these horrible years. She hesitated a moment, choosing her words carefully before she spoke. "I'm not the only one who realizes she has made a mistake by not trusting you."

Robert stiffened. "What are you saying, child?"

Meg explained what had happened in Edinburgh between her mother and Drusilla Buchanan. Robert listened, his expression betraying nothing of his emotions. "Mother thinks it's too late to try to mend your marriage. She's afraid you could never forgive her."

Robert squeezed the arms of his chair, his knuckles blanching white. "Your mother turned her back on me a long time ago."

"I've seen how much she suffered for what she thought you had done. I've heard her crying in the middle of the night. In all the time she was away from you, she never once broke her marriage vows to you." Meg rested her hand over his. "She still loves you. She told me she has often wished she had stayed and fought for your marriage. If you still have feelings for her, don't let what happened in the past ruin any chance you might have for a future together."

Robert closed his fingers around her hand. "Some things can't be mended, my bonnie lass."

Meg squeezed her father's hand while inside she clenched a slender thread of hope to her heart. She refused to let this die. Somehow she would find a way to bring her parents back together.

Chapter Twenty-five

"Your father is right. Some things can't be mended."
Joanna stood near the windows of her sitting room at
Dunleith Castle, staring out at Loch Laren. Moonlight
rippled across the rolling waves, sprinkling silver
across the water. "I think it's best if we leave things as
they are, Meg."

"Mother, I thought you might go to see Father." Meg
touched her mother's arm. "You need to discuss what
happened all those years ago. You need to try to see if
you can repair the damage."

Joanna's features twisted with a flicker of pain. She
handed Meg a crumpled piece of ivory parchment. "I
sent him a note this afternoon, apologizing for my behavior nine years ago. This was his reply."

Meg opened the crinkled paper. The few lines
scrawled in her father's bold hand spoke of forgetting
the past. Since neither of them could go back and
change what had happened, he hoped Joanna would

not allow the matter to weigh heavily on her mind. "You see, he wants to forget the past."

"If he had wanted to reconcile he would have come to see me." Joanna closed her eyes. "It's too late. He can't forgive me for not trusting him, and I don't blame him."

"Mother, I'm certain if you would only see him, and discuss this, you would both see how foolish it would be to throw away any chance you might have for finding happiness."

"I'm very glad you and your father have reconciled." Joanna touched Meg's cheek, the warm scent of lavender drifting around her. "One day you shall understand why it cannot be the same for your father and me."

"I do understand." Meg released her breath in a frustrated sigh. "You are just as stubborn as he is. Well, I am every bit as stubborn as both of you. And I intend to find a way to bring both you and Father to your senses."

Alec set a brass lamp on the floor near the door. The scent of burning tallow rose from the container, twisting around him. He stood in the old music room, facing the new door leading to the east wing, the one that had been hung after the fire. He wasn't certain why he had come here tonight. Perhaps he needed to face his ghosts. He hesitated a moment before turning the key. He eased open the door, exposing the remains of the crimson drawing room.

Although all the debris had been removed, the scent of ashes lingered here. It coiled around him, filling his every breath, tightening his lungs. Moonlight poured through the skeletal remains of the three floors above the drawing room, illuminating twisted timber and the blackened streaks across stone walls.

Ogilvey had told him what he knew of that night. He had described the flames that shot fifty feet into the evening sky. He had told of how Alec's brother had died in those flames. His parents had escaped, initially. His mother had lasted a day, his father three, both eventually succumbing to the damage the smoke had done to their lungs.

Soft footsteps echoed on the parquet behind him. He turned, frowning when he saw Wildon Fethersham. "I didn't think you would be back, Blandford."

Wildon paused a full twenty feet away from Alec, as though he were afraid of coming any closer. He stood with his right hand thrust into the front edge of his coat, staring at Alec. Moonlight fell across Wildon's face. His brown eyes were filled with the same strange mixture of fear and determination that drew his smooth features into tight lines. "It wasn't enough for you to take away my inheritance. No, you had to take away my chance at the Drummond fortune as well. And now you want to murder me."

Alec frowned. "Murder you?"

"Oh, you might call it a duel. But with your skill with pistols, it will be murder." Wildon pulled his hand from the inside of his coat. Moonlight slanted through the French doors, glinting on the pistol he held clutched in his trembling hand. "And if I don't meet you, then I'll be branded a coward. You win either way."

Alec had completely forgotten about the challenge he had issued his cousin. "I believe they do more than brand murderers these days, Blandford."

Wildon swallowed hard. "I have a better chance of avoiding the gallows than I do of avoiding a bullet from your pistol. I intend to say you were killed by accident."

Alec judged the distance between them. Although Wildon's hand was trembling, Alec suspected his cousin could still manage to fire the pistol before Alec could get it away from him. "You can relax, Blandford. I've given Meg my word that I shall not meet you in a duel."

Wildon laughed, a high, thready sound filled with fear. "And you expect me to believe that? I'm not so big a fool as you might imagine."

Alec was about to tell his cousin no one was a bigger fool, when Meg entered the room with Seamus trotting at her side. His heart thumped against his ribs when he realized she had stepped straight into harm's way.

"What the devil are you about, Lord Blandford?" Meg demanded.

Wildon gasped. He pivoted, swinging the pistol in Meg's direction. "What are you doing here?"

"Seamus, come!" Alec shouted.

Seamus lunged at his master's command. Alec dashed for his cousin at the same time that Seamus charged him from the opposite direction. Seamus set his paws in an attempt to stop. With his usual grace, his front feet slipped in opposite directions, his chin hit the smooth parquet, and he kept going.

"Stop!" Wildon yelped as Seamus slammed into his legs.

Alec snagged the pistol from Wildon's hand as the man toppled backward. Wildon whacked the floor, his head thumping the parquet. Seamus trotted over to Alec, trampling Wildon's groin with his big paws on the way. Wildon gasped. He curled onto his side, drawing his knees up to his chest, moaning in pain.

Meg paused beside Wildon, holding her lamp high, frowning as she stared down at him. "Terribly sorry. Seamus has a problem with smooth surfaces."

Wildon groaned in response.

Meg glanced up at Alec. "What was he doing with that pistol?"

Alec shoved the pistol into the pocket of his coat. "He

thought it would be more fair to have a duel when only one of us was armed."

"Damn you, Alec," Wildon croaked.

"That was hardly gentlemanly of you, Lord Bland-ford." Meg pinned Wildon with an icy look. "In fact, it was most cowardly of you. And after Alec had agreed not to meet you on the field of honor."

"I thought he planned to murder me!" Wildon wailed, sounding a great deal like a whining little boy.

"Shall you have him put behind bars?" Meg asked, directing her question to Alec.

Alec smiled at Wildon's stricken expression. "That depends on my cousin."

"I must say, Alec, you might have had the decency to tell me you had no intention of dueling me." Wildon lifted the damp cloth he was holding against his brow to give Alec a dark look. "It would have saved a great deal of trouble."

"It would seem I'm forever plaguing you, Blandford." Alec rested his arm on the mantel in his library. "First I return from the grave, then I spoil your plans for marrying a rich heiress, and finally I decide not to kill you in a duel. It's little wonder you tried to murder me."

"Quite right." Wildon shifted in his chair. "You've ruined me, cousin. I never would have plunged so far into dun territory if I had known you were planning to rise like Lazarus from the grave. It was damn vexing."

"I can imagine. Very inconvenient of me."

"Precisely. I don't know what I'm to do now." Wildon rested his head against the back of the chair. "Creditors, you know. I shall be completely ruined if I can't obtain the blunt to cover my debts. Thanks to you, my chances are slim at finding a wealthy bride. By now all of London is aware of my difficulties."

Alec rubbed his fingers against the smooth white

marble of the mantel. "Your difficulties didn't prevent Lady Hermione from trying to arrange a marriage with my wife."

"Lady Hermione. Such a dear lady. She has the intelligence to look past my present situation. She alone has always seen my qualities." Wildon curled his lips as though he had bitten into a lemon. "Certainly a woman of far superior distinction than her granddaughter."

"There is little doubt the two ladies differ greatly in quality." Alec studied Wildon a moment, an interesting idea forming in his brain. "Lady Hermione is more to your liking?"

Wildon nodded, his expression growing grave. "I have to say, if it were not for her fortune, I would never have considered Margaret Drummond for a wife. The woman can freeze a man with a look. You have my sympathy on that score, cousin. I only wish the chit had been more like her grandmother."

Alec gave a silent prayer Meg was nothing at all like the lady. "Was it Hermione's idea to murder me?"

Wildon frowned, a wary look entering his brown eyes. "About that unfortunate misunderstanding, *cousin*. I do hope you realize I felt compelled to strike before you could do away with me."

"Aye. Yet, a question remains—what the devil should I do with you?" Alec rubbed his chin. "I shouldn't like to live my life wondering if you're going to pop out and try to shoot me. Still, I suppose it would be terribly gauche to have you hanged for attempted murder."

Wildon sat up. The light of the wall sconces revealed the sudden draining of color from his face. "You wouldn't . . . You . . . I'm a relative."

Alec grimaced. "Pray don't remind me."

"Alec, you must own your part in my ruination. I

never would have done such a thing if you had not pushed me to the brink of distraction."

"Aye." Alec suppressed the smile he felt lifting his lips. "I suppose I could have you transported instead. Shipped away to Australia. Though I understand life for criminals there can be harsh."

"Australia?" Wildon said, his voice cracking.

Alec tapped his forefinger against his chin. "Of course, there is one other possibility."

"What?" Wildon dabbed at his brow with his handkerchief. "Anything would be better than what you have named."

Alec allowed Wildon to sit a few moments on the coals before he spoke. "Since you seem determined to marry a wealthy woman, I happen to have one in mind. One who is quite taken with you. And I'm quite certain your lack of fortune will not detract from your charm in the lady's eyes."

"Really." Wildon scooted to the edge of his chair. "Who is she?"

"Lady Hermione Chadburne."

Wildon's mouth dropped open. "You must be joking. The woman is old enough to be my grandmother."

"But I thought you preferred her over Meg?"

Wildon waved his hand. "I meant if the ladies were both of similar age. They obviously are not."

"With Lady Hermione, her age is a definite advantage." Alec grinned. "You can't expect more than ten or fifteen years of wedded bliss with her."

Wildon's eyes grew wide. "You're serious."

Alec pinned his cousin with a deadly stare. "As serious as a judge, cousin. Marry the woman, and I shall not bring charges against you."

"She would never agree." Wildon ran his forefinger under the edge of his high, starched collar. "Think of the scandal such a match would cause."

"Young women marry elderly gentlemen every day. Given your affinity with the lady, I'm certain you could manage to sweep her off her feet. In fact, I fully expect you to charm the lady senseless." Which, in Hermione's case, wouldn't be much of a task.

Wildon flicked his tongue over his lips. "I suppose I could try to persuade her. Of course, it might take some time."

"I warn you now, Blandford. If you're thinking of taking your time, courting the lady without really planning to marry her, in the hopes that it will be too late to bring charges against you, then I shall have to use another tactic. I shall be compelled to drop a few crumbs into the mouths of the gossipmongers of London. I shall make certain everyone soon knows how you sought to murder me instead of meet me on the field of honor."

Color rose, filling Wildon's pale cheeks, turning white to crimson. "You really are a blackguard."

"I shall also require one more thing of you." Alec crossed the room and retrieved two copies of the document he had fashioned while Wildon recovered from his fall. He waved Wildon over to the desk. "You will sign these, when my witnesses arrive."

The parchment shook in Wildon's hand as he lifted one of the documents and read the few short sentences. "This is a confession."

"Aye. Two copies. If anything untoward happens to me or any of my family, this letter will be delivered to Parliament. Soon afterward, you will be hanged. If you're still in the country."

"But what if something happens to you and I had nothing at all to do with it? You're not exactly the most amiable of men. Someone else might very well take a notion to murder you."

Alec shrugged. "I guess you had better hope I live a long and healthy life."

"Good gad!" Wildon leaned heavily on the desk. "You're the devil himself."

"The choice is yours, Blandford. You can go to Australia now. Or convince the lovely, very wealthy Lady Hermione to be your wife." Alec sat on the edge of the desk. "What's it going to be?"

Meg propped her forearm against her pillow and watched, admiring the shift of firm muscle beneath his tautly stretched skin, as Alec climbed into bed beside her. The warmth of his naked body radiated through the soft white linen of her nightgown. He had spent the better part of the evening in the library with Wildon Fethersham. Twenty minutes ago, Alec had come to his bedchamber—where Meg was waiting for him— pleased to tell her all about his plan to handle his cousin.

"Alec, you didn't really persuade Blandford to ask my grandmother to marry him?"

Alec cupped his hands on the pillow behind his head, the thick muscles of his upper arms bunching with the movement. He grinned his devilish Highlander smile and she felt her heart kick into a gallop. "I think they will make a splendid couple."

"A splendid couple? He shall ruin her!"

"Blandford has always been very good about managing his estate. He only got over his head when he thought he had the Dunleith fortune to spend." Alec lifted a golden curl that dangled over her shoulder and spilled across his bare chest. "And I told him I would pay off the debts he incurred while Earl of Dunleith as a wedding present."

"I can't imagine Grandmama actually agreeing to marry Blandford."

Alec winked at her. "Never underestimate my cousin. I fully expect he is capable of sweeping your grandmother off her feet. If he could lift her, that is."

Meg tugged on the black curls just beneath the hollow of his collarbone. "It's wicked of you to foster that pampered puppy on my grandmother."

"She must think he is a worthy gentleman." He flicked open the top button of her nightgown. "She was anxious enough to see you married to the man."

"It's not exactly the same."

"No." The rest of her buttons succumbed to his deft fingers. "It's a much better match. If you think about it, my bonnie Meg, you will see they deserve each other."

Tingles whispered across her skin as he brushed his warm fingertips over the first swell of her breasts. "If she did marry him, he would treat her dreadfully. Take mistresses. Ignore her. My grandmother can be a bit high-handed, but she always means well. I shouldn't like to see her abused."

He slid the nightgown from her shoulders, exposing her breasts to his gaze. His warm palms brushed her skin as he slid the white linen down her arms. "If he did marry her, Blandford would have me to answer to if he should abuse your grandmother in any way."

"If he married her?" With his help, she slipped her hands free of the sleeves he had bunched around her wrists. Wicked Highlander. She had never been and never would be safe from his devilish charm. "Alec, you don't really intend to allow that man to marry my grandmother, do you?"

"I considered it, for a moment." He traced the line of her collarbone with the tip of one long, elegantly tapered finger. The breath tangled in her throat. "But in the end, after Blandford had stewed a bit with the dreadful possibility, I told him I thought better of the entire match. I suggested my wife would be unhappy to have him as a grandfather."

"You were right." Meg leaned forward, brushing her breasts against his chest, the scrape of masculine curls and warm skin sending sensation sparking through her. She smiled as his muscles tensed, his breath catching in his throat. "I have an idea of how I can bring Mother and Father back together. Would you like to hear it?"

"Later." Alec slipped his hand into her unbound waves, sliding his fingers against her nape. He pulled her toward him, until his lips brushed hers. "Much later."

Chapter Twenty-six

It was strange, Joanna thought as she climbed the winding stairs of the west tower of Dunleith Castle. Why would Meg leave a note asking Joanna to meet her in the third-floor tower room? The note had mentioned only that Meg wanted to show her something of great importance.

Of the four doors leading to the circular hall at the top of the stairs, only one stood open. She stepped into the room, expecting to find her daughter. The only occupant of the spacious sitting room stood near one of the three narrow windows, staring out across the loch. And it definitely was not Meg.

Sunlight poured through the square panes, filling Robert's golden hair. He stood tall and proud without a cane. Dark gray wool molded his broad shoulders. Buff-colored trousers hugged his long, muscular legs. With one look, Joanna felt her heart slam against her ribs. Her first instinct was to turn and run. Yet before her befuddled brain could send the command to her legs, Robert had turned and caught her staring.

"What are you doing here?" she asked, her voice escaping in far too sharp a sound.

Robert frowned. "Meg sent me a note. Asked me to come here this morning. When I arrived, Ogilvey ushered me up here."

Heat flooded her cheeks with a sudden surge of suspicion she couldn't deny. "Meg asked me to meet her here this morning. I wonder what she has in mind?"

Robert rubbed his chin, his dark eyes glinting with speculation. "I wonder."

How terribly awkward this was. Joanna kept thinking she should apologize again. But words couldn't explain how she felt. Words couldn't touch the pain. And nothing was more painful than standing here with the man she loved, facing the truth: He could never forgive her for what she had done. Perhaps one day she could trudge over the barren wasteland of the past with this man, but it wasn't today. She hadn't felt this fragile in a very long time.

"I should see if I can find Meg." Joanna turned, intending to escape. The door closed before she reached it. The click of the lock sliding into place ripped through the quiet room, pounding on her heightened senses. "Who is there?"

"What the devil is going on here?" Robert muttered.

"I'm sorry about this." Meg's voice penetrated the solid oak barrier in soft, muted tones.

"Margaret!" Joanna twisted the brass door handle. "Open this door immediately."

"I'm afraid I can't do that, Mother. You and Father have important matters to discuss."

"Margaret!" Joanna pounded on the door. "Don't you dare leave us like this."

"I've left a picnic basket in the adjoining chamber."

Meg's voice whispered through the oak. "You should have everything you need for the rest of the day. I'll be back tonight to see if you've made any progress."

"Tonight!" Joanna glanced back at Robert, who stood by the windows, apparently oblivious to this disaster. "Do something!"

"What would you suggest?" he asked, his deep voice rumbling through her.

Joanna marched to the door leading to the adjoining chamber. She pulled open the door and froze. The door opened on a large bedchamber. The scent of heather and lavender drifted from a porcelain bowl of potpourri sitting on a pedestal table near the door. Ivory silk swags fell from the canopy of the bed, streaming down thickly carved mahogany posts. Sunlight flowed golden through the windowpanes, spilling over the ivory silk coverlet and the large wicker basket sitting in the center of the bed. A perfect setting for seduction. Oh, she was going to strangle her daughter for putting her in this humiliating position.

Joanna marched across the room and tugged on the handle of the door leading to the hall. It didn't budge.

"Locked?" Robert asked.

"Yes." Joanna glanced over her shoulder. Robert was standing in the doorway, with one shoulder resting against the frame, as casual as a man spending the day in the park. "You don't seem very upset over this."

Robert shrugged. "I suspect we can manage to occupy the same room for a few hours without causing any injury to one another."

He was wrong. Simply looking at him was doing horrible things to her insides. She pressed her back against the door. "I'm afraid Meg still has some hope we might reconcile."

Robert held her in a steady gaze, his expression betraying none of his emotions. "Terrible thing, hope. It makes a person believe anything is possible."

"Yes. It does." Joanna curled her hands into fists at her sides, fighting to keep her emotions under tight rein. She would not humiliate herself by dissolving into a fit of tears. Yet they were there, stinging her eyes. She couldn't deny her tears, just as she couldn't deny the love she still had for this man. Could they reconcile? Suddenly pride seemed an insignificant thing in the face of hope. "I shouldn't have sent you that note yesterday."

Robert frowned. "Why not? Have you decided you don't believe me after all?"

Joanna shook her head. "I should have come to face you, and apologize for not trusting you enough to believe you. But I was afraid I would embarrass you and humiliate myself by telling you . . . how much I still love you."

He stood staring at her for a full twelve beats of her heart, his eyes filled with the same turmoil that raged inside of her. *Please forgive me. Please!* She wanted to scream the words. Yet anxiety locked them in her heart.

Through a fine mist of tears she watched as he walked toward her. When he touched her cheek the dam holding back her emotions broke.

"I love you." She threw her arms around his neck and held him as she had dreamed of holding him for so many years. "I never stopped loving you. Please, please forgive me."

He wrapped strong arms around her, holding her as though he never intended to let her go. "I've missed you so much, Jo."

"I'm so sorry." Joanna whispered through her tears. "So terribly sorry."

"Don't cry." He cradled her face in his hands and

351

kissed her cheeks. "My own sweet love, I can't bear to see you cry."

"Will you forgive me?" She smiled up at him through the tears she couldn't prevent. "Take me back into your life, Robert Drummond, and I promise I'll never doubt you again. I shall spend the rest of my days doing my best to make you the happiest man in Scotland."

"You've been a long time in coming home, lass." Robert brushed his lips against hers. "It's good to have you back."

Rain poured over the streets of London. Yet the rain did not prevent members of the haute ton from flooding the Earl of Dunleith's town house on Grosvenor Square. The trip to London for the Season had been Alec's idea. Although he had never cared for the whirl of the Season while he had a commission, he could see where a few months in town each year might be amusing now that he was a married man. This ball was meant to quell the rumors about their hasty marriage. Alec wanted society to see they were both happy to be married to one another.

Meg wended her way through the crowded ballroom, looking for her husband. After the first dance, she had been swept away from Alec, kept occupied by a steady stream of gentlemen intent on partnering her on the dance floor and questioning her about her sudden marriage. The mingled scents of sweet water, cologne, and perfume swirled through air made overly warm by the combined heat of over four hundred guests. Her first ball as the Countess of Dunleith was a crushing success.

Meg climbed the three stairs leading to the reception hall, hoping to find Alec from this vantage point. Candlelight glittered against crystal, filling the room with a warm, golden glow. A waltz flowed from the minstrels gallery. In the crowd, she noticed her father leading her mother in a series of graceful turns on the dance-floor. The pure warmth of joy glowed within Meg as she watched them. Although they were surrounded by other couples, they might have been alone, so intent were they on each other. Love long denied had flourished once more between them. Her parents were like newly married lovers, unable to get enough of one another. With that thought in mind, Meg surveyed the room, searching for her husband. Yet she couldn't find him.

Unfortunately, she did notice Wildon Fethersham, headed straight for her. Although Alec had settled all of the debts Wildon had incurred during his short tenure as Earl of Dunleith, the gesture had not dissolved the animosity Wildon felt toward his cousin. Although Alec tolerated Wildon with good humor, since that day Wildon had nearly murdered Alec, Meg could scarcely find the tolerance to be civil to the man. Why the devil would he approach her?

"You look as though you're searching for someone," Wildon said, pausing on the step just below her. He smiled at her, a smug little grin that made the back of her neck prickle. "If you're looking for Alec, I saw him go into the library a few moments ago."

Meg managed a smile. "How very kind of you to keep track of my husband for me, Lord Blandford. In case you are searching for my grandmother, you can find her in the gold drawing room, playing cards."

One corner of Wildon's mouth twitched. "Very amusing. We shall see how amused you are after you visit Alec in the library. I doubt you'll be smiling."

Meg squeezed her fan as she watched Wildon march away from her. What the devil was that supposed to mean? The man was only trying to make trouble, she assured herself. There was no reason to believe Alec had done anything to upset her. She hesitated a moment before heading for the library.

"Your letter came as a shock." Pamela Elkington stroked her fingertips over the brass unicorn on the desk in Alec's library. A single pale blond curl lay across her shoulder, glimmering in the candlelight. "I had no idea you were planning to marry."

"It came as a surprise to me as well." Alec sat on the edge of the desk near Pamela.

Pamela lifted one golden brow, her blue eyes filled with speculation. "I've heard as much."

"No doubt. Any sudden marriage causes rumors." Alec took her gloved hand in his. "But the truth is, I'm very happy with my bride."

"Margaret Drummond is a beautiful woman." Pamela glanced down at their clasped hands. "Though her reputation is for being a trifle . . . cold. I wouldn't have thought her to your liking at all."

"She may have been cold with other men, but to me she is as warm as summer." Alec squeezed her hand, trying to soften the words that followed. "I love her."

"I have to confess, I was hoping the rumors were true, and that it was simply a *mariage de convenance*." Pamela looked up at him, a glimmer of sadness touching her beautiful face. "I was hoping you might need a companion to warm your nights. But when I saw you dancing with your wife tonight, I realized the rumors were all wrong. There was a warmth in your eyes when you looked at her . . . it was obvious you were both deeply in love."

Alec lifted her hand and kissed her gloved fingers. "I hope one day you find a man who deserves you."

Pamela rested her hand against his cheek. "I wish you every happiness, Alec. You were always a very special gentleman."

The library door opened. Alec glanced over Pamela's pale blond hair to the woman who stood on the threshold of the room. Light from the wall sconces illuminated Meg's face, revealing her surprise. Her gaze flicked from Alec to Pamela and back again. Alec smiled, though inside his muscles tensed when he wondered what his wife would make of this little tête à tête.

"I don't believe you have had the opportunity to meet." Alec rose and lifted his hand toward Meg, inviting her to join them. "Lady Margaret, may I present a dear friend of mine, Lady Pamela Elkington."

Emerald silk flowed around her slender form as Meg crossed the room. Although she would deliver their first child in seven months' time, her body had yet to grow plump with his seed. She took Alec's hand and greeted Pamela. After Pamela wished them both good fortune on their marriage, she left the room, closing the door behind her.

"Lady Pamela Elkington." Meg drifted to the fireplace, where she stood staring down into the flames. "I take it she is *the* Pamela who wrote you that very friendly letter while you were ill."

"Aye." Alec watched his wife, apprehension coiling around his heart. Although he was certain of Meg's love, he still wasn't certain she truly trusted him. Silently he hoped she would realize the little scene she had witnessed was completely innocent.

Meg glanced at him. "She's very beautiful."

Alec grinned. "I've always had an eye for beautiful women."

Meg rolled her eyes toward heaven. "And beautiful women have always come your way."

Alec crossed the room, pausing behind his wife, so close the emerald silk of her gown brushed against the black wool of his trousers. He slipped his arms around her and drew her back against his chest. "What's going on in that beautiful head of yours?"

Meg shrugged. "I was just thinking how easy it is for a man to look guilty when he is completely innocent."

He slid his hand over her belly, imagining the day he would feel his babe move within her. "You're the only woman I want, Meg."

Meg turned in his arms and rested her hands on his chest. "I'm glad to hear it, MacLaren. I would hate to have to boil you in oil."

"So would I." He pressed his lips against her brow, his heart easing when he realized he had his wife's trust as well as her love. The scent of spicy vanilla swirled through his senses and spilled into his blood, more potent than brandy. Desire pounded like a closed fist low in his belly. "There are so many people here, I doubt anyone would notice if we slipped upstairs for a few hours."

Meg lifted her brows in mock surprise, mischief glinting in her green eyes. "And what possible reason could you have for wanting to go upstairs for a few hours?"

Alec wiggled his eyebrows at her. "Let me show you."

"Our bedchamber is too far." Meg slipped her arms around his neck and lifted up on her toes to kiss him. "Lock the door, my wicked Highlander."

Epilogue

The scent of lavender and heather spilled into the crimson drawing room from porcelain bowls filled with potpourri placed on polished mahogany tables around the room. The sweet fragrance mingled with the scent of burning peat from the hearth—the scent of summer melding with winter. Snow drifted past the square windowpanes, dusting the Highlands in a chilly mantle of white. Yet inside the great stone walls, it was warmer than summer. Alec sat beside his wife on a sofa near the hearth, watching as three of his five children played with six plump seven-week-old Irish red setter puppies.

"Come back here!" Colin, the eldest, was chasing after a puppy who had stolen the green ribbon from his seven-year-old sister Isobel's long black curls. Tall, with black hair and blue eyes, his eldest son, Meg assured Alec every day, would grow to be just as wickedly handsome as his father.

Isobel sat amid the medallions of red and gold and ivory stitched into the carpet, giggling as four puppies gamboled around her, tugging at the hem of her dress—which was the same soft green as her eyes—leaping upon her lap, licking her face.

Four-year-old Douglas sat between Joanna and Robert on the sofa across from his parents, hugging a squirming puppy. He tipped his golden head and regarded his grandfather with hopeful blue eyes. "Tell me another story, Grandpapa. Please."

Joanna held her seven-month-old grandson, Patrick, in her arms. She smiled at her husband, pride and affection shimmering in her eyes as she listened to Robert begin another story about Fionn's brave shoulders.

Seamus lay by the hearth beside his son, Wallace, ignoring his playful grandchildren. Katrine—the dam of the litter—lay on the carpet near Alec, watching her progeny with a watchful eye.

Dressed in a startling shade of purple, Hermione sat in a wing-back chair nearby, with Patrick's twin, Alexander Robert, in her arms. She surveyed her family, smiling like a queen pleased with her court. She had long ago realized there was no point in fighting the Scottish any longer. Not when she was so dreadfully outnumbered. Through the years, she had made peace with Robert and Alec, accepting them as part of her family. Still, she was convinced Meg should take more of her advice in decorating the castle. Hermione was certain the crimson drawing room would look divine if Meg would only allow her to transform it into Roman ruins.

Meg rested her hand on Alec's chest, above the heart she owned. "You're smiling as though someone has just told you a wonderful secret. Care to share?"

"I was just thinking how very lucky I was the night Robert asked me to kidnap you." Alec hugged her close to his side, smiling into her beautiful face. "You've given me everything I could ever want in this world. Home and family, and a bonnie lass to warm my days." He brushed his lips across hers. "And my nights."

"You once asked me if I believed in magic." Meg cupped his cheek in her warm palm. "Every day with you, I'm more and more certain there is magic all around us, my wicked, beloved Highlander."

AUTHOR'S NOTE

For several years I've been telling my Irish Setter, Seamus, he could have a starring role in one of my books. Each time I tried to cast him, another dog, or—to his horror—a cat got the part. Finally, I found the perfect role for him, a lovable klutz. I hope you enjoyed the time you spent with Alec, Meg, and Seamus.

A few years ago I had the pleasure of touring Scotland. One glimpse of the Highlands and I knew I had to set a novel in that beautiful location. Although Dunlieth is a fictional part of Scotland, it is based on several areas in the Central Highlands. I also used Culzean Castle near Ayr as a model for Dunlieth Castle, placing it on the fictional Lock Laren.

In my next book, I wondered what would happen if a rogue suddenly found himself the guardian of a family of three sisters. Justin Hayward Trevelyan, Duke of Marlow, had earned the title of the Devil of Dartmoor by becoming one of the most notorious rakes in England. Yet even a devil can be redeemed when he meets the proper angel. Set in 1816 England, *Devil's Honor* is the story of a bitter rogue who is taught how to love by his charming ward.

I love to hear from readers. Please enclose a self-addressed, stamped envelope. You can write to me at:

P. O. Box 584
Glen Carbon, Illinois 62034-0584

E-mail: DEBRADIER@AOL.COM

DEBRA DIER
LORD SAVAGE
Author of *Scoundrel*

Lady Elizabeth Barrington is sent to Colorado to find the Marquess of Angelstone, the grandson of an English duke who disappeared during an attack by renegade Indians. But the only thing she discovers is Ash MacGregor, a bounty-hunting rogue who takes great pleasure residing in the back of a bawdy house. Convinced that his rugged good looks resemble those of the noble family, Elizabeth vows she will prove to him that aristocratic blood does pulse through his veins. And in six month's time, she will make him into a proper man. But the more she tries to show him which fork to use or how to help a lady into her carriage, the more she yearns to be caressed by this virile stranger, touched by this beautiful barbarian, embraced by Lord Savage.

_4119-7 $4.99 US/$5.99 CAN

A Quest of Dreams DEBRA DIER

Bestselling Author Of *Shadow Of The Storm*

To Devlin McCain, she is a fool who is chasing after moonbeams, a spoiled rich girl who thinks her money can buy anything. But beneath her maddening facade burns a blistering sensuality he is powerless to resist, and he will journey to the ends of the earth to claim her.

To Kate Whitmore, he is an overpowering brute who treats women like chattel, an unscrupulous scoundrel who values gold above all else. Yet try as she might, she cannot deny the irresistible allure of his dangerous virility.

Hard-edged realist and passionate idealist, Devlin and Kate plunge into the Brazilian jungle, searching for the answer to an age-old mystery and a magnificent love that will bind them together forever.

_3583-9 $4.99 US/$5.99 CAN

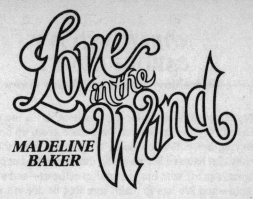

Love in the Wind

MADELINE BAKER

Author of Over 10 Million Books in Print!

Shattered by grief at her fiancé's death, lovely Katy Marie Alvarez decides to enter a convent. But fate has other plans. En route to her destination, the coach in which Katy is traveling is attacked by Indians and Katy, the lone survivor, is taken captive. Thus she becomes the slave of the handsome, arrogant Cheyenne warrior known as Iron Wing. A desperate desire transforms hate into love, until they are both ablaze with an erotic flame which neither time nor treachery can quench.

_4227-4 $5.99 US/$6.99 CAN

NOBLE AND IVY
CAROLE HOWEY
Bestselling Author of *Sheik's Glory*

Ivy is comfortable being a schoolteacher in the town of Pleasant, Wyoming. She has long since given up dreams of marrying her childhood beau, and bravely bore the secret sorrow that haunted her past. But then Stephen, her cocksure brother, ran off with his youthful sweetheart—and a fortune in gold—and Ivy has to make sure that he doesn't wind up gutshot by gunmen or strung up by his beloved's angry brother.

Noble—just speaking his name still makes her tremble. Years before, his strong arms stoked her fires hotter than a summer day—before the tragedy that left a season of silence in its wake. Now, as the two reunite in a quest to save their siblings, Ivy burns to coax the embers to life and melt in the passion she swears they once shared. But before that can happen, Noble and Ivy will have to reconcile their past and learn that noble intentions mean nothing without everlasting love.

_4118-9 $5.50 US/$6.50 CAN

Dorchester Publishing Co., Inc.
65 Commerce Road
Stamford, CT 06902

Please add $1.75 for shipping and handling for the first book and $.50 for each book thereafter. NY, NYC, PA and CT residents, please add appropriate sales tax. No cash, stamps, or C.O.D.s. All orders shipped within 6 weeks via postal service book rate. Canadian orders require $2.00 extra postage and must be paid in U.S. dollars through a U.S. banking facility.

Name _____

Address _____

City _____ State _____ Zip _____

I have enclosed $_____ in payment for the checked book(s).

Payment <u>must</u> accompany all orders.☐ Please send a free catalog.

PATRICIA GAFFNEY Fortune's Lady

"Like moonspun magic...one of the best historical
romances I have read in a decade!"
—Cassie Edwards

They are natural enemies—traitor's daughter and zealous
patriot—yet the moment he sees Cassandra Merlin at her
father's graveside, Riordan knows he will never be free of
her. She is the key to stopping a heinous plot against the
king's life, yet he senses she has her own secret reasons for
aiding his cause. Her reputation is in shreds, yet he finds
himself believing she is a woman wronged. Her mission is
to seduce another man, yet he burns to take her luscious body
for himself. She is a ravishing temptress, a woman of
mystery, yet he has no choice but to gamble his heart on
fortune's lady.

_4153-7 $5.99 US/$6.99 CAN

Dorchester Publishing Co., Inc.
65 Commerce Road
Stamford, CT 06902

Please add $1.75 for shipping and handling for the first book and
$.50 for each book thereafter. NY, NYC, PA and CT residents,
please add appropriate sales tax. No cash, stamps, or C.O.D.s. All
orders shipped within 6 weeks via postal service book rate.
Canadian orders require $2.00 extra postage and must be paid in
U.S. dollars through a U.S. banking facility.

Name _____

Address _____

City _____ State _____ Zip _____

I have enclosed $_____ in payment for the checked book(s).
Payment <u>must</u> accompany all orders.☐ Please send a free catalog.